Sea Dragon's Command

Royal Dragon Shifters of Morocco #3

Ava Ward

A Red Letter Hotel Paranormal Romance

COPYRIGHT

First Kindle Edition, 2019
ISBN 978-1-079492-99-6

Edited By: Jean Lowe Carlson.
Proofread By: Jean Lowe Carlson and Matt Carlson.
Cover Design: Copyright 2019 by Damonza. All Rights Reserved.
Chapter Graphics: FreeTiles http://www.dafont.com/ Free Commercial Use.

ACKNOWLEDGEMENTS

To everyone who made this third book possible, you are the best! Special thanks to Lela and Josh, Louie and Brenda, Sam and Ben, Marc and Claire for their support. Thanks to Amber, Carol, Jo, and Dave S. for helping me celebrate the fun. Thanks to my family Wendy, Dave, and Stephany for being as excited about this as I am.

Special shout-out to my Beta Readers and Launch Team – Joy, Linda, April, Tanya, Jules, Georganne, Carrie, Fiona, Nikhil, Michelle, Kimmy, Penelope, Queen, Eileen, Marco, Jessica, Erin, Rosemarie, Christiane, Alfreda, Sierra, Joel, Jean, Brittany, Claire, Susanne, Kona, Ruth, Stephanie, Katie, Lynda, Melissa, Terry, Jeanette, Dottie, Raquel, Mike, Bill, Susan, Wendy, Melissa, Kim, Amy, Cori, Bobby, Alison, Angie, Kam, Cyndi, Daniel, Elizabeth, Terri, Robin, Felicia, Christine, Kahlia, Victoria, Julie, Susan, Juan, Hannelore, Jen, Bobbi, Tina, Jody, Shannon, Marlys, Sandra, Tara, Kathy, Heather, Jewell, Deborah, Sue, Catherine, Liz, Phyllis, Joanne, Cathy, Esther, Janet, Krystle, Joy – you are amazing!

And as always, the most thanks to my husband Matt, for his never-ending support of my obsession with writing. I love you, baby!

OTHER WORKS BY AVA WARD

RED LETTER HOTEL PARANORMAL ROMANCE

Royal Dragon Shifters of Morocco
Royal Dragon Bind
Crystal Dragon's Kiss
Sea Dragon's Command
Blood Dragon's Heat

SHORT FICTION

The Man in White
The Grasses of Hazma-Din

ABOUT SEA DRAGON'S COMMAND

Her magic is running wild. Can he help her tame it before it destroys her?

Layla Price's magic has been unleashed. Set free during a confrontation with her enemy Hunter, her fury as the world's most dangerous Dragon-shifter knows no bounds.

But her power is a grave risk to her friends, and as Layla trains with the uncompromising Royal Siren Reginald Durant to tame her magics, she struggles to master her ability.

When her mate Adrian is framed for murder, she must go undercover – risking her life in a dangerous game to draw out her nemesis.

And when she finds Hunter, will her magic be controlled enough to finally take him down?

Or will Reginald's training fail her – leaving her powerless against her enemy?

AUTHOR'S NOTE

Welcome to the passionate world of the Royal Dragon Shifters of Morocco!

This series is a *billionaire reverse harem dragon-shifter romance,* involving a strong, intelligent heroine who attracts multiple sexy bad-boy billionaire dragon lovers over the course of the series.

The world is racy, opulent, and sensual, with intense action sequences, political intrigue, and dangerous enemies. The themes are uplifting with HFN endings and for the best experience, the books should be read in sequence.

Thanks for joining the Royal Dragons at the Red Letter Hotel! *Are you ready for the heat?*

CHAPTER 1 – SIREN

Standing on the high stone veranda, Layla Price stared out over the evening gardens of the Red Letter Hotel Paris. Winter had arrived at the Palace of Versailles in the Twilight Realm, the leaves fallen from the maples, the topiary's animalistic charm gone to sticks. Dressed in a 1940's white silk evening gown with an elegant train, the starkness of Layla's ensemble echoed the season. At the end of November, there was a cold bite in the evening wind. Layla stood on the sprawling veranda in her thin silk because a party raged behind her, one she was supposed to be attending.

But the cold was preferable to what she'd been facing inside.

Through the vaulted French doors of the glass atrium behind her, Layla could feel a press of magic flooding her in disrupting currents. Clutching a chardonnay, she shivered at the cacophony of power issuing from the atrium. Magical scents heaved around her on the veranda; a wall of fragrance like walking into Macy's at Christmastime. As a Desert Dragon, her inner heat warmed her silk gown and the strings of silver beads that spanned her back; her shivers weren't from the cold, but from the power roiling through the hall behind her.

The power of the Owners Board of the Red Letter Hotel.

Jangled, Layla felt assaulted by the combined magics of the Hotel Owners. She felt her own inner Dragon rise, coiling through her veins ready to lash out and strike that power back. As she faced the wind, taking deep breaths to get her shit together, she heard a smooth step behind her. Glancing back, Layla saw it was Reginald Durant, Partner to her Courtesan-in-Training since Samhain.

Royal North Sea Siren and Head Courtier of the Paris Hotel.

Layla set her jaw, ire spiking through her like bourbon set fire with a blowtorch. Reginald was a thorn in her side these past weeks, an iceberg that never cracked, ever since he'd insisted she train with him as a Courtesan or lose her job at the Red Letter Hotel Paris back in October. Like he'd stepped out of 1700's France, he wore a coat and trousers of ice-blue silk, embroidered with ships and leviathans in gold thread. White stockings and black shoes with gold buckles complemented his ensemble, his white silk cravat ending at a trim waistcoat that fit his lean dancer's frame and sculpted shoulders perfectly.

Reginald's eyes were a pale snow-blue as they met Layla's in the last of the evening's light. Wearing his customary white wig and face powder with cupid's-bow rouge on his full lips, his bone structure was so defined and masculine as to be haughty as he stared Layla down.

"Layla Price. Come back inside, you'll catch your death."

"I'm a Dragon. We don't get sick." Layla set her jaw at his smooth baritone. Fire rising in her veins, she turned towards Reginald with poise just like he had been drilling into her these past weeks.

Though she downed her wine like a tavern wench, just to watch his eyes flash.

She enjoyed baiting him. Her relationship with Reginald had been like a bad arranged marriage all November, making Layla feel like she was in the worst version of the *Princess Diaries*. Born centuries ago, Reginald had perfected his courtly manners in times when it had been an art, while Layla had grown up in the extremely casual atmosphere of Seattle. Even her best manners when she'd bartended for high-class establishments fell woefully short of his standards.

But strangely enough, though he'd insisted she be exclusive to him for the duration of her training, he hadn't set a finger to her these past weeks, except to adjust her gown or escort her. It was confusing and frustrating, and some part of Layla was growing restless at living with such a devastatingly handsome yet cruelly stern man every day and night. It made her inner Dragon roil, flooding a charred bourbon-orange scent from her skin as Layla lifted an eyebrow at him.

"Are you defying me, Courtesan?" Reginald's gaze was frosty as he stared her down, the sensation of a chill ocean easing from him as they faced each other in the twilight.

"I might be." Layla grumped back, setting her wine glass aside on the stone railing of the veranda. "And I'm not a real Courtesan yet."

"All too true. They are far more respectful than you are being right now."

Reginald's haughty gaze was dominant as he leaned into his power, until Layla could hear ocean surf in her ears. She was inundated with a chill, as if seawater had been poured through her. Sirens had mesmeric powers and Reginald used those magics now, punishing Layla for her impertinence.

Layla held herself back from razzing him more in her ire. She'd been disrespectful the first few days they'd been in each other's company and he'd punished her for it – making her move into his apartments on the fourth floor of the Hotel to continue her training under his extremely watchful eye. Ever since, she'd been around him night and day except when he was hired for an Assignation. In addition to etiquette, her primary lessons these past weeks had been on stilling her temper – all while wanting to blow up at Reginald every day for trying to dominate her.

"You will remember your training, Courtesan." Reginald spoke as his power surged, not about to let her win this battle. "If you value this Hotel and everything Adrian Rhakvir has tried to do for you these past months, you will stow your snide commentary and face your changing role at this establishment with grace and open eyes. For it is not just your own downfall you orchestrate if you perform badly as a Courtesan, especially tonight. Come. Attend me."

With that, Reginald turned, snapping his fingers for Layla like a dog. Fury spiked inside her, blistering the chill air. But it was neither less nor more than Reginald's other chastisements these past weeks, and tonight Layla set her teeth.

"No. I'm not going back inside." She bit tersely, turning back to the night.

"No?" Reginald spoke, that one word pricking Layla's spine like an icicle.

"No." Layla repeated stubbornly. "The magic of the Owners is terrible, and I don't have any resistance to it. I can feel them; their desires, their urges, their manipulations. It's sick inside that hall. All my Dragon wants to do is bite and snarl and burn them all. Ever since Hunter destroyed my hamsa-cuff in October… I can't keep anyone out anymore, especially not people who are this powerful. So you're just going to have to go through the evening without me. I'm done."

Layla shivered as the stars began to emerge, the last of the evening's gloaming dying out over the gardens. As if recalling her destroyed hamsa-cuff, her left wrist prickled and Layla looked down, watching the hamsa-hand burn mark on her inner wrist flare. Vicious and red, it came out now when she was feeling intense emotions – though the mark no longer held the power to contain her magic with the cuff destroyed.

As her burn prickled, Layla felt Reginald move up behind her. She thought he would say something terse but instead he stepped close, smoothing a hand down her back. His fingers were warm, as if the Siren carried a deep heat inside. Touching the beaded strings of the

9

gown, his fingertips caressed Layla's back, and the sound of an ocean eased into her, no longer pummeling but soothing. His lips brushed her hair, that small touch making things low in Layla's body tighten deliciously. Setting his lips to her bare shoulder, he kissed her gently.

"I don't blame you for not wanting to go back in there. The Hotel Owners are a cruel bunch."

Layla blinked, stunned at his sudden change. She glanced over and for a moment, their lips were only a breath away. It was the closest she had ever been to him, and she blinked her jade-green and gold eyes, meeting his – a stormy pearl-grey now as if they carried deep emotion behind his glacial austerity.

Easing back with a sigh, Reginald reached up, removing his white 1700's wig. His actual hair was a bright flaxen gold and bound in a tight club, the strands fine as silk. Setting the wig on the stone rail of the veranda, he moved to a fountain's basin nearby and slipped his hands in, splashing his face with water. Removing a silk handkerchief from his vest, he dried his face – taking off all his makeup and rouge with it.

Reginald was stunning without his makeup. The Siren's lips were full, his cheekbones so high they could have cut glass as he narrowed his blue eyes at the night. Layla watched him palm his hands back over his beautiful hair, his straight golden brows scowling. At last, he turned to meet her gaze, his eyes more compassionate than usual, though still stern.

"You did the right thing, Layla, to come out here to compose yourself. Never display your ire at a party. Petulance or furious magical eruption earns a Courtesan a bad reputation."

"Why should I care about my reputation?" Layla lifted an eyebrow, wondering why he was being so frank tonight, and why he'd removed part of his Courtier's costume.

"As a Courtesan, your reputation is *everything*." Reginald's gaze was piercing as he stared her down. "Elegance and poise will keep you safe in dangerous situations; so will wit, and the ability to deflect conflict. The more elite you can make your reputation, the less any partner will be tempted to ruin you. People do not smash priceless Ming vases when they are angry. They do throw ceramic dinner plates at the wall, however. Among this crowd, tonight," Reginald nodded at the party, "you can be certain you wish to be seen as a Ming vase and not a dinner plate."

That stopped Layla. She'd never considered that elegance was actually a safety measure for a Courtesan. It made her reconsider her training with Reginald and she paused, her ire with him easing. Turning, she glanced at the party and Reginald did also. Together, they watched people moving through the blue glass pavilion, soaring up to the deep cerulean sky – an enormous amount of magic still seething through the hall before them.

"Why did you bring me to the Hotel Owner's Gala tonight, Reginald?" Layla asked.

"Because we are working on your ability to control your powers." Reginald lifted a golden eyebrow at her. "Your first showing as a Courtesan-in-Training at tonight's gala with the Owners requires your utmost control, Layla. I have drilled you in controlling your magics and your tongue and posture these past weeks, so that when we are among such esteemed and dangerous company, we can be what they wish to see of us. And protect the truth of what we are from their talons."

"Is the Paris Hotel in trouble?" She asked, curious now, sensing the danger he was hinting at. "Because of everything that's happened since Hunter infiltrated our branch at Samhain?"

Taking a deep breath, Reginald gazed at her in the deepening twilight, his pale blue eyes unreadable. But then he spoke, the barest smile of approval lifting the corners of his full lips. "Your observation is astute. The Paris Hotel is in trouble, yes. Because of your abduction at Samhain and Adrian and Dusk's near Dragon-brawl right in the middle of the celebrations, many questioning eyes are turned our way. The Hotel Board of Owners are wondering if Adrian is a good fit to lead this branch. Or if he should be removed from his duties as Hotel Head."

"Why would the Board fire Adrian as Hotel Head?" Layla asked, an uneasy feeling moving through her as the wind gusted.

"Adrian needs patrons and investors in the Paris Hotel to keep it safe, Layla." Reginald responded soberly. "We weren't able to keep the events of the past month a secret, and guest bookings have been canceled right and left. Investors have pulled their support, and it's costing our Hotel branch a fortune. We're running in the red, currently supported by Adrian's personal wealth. Adrian needs to convince the Board this week that he can keep our doors open, and return our Hotel to profitability. Otherwise, the Board may replace him as our Head."

"What would happen then?" Layla blinked, shock racing through her at the truth of the situation.

"Many Hotel branches are run by excellent Board members. Others aren't. We wouldn't have a choice in the selection of a new Hotel Head." Reginald's golden brows tightened in a frown, and Layla watched him tap his fingers upon the stone rail of the veranda, almost like a nervous tic. Reginald didn't have nervous tics, and Layla noted it – how worried he truly was about the entire situation. "Come." He spoke at last. "Let us go back inside. The party has barely begun, and we must make a good impression for the evening."

"I can't go back in there, Reginald." Layla breathed, tension spiking through her again. "I can't shield against their magics. They're just… too intense."

"Yes. The Hotel Owners are probably the most powerful group of magical entities you are ever likely to meet," Reginald breathed darkly. "Even I have trouble shielding against many of them, especially those of the Crimson Circle, their innermost elite. Though less than a fifth of them have come tonight for Adrian's fête, there are some with strength here."

"What if my magic flares tonight and someone powerful feels it?"

"I will shield you. Trust in your Partner. Come."

But his haughty certainty did not inspire confidence in Layla. Trepidation writhed inside her, feeling the miasma still surging from the hall. Layla's unpredictable magic flared suddenly, trying to strike all that odious power back. She'd always had a temper, but her newly unleashed Royal Dragon Bind magic made her every emotion thirty times more volatile now without her hamsa-cuff to control it. Waves of heat and fire washed through her, and Layla was devoured by a reckless desire – to fight all those whose magic assaulted her.

To fight each and every Hotel Owner at the party.

"Layla. Breathe through your flare. I can control it for you, but that's not why we train."

Reginald's elegant features were exquisite as an iceberg as he stared her down, weathering the magical gale that raged around Layla. Caught in her passions, she couldn't help but feel a love-hate attraction to him – a blistering push-pull that had colored their interactions these past weeks. Haughty and elegant, there was something intensely compelling about the Head Courtier with his perfectly masculine shoulders, his slim waist and thighs fitted close by sleek blue silk. Layla both hated and loved his lean grace and effortless style, golden rings with diamonds and aquamarine shining through the night just like his eyes.

Suddenly, Layla's lack of control over her attraction to him – and

13

Reginald's ability to withstand it – pissed her off. A sandstorm built inside her, bursting with golden flame in the night. Her magic was a bonfire, flared by the magic assaulting her from the hall. That passion slammed into Reginald Durant, twisting deep into his body, raking him with talons and fangs. She felt it careen into him with anger and sex – and she felt his Dragon rise in return. Like a leviathan of power and carnality, his Siren-magic was suddenly surging up, coiling around her in an oceanic wave as his nostrils flared. Striding forward, he clamped a strong hand on Layla's wrist. Pouring the entire ocean through her in a torrent of furious – and delectable – passion.

"Enough, Courtesan!"

It was the strongest he'd ever touched her. Reginald's Siren-magics flowed deep into Layla's body and she cried out, stumbling as Reginald's passion tore through her. His breath was hard as he caught her around the waist, his pale blue eyes blazing in the twilight. As if that show of dominance had only pushed his own Dragon higher, Layla felt his magic surge with coils of carnality unlike anything she'd ever felt from the Siren. His power surrounded her, stroking, strangling, caressing – devouring and dominating her with a vicious lust.

As his power swamped her, Layla's inner Dragon roared in triumph. For weeks, Layla had been denied intimate contact with anyone, including her bound Dragon lovers Adrian Rhakvir and Dusk Arlohaim. Her skin was roaring with need, her body humming with passionate rage, and she suddenly realized what was pushing her ire with Reginald tonight. She hated leaving her position in Concierge Services; she hated the idea of sleeping with people for hire as a Courtesan. She hated being paraded in front of the Owners, and she hated that Reginald had trapped her into it.

But most of all, she hated that she still couldn't control her Dragon yet.

And that he could.

Reginald's breath rasped; pressed close, their chests heaved together. His eyes were wide, pearl-grey with bright flecks of gold in them now. Layla gasped as she watched the roaring passion in his eyes. Pressed close, she felt his strong breath rise and fall, his hands viciously hot where they gripped her – tightening hard.

But with a slow inhalation, Reginald mastered his inner Dragon. Layla felt him wrangle all that enormous carnality as his gaze slowly bled from pearl-grey back to a pale ice blue. As he gazed into her, deep and dominant, he sent that chill control into Layla. A sluicing sensation rolled her. The Head Courtier was a Dragon of the oceans and Layla felt the leviathan of his control as darkwater coils slid through her body. The terribly arousing, dominant sensation made her weak, collapsing into the Head Courtier as he held her fast.

"Do not challenge a Siren, Layla Price." Reginald's voice was low by her ear, his breath chill yet somehow hot. "Strike me again with your magics and watch how fast I obliterate you."

Sinking under his floes, Layla's heart hammered as a chill, sensual darkness devoured her. A delicious shudder slid through her as wetness spread between her thighs. Reginald smiled at her wreckage. Dominant, ruthless, his eyes were a dark grey now with flecks of gold that sparkled like the sun on an Arctic sea. Music lifted within Layla; a chorus of voices and reed pipes that sang in impossible harmonies.

Aching harmonies of danger, heartache, and sin.

Lifting a hand, Reginald arrested Layla's jaw with spread fingers. Running his thumb over her lower lip, he pulled it down. Opening her mouth, he glanced to her lips. As if his power went where his gaze commanded, Layla suddenly tasted the ocean sliding over her tongue; salt-spray and brine, and the creamy texture of the oyster. The sensation made her writhe against him as it licked to the back of her throat; thick and meaty. She had no choice but to swallow it, her entire body spasming with all that delicious heaviness sliding down her throat.

Deep inside her, its thick heat lingered. Layla shuddered against Reginald, undone. It was the most impossibly erotic thing she had ever felt, even more than her rumbling sexual encounters with Dusk and her heated passion with Adrian. She gasped, hoping he would do something about her wretched need.

Praying that he wouldn't.

"Feel me, Layla Price." Reginald breathed by her ear. "Defy my command again and I will assault you with my storms until you beg me to drown you. Tonight, you will show *composure*. You hold power as a Courtesan that you never could have achieved as a Concierge. Even though you are still in training, you will honor your new position as you follow my lead tonight. Am I clear?"

"Yes." Layla could hardly breathe. Cradled against Reginald's chest, his power made everything she'd felt inside the atrium feel insubstantial. His body was hot, so hot; even as waves of chill pleasure rolled through her, playing with her the way an orca plays with a seal. His lips smiled as she shuddered against him. Reginald had rolled her with his Siren's power.

And she loved it, dammit all to hell.

Looking up, she found Reginald watching her. Stroking his thumb over her lower lip, he pressed her with the softest kiss. Shivering with ecstasy, Layla melted into his mouth as he licked his pleasure into her, dark and exquisite. She felt him smile as he pulled away, leaving her gripping the stone railing of the veranda as if it was the only thing that could keep her afloat in his storm.

Their gazes connected.

Reginald's smile vanished as he stepped back.

"People have killed for my pleasure, Layla Price. People have died for it. People have taken their own lives because they could not have another night in my bed. Consider this: what might someone do to have my embrace? What might they risk; who might they betray to have my kiss again – or yours? What might any of these Hotel Owners do to support Adrian if you charm them tonight? This is the power of a true Courtier or Courtesan of the Hotel. Learn it. Come."

Head Courtier Reginald Durant made a sweeping gesture toward the glass atrium, as he watched Layla with his pale blue eyes. He didn't take up his wig, only extended his arm in an escorting position, waiting. Still flushing with the heat of his lesson, Layla took his arm. Trapping her hand lightly on his sleeve, Reginald twined his long fingers into hers, binding their hands together gently. It was an intimate gesture, kind, and for the first time Layla questioned her fury with him – wondering if maybe he wasn't as much of a bastard as she'd made him out to be.

Perhaps Reginald Durant really was trying to help her succeed with her magic.

And the danger they faced tonight.

CHAPTER 2 – OWNERS

Leading her back across the evening veranda, Reginald escorted Layla into the Hotel Owner's party. The fête was in the Blue Pavilion tonight, a massive domed atrium of cobalt crystal lattice with diamonds set into the ceiling to mimic a starry night sky. It was like an observatory, though the space was open with waterfalls and niches of greenery to meander through. The Pavilion was home to thousands of night-active moths, and as Layla and Reginald were admitted through the veranda doors by six Guards in crimson uniforms with pikes, they stepped through a shimmering netting and into a night-scape alive with life.

Luminous moths swirled lazily through the enormous blue dome. The twilight was waning outside, but underneath the dome it was always night. Around the space, veins in the greenery brightened as the twilight died, every tree and flowering vine vivid with phosphorescence. A string quartet played music and elegant people mingled with drinks or lounged in rattan chaises upon sprawling rugs. A moth as large as Layla's hand with fuzzy wings and long feather-feelers landed on her shoulder, glowing silver-white like her gown. Its feet tickled her as it walked around, trying to decide if she was a mate.

As they entered the pavilion, the cacophony of magic from the Hotel Owners suddenly closed around Layla again. Inundated with the combined power of over fifty people in the atrium not restricting their magics, it was like the Samhain Masquerade but worse, as seeking tendrils and thundering flows were suddenly wrapping around Layla, tasting and testing. Stiffening on Reginald's arm, she tried to breathe through it, navigating those flows like a river by floating among them as Reginald was teaching her.

But they were awful. The Samhain Masquerade had been a night of passion, and Layla's inner Dragon had roared with delight to surrender to the eros she'd felt then. But this party was about power, and as Layla entered the fête, she felt the Owners baiting her, trying to manipulate her with their magic. It was casual for them, all par for the course; but Layla's breath was suddenly high, her heart racing to be inundated in that vicious energy again. A scalding sensation built on her skin as her Dragon snarled inside her, coiling up into a pre-strike knot with fangs bared.

Reginald's fingers smoothed over hers upon his sleeve, and Layla felt an invisible wall of water surround her, much like Dusk did with his crystal shields. It was Reginald's version of a shield, flowing but strong, and Layla inhaled a grateful breath as she felt the drives of power sluiced away from her.

"Thanks." She spoke, relieved.

"Of course." He returned quietly, with a small smile.

They began to navigate the party, as they had been doing for a scant ten minutes prior, before Layla had panicked and stepped out to the veranda. Reginald was gloriously effete as he led her around, his haughty poise and piercing blue eyes instantly making even the Owners with the wretchedest magics attend him like he was royalty.

And in a way, he was. Reginald Durant was considered one of the top five Courtiers in the world, and commanded a price for his Assignations that reflected it. He was a celebrity, even among the Hotel Owners. As Reginald introduced Layla to a number of people she'd never met, all of them ancient and dripping with Twilight Realm money, not to mention ridiculous amounts of magic, Layla watched how the Owners treated him. They gave him bows and deferential nods, using his proper title as they watched him with avarice. Though Reginald looked human, albeit ridiculously handsome for one, everyone here knew exactly what he was, and treated him accordingly.

A Royal Siren, and an expert in the arts of passion.

Layla used her Concierge skills as they went around, memorizing names of Owners as she was introduced, their Lineage, and anything else notable about them. Though many looked human, they weren't; humans were not allowed to own a share of the Red Letter Hotel. Maneuvering around the hall, Reginald didn't linger – the Head Courtier was eye candy for the night, his date in the same category.

After twenty minutes of banal conversation, Layla was relieved to see her bound Royal Crystal Dragon lover and Head Concierge Dusk Arlohaim enter the pavilion with the Hotel's Madame, Etienne Voulouer. Dressed in a classic white tuxedo jacket, surprise took Dusk's handsome face as he saw Layla, as if he hadn't known she'd be in attendance. His smooth lips fell open, a wave of iridescence passing through the serrated ridges of midnight-blue scales at his temples and outer cheekbones, as well as his artfully-styled dark hair.

Dusk's vivid summer-blue eyes pierced her, sliding down her clinging silk gown with a pleased smile. Exceedingly sexy with his strong soccer-player's body, he turned, making a bow to the Madame. Leaving her, he maneuvered to where Reginald and Layla were speaking to a lizard-woman with iridescent green scales that matched her slinky green gown.

"Layla Price! You are a vision."

Dusk's hand flashed out before Reginald could pull her away – catching Layla's fingers and raising them to his lips. Pressing them with a soft kiss, he pressed a low tremor of his sexual magic into Layla with it, his sky-blue eyes simmering with all the pleasures they'd been denied these past weeks.   She was instantly on fire. Layla felt the full force of his vibrations hammer her – making her own magic roar. Passion seethed through Layla from her fingertips to the depths of her groin. But before her enormous energy could surge out to any Owners, Reginald thickened his shield around her in a furious wave.

But it wasn't enough. Layla's magic was rampant, careening into Dusk, her Dragon roaring to be touched by a mate long denied. Like two enormous beasts coiling through each other, Layla felt Dusk's magic surge to hers like a tower of crystal being thrust from the center of the earth. Layla shuddered; a wave of etheric golden flame burst from her. Heads turned and Owners raised eyebrows as Dusk shuddered – his gaze locked to Layla's and a bright cord of power braiding between their bodies in a golden-diamond rush.

Reginald plucked her hand from Dusk's in a brisk maneuver. Gripping Layla's wrist in cold fingers, he stepped between them, parting their Bound magics like the prow of an ice-breaking ship. Holding Layla's wrist, he poured his Siren-song through her bones as he stared her down, flooding her with the drowning ocean. She jolted, but managed to stay standing as Dusk's Bind to her was sluiced back.

"That is enough of that." Reginald murmured low. Turning to Dusk, he regarded the Hotel's Head Concierge with a frigid stare. "Touch her again, Dusk Arlohaim, and face my wrath. Layla needs composure tonight. Not your idiot antics."

"Idiot antics my ass." Dusk's sapphire gaze sparked with hot diamond-light as he sipped his bourbon on the rocks, trying to cover a deep shudder. Fierce anger shone in his eyes as he stepped close to Reginald with a falsely pleasant smile. "If this party tonight wasn't so important to the Paris Hotel, I'd be kicking your ass all the way to China right now for your machinations this past month, Reginald. Layla's not yours."

"And she's not yours again until she is *quite* done with me."

21

"Kids, please." Though breathing hard, Layla had her wits about her enough now to see that Owners were staring, trying to figure out what was happening between the Head Concierge, Head Courtier, and the unknown ingénue. "If this party is as important to Adrian and our Hotel as you say it is, let's get it together, shall we?"

"You're right, Layla." Dusk spoke briskly, ever the problem-solver. Pulling his magics back and stowing them solidly behind a barrier of invisible crystal shielding, Dusk took a deep breath. Turning to Reginald, he raised his glass and smoothed his face into a *fuck-you* pleasantry, though his low voice was snarling. "Here's to you, asshole. I'll be nice tonight, but only for Adrian's sake – and Layla's. Shall we mingle and talk up our Hotel?"

"Indeed."

With haughty grace, Reginald did not respond to Dusk's furious attitude as he took up Layla's hand again. Turning his back, Reginald led Layla away. But though their little show was over, owners were watching on all sides now as Reginald stopped to pluck a fresh glass of chardonnay from a caterer's tray for Layla, then took a red Bordeaux for himself. Reginald nodded at a tall, handsome Vampire with dark black eyes and sleek chestnut hair who was watching them, and angled Layla in that direction. Dressed in a classic tuxedo with long tails from the Victorian era, the Vampire was lean in a way that might have been spectral had he not had such beautifully masculine features and full, smiling lips. As Reginald and Layla arrived, tendrils of sucking darkness licked into Layla. She didn't know how to combat magic like that, but Reginald did; with a wave of his hand, he sluiced back that tendril.

"Your abilities against my kind have improved, protégé, since I saw you last." The Vampire spoke to Reginald with an amused smile on his full lips. The affable smile showed the tips of his vicious canines, and Layla was certain it was intentional.

"It has been a long while since I was at the Florence Hotel under your tutelage, Quinn." Reginald spoke back, though he was peaceable. Turning to Layla he said, "Layla Price, may I introduce the Barone Quindici DaPonti, Master of the Dark Haven of Florence, and an old mentor of mine at the Red Letter Hotel Florence. Quinn, this is Layla Price, Concierge of the Paris Hotel and Royal Dragon Bind of the Desert Dragons of Morocco and the Mediterranean."

It wasn't lost on Layla that Reginald had not mentioned to the Vampire she was training as a Courtesan. She hadn't known Reginald had worked at the Florence Hotel, but she didn't get to ask about it as Reginald made a gesture, indicating Layla should make the Barone's acquaintance more formally. She did, dipping into a slight curtsey and nodding in the manner Reginald had been teaching her. "Barone DaPonti. A pleasure."

The chestnut-haired Vampire laughed in a pleasant baritone, his wineglass sloshing a little too thickly as he did so – blood, not wine. "Ms. Price, excellently well-met. And you may call me Quindici, or Quinn. Many do."

"Quindici." Layla rose, cocking her head. "Were you the fifteenth child in your family?"

"Technically, yes." The Vampire Barone flashed fang again as he smiled pleasantly. "I was the fifteenth creation of my Sire, the Dark Temptress Emiliana DiClario, formerly of Rome though now long dead and dusted. She had no time for nomenclature, and so her children are named according to turn order."

"It's Vampire custom to take a new name when you are turned." Reginald supplied mildly.

"Well, I suppose numbering you would keep you all straight." Layla mused.

23

Her words made the Barone laugh again. He seemed to be of a pleasant nature, though the intensity of his presence indicated a highly calculating mind beneath it. Layla suddenly found herself wondering if the laughter and smiling wasn't a calculation also, as Quindici turned sober, watching the crowd as he addressed Reginald. "There are a number of Owners here tonight vying for Adrian's job, Reginald. If he fucks up even once more… I think they'll have it. Or you might."

"I no longer desire the leadership of this Hotel, Quinn, as you are quite aware." Reginald responded with a glance at Layla. They had suddenly delved into a very serious conversation and Layla perked – none of the other Owners having gone into this particular topic. "Do you have names I may relay to Adrian?"

"Lawrence Koss of the European Fumaroles," the Vampire spoke low, nodding subtly to a man twenty paces distant, a solid Germanic fellow with brick-red scales cascading from his temples and hands. "Visiniya Yffe of the Arctic Selkies," he nodded to a woman in a gown of white seal fur, her long white hair cascading down her back. "Bintni Rabii of the Kali-Makti," he nodded to a stunning woman with black skin and heated red eyes, built like a brick house with long black hair and a necklace of skulls draping between her breasts.

"Anyone else?" Reginald asked with a glance at the Vampire.

"Well, besides you-know-who," Quindici grinned at Reginald with a sly look, "there is of course, myself."

"You?" Reginald raised a doubtful eyebrow at the Vampire.

"Would you and Adrian rather have anyone else head up this Hotel if Adrian is dismissed?" The Vampire murmured slyly, a knowing glint in his black eyes. "Tell me that either Adrian or you have an ally amongst the Owners closer than I, and I will gladly back down. But last I counted, though your standing amongst the Owners is high, protégé, your allies among the inner circle of the Board are few – and Adrian's are fewer. To which of us may go the safekeeping of your dearest beloveds should Adrian fall, I wonder?"

The Vampire's pointed gaze at Layla was obvious, and Reginald scowled. "What's in it for you, Quinn?"

"Adrian and you have… ample income. And, from what I hear, Adrian pays those he employs for more… *clandestine* operations." The Vampire examined his exquisitely-buffed nails as his eyes glittered with dark pleasure.

"You need mercenaries?" Reginald's eyebrows lifted. "What for?"

"The Dark Haven of Pisa needs a little… change of operations. To be brought in line with my Dark Haven of Florence, ideally. I do not wish to waste my own Vampires for such a venture, but use a little more… firepower. So?"

Taking a harsh breath, Reginald glanced to Layla. She saw something uncertain move through his pale eyes, before he turned back to the Vampire. "Your word. If I tell Adrian to get what you need, and anything happens to Adrian, that you'll do everything in your power to keep this Hotel and everyone in it safe."

"On my maker's ashes, I swear it." The Vampire smiled slyly.

They clasped wrists. But glancing at Quindici, as he smiled at Layla again with a flash of fang, Layla knew Reginald had just made a deal with a devil on Adrian's behalf. Perhaps Adrian would have condoned it, perhaps he wouldn't have, but as Reginald led Layla away, she could still feel Quindici's eyes on her. A devouring darkness eased out, slipping up her thigh. Stepping briskly, Layla shook it off, and she heard an echo of laughter in her mind.

"What was that all about?" Layla asked Reginald.

"Not here; not now." He spoke softly, clearly not about to go into any detail about why he and Quindici had spoken. Angling her over to another group, Reginald stopped to speak with three squat mole-looking Owners with dark beady eyes. It was all banal pleasantries again and Layla was tuning out, when suddenly she felt a wash of interest move over Reginald's shield from the old mole-man standing next to her in a black tux. With a lecherous gleam in his eyes, his hand lifted – fondling Layla's breast through her clinging white silk.

It startled Layla so badly that she froze. No one else here had treated her like a piece of meat, and to have it so blatantly done suddenly made her heart hammer in shock. Without losing a beat, Reginald maneuvered Layla behind himself, corralling her into the greenery and cutting her off from the mole-man. The old lecher scowled, trying to strike through Reginald's magics. But with a scathing glance, Reginald washed a wave of power so hard over the mole-man that he stumbled and nearly fell on his face.

"Try that again, Remi Dufresne," Reginald spoke with menace, "and I will have you banned from this Hotel, I don't care who you are. She is not your Assignation for the night. Nor would I ever allow her to accept an Assignation from you."

"But she's yours, Reginald." The man startled, blinking his beady eyes at Reginald. "Sirens share their mates, do they not?"

"She is not mine. She is her own creature." Reginald returned darkly. "And I wouldn't share her with you even if the world was burning down. Test my patience again and watch it fail."

Layla felt Reginald's darkwater energy expand, filling the space between them like a nightmare of the deeps, swirling with terrible black currents. The mole-man was apparently not Reginald's friend, not like the Vampire, and the man set his jaw in a furious scowl. But he wouldn't push past Reginald's body or his inundating magics, and Layla felt relief flood her. Reginald had skills in courtly grace and charm, but he was also a vicious power to be reckoned with, Layla realized – a dominant in any situation.

The mole-man backed down. With a snort, he turned away, plucking a glass of champagne from the gilded tray of a Caterer and tossing it back. Moving to Reginald's side, Layla slid her fingers around the arm of his embroidered coat. He glanced over, his golden eyebrows lifted as if asking what she needed.

She mouthed *thank you* – meaning it for the second time tonight.

A small smile flickered over his lips, as if it pleased him that she had thanked him. But then he changed. All of a sudden, Reginald's pale blue gaze pressed hers with a deep thoughtfulness. Layla felt him flare his magic then, flashing a white-capped power through the entire pavilion. All around, heads turned with eyebrows raised. His demonstration of power arrested the full attention of the room, and once talk had silenced, Reginald moved. Lowering slowly to one knee, he knelt before Layla like a knight with his lady.

Raising her fingers to his full lips, he gave them a gentle kiss – letting that kiss linger as he watched her with his pale blue eyes.

Layla blinked. All around, people stared with open mouths, shock rioting through their magics, followed quickly by intrigue. Layla saw Dusk's lips fall open in astonishment a table away, his sapphire eyes wide. Next to him, the Madame was smiling with a subtle, catlike delight in her enormous 1950's peacock ballgown made of real peacock feathers. Layla realized from their reactions that the Head Courtier was doing her a grave honor, showing his obeisance in such a high-level crowd. Demonstrating to the Hotel Owner's Board that she was of elevated position, and not to be trifled with. It was like what Hunter had once done for her as Adam Rhakvir among the Dragon clans, but far more.

Adam had held standing in his own clan, but Reginald held standing among the highest elite of the Twilight Realm.

As he rose, Reginald lifted Layla's hand, his piercing gaze sweeping the assembly with a subtle challenge. The mole-man scowled, though his demeanor was broken as Reginald's glance found him – his eyes skittering away from the Royal Siren's command. At last, the party continued, people breaking into chatter though numerous eyes still watched Layla and Reginald. Reginald began escorting Layla over to a statuesque Faunus woman with sleek tawny fur and corkscrewing horns with gold torques curling up them – when a smooth baritone voice suddenly made the Head Courtier turn.

"Reginald Durant. Still slumming it for money with the plebes, little brother?"

Layla's eyebrows rose at the slur as she turned with Reginald – to find herself facing a man who could have been Reginald's twin he was so impossibly handsome. And as the two stared at each other, hatred seething between them, Layla marked it for the only thing it could have been.

The hatred of family.

The Hotel Owner who looked like Reginald's twin was handsome in the extreme. If Reginald had ditched the 1700's couture, he would have ended up looking something like this man; about the same height and build with the same bright gold hair, but cut short and well-styled. He looked like a male model straight out of a Calvin Klein underwear ad in his modern charcoal suit jacket and expensive silk details, with Reginald's full lips and austere high cheekbones. But where Reginald had ice-blue eyes that could change to the color of stormy oceans, this man had pure-white irises with a ring of pale blue around them – that made his impossible beauty look even colder than Reginald's.

"Bastien." Disdain dripped from Reginald's lips like cool poison as he faced the man Layla understood now to be his brother. "Done fucking your way through all of Greece, plying anyone with power to your manipulations?"

"Greece is *passé* these days." Bastien gave a biting smile, vicious though still somehow classy as he gestured with his dry martini at his brother. "You should keep up with your Lineage's whereabouts, Reginald. It's all about Ibiza these days. Or Maui. Or Cabo. Sirens are anywhere there's a high-end beach party, except rotting away at this stuffy old Hotel sleeping with grannies for cash."

"Hardly." Reginald's gaze devoured his brother as if he would eat Bastien alive.

"And who is this *winning* creature?" Reginald's brother turned to Layla with a haughty lift of his golden eyebrows – just like Reginald.

"Layla Price, Royal Dragon Bind of the Moroccan Desert Dragons. May I introduce my brother, Sebastien Durant, Royal and Clan Second of the North Sea Sirens."

"*Enchanté*." Bastien reached out to take Layla's hand, but Reginald swiftly blocked it, something furious flashing through his gaze.

"Touch her and lose your hand."

"It's just a simple kiss." But Bastien's gaze skewered Reginald like a harpoon, a scary kind of hatred in it as he flashed a nasty smile and sipped his martini.

"No touch is simple with you." Reginald snarled, something Layla had never heard the exquisitely composed Reginald do before. From the tension now bristling between them, Layla understood that Bastien had significant Siren-abilities through touch, and had meant Layla harm. "As Head Courtier of this Hotel, I forbid you to lay a hand on Layla while you are here."

"And *you* are limiting your potential, little brother, masquerading as a perfumed fuck-boy all these years." Bastien set his jaw, his white eyes glittering with malice and haughty disdain. "Taking on ingénues to train when you should be out claiming your birthright as a North Sea Siren. Have you forgotten your clan, Reginald?"

"Haranguing me about my choices again, Bastien?" Reginald had gone icy at Bastien's words, his voice soft and terrible. "For last I recall, they are mine to make."

"They are *father's* to make." Bastien's white eyes flashed with wrath. "He is your King and you defy him, playing the fop for rich matrons and denying your place at his side. You are a *Royal Siren*, Reginald. Your power is the duty of your clan."

"My power was not made for war." Reginald went very still beside Layla.

"That is *precisely* what your power was made for." Bastien's gaze was terrible as he stared his brother down. "And yet you deny father your talents during this conflict that has lasted so very long, while the rest of your brothers play their part. We are doing what needs to be done to end a blood-feud *you* started. While you run like a cowardly eel, hiding here in silks and lace."

"Last I heard, you were nowhere near the North Sea," Reginald retorted, scathing. "Fucking your way through the wealthiest Siren-clans of the Mediterranean gains father little."

"It gains father much." Bastien Durant swigged back his martini and set it decisively upon a side-table. "My actions gain our King allies. Far more than could ever be said of you."

"I send our King a generous tithe of my quarterly earnings for his sorties."

"Money isn't power, Reginald." Bastien's perfect lips lifted in a mean snarl. "Magic is power. And father needs yours at home."

"My magic is needed here." Reginald lifted his chin, his ice-blue eyes flashing fury. "My self-banishment contained the event that sparked this conflict, Bastien. Removing myself from the North Sea and swearing to the Blood Dragons that I would never return to their shores was good enough for King Huttr Erdhelm. The truce was written. But father broke that budding accord when he attacked Frostjavin. He saw an opportunity to invade the Norwegian fjords while they were weak from what I'd done. His actions caused the war. And only his actions provoke it."

Layla blinked at this astounding information seething between the two brothers. This was news, that Reginald had somehow started an entire war between the North Sea Sirens and the Blood Dragons of Sweden and Norway. It was something that had never been mentioned at the Hotel – not by Dusk, or Adrian, and not even by Rikyava

Andersen, the Blood Dragon Head Guardswoman whose uncle was King Huttr Erdhelm.

But before Reginald and Bastien's argument could inflate more, a stir occurred near the doors – as Layla's bound Royal Desert Dragon Adrian Rhakvir came striding into the pavilion.

Layla's breath stopped as she felt Adrian arrive, his desert-jasmine energy swirling through the room in a hot wave of power. Tall and striking, Adrian had an intensity that other Owners in the room simply couldn't match. His lean physique was honed, his shoulders sculpted and strong. His cheekbones were beautifully high, his jaw sharp with a soft black stubble, his thick black hair rakishly styled. Wearing a navy three-piece suit that caught the light, his royal plum shirt was open at the collar, matched by a silk pocket square. A gold pocketwatch on a chain was tucked into his waistcoat, a ruby and platinum ring flashing on his index finger with a snarling dragon.

But it wasn't Adrian's striking good looks or his heady cinnamon-jasmine scent that arrested Layla as he entered the pavilion, giving effortless greetings and clasping hands as he beamed his perfectly intriguing smile. It wasn't his swirl of desert wind that caught her as his intense Mediterranean-blue eyes found hers, piercing her and making her catch her breath. It was the way she could feel him, like a golden cord of heat and passion bound them together through the very depths of their souls.

Like they were a part of each other – and always would be.

Layla and Adrian's magics rushed out, greeting each other in a sensual slide of heat and coils and muscled power. Layla could feel him through her every sinew, and she knew Adrian felt her too, his aqua eyes blazing even as he kept making his greetings. Layla's magics weren't bound by her talisman anymore, and they wanted to devour Adrian. To revel in him. To writhe inside his body and haul him close.

Her Dragon surged forward to try and catch him; to make him enter a heated dance with her. But cool fingers stole around Layla's wrist and she closed her eyes, feeling Reginald's Siren corralling her back. He was more gentle about it than he'd been with Dusk, and Layla steadied, feeling her Bind with Adrian sluiced under a deep white wave. Her Dragon calmed beneath that oceanic power, but it left her feeling barren as she opened her eyes – finding Adrian's face fallen into hurt as he felt their Bind washed away also.

Which he had to cover quickly as a group of Hotel Owners came over to speak with him.

Layla understood Adrian's bleak look; she felt that way, too. It had been nearly a month since they had last been alone, courtesy of Reginald's strict limitation of Layla's exposure to her Bound men while she trained. Not to mention the fact that Adrian was always traveling for his numerous business ventures. She'd been allowed to train in fighting-magics down in the Guardhall with Dusk these past weeks, but not to see Dusk or Adrian in any kind of intimate setting.

And feeling her Bind with Adrian washed away now was torture.

"My, my." Layla had forgotten they were still engaged in conversation with Reginald's brother Bastien, until his ocean-smooth voice suddenly grated upon her ears. "The Royal Dragon Bind is causing trouble at the Paris Hotel, I see."

"That's none of your concern, Bastien." Reginald gave his brother a frigid look.

"As a Hotel Owner, it is my concern, actually." Bastien Durant had claimed a new martini and now sipped with a cruelly teasing glint in his eyes, flaunting what he was and what Reginald was not. "Adrian Rhakvir is under a lot of scrutiny. Everyone smiles to his face, but many of the Owners are talking behind his back; that perhaps Adrian has lost his ability to control this establishment, and the *creatures* employed in it – if he had any control over them at all." Bastien gave a pointed glance to Layla. "Depending on how things go, someone else may be appointed to Adrian's position here, soon."

"Not something you would ever want, when you have *Ibiza*." Reginald spoke frigidly.

"Oh, I don't know." Bastien sipped his martini with a cruel smile. "Paris has its charms."

Bastien had opened his lips to bait Reginald more, when a series of gamelan-style gongs sounded in the pavilion. Over near the garden entrance, a trio of gilded screens had been erected, and as everyone turned, the Madame took center stage, beckoning people to gather. It seemed they were to have some kind of entertainment, and as Reginald guided Layla over to a good viewing spot by a cobalt column with white trumpet-flower vines crawling up it, Layla felt Adrian step to her other side.

He glanced over at her, a wry smile curling his beautiful lips. Layla sensed Adrian wasn't about to do anything rash tonight, but though he didn't reach out to touch her, he did move close to her side as the crowd thickened before the gilded screens. The Madame was saying something about the entertainment, but Layla wasn't listening. All she could feel was Adrian's hot, sensual energy curling around her; stroking her neck and collarbones, kissing her lips. Tucking his hands in his pockets beside her, Adrian gave a clever, renegade smile – watching the speech even as he stole kisses from Layla on the sly with his magics.

Layla's eyelashes fluttered as her lips fell open. Delight rushed through her as Adrian's magics pressed her lips, licking softly, exploring. She could feel him as if he stood before her, cradling her neck with one hand and sliding the other around her waist to draw her close. It was all Layla could do to not moan as he kissed her, as he touched her deep and slow all the while standing perfectly at ease right beside her.

Feeling what was going on, Reginald stiffened, sliding a hand around Layla's waist as the gilded screens were pulled back. The view before them opened to two Courtiers and one Courtesan lounging in a group of antique crimson chaises. Dressed in draping black lace that covered little – her in a tight-corseted gown, them in men's Victorian dressing-robes and all wearing lace demi-masques – the trio began to engage in what Layla realized was to be a public Assignation for the Owners.

It was the best of what their Hotel had to offer, the tryst elegantly Parisian as it began with slow titillation and sexy foreplay, the men two of Reginald's best Courtiers and the woman Sylvania Eroganis' own protégé. But as it began, decadent and sensual, all Layla could feel was Adrian's hands stroking her. Adrian's lips kissing hers gently, teasing her, seeing how much she could keep her composure as they stood side-by-side and watched the show.

Layla could feel Reginald's energy rising, washing away Adrian's touches in a stealthy way that affected no one else around them. Adrian fought Reginald, licking in with his hot power to take Layla again and again. Eros was building inside her, and before her as the Assignation participant's clothing was shed. As hands started to play harder in the scene, and the two Royal Dragons fought subtly for possession of her, Layla could feel the temperature of the room heat, the Owners riveted as they watched the show. And as Adrian kissed her, Reginald trying to wash his attentions away in a scintillating game that left Layla burning up between them, she felt the entire situation pushing her over the edge.

Layla's Dragon raised its head, stirring its red-gold coils in an eager wave, wanting to revel in all the passion rising around her. Gripping her hip, Reginald crushed her close to his side now, digging his fingers in almost cruelly and piercing Layla with his Siren's cold to subdue her, so hard it made her sway. As the Assignation trio began to engage in coitus upon one gilded couch, the woman in the middle while the men took her at both sets of lips, Layla felt her Dragon roar, wanting the same situation between Reginald and Adrian. Layla shuddered hard, crying out softly, and Reginald's hand spasmed on her hip to stifle her.

Even as Adrian's power poured down her throat – touching her and taking her deep.

It might have been contained. Reginald, Adrian, and Layla might have been able to remove themselves from the hall to sort it out with words or even pissed-off petulance somewhere far from the party. But without warning, Bastien Durant's hand shot out from where he stood right behind Layla, gripping her wrist. Suddenly, Layla was drowning not only in Adrian's heat and Reginald's stern command – but in an entirely different kind of ocean, roaring with cruel power.

Reginald's control of Layla's Dragon was ferociously ripped away as Bastien crushed his fingertips into Layla's wrist. But rather than possess her, Bastien simply tore down the wall of protection Reginald had created between Layla and Adrian, undoing all the subtlety of the situation happening between them. Adrian's energy came roaring at Layla in a powerful wave of sex and lust, as the Assignation hit its climax. Coils of scalding power swamped Layla; delicious barbs raked her flesh.

And Layla's Dragon was suddenly roaring out – seething through the party.

She didn't just revel in the eros around her; she devoured it. As Layla's inner Dragon ate all that enormous heat in the pavilion, she roared, flaring her power in a disastrous wave. Sex and passion exploded through the room in a wash of golden flames and blistering wind. People cried out with passion and pain as Layla's power scorched them; magical shields were slammed up on every side as Owners staggered back. Adrian stumbled hard as the full force of Layla's power hit him, and even Reginald grunted as that wave of scalding energy slammed him also.

Layla could barely see the room; her body was a morass of pleasure, cascading through her in rioting waves. An enormous space had cleared around her, Reginald the only one withstanding her sudden gale as he tore Layla's wrist from his brother's hand. Stepping behind her quickly, Reginald gripped her by her throat and abdomen with a growl, hauling her close as she seized with pleasure in his arms. Beside her, Adrian was down on one knee, shuddering as his magic burst into simmering aqua and crimson flames, twining deep into Layla's and forming a devastating loop – expanding tenfold.

Moths lit up like torches all around the pavilion, chaises singeing and rugs charring. Wineglasses were dropped, shattering upon the pavilion's blue glass floor. Fierce winds whipped the air from Layla and Adrian's twined magic, carrying a stinging heat. The Assignation had ceased in the sudden outpouring of power, the participants clutching clothing as they retreated to the far edge of the hall.

But all Layla could hear was a scream of desert wind in her ears, and Adrian's roar.

Even Bastien Durant had stepped back with surprise in his cruel white eyes, the Owners shielding hard as they retreated to the edges of the atrium. Struggling to get to Layla, Adrian was being held back by Dusk and the Head Guardswoman Rikyava Andersen, who had arrived on the scene in a blitz of whirling blood droplets and a smell of battlefield char. With a curse, Dusk hauled Adrian toward the pavilion exit, but Adrian fought him like a mad thing. As Dusk wrangled one of Adrian's arms, Rikyava seized the other and bent it behind Adrian's back. He struggled, breathing hard as he stared at Layla with fire in his eyes and red-aqua flames searing around him.

Layla struggled also, needing to be free of Reginald's icy grip. She could barely draw breath, even with Reginald's Siren-magic commanding her like a black winter ocean. She needed to eat at Adrian's mouth; to drink from his lips. She needed to feel his coils around her; binding her, his fangs sinking deep inside her. She screamed at the sensation of it; and she felt Reginald's strong hands seize the back of her gown and rip it open, silver beads scattering. Somehow his chest was already bare and Layla felt her skin pressed to his firm flesh. Gripping her by the throat, Reginald massaged her neck; holding her, possessing her.

Corralling her back from Adrian's disastrous heat.

Layla finally felt Reginald's ocean drown her and she sank back against him, dazed. She shuddered hard, feeling his control; needing it. Fear slid through her returning awareness; that if Reginald ceased touching her, her and Adrian's roaring devastation would return.

But the Head Courtier didn't let her go. Continuing to massage her throat gently but firmly, he whispered something in her ear that carried his oceanic susurrations. Pressed against Reginald's embroidered coat and bare skin, she could feel his strong, lean chest rise and fall. His breath was steady, his body warm, and at last Layla remembered she could breathe through her rioting lust.

"Easy, Courtesan," Reginald murmured, still holding her close. "Feel me breathe and be easy…"

Layla could finally think again. At last, she was aware of the party. Everyone gaped in a wide circle around them, drinks and everything else forgotten. No fewer than thirty Hotel Guards in crimson hovered nearby, not rushing in yet, but watching Reginald. Adrian, Dusk, and Rikyava were no longer in the hall. Layla didn't know how many minutes it had been, but it seemed she'd lost time inside her roaring maelstrom.

At last, Reginald gave the Hotel Guards a terse nod. The Guards moved in but not to Layla, instead beginning to clean up all the shattered glass from dropped champagne flutes and wine stems. All around, Layla could see Owners either shivering or scowling or both. The woman with green lizard-scales had fainted and was being carried off by a lean man who shot Layla a look like daggers – from eyes that seared with gold-umber flames.

"Layla, can you hear me?" Reginald spoke softly by her ear. "I need to let you go. Too many people are staring. You need to stand on your own. Are you ready?"

Layla gave a weak nod. She didn't know if she could; her knees felt like jelly from the ecstasy that had just poured through her. She had been devastated by her reaction to Adrian's magic and their Bind – something so desired for weeks suddenly granted in a terrible, hedonistic rush because of Bastien Durant's cruel interference.

Her body was unsteady as Reginald pulled away, but somehow Layla managed to stand on her own, Reginald thankfully leaving her hand upon his arm to steady her. Layla couldn't meet any eyes. She knew she was fiercely flushed, having practically fucked Adrian in front of the entire Board. Adrian was nowhere to be seen, though Dusk had returned in his elegant tux, his eyes dazzling with blue-diamond fire and his breath heaving as their gazes connected.

The look he gave Layla was bleak – bad.

Layla's gaze caught upon Sylvania Eroganis, the Hotel's Head Courtesan. Dressed in a glorious gown of barely-there silver lace that showed her body piercings with their strings of pearls, the Silver Passion's straight silver brows were knit in concern, a look Sylvania never made. Beside her, Madame Etienne Voulouer stood in her enormous peacock ballgown, clasping hands of Owners and already charming them with blithely incessant patter.

Damage control, Layla thought, as she watched Sylvania turn to other Owners and begin laughing with her dulcet tones as if nothing had happened. Courtiers and Courtesans working the party tonight were chatting and laughing blithely, engaging Owners to smooth over what had just happened as if Layla and Adrian's magical outburst had never been. Layla realized they were all doing damage control, not just because of what had happened with her, but because of what had happened with Adrian.

Reginald's hands were gentle upon Layla, slipping to her bare shoulders. Rikyava had returned, whispering something to the Madame, urgency in every line of her statuesque Swedish frame and one hand on the rapier at her hip. Layla startled to note that Rikyava's cheekbone was bruising, dark and ugly. Had Adrian punched her? Concern washed through Layla as the Madame's eyebrows rose in alarm. Turning to Sylvania, the Madame spoke quickly and the silver woman blinked then turned, moving swiftly from the hall with Rikyava.

People were finally mingling again. Talk had resumed, the space around Reginald and Layla diminishing though people were still glancing at Layla like she was a rabid animal. Layla felt like it. What impression had she made tonight, completely losing control of her magic in front of the Hotel Owners?

"Well." Bastien Durant's gratingly smooth tones skewered Layla as he sipped his martini. "I think we've seen all we needed to see tonight, about how well Adrian controls this establishment."

Reginald's gaze whipped around to his brother. His nostrils flared, his eyes burning a wrathful blue-white as he concentrated his fury upon Bastien. Layla felt something lash out from Reginald like a typhoon, striking his brother in a harsh, vicious whip.

Bastien flinched, his white eyes widening at the sudden attack.

"You *dare* strike your Clan Second—!"

"Your ocean will run dry by my hand someday, Bastien." Reginald interrupted him, in an utterly cold, dead voice. "Come, Layla."

Escorting Layla out of the Blue Pavilion, Reginald did not glance back at his wicked brother, but led Layla from the hall with one hand around her waist in a promenade that placed him behind her so the ruined back of her dress wasn't visible. But all the same, Layla felt bare as they left the soirée. Bare to the stinging criticism now whispering through the Hotel Owners, bare to their scathing glances.

Bare to her embarrassment and shame – that she had no control over her Dragon and now everyone knew it.

Her cheeks were burning as they made it to the veranda. Tears stung Layla's eyes as she blinked at the cold stars, shining bright in the stark winter sky. Her breath hitched and she set her jaw. But Reginald felt it, for he shifted, clasping Layla's waist and guiding her gently away into the barren topiaries. Out in the shroud of winter darkness, Layla smelled only the cold night and Reginald's fresh ocean scent. But past a thick copse of hedges, she couldn't hold it in any longer.

With a sob, she sank to a stone bench – losing it.

CHAPTER 4 – FURY

Reginald sat beside Layla, tucking her close to his body as she cried. Cradling her, he made soothing sounds as he rocked her quietly on the stone bench out in the cold nighttime gardens. It was the most tenderness he'd ever shown her, and it made Layla cry harder, hating it and needing it at the same time. Moving behind her, Reginald turned them diagonally on the bench so he could pull her close and cradle her back to his bare chest.

Sobbing hard with fury and embarrassment, Layla's breath hitched. Reginald said nothing; simply held her. Layla had a sudden vision of a quiet harbor in a sheltering cove filled with Viking ships with smoke rising from thatched-beam farmsteads. Reginald was her safe harbor as the stars shone bright above, as a chill wind snaked through the hedges. Kissing her temple, his embrace warm, they shared a deep moment as Layla's lust and fury at last blew away.

"Thank you," she finally sighed, relaxing back into him. "For the third time tonight."

"You're welcome." He murmured, brushing her curls back so he could kiss her shoulder. Layla breathed quietly, feeling Reginald's warm, strong chest still pressed against her. Broken strings of beads draped at her sides from his fast action, but her slinky dress managed to stay on. He'd not relinquished their contact, and Layla burrowed back into him, relishing the quietude.

Her nose turned into his neck, breathing in his mild ocean scent above the high collar of his embroidered coat. He raised his chin, letting her smell him. Breathing him in, Layla could see sunlight on the sea again; boats casting fishing-nets and lines. She heard him sigh as the vision was washed away in a curling white tide.

"Those are not your memories, Layla," Reginald spoke. "Best leave them alone."

"I'm seeing your memories?" She asked, confused.

"Being a Royal Dragon Bind means you have resonant magic similar to Dusk's," he murmured, stroking her curls from her neck again. "I've had to thrust my power deep inside you tonight. You are reading my power, my emotions. My memories."

Reginald slipped into silence. Time faded as Layla sat with him, watching glimmering fairy-lights dance like slow fireflies through the winter hedges. The garden was beautiful tonight, but she barely registered it, her mind pouring back over the disaster that had happened inside the Blue Pavilion. Reginald must have felt it, because at last he heaved a sigh, then rose from the bench, extending his hand.

"Come. You need to blow off steam. Let us retire to the Guardhall for the remainder of the evening. There is no need to return to the party."

Layla didn't know if Reginald's statement was a chastisement or simply an acknowledgement of futility. But as she gazed up at his austerely handsome face, she saw no anger in it. He was simply fatigued, with that same mixture of emotions that he'd only begun to show her tonight.

Taking his hand, Layla rose. Without any further talk, Reginald led her back to the Hotel, though nowhere near the Blue Pavilion. Moving down a number of stairs to a stone door that led to the rear of the Guardhall, Reginald stepped into a foyer, Layla behind him. The stone foyer led into a vaulted dressing-area for the underground catacombs of the Guardhall, an auxiliary entrance that Guard personnel

43

often used. Well-built men and women of different Twilight Lineages idled at lockers and benches, donning workout gear or crimson 1800's Guard uniforms. A few looked up as Layla and Reginald entered, but soon went back to dressing.

Layla understood their nonchalance. She was a fixture down here in the Guardhall these past weeks, training daily with Rikyava or Dusk and sometimes both to blow off magical steam now that her hamsa-cuff was gone. Reginald had encouraged her to train in fighting since they'd become partnered, and he was encouraging it yet again as a solution to the debacle tonight. As Layla moved through the underground catacombs after his fencer's grace, Guardsmen and women in crimson uniforms gave the Head Courtier curt nods. Layla couldn't help but feel curiosity as she moved to her locker and pulled out a dark green tank top, charcoal yoga pants, and black ballet flats. Reginald had never come down here before with her, and she wondered if he was going to join her in sparring.

But he didn't move to a locker of his own, just idled near Layla and nodded for her to dress. She did, shucking the ruined gown and trying to fold it neatly into her locker. It was salvageable, and she intended to ask the Head Clothier Amalia DuFane to repair it. It was something Dusk would have done, and Layla smiled a little as she donned her yoga gear. Since their Bind, she was thinking more like Dusk – saving everything in a strangely frugal way, yet enjoying every delicacy as if there would never be any more.

It softened her wrath, but not by much. Layla still simmered as she pulled her long curls back into a ponytail and slipped on her flats. She wasn't feeling embarrassed anymore, just furious. A seething sensation like hissing surged through her and where it went, Layla's fury boiled. Bastien Durant was so on her shit list. If she ever saw him again, she was going to unleash all her wrath on him, Hotel Owner or not. But Layla couldn't do that if she had no stopping point. And even as she seethed, that thought pushed her determination.

She would conquer her magics, or exhaust herself trying.

With a brisk nod to Reginald, Layla grabbed a sweat-towel from a stand nearby and flipped it over her shoulder, indicating she was ready. She saw his lips quirk as he took her in, dressed for a fight now rather than a party. Layla supposed the party had been its own kind of battle. But the real battle was still taking place inside her, as her Dragon rioted through her veins with rage.

Making even seasoned Guard personnel nearby raise their eyebrows and edge back from her stinging heat.

"Are you ready?" Reginald asked.

"Ready to fuck some shit up." Layla growled, reaching up and pulling her ponytail tighter.

Reaching out, Reginald gestured her towards the dressing-hall exit, though he didn't touch her. Layla felt a growl boiling inside her as she stepped towards the exit, needing some fight-training badly now. As she hitched a hard sigh, rage flaring her cheeks as she pushed out the stone door of the dressing-area, which pivoted smoothly beneath her hands, Reginald glanced over with a far less austere smile than usual.

"That was quite a show back at the party." He spoke casually.

"That was a disaster!" Layla growled, pissed. "How am I ever going to be able to show my face among the Hotel Owners again? And now they think Adrian can't control this branch!"

She thought Reginald might chastise her for language, but he only escorted her calmly, moving like a gentle surge of the ocean beside her. "I think you've raised their interest, actually. What was a disaster in the moment may actually prove a benefit, Layla. It is always better to make an impression like a thunderstorm than a limpid breeze. They will *all* remember the Royal Dragon Bind now. And the Owners who were not there, many of the more powerful ones, will hear tales of you. They will become wary of the Bind's power – even if they don't know what that is quite yet."

"I don't feel powerful." Layla grumped as they turned a corner into the wide main catacomb, moving into a bustle of Guard personnel going briskly about their duties. "How do I show the Owners power if I can't control any of it yet?!"

"You will, eventually. And the brute force of barbaric, untamed magic is often more frightening than a honed blade." Reginald reached out absently, stroking her back, his fingers brushing one of her sable curls at the end of her long ponytail. Even though he was tightly controlling his magics, his touch made things low in Layla's body clench. Heat simmered between them and her breath caught, feeling his steady fingers caress her. She felt Reginald realize what he was doing and adjust his magics – pouring an oceanic calm through her instead of his ardor.

But Layla knew what she'd felt. Reginald was suppressing an attraction to her, and as Layla glanced at him, she was suddenly arrested by his handsomeness, as if gold could have been made into an Adonis of the ocean. He looked over, and Layla saw something she hadn't seen before. Reginald had a kindness in his face that Bastien, for all his statuesque beauty, didn't have. Reginald's pale blue eyes were haughty, and at times they could be cruel, but as he and Layla arrived at the alcove that led in to Rikyava's office, all she saw in him was an ancient sadness.

"Reginald." Layla turned, something moving in her heart for him. "Were the things Bastien said tonight true?"

Lifting a hand, he cupped her cheek with his long fingers, his brows knit. "Yes. But my words to him were more true. I have a dark past, Layla, and my family seeks to chain me with it. The Durant Sirens have ruled the North Sea for over three thousand years, and at one time, I was next in line to be King, despite being the youngest in my family. Siren inheritance follows power, and I have more than most. Bastien criticizes me because my family wishes to chain my power to their talons, and I won't let them."

"Because they would use you in their war against the Blood Dragons."

"Yes." Reginald's gaze tightened, his eyes becoming sharply icy. "And I cannot let that happen."

"Does this have something to do with your memories I glimpsed?" Layla asked, having a deep intuition that it did.

"It does, but we have no time for details now." Reginald spoke, effectively telling her that he wasn't ready to share. "But while Bastien seeks to tear down my place here at the Hotel, by defaming me and attacking those I associate with, what my odious brother doesn't understand is that he triggered a demonstration tonight. While it has proven that you and Adrian don't have control over your Bind yet, it also showed something far deeper to the Hotel Owners. It showed that you have power in that connection. A power to be noticed; a power to be feared. A power that could trump their hegemony, if applied in the right fashion."

Layla understood what he was telling her. That she had the power, bound to Adrian and Dusk, to be a threat to the entire Hotel Owners Board.

"Do we need to meet with the Owners again this week?" She asked, dreading the answer.

"No." Reginald spoke succinctly. "Better to leave them guessing at just how much you may be raging right now, bonded to Adrian Rhakvir and denied the right to mate with him. And how much power that may be generating for you."

"What?" Layla blinked, confused.

"Your magic is behaving around Adrian and Dusk as if you are life-mates, Layla, something most Dragons take decades to find, or centuries." Reginald's brows knit again as he watched her. "But Adrian's energy, and Dusk's, race to you like you're the only woman in the world. You've bound them fast. For you, they would do anything. Adrian made a fool of himself tonight, but it wasn't his fault. All of you are powerful individuals – but connected, it is like touching a live power plant with your bare hands. Something that none of you are adjusted to yet, especially since you've not been able to explore it this past month."

"And whose fault is that?" Layla growled angrily, crossing her arms.

"Mine. On purpose. Come."

With that enigmatic answer, Reginald led Layla in through the stone doors of an octagonal office absolutely stuffed with a hodgepodge of papers and wall-to-wall cabinets full of weapons. The chaos of stone and clutter was Rikyava Andersen's office as Head of the Hotel Guard, and as they arrived, the statuesque Swedish Guardswoman looked up from examining a cruel-looking ebony spear with a long obsidian blade. The spear had sigils like Norse runes inset all along the shaft in gold, and they flared a caustic violet to Rikyava's touch as she examined it, the color filtering into the blade like vivid purple ink. But seeing them enter, Rikyava turned, setting the spear aside in a rack, her straight blonde eyebrows rising.

A nasty bruise purpled the Guardswoman's cheekbone, extending all the way to her eyebrow and ear. Layla's lips fell open, knowing it had been Adrian who'd done that tonight.

"Rikyava, are you ok?" Layla rushed forward, her hands rising to Rikyava's face to examine the bruise, though she really couldn't do anything about it.

"It's fine. Layla, it's fine." Rikyava smiled wryly as she trapped Layla's hands, lowering them away from the bruise. "I'm not going to lose an eye or anything, so I call it a win. Adrian really doesn't sucker-punch all that hard."

"How is he, Adrian?" Layla's brows knit, worrying for him.

"He'll be fine." Rikyava patted her hands, though her smile was tense. "He's just upstairs in his apartment having a few drinks to chillax. Dusk and Sylvania are with him, helping calm his Dragon so he can sleep it off."

"You didn't use *that* on him." Reginald's gaze was frosty as he nodded at the ebony spear. Something in his glance was dark as he and the Head Guardswoman shared a look.

"I didn't need to." Rikyava spoke firmly. "But I'm having the Guard get them out and start practicing with them, just in case."

"Astute." But Reginald's voice was still chill as he glanced at the spear again.

"What does that spear do?" Layla asked, frowning.

"Forbidden Spears paralyze Dragons, Layla." Rikyava spoke brusquely, though her words were soft. "They're intensely effective magical weapons, used especially if someone gets out of hand in Dragon-form."

"You think you might have to paralyze Adrian from going full-Dragon sometime?" Layla blinked, understanding. "Because of he and I's Bind?"

"Hopefully not." Rikyava gave a hard sigh, running a hand over her long blonde ponytail, her lavender eyes tight. "But everything that happened between you and him this evening just makes me worry. It's not the first time your Bind has triggered you both. Let's just say I'm hoping it doesn't come to using the Spears, but it's my job to protect the Hotel and everyone inside it. Sometimes… protecting your friends means taking one of them out.”

Layla's gaze pinned Rikyava. “Are you saying that if Adrian went ballistic in Dragon-form because of our Bind that you would kill him?”

“I would do everything in my power to prevent him from doing harm, and from harm coming to him.” Rikyava spoke quietly, though her firm gaze upon Layla brokered no bullshit.

“Hopefully, we may all find a better way.” Reginald interrupted calmly. “Rikyava, I need to tend a few things with the Madame after tonight's antics. Would you mind occupying Layla and helping her discharge a while?”

“Sure.” Rikyava spoke with a genial nod. “Unless someone else goes ballistic at the party – though I think we've probably seen the last of the pyrotechnics. Come on, Layla. Let's get set.”

Moving toward the doors, Rikyava gestured for Layla. Layla thought Reginald might give her some final instruction for the evening, but he didn't. With a short, elegant bow, he simply departed, his ice-blue gaze straying one last time to the black spear. It was a hard look, as if the odious weapon was something never to be used unless one was at the very end of need.

Layla shivered, hoping to god they weren't there yet with Adrian. But Rikyava beckoned again, and Layla moved after her out of the office, striding across the vaulted main hall and turning left towards the magical fight-halls. Heading in through the open door of one hall, as large as a basketball court and entirely coated in a thick flow of rose quartz, Rikyava beckoned Layla in, then shut the three-foot-thick door behind them. Moving to a rose quartz bench, Rikyava shucked her crimson Guard jacket as Layla did a few stretches.

They turned, facing each other, and Rikyava gave a wry smile. “Ready to blow off some steam, girlfriend?”

"Absolutely." Layla sighed as she stepped out into the center of the hall.

CHAPTER 5 – FIGHT

Whirling in a fast maneuver, Layla swept her leg along the rose quartz floor of the practice hall, then followed it with a curling double-wrist gesture like a lotus, and a quick exhalation of *HA!* The sound came from deep inside her, a heave of energy from her core supported by her diaphragm, not unlike a sound she might have made in a power yoga class back in Seattle. Like a combination of ballet and a fast martial art, the maneuver took all her core balance to pull off. She felt it sweep up her Dragon-magics like a sand-funnel, her standing leg anchoring her to the rose quartz as energy channeled from her core through her wrists in a blistering wave of heat.

The sharp exhalation should have pushed Layla's Desert Dragon magics into a quick, precise strike at the stuffed dummy propped on a pole in the training-hall, knocking it over in a blast of hot wind. But what she got was a scalding wave of real golden fire manifesting in the air between her fingers – hurling out at the dummy and charring it into a sudden fireball.

Laughter rang out behind her – Rikyava's roaring, amused laugh. Panting, Layla lowered her hands, blinking at the conflagration. Stepping up behind her and still chuckling, Rikyava waved a hand. A halo of blood droplets shot from the Guardswoman's palm, engulfing the blazing dummy and snuffing Layla's fire out to wisps of smoke. Stepping over, Rikyava clapped a hand on Layla's shoulder with a grin, amusement sparkling in her lavender eyes.

"Well, shit. Not exactly what we were going for with that last move, but effective."

Layla shook her head as she growled in fury, her long ponytail brushing over her bare shoulders. Setting her hands to her hips, she actually roared at the dummy as her Dragon screamed in her veins with exasperation.

"Fuck! Am I ever going to get control over my magic?"

"Patience, padawan." Rikyava grinned, reaching up to pull out the ponytail holder from her long Swedish-blonde hair and scratch a hand through her luscious mane. "You may think you're not making progress, but you got most of that maneuver right just now. Everything was good except your hand position. You're too damn tense. Remember what I told you before about Desert Dragons: tense muscles make fire, soft muscles make wind. You're one of the few Dragon Lineages that can manifest fire, Layla. Learn the difference between tense and loose muscles, and you might be able to even breathe fire eventually."

"Like that's going to help me. Dammit!"

Wiping sweat from her brow with her forearm, Layla turned toward her friend. Dressed in her white silk undershirt with black Guard breeches and tall black boots, Rikyava was built in all the right places, tall and statuesque. Grinning as she walked over to a basin set into the nearest wall, flowing with a waterfall, Rikyava reached in, pulling out two chilled glass bottles of water with stainless steel tops.

Opening one, she swigged it, then gestured to Layla with the other. Moving forward, Layla twisted the top off her bottle, the condensation on the glass cool to her fingers. Swigging water, she enjoyed the chill sensation cascading down her throat, the water bottled from an artesian spring far beneath the Hotel.

"Actually," Rikyava spoke, wiping her lips with her forearm. "Desert Dragons are famous for fire-breathing, and it's super intimidating. Adrian's excellent at breathing fire. It's part of why he's won so many dominance-battles, and why people give him respect though he's still young. He can make fire-walls, weave fire into whips and spears, even in human form. Pretty cool, really. You might be able to do those things eventually. You're learning battle-magics far faster than anyone I've trained, and a lot of maneuvers that make sense to you are things Dusk and Adrian are good at. As if you're channeling them through your Bind when we train."

"It feels that way sometimes." Layla nodded, swigging her water and wiping a sheen of sweat from her neck. They'd been training for nearly two hours, and still Layla's body felt infernally hot, as if the Dragon inside her could keep going all night after the rage and embarrassment she'd experienced at the Owner's party.

"You feel like you're channeling your guys when you fight?" Rikyava lifted her straight blonde brows, nodding to the rose quartz bench by the wall. They moved over and sat, Layla kicking off her ballet-flats and grounding her bare feet on the cool quartz flow with a sigh.

"I do." Layla nodded, glancing over to Rikyava. "Some of the movements just feel so right in my body, like I've known them for decades. It's like I have a whole repertoire of having danced for the New York Ballet, but I've never even stepped on stage."

"*Lucky*." Rikyava imitated Napoleon Dynamite with a grinning pout. "Most Twilight Realm folk study for centuries to have the fluidity you're picking up on. Which brings up the point: how come you're so tense, Layla? It's not like this is hard for you. I'd prescribe meditation and yoga and Rake André's drinks to relax you, except I already know you do those things. So what gives?"

With a hard sigh, Layla leaned back upon the smooth rose quartz wall. Gazing up at the ceiling of the training hall, she let her gaze wander over the lofty pink vaults. The entire room was rose quartz, from the glassy floor to the high vaulted domes. Some long-ago Crystal Dragon had grown it when the Hotel was built, this hall originally carved out of bedrock, then improved with a three-foot-thick layer of crystal to act as magical insulation. It was lovely, glowing far above and all around them with its own light like being inside a giant pink candy dish.

"Layla? Earth to Layla." Rikyava chuckled beside her. "Where you at, girlfriend?"

"Sorry." Layla heaved another sigh, her dark eyebrows pinching into a frown as she glanced back to her friend. "I think it's Reginald. I think he's why I'm so tense lately."

"You think?" Rikyava joked wryly, her violet eyes teasing. "How's your house-arrest going with the big bad Siren, anyhow?"

"Awful." Layla shook her head, still leaning back against the wall. "Living in his apartment with him night and day just grates on me, Rikyava. The only time I have to myself is when I'm down here training, or when he's out having an Assignation. For three weeks it's been *stand up straight. A Courtesan doesn't pout. Not that fork, the other one. Ankles crossed, don't splay your legs like a dock worker on the subway.*"

"Figures." Rikyava snorted, taking another swig of water. "That man is insufferable. When the Hotel Departmental Board voted to make you a Courtesan three weeks ago, I was fucking livid. Everybody could see that was *so* not the right decision for you."

"I don't know, Rikyava." Layla smoothed her feet over the crystal flow, feeling its grounding. Deep inside, her Dragon stirred restlessly, just as it did every time she thought about becoming a Courtesan, or Reginald. With a languid roll, it lit her veins with fire, and Layla was suddenly simmering not with battle anymore, but sex. Lustful thoughts filled her; sensations of scales sliding over skin like hot silk. She shivered and an etheric golden fire sloughed off her body – the kind that didn't burn, but the sign that her eros was taking charge rather than her fury.

"Ooh… easy." Rikyava shivered next to Layla with a knowing smile. "That sex-magic of yours could make Caligula shy."

"That's just the thing." Layla glanced over, feeling a surge of frustration now. "I might not want to become a Courtesan, but my Dragon does. She doesn't care that I have issues about sleeping with people for money, or about monogamy. And the more Reginald denies me any touch these past weeks, the stronger it's getting. I feel like I need to up my fighting sessions to three times a day just to blow off all my pent-up sexual frustration. I thought I had a high libido before my Dragon woke. Now… it's just insane."

"Why do you think most Dragons take a number of partners, more than almost any other Lineage?" Rikyava chuckled with a knowing look in her lavender eyes. "Because it's either fuck or fight, Layla. Most of us with normal day jobs don't want to be all tied up in a fighting rage all the time. So fuck it is."

"Except I'm stuck in the opposite situation right now thanks to Reginald's ultimatums. More celibate than a nun on Sunday." Layla growled, feeling a conflicted heat rise inside her. Reginald had been odious with her for weeks, yet suddenly tonight had showed a deeply tender side, protecting her from the Owners and helping ease her fury afterwards. As Layla thought of him, of how kindly he'd held her out in the gardens, her Dragon coiled over with a languid, sexual movement – not conflicted about Reginald in the slightest.

"But isn't Reginald training you in all the sexy stuff?" Rikyava frowned now, cocking her head. "I thought everybody had to learn those things during their training to become a Courtesan. And since Reginald's not allowing you to see Adrian or Dusk, I thought you two would totally be boning by now."

"Nope." Layla growled, sliding her feet over the quartz floor again as her Dragon coiled restlessly inside her. "Before tonight, the most Reginald and I touched was when he fixed my hair, or if we were practicing dancing. He's sat with me through Assignation demonstrations on various topics, but that's all. Which just drives me even more crazy – watching people have sex and having to sit primly on a chair next to Reginald and discuss it like it's an art class."

"Like tonight." Rikyava's gaze was knowing as they finally came around to speaking of everything that had happened at the Owner's party. "When that Assignation demonstration started in the Blue Pavilion, I felt your Dragon's power spike, Layla. Hard. I was outside in the main hall of the Hotel, and good thing I was, when Adrian went ballistic. What happened, anyway?"

"Reginald's brother happened," Layla sighed, hating recalling it though it was nice to tell a friend. "Bastien Durant. Adrian was teasing me with his magics during the Assignation demonstration and Reginald was trying to fend him off. I think we all could have settled it like human beings if we'd just left the room, but Bastien had to reach out just then and tear down Reginald's protection. Voilà. Crisis instigated."

"No shit." Rikyava went silent a long moment, and Layla wondered if she was thinking about that black spear again. "I hate Bastien Durant. I've met him a few times, and every time, he's a fucking dick."

"I thought Reginald was the dick of the family?" Layla smiled sidelong at her friend.

"Not even close." Rikyava scowled, propping one boot up on the bench, not in a teasing mood now. "Reginald is a hard-ass, but most of his family make him look like a summer breeze, trust me. The Durant Sirens are like the Chicago mafia of the 1920's. They're bad news, *really* bad news, most of them. You think Reginald's dominant? Think again."

"Do you hate him? Because of your clan?" Layla hedged, wondering about the situation between the Blood Dragons of Norway and Sweden and the North Sea Sirens.

"Reginald?" Rikyava blinked at her, astonishment and something complex moving in her gaze. "I don't hate Reginald, Layla. Even though my clan is at war with his, he and I… we don't dwell on the politics of our clans. Like him, I chose to take a job here at the Hotel because I wanted to escape my clan's responsibilities. Fortunately for me, my uncle King Huttr respects my decision. To him, battle is battle, and even if I'm doing it here for the Hotel, it still earns our clan prowess. Reginald's father, King Léviathan Durant of the North Sea Sirens, doesn't see things that way. He sees what Reginald is doing here as a betrayal of their clan. He doesn't see what the rest of us do…"

"That Reginald is a celebrity here?" Layla spoke, thinking about how he'd been treated at the Owner's party.

"More than that." Rikyava glanced over, that complex look in her gaze again. "Reginald holds more power in the Twilight Realm than any of us here at the Paris Hotel, even Adrian. He's built his empire in the bedroom, but he's no pushover. He has immense influence, Layla. You're lucky he's training you. You don't even know how lucky, even though he's a dick sometimes."

Sobering, Layla thought that over, thankful that Rikyava could always put things in perspective. "But seriously. Why is Reginald training me with so much restriction? Is he just trying to drive me nuts? He knows how hard I'm chafing; he basically admitted it tonight. I mean, everything that happened at the party could have been avoided if he'd just let Adrian and I be alone together these past weeks."

Rikyava laughed, still chuckling as she sipped her water. "I think

Aldo's trying to drive your Dragon nuts, girlfriend."

"Why?" Layla glanced over, sensing Rikyava was right but still confused, as it echoed something Reginald had hinted at. "Why would he want to drive my Dragon nuts?"

"To make you stronger." Rikyava set her water bottle aside on the bench. "Look, Layla. When Dragons get pent-up, their magic intensifies. When pro boxers have a fight coming up, or pro weightlifters have a competition, everybody knows they don't fuck. They take all that raging energy and channel it into their sport. Same is true of Dragons. The more Reginald frustrates you, holding his sexy eye-candy at bay while you have to live with it daily, not to mention keeping you away from your bound men, the more he cranks your magic up. Your power is growing at alarming rates, Layla. I don't know if you're aware, but you are a long way from where your magic started back in August, talisman or no. Normally, Dragons take decades or centuries to develop their magic. You just suddenly flipped yours on – and Reginald is taking that power and purposefully blocking it to see how high it'll ratchet up. And how quickly."

"Does he care that it's driving me insane?" Layla wondered.

"He's probably seeing how far he can push you before you break." Rikyava eyed her knowingly. "Today was damn close. I don't think he expected it, but he and I are going to have a talk anyhow. Even though he's dominating you hard right now, he needs to be more careful when other people are around."

"How exactly is he dominating me?" Layla glanced over, her brows knit.

"Withholding touch is a major power play with Dominants." Rikyava grinned, sly now. "He's driving you crazy on purpose, and that sucks for you, but it's not as bad as what you're really chafing at."

"What am I really chafing at?" Layla frowned deeper.

"That Reginald's trying to force you to play Submissive to him. But Layla-girl don't play that game, does she?" Rikyava chuckled.

"I don't think so." Layla scowled now. Being a pushover in the bedroom was so not her style. And yet, as she thought about being flooded with passion by Adrian or rolled by Dusk's vibrations, it suddenly made her exquisitely hot. And the next thought troubled her further – thinking about being sluiced with Reginald's oceanic tides as he laid her back on silk sheets.

"Nope. That is so not going to happen." Layla spoke again as she tried to banish the thought. But it wouldn't go. Over and over, as Layla gazed up at the pink crystal vaults, she saw Reginald – dancing with her, stroking her skin with his long white fingers, the swell of his strong dancer's shoulders under his 1700's frock coats.

"Fuck." She breathed softly. "Fuck, fuck, fuck…"

Beside her, Rikyava's brows had risen. But before the Head Guardswoman could say anything, it was as if thinking about Reginald had summoned the devil himself. The reinforced crystal door to the training-hall was suddenly hauled open, and in he strode with a brusque, dancelike grace. Still in his sky-blue outfit of the night and without his wig or makeup, Reginald was devastatingly handsome with his natural features and golden hair bared. Layla thought he'd snap his fingers at her to come get ready for bed, when he opened the door wider.

And Dusk followed him in.

Layla blinked. It was the last thing she expected tonight, to be permitted to see Dusk.
But as she smelled his river-water scent flood the hall, relief filled her. Though his gaze flickcd to Reginald, there was far less ire in Dusk's eyes than previously. Stepping close and sinking to one knee before Layla, Dusk actually glanced at Reginald before reaching out to take

her hand.

"She is calm." Reginald gave a small nod. "You may touch her."

Dusk gave him a nod back, though a small prickly moment happened between him and the Siren. Reginald wasn't about to apologize for what he'd demanded of Layla these past weeks, and there was no love lost between the Head Courtier and the Head Concierge. But as they watched each other, Layla realized something had changed between them this evening. Dusk was finally paying attention to the control Reginald helped provide Layla over her passions – and for the first time, Layla could feel Dusk was grateful about that.

"How are you?" Dusk's soft words drifted up to the high vaults as his fingers stroked Layla's. He remained kneeling though she could feel a slow vibration in his touch. Whether it was meant to keep her calm or arouse her, she didn't know, as it did a bit of both. But it was a sedate arousal, and as Dusk stroked her, she saw him share a glance with the Head Courtier again.

"Better." Layla sighed as she gripped Dusk's fingers gently, grateful for his touch. "But I'm still fucking furious. I can't believe things got so out of hand tonight. I feel like I just need to fight all night. Maybe all day tomorrow, too."

With a deep inhalation, Reginald moved towards the bench. Glancing at Dusk, he nodded his chin at Layla. "She needs the touch of skin tonight. You have my permission to be with her, Head Concierge. Be gentle, please. Return her to my rooms before dawn."

With a sudden shock, Layla realized what Reginald was saying. But before she could say anything, he turned away, a glance like sadness passing between himself and Rikyava. Maybe it was chagrin at what his horrible brother had pushed Layla to tonight and how it had affected Adrian and their Hotel; maybe it was wretchedness at his role in provoking Rikyava's clan to war. But as quickly as that look came it was gone, and Reginald with it – striding back to the door and turning the corner.

"Aaaaand," Rikyava rose, "I think that's my cue, too. Cheers, kiddos. Keep it kosher."

With a wink, the Head Guardswoman departed also, closing the thick crystal door behind her with a soft whoosh of air. Layla and Dusk were quite suddenly alone in the hall, the vaulted space moving with soft currents of air and the burble of the waterfall.

"Did he just…?" Layla blinked at Reginald's departure, then looked to Dusk. "Did Reginald just give his blessing for us to get it on tonight?"

"Once a Head Courtier, always a Head Courtier." Dusk lifted an eyebrow with a wry smile. "It's a formality, Layla, for a Partner to give their blessing to a Courtesan-in-training to have an Assignation."

"Which is what he's insinuating, that you and I can have some alone time tonight." Layla scowled, anger seething through her. "Like you've paid for me?"

"Never." Dusk chuckled, then slid up to the bench beside her. "You are too priceless to pay for. Come here."

Pulling off his bowtie and unbuttoning his tux shirt, Dusk angled their bodies so Layla could lean back against him. She found herself relieved by the warmth of his body and the silken touch of his chest on her back. With a sigh, Dusk wrapped his arms around her and Layla felt quietude ease through her. Dusk was controlling his passion now; mightily. And Layla still had Reginald's oceanic sensations moving deep through her, controlling hers.

Dusk kissed her shoulder and Layla found her head tipping back as she sank into it. His fingers stroked the front of her neck; soothing. It was gentle even in its eroticism and Layla sighed, abandoning herself to it. She'd wanted this so badly, all month. Needed it. Her mind drifted;

her body drifted in a smooth, sedate space as Dusk touched her. Time faded, replaced only by breath and the steady caress of his fingers. Their bodies pressed close, Layla could feel Dusk's deep heat rising now; not a flashing, fierce heat like Adrian, but like the last heat of day lingering in a slab of stone – a sensation one could revel in if one remained very still.

"Come on." Dusk's voice was gentle by Layla's ear. "Let's go somewhere we can relax."

"Where?"

"Just trust me." Dusk gave her a look and Layla acquiesced. She could use some relaxation just about now. Could she ever.

CHAPTER 6 – DUSK

Rising, Dusk guided Layla up from the rose quartz bench with him,
then turned and led them through the Guardhall and back up the stairs,
until they pushed out a set of doors into the deep evening gardens once
more. The gardens were somber and sensual tonight, with swirling
glow-globes lit upon pedestals and magicked white firefly-lights
glimmering through every bare topiary in the midnight hour. Being out
in the chill again with the stars winking high above was soothing, and
Layla drew deep breaths – trying not to think about the Owners party,
or Adrian.

Or Reginald.

Glancing over, Dusk kept his silence as they walked. No sighs
came from the clusters of illuminated topiaries this late in the season,
the December air too brisk for outdoor lovemaking. It made the gardens
seem more expansive than usual, and Layla could feel Dusk thrumming
a low vibration through their intertwined fingers as they walked, both
heightening and soothing that sensation of expansiveness. The lights in
the topiaries mimicked the stars far above, and the stars reflected in the
pools all around, until Layla felt like she walked among the midnight
sky. She shivered, but it was a good thing, feeling crisp and clear for
the first time all night as her breath puffed in the frigid air. Looking
over, Dusk saw her shiver and removed his white tux jacket, tucking it
around her bare shoulders.

His attention was everything Layla needed tonight. Dusk was
being a gentleman, using his magics to soothe her rather than fluster her

or give in to his own sexuality. Deep inside, Layla's Dragon stretched like a cat being petted, its big golden eyes slipping half-closed in contentment as they walked. After a few minutes, they rounded a hedge and came upon a small bath-house. Made of vaulted crystal, the modest dome was set with wrought-iron so delicate it looked like a bird's nest. Stepping up to the enclosure, no larger than Layla's apartment and surrounded by tall hedges, Dusk opened a wrought-iron door and beckoned Layla in.

She entered, hearing the sound of a waterfall inside. There were numerous outbuildings on the grounds of the Hotel and this was one she'd never been in before, not even on her tour. A thin mist curled through the air inside the bath-house, obscuring the view, but a rose quartz floor glowed with a pool of milky water set into the ground, a cascading waterfall emptying from the wall into the pool. Vines trailed up every wall and high into the dome, enormous white trumpet-blossoms opening to the night.

It was an intoxicating space, and as Dusk closed the door and set an amethyst bar to lock it, Layla realized she could no longer feel a whirling dervish of eros cascading through her. It stunned her, realizing she'd been feeling so much from other people at the Hotel, like a low-frequency vibration inside her bones that irritated her over and over. She'd not even known it was there until it was gone, even more thoroughly than from the magical insulation of the fight-hall. Layla stood in the sudden silence, relieved, only the fall of water vibrating through her as it cascaded into the pool.

"Wow. That's something." She breathed to the curling mist.

"Quiet in here, isn't it?" Dusk gave her a knowing look as he stepped to a chaise nearby.

"You can say that again, Mister Garrison." Layla randomly quoted South Park, eliciting a soft laugh from Dusk, and a grin. "How did you find this place?"

"Trial and error." Dusk gave her a wry smile as he stepped out of his black oxfords. "It's the one place I truly feel relaxed here at the Hotel. Even the fight-halls and my apartment don't ground out the vibrations of other people's emotions nearly as well as this place, though I've done my best with my apartment. This is my sanctuary, free of all outside vibrations. Here, there exists only the beauty of silence – and you, right now, with me. Shall we?"

Giving her a relaxed smile, Dusk began to strip off his bowtie, laying it upon a chaise near the door next to a wrought-iron stand of white towels and robes. Glancing to her, he began unbuttoning his shirt. Layla tried to not stare as he stripped his shirt away, but failed. Dusk was handsome in the extreme, lean and cut with defined muscles that one didn't really see in his immaculately slim suits. With incredible shoulders and strong legs like a World Cup soccer player, his torso was a dusky color through his tanned skin, a midnight dark oilslick hue on his outer arms, shoulders, and down his sides. Over his chest and washboard abs, the color faded to the same lovely bluish hue of his lips, rippling with a sheen as he turned and set his shirt down.

Seeing Dusk's sleek musculature was astounding. It was only the second time Layla had seen him naked, and as he began to undo his pants, she watched how his serrated ridges of Dragon-scale flowed down the back of his neck. Unable to tear her gaze away, she followed those scintillating ridges – edged in gold since her Bind – as they spread out over his shoulder-blades and down his back in a sexy v-shape, dipping below the band of his slacks.

From the backs of his hands, scales continued up his outer arms, connecting to the lines behind his shoulders. As Dusk stripped with unabashed grace – his silk cobalt thong coming down also – Layla saw how those midnight ridges curled in over his hips, diving to his groin and ending just shy of his cock. Which was well-proportioned and quite aroused, the same blue-grey as his inner thighs.

Dusk caught her gaze, holding it with a riveting presence. It was the first time Layla had seen him fully nude and blushing furiously, she turned away. But she could feel his body as he moved close, not touching her but lifting his hands to the white tux jacket and sliding it from her shoulders. She could feel the deep passion of his touch as his fingers slipped across her collarbones, gathering his jacket from her skin. Standing behind her, he laid the jacket carefully down on the chaise, before his hands slipped to her waist.

With a slow glide, his hands eased up over her hips, palming her sides as he gathered the fabric of her top and slid his hands up beneath it. Pleasure washed through Layla at his touch. His pleasure; her pleasure – the pleasure of the slow, deft slide of Dusk's smooth hands up her skin. Layla didn't know where she stopped and he began as she smelled oranges and rainwater in the cavernous night. Dusk's energy held hers with a smooth ripple and Layla sighed, letting it sweep her as he slid her shirt slowly up. Slipping his thumbs beneath the built-in bra, he eased his hands up the outside of her breasts.

And then her arms raised, her top coming up and off, shed to the floor.

Dusk's hands smoothed back down her arms, cupping her breasts gently and making her sigh before sliding down beneath the band of her yoga pants. Palming her skin, he slid his hands down, shedding her pants to the floor and helping her step out of them, along with her black flats. Easing up, he let her feel the sleek deliciousness of his skin, the ridged hardness of his serrated scales, and the firm hardness of other things against her body. Palming her waist again, his hands so hot now yet gentle with strength, he slid his fingers slowly down inside the band of her lace thong.

Corralling her with one hand at her hip, his other hand continued its glide down and in, stroking over her low belly. His fingers pressed deep, massaging her, before he slid them down over her mons. Gliding his fingers down, his middle finger slid sweetly into her cleft, though he didn't enter her with his fingers, just cupped her close.

Moulding his hand to her sex and his body to her back, he breathed by her neck, pouring a deep rumble of passion through Layla. She cried out softly; instantly throbbing and wet. With a soft smile and a sweet rub of his fingers, he kissed her neck gently, then moved his other hand from her hip – sliding her thong down and letting it fall to her feet.

Holding her hip and corralling her close, he began to stroke her slowly with his fingers between her legs. Layla's breath caught as she surrendered to it, leaning back into him and winding her hands up around his neck. He continued to stroke her, slipping his fingers over her sweetly; exploring every lip and crevasse, though still without entering her. Breathing hard and fast now, Layla sighed as he found her clitoris, as he teased it with sweet, slow strokes. Sliding his hand up from her hip, he cradled her ribs, then her breast; rolling her nipple gently between his fingertips as he stroked her slowly below.

His fingers were so deft. Layla gasped with pleasure in his arms, undulating, feeling him so close. No lover she had ever been with had known what he was doing as much as this, and she undulated hard in his arms as he heightened her pleasure with his hands, knowing how far to take her but arresting it just shy of completion. Layla cried out, needing him, needing release, feeling how wet she was below as she shuddered against him in delicious agony. With a soft smile at her neck, Dusk kissed her gently – and then stroked her with one last lovely glide before turning her in his arms.

Breathing hard in the misty enclosure, power and sexual heat rushed through Layla as she came to face her bound lover. Looking up, she saw a beautiful mystery in his dark sapphire eyes as he gathered her close. Their bodies eased together beneath the blossoms and starlight, enormous blooms unfurling around them in the midnight hour with an intoxicating scent. Inhaling, Dusk's eyes closed as he set his forehead to Layla's, and she was aware of a deep, thrumming vibration that moved through his body as he breathed.

There was no rush here tonight; there was no hurry. Dusk meant to take his time with her tonight and Layla found herself absorbed in his lower-than-sound sensations, feeling them carry waves of his emotions to her. Fear, calm, passion; awe. Her body thrilled where her bare breasts touched his sculpted chest, her hips pressed close to his with his hands cradling her low back.

Breathing deeply, serenely, Dusk's lips moved to her ear.

"I feel you," he murmured. "Ever since we were bound together. I feel you like a hot desert sky in my body; like a deep midnight canyon in my mind. I feel sand and wind, and the currents of the dark earth moving inside you. I feel the slow eons of time and the fast fury of the sand-funnel. You're like music inside my body, Layla. I feel what you are... and it holds me so fast."

Layla's breath stopped; her heart skipped a beat. Intoxicated by the moment, she moved close. Smooth as satin, Dusk's skin slipped over hers, touching from groin to chest. With a sigh, his strong arms clasped her closer – her heart pounding from the deep ripples passing through him. Layla passed her lips over his chest, feeling that amazing sensation of their togetherness.

"What do you think I am?" She asked.

"Incredible," he breathed. "You are incredible, Layla Price. And I am so lucky... to be bound to you."

Setting his smooth lips to her shoulder, Dusk kissed her, gently.

Tears rose in Layla's eyes and her heart clenched, feeling this gift of solace and love he gave her tonight. No matter their relationship by day, no matter how they had to be in the coming weeks, she was grateful for him. A hard lump rose in her throat and she slid her hands up to cup his jaw.

"I love you, Dusk Arlohaim," she breathed.

"I love you, too, Layla Price," he breathed as he pulled back, gazing deep into her eyes.

And then he kissed her.

His lips pressed against hers; soft and slow, opening her body to his vibrations. Layla opened her lips and her heart at the same time, letting him take control with his soft licks and rumbling pleasure. His skin slid over hers as they kissed, impossibly smooth; his hardness pressed against her hip, ready and full. His hands gripped her, so sure, so certain – and so loving.

It was everything Layla wanted, everything she needed tonight. As she surrendered to Dusk's kiss beneath the starlit dome, she suddenly felt whole. With strong hands, he guided her gently down beside the pool, his thrumming passion sweeping her. And as she lay back beneath him on the firm stone, Layla finally released her tension from the past weeks. She released everything as she wound her legs up around his muscled hips, feeling tiny ridges of midnight scale press intoxicatingly into her tenderest flesh.

For a moment, they paused together. Gazing up into his face, seeing Dusk's eyes burn hot like stars, so impossibly bright, Layla felt infinity. An endless pleasure rolled through her as he breathed, his slow thrumming shuddering everything inside her. She felt suddenly like she wasn't upon the earth but somewhere in the stars, feeling the wild, slow dance of the universe.

And then he pressed inside her – filling her with that slow, thrumming pleasure.

Filling her to the brim with the sound and feel of underground rivers and ageless time and diamond-bright stars, Dusk penetrated Layla with the passions of the unseen cosmos. She cried out, arching against him, feeling time pause as they breathed together at the height of his thrust, feeling infinity expand around them in an endless unfurling. Dusk gazed down at her and she saw him feel their Bind, his eyes sparking impossibly bright as a wash of light poured through his body. Layla felt it too; a slow pulse of gold and diamond energy that bound them together from the seat of their beings – luminous and wild.

With a deep mystery, Dusk began to move to that slow rhythm. Layla's breath caught as she stared up at him, feeling him. He was moving, but it wasn't so much him that was moving as it was the cosmos moving him; moving them both. She fell into that dark passion, that endless churn, and as he drove deeper inside her, she felt her magic become unbound. Coiling up from the deeps with glittering diamond-gold eyes and a wave of slow fire, it made them both shudder. Dusk thrust harder as Layla gripped his hips with her thighs – winding herself around his strong body as they both cried out in deep pleasure.

Dusk gasped as he fell to his elbows. Cupping a strong hand behind Layla's neck, he trapped her to his chest as he fucked her deeper, harder; slower. Layla cried out as she bit his chest, passion coring her as Dusk flooded her with his vibrations, losing himself to the pleasure of the earth. They fucked hard, and deep, Dusk growling with sub-basso tremors as he thrust into her again and again, changing the position of his hips to drive himself in with a rolling thrust that undulated his entire body. The uncoiling of his Dragon drove him, and Layla felt it expand like some massive thing, filling the crystal bath-house and driving far into the earth. As Layla cried out to feel him so massive and strong inside her and all around her, Dusk roared from the seat of his being.

From the seat of his power.

Thunder shuddered the bath-house; the thunder of the mountains. Thunder shuddered the night around them; the thunder of stars going supernova. Thunder shuddered everything inside Layla and her Dragon was suddenly roaring, pushing them both. She rode Dusk's power and he rode hers, slamming into her deep and hard until their climax exploded out in a powerful wave of energy. Crystals full of diamond-gold fire burst out into the air around them, scattering across the stone as Layla screamed with pleasure, biting Dusk's shoulder and convulsing as he thrust deep inside her one final time – releasing at last.

With a gasp, he came crashing down, trapping her beneath his body as he shuddered – on and on and on. Layla laughed. She couldn't help it. Inside her mind were only stars, and inside her body was only pleasure, and inside her heart was only love, so big and expansive and warm with golden-bright light. It was bliss; pure bliss. As Layla laughed, with a rumble and a cough, Dusk laughed, too.

And then they were in a fit of laughter, so bad it made Layla spasm in coughing and she had to slap him lightly to move so she could breathe.

He did. With a growl, Dusk did an impressively quick push-up, launching off Layla and plopping to a seat beside her on the rose quartz floor. He was still chuckling as she gasped for air, shuddering with aftershocks. Her hand fell to the floor beside her and landed on a scatter of small fragments. Picking one up in her fingertips, Layla lifted it – discovering it was an actual crystal about an inch long and clear like a diamond. Deep within its core, an endless diamond-gold fire writhed like stars being born, shining through all the facets. Amazed and spent, Layla laughed again, wondering at what they had wrought together in their climax.

Reaching out, Dusk smoothed a hand over her naked abdomen and ribs – rolling another deep wave of pleasure through her.

"Stop!" Layla laughed, coughing and letting the crystal drop from her fingers, then trapping his hand to her ribs. "Ohmigod, stop!"

"Pretty good, huh?" Dusk gave another sexy chuckle, though he left off shuddering her with his magics. His other hand gathered a handful of crystals from the floor and he admired them with an incredulous look, shaking his head with a grin. "I told you that being with me when I'm healthy was worth waiting for."

"Pretty *damn* good. And it was worth waiting for." Layla gasped, grinning as their eyes met. She laughed, still breathless, still feeling endless waves of pleasure rolling through her. Watching her, Dusk's face softened, a handsome wistfulness taking him. Letting the crystals fall back to the floor, he leaned over her, gazing down with a complex and lovely passion in his bright eyes.

"It was." He echoed softly.

And then he kissed her – on and on and on.

CHAPTER 7 – DAWN

Layla still couldn't sit up off the rose quartz floor, her Dragon glowing as she and Dusk languished in the crystal bath-house. Sitting beside her, Dusk smoothed his palm over her belly and Layla let him, glorious with delight and feeling entirely boneless. He didn't rumble her, only touched her with the exquisite silkiness of his palm, stirring the mist as the fire-crystals of their lovemaking twisted with ethereal flames beneath the wan light of the dome. Layla closed her eyes, a deeply contented smile lifting her lips as he rubbed her belly and breasts.

"Who's ready for a swim?" Dusk chuckled, teasing and sexy.

Smiling, Layla opened her eyes. "I think I'll drown. I can't even move, really."

"You don't need to move. Just hang on."

She was about to ask him what he meant, when Layla felt herself being scooped up from the floor. In one incredibly lithe, strong movement, Dusk cradled her to his chest, then turned and slung his legs into the milky pool and slid them both down into the water. Layla barely had time to blink before she was up to her chest in milky water, cradled close to Dusk's strong body and wrapping her arms up around his neck – watching their fire-crystals flicker all around them like thousands of tiny candles beneath the stars.

They kissed, for a long time. Turning her on his lap, Dusk clasped Layla close with her back to his strong chest, Layla resting her head on his shoulder as she felt the deep pleasure of him breathe. Cupping her ribs as he slid a hand down, he chuckled by her ear as he slipped his middle finger into her cleft again. His low, masculine rumble rolled through Layla again as he stroked her in languid circular movements; then smoother, quicker, more concentrated.

All around them, the fire-crystals brightened, flaring hotter as Dusk's rumble stirred them, as he stirred Layla's passion with his fingers. Concentrating in her pelvis and groin, he vibrated that energy into her clitoris through his fingertips. Layla writhed as that rumble built, little lights brightening all around them.

Just when she couldn't take it anymore, he thrust two fingers inside her, taking her deep and fast; hard. Wrapping an arm around her so she could feel his strength, trapping her close, Dusk held her firm upon his pleasure. All that pleasure was suddenly cresting in a hot, bright wave, rising up through Layla with a gasp and a clench of powerful coils as the climax pummeled her – shuddering her hard before it sighed away.

"My god!" Layla gasped, undone as Dusk rolled his fingers deep inside her, smoothing his other hand over her ribs and cupping her breast tenderly.

"I don't think I will ever tire of doing that to you, Layla Price." He chuckled by her ear, grinning into her neck and kissing her as he continued to slide his fingers deep inside her – though it was soothing now rather than arousing.

"I don't think I will, either!" Layla gasped in sweet oblivion, her head falling back on his shoulder as she breathed hard, undulating with his deep touch.

"Maybe I'll do it while you're training with Reginald," he chuckled, grinning at her ear.

"Don't you dare." She tried to make it sound like a warning, but she was so pleasured right now that it didn't matter. Everything throbbed in the most languid, wonderful way, their lovemaking like a spiral of passion and joy that had not yet released either of them.

"You are an amazing woman, Layla," Dusk murmured as he finally slid his fingers out of her. Layla gasped with pleasure and he slid both hands up, cupping her breasts, massaging them, caressing his hands over her ribs. "I can't tell you how much I needed this, with you, tonight."

"I really needed you, too." Layla sighed with a small smile.

"I couldn't tell."

She felt him grin as he caressed her. His touch was even smoother in the milky water of the pool, like the water had been created to make his skin pure bliss. Layla languished, wondering how many hours had passed since the party, though she didn't really care. The Hotel could wait. Reginald could wait. Adrian could wait. She was relaxed here in Dusk's arms, and he was right – they needed this. But something still niggled at her, and at last, she had to voice it.

"Does anyone know we're here, Dusk? Like… if something bad happens with Adrian or the Board tonight?"

His chuckle was very male as he smoothed his hands over her belly beneath the water. "Rikyava can scent my whereabouts, and probably yours too by now. She's got an intensely keen ability to smell magic. I'm sure she knows you're not in Reginald's room and I'm not in mine. She's got the Guard on high alert tonight. If anything happens that we need to be aware of, she'll come find us."

"Fair enough." Layla settled back on his chest as he smoothed his hands over her ribs beneath the water. Cupping her breasts again, his gentle but firm touch made her arch as he ran his thumbs over her nipples. Closing her eyes, Layla surrendered to the sensation, Dusk adding a sub-sonic rumble that tingled her as he gently kissed her neck.

"I don't think I can go again right now," she murmured, a smile creeping up her lips.

"I can't either. Once was plenty for now. But it doesn't mean we can't enjoy each other. And have more later." Dusk kissed her neck again and Layla turned into him, letting his smooth lips find hers. They devoured each other a long moment, Dusk taking Layla's lower lip in his teeth and grinning as they finally released.

"You are so bad," Layla murmured at his lips.

"You like me bad. Bad is better." He grinned.

"Yeah. But bad boys can be exhausting."

"You attract a lot of bad boys, Layla." He murmured at her neck, smoothing his hands over her belly again in the water. "I've said it before and I'll say it again. Me, Adrian, Adam when we still thought he was Adam. Reginald."

"You told me about Reginald, way back when." Layla spoke thoughtfully, stroking Dusk's muscled thigh beneath the water. "I didn't believe you at the time, but now…"

"Now you're starting to see it, aren't you?" Dusk's voice was sober now. "He may be an asshole, but Reginald's strangely tender with you. In a way I've not seen with anyone, really. It gives me hope."

"Hope of what?" Layla turned her head so she could see his face.

Dusk's eyes narrowed, thoughtful as he met her gaze. "That he actually might be an ally to us rather than a thorn. Reginald and Bastien hate each other, but I thought Reginald hated Adrian more. Now, I'm not so sure. I think because of you, Reginald is willing to play ball with Adrian."

"What do you mean?" Layla asked, watching him. "Play ball for what?"

"You know that the Paris Hotel is in trouble right now." His gaze was eloquent.

"Reginald told me." Layla raised her eyebrows. "What does that have to do with Reginald stepping up to bat for us against his brother?"

"Bastien Durant is the front-runner for Adrian's position as Hotel Head if Adrian is dismissed by the Board." Dusk spoke darkly.

"You're joking." Layla blinked, horrified that if things went badly, that asshole of a Siren might become their boss at the Paris Hotel.

But Dusk wasn't joking, continuing with a sober darkness even as he smoothed his hands over Layla's skin. "One of the reasons I curry powerful friends is so I can go where I will when I will, Layla. I enjoy my freedom, and peace. But now a war has come to us. Since Adrian bound you, it's stirred up a hornet's nest of enemies who don't want to see Adrian come into his full power. Hunter kicked that hornet's nest at Samhain, but it was already buzzing. Right now, it's a simmering conflict in the shadows between Adrian and the people who don't want to see him rise any higher... but what if it wasn't anymore?"

"How bad could it get?" Layla asked, listening intently.

"Bad." Dusk breathed, moving one hand through the water, the other still wrapped around Layla's ribs. "Twilight Realm wars are bad news, Layla. There are reasons we have strict laws against feuding. And people to enforce them."

"The High Court?"

"The High Court," he nodded, "and their watchdog enforcers, the Intercessoria. If things get bad, you'll see Juds – the Intercessoria Judiciary. Believe me, we do *not* want Juds sniffing around this place. There are many people on staff here who are here specifically because they wish to keep a low profile with the law."

"Like you." It all clicked into place for Layla. "And Reginald. Starting a war between the North Sea Sirens and the Blood Dragons like he did. Supposedly."

"Reginald told you about that?" Dusk frowned at her.

"Not really. Bastien was berating him at the party, and I learned a little." Layla sighed. "But why are you hiding from the law here at the

Hotel?"

"You know that my clan and the Tunisian Crystal clan killed each other off." Dusk spoke, a darkness in his sapphire eyes.

"Yeah?"

"Well," he continued with a sigh, "once I was an angry youngling with a murdered clan and no one to restrict my rage. Adrian's father Issam helped me; took me in and gave me a safe place in the Sahara to vibrate out my fury without triggering active fault lines. But I killed three villages of humans in my grief before he found me – and the Juds never forget something like that, no matter that it happened when a person was only six years old. If you think the Hotel has a long memory, it's nothing compared to the Intercessoria. Generous donations can eventually buy off the Hotel. The Juds – nothing can buy them off your scent. No matter how young you were when you committed your crime."

Layla considered that, understanding that the Intercessoria Judiciary were the kind of elite police force that held ultimate authority. The kind who put people away in dark oubliettes that never saw the light of day.

"If anything happens here, anything we can't solve internally – will Juds get involved?"

"You can count on it." Dusk's voice held a growl now and it was not a nice sound, nor was the prickling, tense vibration that accompanied it. Layla smoothed her hand over his thigh and he took a breath, leaving off. But she'd felt enough to know, and had felt enough earlier in their passion, that it was only the barest hint of Dusk's real power, the edge of a very deep fault line.

If he ever decided to shake the base of that fault line in anger, Layla could only imagine the result.

Behind her, Dusk gave a hard sigh, then lifted Layla to settle her

79

in a more comfortable position on his lap. But they could both feel the mood waning, the hour late and the difficult day all too near now that they were speaking of dire things.

"We should probably get you back." Dusk's voice was low as he kissed her neck. "As much as I hate it, we have things that need attending."

"Like sleep," Layla agreed.

"Sleep is for the weak." Dusk chuckled, stroking Layla's neck.

"You don't believe that."

"No, I don't. Sleep keeps Dragons sane." He kissed her neck, then lifted her as he rose, cradling her close as their torsos came out of the water. Dusk was only a few inches taller than Layla, and it was the perfect height for her to wrap her arms around his neck and kiss him, deep and slow. His hands heated on her skin, pulling her close as he kissed her back. When he finally pulled away, he was breathless, smoothing his hands over her ass in the water.

"I thought you were pining for Adrian," he chuckled, giving a sexy growl with a smug smile.

"I am," Layla grinned back, nuzzling his nose. "But you might just be changing my mind about whom I feel like spending time with. Especially after I've had a bad day."

"I'll take it." But Dusk's grin got serious then, his summer-blue eyes pinning her as something complex moved through his gaze. He paused as if he wanted to say something, then stopped.

"Penny for your thoughts?" Layla asked gently, lifting up to kiss his lips again.

"Layla. I hope you know…" Dusk frowned, then smoothed a hand over her ass again as he watched her. "I'm not requiring exclusivity from you, as my lover. Even though we've been bound by magic, you and I are friends, and I have other long-term lovers here at the Hotel that I've had for a very long time. You captivate me," he reached up, brushing a strand of her wet curls back from her neck, "but… I'm not monogamous. I never have been, not even when I was young. Can you handle that? Could you do this, with me… if I had other partners now and again?"

Layla thought about it, watching his handsome, serious face. It was a deep question, and not one she'd precisely considered yet. She'd never tried being with a man in an open or polyamorous relationship before, and from her prior experience with Gavin and his secret harlots back in Seattle, Layla felt a sudden grip of tension coil through her.

But as soon as it came, it changed. Standing with Dusk, breathing with him, she could feel his deep honesty, bringing the question of monogamy up now before anything got truly messy. She could feel his dark worry; that he would fuck up everything good he had with Layla if he tried to stuff himself into a monogamous life and failed. And though a coil of anxiety churned through her, thinking about him being with other women, Layla knew her life wasn't headed in a monogamous direction anytime soon – and it seemed wrong to demand Dusk do so.

Her new life at the Hotel was about her; not about any man. Even though Adrian had been the instigation for it, Layla had come to the Hotel because she needed to find out who she really was. She was learning how to control her Dragon-magics, and doing so required that she be Reginald's for the time being, even if they weren't sleeping together. Discovering who she was meant opening to her Binds with both Adrian and Dusk – and who knew what the outcome of that might be.

Gazing into Dusk's handsome face, she realized she could try to work with it. He'd had other partners for decades before their Bind. It wasn't comfortable for her, and Layla didn't know how she might feel if she heard from someone else that they had slept with him, but she didn't want to deny him something he needed – especially when she had a complicated situation herself.

"I think I can work with that." Layla spoke at last with a small smile. "I can try."

"Are you sure?" Dusk's brows lifted, an answering smile lifting his face hesitantly as he searched her eyes. "What are you thinking? I thought you'd be mad, but it seems like you're… strangely ok about me having other partners."

"I mean, I can't say I'm one hundred percent ok with it." Locking her hands behind Dusk's neck, Layla pressed her hips to his. "It makes me churn inside to think of you with another woman, but you had a whole life here before I came along, Dusk. I'm not going to bowl on in and demand that you change who you are because some magical resonance happened between us. I care about you. And you've been there for me more times than I can count since my life changed back in August. The least I can do is try to be understanding about what you need. Because lord knows Reginald isn't going to let us boink like this everyday. Just because I'm frustrated as hell doesn't mean you have to be."

"Boink." Dusk chuckled sexily, gripping her close by a hand around her waist, and one down at her ass. "I'd boink you any day. You are my favorite boink, you know."

"I hope so." Layla grinned, nuzzling his nose.

"No, I mean it." Dusk's gaze was serious again as he lifted his lips, kissing her. "I would rather be with you than any of the rest. My partners are amazing women and men, Layla, but you, this… you smite me in a way I can't describe. I want you in my life. If it means giving up my other regular partners, I'm willing to give it a go, but…"

"I don't want you to," Layla spoke softly, holding his sober gaze with one of her own. "I want you to get what you need, Dusk. I want

82

you happy when you and I get to be together, not frustrated and angry."

He took a breath, and then sighed in a wave of vibration so deep that Layla realized it was relief. He'd truly been worried she was going to demand exclusivity from him, or even celibacy. Lifting her hand, Layla stroked Dusk's dark waves back from his temple, feeling something tender blossom between them. "I'm not saying I'm not jealous," Layla smiled slightly, "because I am. I do want you all to myself, especially now that I know how it can be between us… but I also realize the practicality of our situation."

"You sound like Adrian," Dusk chuckled, something glowing in his sapphire eyes now. "When he's not all spun up about you, that is."

"I came here for me, Dusk," Layla spoke firmly. "I came to the Hotel because I needed a change in my life. I didn't come here initially for Adrian or for any man. Becoming who I truly am is *my* adventure, my life. And I'm going to live it how I choose to – not the way any society told me to. I'm learning that Dragons are passionate, sexual creatures. I'm trying to adjust to that, to learn new ways of being. Because I don't want my life tied up around any man. And I don't want to demand that of you, either."

"I like the sound of that. Independent women are my kryptonite, you know." Dusk chuckled, nuzzling her nose.

"Do Crystal Dragons have kryptonite?" Layla spoke back, enjoying his soft skin.

"Only sexy, witty, amazing women that my Dragon can't get enough of. And I can't either." Pulling her in, Dusk kissed her hard this time. Pulling her hips to his with his strong hands, he massaged her ass as he devoured her – making her feel how hard he was becoming yet again. By the time he released her, Layla was wet below as she stared up into his rakish, sexy gaze.

"Gotcha." He growled with a grin.

"Gotcha yourself." Layla laughed, breathless.

Dusk released her with a bright laugh, stepping smoothly out of the milky pool to the floor with a ripple of his strong thighs. Extending a hand, he helped Layla out of the water, which was all the more impressive as she watched the exquisite muscles in his body contract to help her step out. He was glorious with all that sexy, lean muscle and iridescent lines in so many shades. He saw her watching and a ripple of dark luminescence rolled through his sleek ridges, lighting his eyes.

"What was that for?" Layla grinned, knowing it meant he was feeling intense emotions.

"You make me hot," Dusk murmured, his blue gaze pinning her. "What else can I say?"

With a low chuckle, he turned, taking up a fluffy towel and drying off. Layla stepped to the chaise, taking up a towel also and wringing out her wet hair. Dusk's gaze traveled up her naked body as she toweled off, a lecherous grin on his face. Layla gave him an eyebrow, her lips curling into a grin also as she ogled him back; plenty of delicious things to peruse on his well-built body. Adrian might have been lean and mean, but Dusk was fit as shit – and now Layla knew the feel of all that hot, powerful muscle beneath her hands and between her thighs as he fucked her.

Her cheeks heated and she turned away, toweling down.

"I felt that." Dusk's chuckle was murderous behind her.

"Good." Layla bent over and wound her hair up in the towel. As she did, Dusk stepped to her rear, seizing her hips and hauling her back against his body, roughly. Layla gasped as her hand flashed to her towel to keep it from falling off, a shiver of delight passing through her. His strong fingers gripped her hips as he ground against her, letting her feel his deep heat where he pressed up against her ass, hot and hard.

Layla writhed, feeling it – wanting more.

But Dusk released her with a dark chuckle and when she straightened, he was hauling his blue silk thong and pants up over all that hard length – but not before she got a good, solid eyeful.

"You are going to be fun, Layla Price." Dusk's gaze was as hot as his sex, ramming through Layla with a delicious rumble.

"And *you* are going to be a handful." She sassed, stepping into her beige lace thong and pulling it up.

"I'm more than a handful." He grinned, sliding one hand down his trousers and over the thick imprint she could still see.

Layla breathed out shakily as she laughed and nodded. Dusk was far more than a handful and she loved every inch of it. Her cheeks colored again as a wash of heat passed through her, a blossom of orange-peel bourbon scent rising through the swirling mist.

Dusk scented it and laughed, turning to take up his shirt from the chaise.

They dressed with more teasing and flirtation, until finally Layla and Dusk were both laughing as they stepped fully clothed from the crystal bath-house. It had been a wonderful night, and lighthearted energy swirled between them as they made their egress. But as they stepped out into the night, Layla suddenly smelled a scent she recognized in the chill air. A curl of cinnamon-jasmine musk brought her up short, her gut dropping down through her toes.

And the blaze of Adrian's hot aqua eyes was like a spike through her heart, as he stepped from the midnight shadows of the hedge.

CHAPTER 8 – BLACK

Dusk froze beside Layla on the steps of the crystal bath-house, his arm halted as it was about to slide around her waist. Stepping from the stark moonlit shadows, Adrian's aqua eyes burned in the deep night. If fury had a color, if the entire Mediterranean Sea could suddenly become a tornado of wrath, he held his distance, and Layla was glad he did. Fear ripped through her, watching his eyes burn. Her every sense prickled on the midnight wind, hairs rising all along the backs of her arms. Dusk settled his hand to her waist, drawing her close. Not a move that was possessive, but protective – as if he was as afraid as Layla at what the furiously jealous Adrian might do.

"It just happened, Adrian." Dusk's voice was low and reasonable as he spoke through the chill night.

"*Bullshit.*" Adrian's voice was a frightening snarl from the hedge-row. "It's what you always do, Dusk, steal from other men. You're as bad as Reginald."

"I didn't mean for it—"

"Fuck you! You know you did!"

"Hey!" With a hot flare, Layla stepped toward Adrian. Dusk's hand on her waist restrained her now, as she laid into her Desert Dragon with a vicious snap of power. "Cut the shit, Adrian! Just because you bound me first with your tempestuous gifts doesn't mean I belong to you! You fucked with me during the Owner's party tonight because you were jealous I was on Reginald's arm, and shit got heavy. I needed to release steam after all the embarrassment that caused, and I chose Dusk tonight. End of story. If you can't handle that, you need to grow up."

Even from a distance, she saw Adrian startle. The burning in his eyes died, replaced by shock. And then he narrowed his eyes, something dire surging between him and Layla upon simmering winds. "Grow up? What am I, sixteen?"

"You heard me. And maybe you are." Layla stood her ground, raising her chin against his incredible pull. Dusk had formidable energy, but Adrian had an annihilation that raced through her marrow, searing her blood like liquid fire. He was dangerous, but not because of his fury.

He was dangerous because of the way she needed him – like she needed her very last breath.

Adrian's beautiful lips fell open. Layla felt that cinnamon wind swirl around her, shaking the bare hedges. Moving forward, he stopped ten feet shy of where Layla and Dusk stood, his hands thrust deep in his pockets, his entire frame rigid with power and wrath. "Do you think I'm some kind of child?" He breathed, that utterance swirling around Layla's bare ankles and slipping up her legs, caressing her thighs. It made her shudder as pleasure flooded her.

"No," Layla spoke, willing herself to stand firm beneath Adrian's passionate onslaught. Balling a fist, she felt her own searing heat concentrate; bolstering her. "But I've spent all my life trying to do what others wanted, Adrian; trying to do everything right despite my temper and passion. You opened me to a new world; to something powerful in myself. But I don't owe you my body or my power if you can't figure out a way to tame your jealousy. I'm a Royal Dragon Bind, Adrian. Being monogamous goes against the nature of my magic, and I'm trying to accept that, even as much as it bothers me. You need to handle it also."

"I'm trying." His gaze intense, Adrian moved forward, his hands coming out of his pockets. "But seeing you with Reginald tonight and now Dusk—"

"I know." Layla stepped closer, Dusk releasing her as she stopped a few feet shy of Adrian. "None of this is ideal. You don't think I know that? You don't think I hate living with Reginald? Suffering his odious platitudes day and night?"

But even as she said it, something inside Layla gave a restless stir, feeling something else for the Siren since tonight.

"Have you slept with him?" Adrian's gaze blistered as he stared into her eyes, sensing her feelings through their Bind. Layla saw the gold in his eyes flash; molten, brutal.

"No, Reginald hasn't even touched me, Adrian, not really." Layla spoke, feeling like they were at the crux of it now. Though her words weren't entirely true; Reginald had touched her with his magics quite deeply tonight – twice.

"What I felt today at the Owner's party was a lot more than touching." Adrian's energy blistered around Layla, a burning sand funnel in the night, full of wrath. And then his gaze slipped to Dusk. "And now you're with him. When will it be me, Layla? When will it be my turn to be with you?"

Suddenly, Layla saw the problem: there just wasn't enough of her to go around. Not for casual time, and certainly not for lovemaking. Even though Dragons were generally polyamorous, her Binds with Adrian and Dusk drove deeper than that; deeper than any kind of normal relationship. Layla had proven that tonight with the intensity of her lovemaking to Dusk, and watching Adrian now, seeing him so frustrated and furious from his chosen celibacy since their Bind, everything suddenly made sense.

With a slow inhalation, Layla gathered herself as everything became clear. Her Dragon went quiet, calm and collected instead of pissed off at Adrian. Moving forward, she took up Adrian's hands, kissing his fingers gently. She felt a shudder pass through him, his lips parting as he gave a soft sigh. They'd shared something powerful earlier today in the Pavilion, and Layla had been a selfish asshat to only be thinking about her own problems right now. Adrian was hurting; he was thrumming with power and passion for her, unconsummated for months longer than Dusk.

Layla realized his determination to be celibate for her took an iron fist – and a deeply dedicated heart.

"I'm available until dawn," she murmured, gazing up into Adrian's beautiful aqua-gold eyes. "Reginald gave me a reprieve for the night. And dawn is still a few hours away yet."

Adrian's breath stopped. Something so desirous flashed through his beautiful eyes that Layla felt it like a punch to the gut. It shuddered her whole body to feel the depth of his need. As if they were connected by a burning cord that he had suddenly flared with a disastrous recoil, she felt like her heart was being ripped out to see him suffering that much.

Reaching up, Adrian caressed her curls back from her face, his hand so hot it scorched. His touch triggered Layla's Dragon and a spiced wind surged from her, coiling around him with talons and muscled barbs. Adrian exhaled, falling into her, their bodies touching hip to chest. A lower-than-human growl rippled from his throat as his magic suddenly raced around her, his hands gripping hot at her waist. Vibrant, Adrian's power simmered the air with etheric crimson and aqua flames that licked along Layla's skin like burning tongues as he gripped her. It was painful yet terribly pleasant, and she shuddered, flooded with heat as her pulse pounded and her head whirled. As her knees buckled from the power of Adrian's pleasure, Dusk stepped in fast behind her, catching her in his arms.

But even though Dusk poured his soothing vibrations through her, he couldn't quell Layla and Adrian's disastrous passion. Layla surged like a mad thing in Dusk's arms, her mind and body awash in sensations that were far from human, and entirely ecstatic. A tirade of memories ripped through her; of desert sands and arroyos, and palaces of colorful zellij tile. Deep inside, she felt her Dragon roil, rising in a wave to Adrian's vast call.

The call to have his Bound mate.

Dusk held her fast, making a soothing vibration at her ear as Adrian continued to grip her hard with fingers like talons, growling his not-human sound and calling her beast. But Dusk's ministrations weren't enough to counteract Adrian's desperate hold over her, and Layla gasped in Dusk's arms, struggling to be let go. She wanted to fuck Adrian's brains out right then and there. She wanted to shift into her Dragon and rip Adrian apart as they fucked like animals in the night.

But as if Dusk sensed what she really needed, he held her fast, grounding her as Adrian flooded her with carnal heat and need. Holding her back from changing into her Dragon. Holding her back as Layla felt fire on the wind; as scorched cinnamon and jasmine devoured her.

It wasn't enough. She needed more – more of both of them. Layla writhed in Dusk's arms, gasping as she wound a hand up behind Dusk's neck and one up around Adrian's, pulling them both close. Her body struggled with pleasure between them as Dusk poured his calming vibration through her bones while Adrian flooded her with passion and fire. Turning her face into Dusk, she buried her nose in his neck, keening with pleasure and need as Adrian pulled her close by the waist, his lips finding her collarbones.

Kissing her, biting her; Adrian flooded his passionate growl and burning heat into her as he pressed his lean body and his hard arousal against her. She could feel him through her yoga pants, so exquisitely hot and firm that she bucked and cried out. Stroking her wet curls, Dusk set his lips to her temple, his grounding vibrations barely enough to keep her from shifting. Crushed close to Dusk's strong, warm chest, she was trapped between the delicious bodies of her two bound men.

Trapped – and flooded with both their pleasures.

"I need you." Adrian was breathless as he pressed his forehead to her neck, undone.

"I barely have control over my magic, Adrian," Layla gasped back, writhing between her men's bodies, so hot and needful. "What if I shift into my Dragon?"

"I don't care."

"I do."

"I can ground her." Dusk's voice was soft behind her shoulder. "If you want to take her, Adrian... I can ground her. Layla's still got some of Reginald's control pouring through her tonight, and I can augment it. I can ground her with my power long enough that we can all get what we need tonight... If you're willing."

Adrian paused. Layla felt his magics roil in frustration, in need. But Layla felt Dusk's energy then, reaching out to Adrian through her body like a cool river – flowing into Adrian's chest to ground his tempestuous fire as much as it grounded Layla's.

Suddenly, she felt Adrian's enormous need pull back a bit. Adrian drew a deep breath and Layla felt a sudden calculating thoughtfulness come clear in him. As if he was truly considering Dusk's offer, Adrian's raging lust paused, and Layla felt him thinking with the side of him that ruled his clan and the Paris Hotel with renegade efficiency. In that moment, Layla suddenly understood why she and Dusk and Adrian were bound in a trio – because they needed each other.

Dusk was the balm to she and Adrian's scorch; he was the earth and water to their fire and wind.

Adrian kissed Layla's neck as he exhaled. She felt him close his eyes, his long eyelashes brushing her skin. And then he murmured, "*In the blackest of your moments, wait with no fear.*"

A deep shudder passed through him on the heels of his Rumi quote, and then Layla felt him become decisive like a war-general. Power surged through him, hauling back his eros strongly enough that he was able to pull back from her and pin Layla with his eyes, then Dusk.

"My rooms. Now." Adrian growled deeply. "And fuck Reginald's ultimatum of dawn. This will take as long as it's going to take. Are you both with me?"

"Adrian." Dusk nodded behind Layla – though she could feel how much he was grinning.

"Yes." Layla breathed, wanting nothing more than what Adrian was proposing.

"Let's go then, before I lose control. Because the heavens will shatter if I do." And then Adrian was turning, striding off into the darkness with a terribly alluring glance for the both of them to follow.

Surging with heat, an electric sensation filled Layla at that searing glance from Adrian's beautiful eyes. Dusk gave her a squeeze around the waist, as if encouraging her to get moving and Layla startled, realizing this was really happening. Stepping away from Dusk, though he continued to hold her hand, grounding her, Layla started along the gravel path after Adrian, back toward the Hotel.

As she caught up, Adrian gave her a hot sidelong glance. The three of them walked in silence through the midnight grounds. Crunching along the path, most of the rooms on the second and third stories of the palace quadrangle were dark now, though the lower halls still held light from the chandeliers. Skirting the fountains, they made their way to a side-door and entered the Hotel. Moving up the nearest staircase, it was a short minute until they were all up to the fourth floor and past the twin Sphinx guardians – facing the snarling red Dragons at Adrian's door.

Lifting Layla's hand, Dusk kissed her knuckles. "Are you certain you want this, Layla?"

He looked at her, the real question in his summer-blue eyes. *Are you ok doing a threesome?*

Layla paused, glancing from one man to the other. They both watched her, something dark simmering from each of them, though in a slightly different way. Layla had never been with two men before. She didn't know how it would go, what tempers or awkwardness might arise, or uncomfortableness. Dusk and Adrian had a history of fighting over women, and watching them both now, that history was still there, reflected in the tension in each of their bodies. Their jealousy and wrath with each other hadn't gone away; it hadn't gotten any easier just because Layla had bound them together into some strange sort of moebius with her. If they were going to fight and bicker, two adopted brothers raised under the same roof, they were going to do it in bed, Layla was almost certain of it.

And yet.

Layla thought back to when she'd nearly died after Hunter's abduction. Adrian and Dusk had worked together to revive her, sleeping with her, holding her close, pouring their magics through her body – both at the same time. They'd been almost civil with each other the morning she'd woken, and had eaten breakfast together almost like all tensions between them had been absolved. They hadn't, but Layla'd had a glimpse of how dynamic the brothers could be when working with one another rather than in opposition.

And watching them both now, she could feel how much power the three of them could have – if they could get it right.

"I want this," Layla murmured, shivering with a deep arousal. "I want to try."

It was enough for Dusk. He nodded, stepping close to bring her his body heat, kissing her. Layla let herself sink into it; let herself be held by his strong arms. Dusk was real and he was here; he wasn't afraid of her or intimidated by what she might become. And *trying* was something he understood – something Layla needed right now.

But then Adrian reached out for her. Twining his fingers through hers, a searing, delicious heat went rolling through Layla's body and she shuddered from the vastness of Adrian's power. It lifted hers, mixed with hers, teased hers to come out and be inundated with glory from that subtle twining of his fingertips. Layla turned, feeling Adrian's pull like a sand-funnel – inescapable. Their gazes connected and heat roared between their bodies, leaving Layla without air as Adrian burned it all up with his dark, sexy intensity.

Calling to her through his touch like a night on fire.

She came. Adrian led, opening one double-door, and Layla stepped into his apartment after him – leading Dusk by her other hand. Adrian shut the doors, locking them as Dusk pulled Layla back against the gilded paneling and his hot, firm body – kissing her neck, cupping a hand beneath her wet curls as he pulled her back to his front. Before her, Adrian stepped in. Staring her down with aqua-gold fire blistering in his eyes, there was something eager there and something mean as he lifted Layla's hands – and then pinned them above her head upon the paneled wall to either side of Dusk.

With a sub-human growl that seared fire all through Layla's body, Adrian let her writhe – and then dove in, kissing her hard.

Layla succumbed to him in a rush, devouring the heat of Adrian's lips and body as he devoured hers. It wasn't slow and it wasn't kind –

and it was everything Layla wanted. Heat roared between them as their Dragons feasted; tearing at each other, roiling through each other with a raw passion and an indescribable bliss. She wanted to pour herself through him; to pour herself around him. She wanted him to grip her and carry her to bed, to throw her down and fuck her hard – and make her forget everything but his terrible, incredible heat.

Her eyes rolled up as Adrian kissed her, as she writhed and bucked against him, pinned, decadently unkind. Fever blistered Layla's veins. As Adrian thrust his hips against hers, making her feel how hot he was for her, how hard, she gasped, one hand spasming out of his grip – and slapping to Dusk's, there to ground her as Adrian devoured her.

Magic poured through Layla – blistering winds and cool underground rivers. She screamed as Adrian slammed her and Dusk back into the wall as he thrust his body hard against hers, hauling her yoga pants down so she could feel every inch of him pressed against her lace thong now. Layla's legs locked around his hips; they weren't going to make it to the bed. But then Adrian hauled her up with his hands beneath her ass and with a growl turned, still kissing her as he moved them to his massive four-post bed.

With a roar, he threw Layla down to the duvet, fire in his eyes with what he was about to do to her. But as Layla landed, she gasped suddenly. She'd landed in a puddle of wet. Adrian saw her face and halted, as Layla lifted her hand from the soaking duvet. There was something beneath the feather comforter, and she'd landed right next to it. Looking at her hand, she saw it had come up coated in something silver and wet, like mercury.

"What the hell?" Layla's passion broke as she stared at her hand. Adrian was frowning, glancing at the slender lump that had been outlined beside Layla as she was thrown down.

But Dusk was sweeping forward, horror on his face as he cast

95

back the duvet and sheets next to Layla – and uncovered the Head Courtesan Sylvania Eroganis. Beautiful as moonlight but pale as death, an enormous puddle of silver starlight soaked all through the canopied bed.

Sylvania's blood.

CHAPTER 9 – PAIN

Layla gasped at the pool of silver starlight blood on Adrian's bed, her eyes wide. Adrian shouted as Dusk flung himself to Sylvania's body with a cry, putting his fingers to the Head Courtesan's throat, feeling for a pulse. Her ardor forgotten, her Dragon coiling in a black terror, Layla was up fast, hauling the duvet and top sheet from the bed but not seeing where to staunch the bleeding. The Head Courtesan was naked in the sheets and rivers of silver moonlight gushed from her ears and nose, from the corners of her mouth and from between her legs, staining the bed.

Dusk's fingers fell from Sylvania's white throat. His head whipped up, fury in his clear blue gaze as he roared, *"Rikyava! Rikyava!!"* shuddering the heavy wooden bed and every pane of glass in Adrian's apartment. Layla felt a thundering spike rush through the air, and then she felt a searing response back – fevered like brimstone and burning battlefields.

She felt the Guard coming, racing toward Adrian's apartment. Rikyava came from her own quarters on the fourth floor, the rest of the Guards rushing up from the lower levels. As they came, Dusk lifted Sylvania off the bed to the floor, placing one palm on her chest, the other over her pierced navel. A harmonic surged through the room, rushing deep into Sylvania's body like an orchestra of light as Dusk worked his healing energy. Adrian went to the Courtesan's head, leaning over her and sliding his hand beneath her neck – pouring his life-giving heat down the Courtesan's throat like giving magical CPR.

But it wasn't having any effect on the pale Silver Passion.

"Come on…!" Dusk growled.

His hands doubled their efforts at Sylvania's heart, then tripled them, a symphony of music cascading through Adrian's apartments with a thousand impossible harmonies. It flooded Layla, making her tremble and shake as Dusk tried to revive the Head Courtesan. With a florid curse, he pushed furious vibrations through Sylvania, wrenching his efforts up so fast they set a pair of two-ton Moroccan vases beside the doors rattling. Setting his hands to the wooden floor, Dusk roared, blasting the wood apart with his frustration before placing his palms upon Sylvania once more.

Adrian was doing no less at Sylvania's beautiful, pale lips. But even his sandstorm of heat and power was having no effect. As Rikyava and the rest of her Guardsmen dashed in with pikes brandished, a hurricane of blood droplets surging around the wrathful Rikyava, Layla could see what Dusk and Adrian didn't want to acknowledge.

That it was too late.

Silver blood pooled beneath Sylvania's body on Adrian's damaged floor. So much blood. Luminous and stunning, it was a terrible contrast to the dark teak wood and the pale, naked woman laying in the middle of it. Racing in without a care for the blood as Adrian and Dusk worked, Rikyava knelt, her fingers to the woman's throat, feeling for a pulse as the rest of her cadre raced through Adrian's apartment with pikes brandished to sweep for an assailant.

But after a moment, Rikyava growled, looking up at Adrian and Dusk, her brimstone eyes bleak. "She's dead. Stop. She's dead Adrian, Dusk. She's gone."

Dusk roared, rattling vases and hanging votives all around. Rising, he slammed a fist into Adrian's apartment wall, shattering blue tiles in a massive shockwave. Adrian rose also, his face pale and shocked, and reached out, gripping Dusk's shoulder. Dusk shuddered, breathing hard, something wild in his all-diamond eyes. But it was Adrian who took command of the situation, gripping Dusk's shoulder and guiding him close so they could speak.

"Use the Orb. Call the Madame and the Head Courtier. I need you calm, Dusk. Can you do that for me?"

As Dusk shuddered under Adrian's firm grip, he closed his eyes. Still breathing hard, he seemed to master himself, though Layla saw tears leaking from beneath his dark eyelashes. Retrieving something from the inner pocket of his white tux jacket, Dusk set it to the center of his brow. A small opal stone, it was no larger than his thumb, but emanated an unearthly light as he held it. Layla could feel Dusk concentrating his vibrations; pouring them into the opal stone like pouring water into a thimble. Taking another breath, he lowered it to his lips, then murmured the names of the Madame and the Head Courtier.

Placing the stone back inside his jacket, he opened his eyes as Adrian gave him a small shake and let him go. Staring at Sylvania's dead body, Dusk's gaze was terrible. Layla followed his sightline, staring at the body also. She'd seen dead bodies before, both when Mimi had died and when she'd had to identify her parents in the morgue after their car crash. Those had been awful, Mimi's body shriveled like burned paper from the cancer, Layla's parents little but pulped meat beneath the morgue drape with only their faces recognizable.

But this corpse looked almost divine. Haloed in moonlit blood upon the dark floor, Sylvania's lovely face and silver hair were angelic, flowing around her in a beautiful shroud. Her starlight eyes were open, her silver irises burst with a stippling of blood yet still luminous. Stepping in with tight eyes, Dusk hunkered and set one palm to the dead woman's chest, gently. Producing a low hum, he sent a deep pulse into the body, his head lifting as he closed his eyes.

Rikyava hunkered at his side, her violet irises brimstone red as she watched Dusk.

"No blade wounds, no talon or claw marks." He spoke to Rikyava at last. "Her skin's unmarred, and she wasn't raped. She's been vibrated apart from within. Her heart's burst; all the blood came through her ears, her lungs, and digestive tract."

"Can you find her last memory? Any imprint of the magic that did this?" Rikyava growled. Her Guardsmen trotted back from the far corners of Adrian's apartment, shaking their heads.

"Apartment's clear, no sign of a break-in, no sign of struggle," one strapping, big-shouldered Guard with Viking-red hair spoke.

"Check the Sphinxes," Rikyava growled to them tersely. "Run a diagnostic on Adrian's guardian Dragons. Send Riko, Guy, and Hermetta to the other Department Heads down the hall, knock on doors but keep it discreet. Find me a witness. Go."

The man nodded tersely, flicking his fingers at his cohort. They departed fast, leaving a cadre of four behind inside the apartment.

Still kneeling by Sylvania with his hand on her chest, Dusk closed his eyes. Throwing back his head, he vibrated a brief tremolo through the body, pulsing it in waves, but varying the pitch and duration in musical notes that trembled through the air. They were tightly controlled and as Layla listened, she thought it was almost like a kind of sonar Dusk created from his magic.

Rikyava had bent over the body also. Lips parted and blood-red eyes keen, she looked ferocious as she inhaled air over Sylvania's bloody ears, nose, lips – even down at her groin. Closing her eyes, the Blood Dragon breathed deeper, and with a sudden shock, Layla realized the Head Guardswoman was actually smelling the scent of Sylvania's blood and deducing something from it. Placing her fingers in the starlit blood, Rikyava lifted it to her lips, tasting it. Her eyes widened at the same time Dusk finally opened his eyes.

Their gazes connected.

"This can't be right." Dusk murmured softly.

"Damn straight." Rikyava breathed back. Her gaze shifted to Adrian. "I smell it, but I don't believe it."

"Neither do I." Dusk spoke, a dark frown devouring his features. Pushing up from the floor, he glanced at Adrian also.

"What?" Adrian asked, frowning. "Did you find anything?"

"Oh, we found something." Rikyava rose, turning to face Adrian. "And what we found… was you."

"What?!" Adrian's eyes flashed gold, astonishment cascading over his face.

"Your scent's all over her, Adrian," Rikyava growled low. "Your magical imprint is all through the blood, along with her own."

"I managed to dredge up her last memory from the fading recesses of her mind, Adrian," Dusk's gaze was level. "The last face she saw was yours. Here. In your apartment."

"When did you last see Sylvania today, Adrian?" Rikyava had moved toward Adrian, one hand carefully at the rapier on her hip. "Was it when she came up to tend you after the Owner's party with Dusk?"

"Yes, but Dusk was still here when she left. She left first, and she didn't come back afterwards." Adrian's eyes had gone wide, fear flashing through them. "I didn't do this, Rikyava. My magic… it can't do something like this. It's never done anything like this before!"

Rikyava frowned. "Dusk. Is that true?"

"It is." He spoke quietly. "And I was still talking to Adrian when Sylvania left. I don't know if she came back after I went down to find Reginald, though."

"She didn't, I swear it." Adrian shook his head. "I haven't seen her since we were both here in my apartment together, Dusk. After you left, I went out for a long walk through the forest, out by the barns to clear my head. I haven't been back to my rooms since you were here."

Rikyava and Dusk shared a long look. Layla could feel tension simmering through the apartment like live electricity. "Did any witnesses see you out on the grounds tonight, Adrian?" Rikyava asked.

"I stopped by the barn on my way to the forest. There were a few grooms there. Ronin, Sareyya, and Canticle." Adrian's brows were furrowed, but Layla could tell he was trying to be as helpful as possible to clear himself of this terrible crime. Just then, Rikyava's red-bearded head Guardsman came jogging back into the room.

"The Sphinxes have only seen the imprints of people who have apartments up here today. No additional guests except Layla, just twenty minutes ago. And Adrian's guardian Dragons show no sign of forced entry. They also showed the Head Courtesan, Head Concierge, and the Hotel Head leaving separately from this apartment about three hours ago."

"But." Rikyava eyeballed her captain, knowing from the man's shifting glance at Adrian that there was more.

"But the Sphinxes did see the Hotel Head and Head Courtesan come back up here together, about an hour ago." His gaze shifted from Adrian, as if he couldn't bear to look the Hotel Head in the eyes as he gave his news. "The guardian Dragons at Adrian's doors recorded one access prior to twenty minutes ago – Adrian's eyes, breath, and finger-prints. One hour ago, at the same time the Head Courtesan came back up here with him."

Rikyava's gaze swung slowly to Adrian.

"I didn't do this, Rikyava," Adrian breathed. "I swear to every god in all the heavens. I would never kill Sylvania. *Never.* And I've never been able to do something like this with my magic."

Slowly, the Blood Dragon drew a deep breath. Turning to her captain, she said. "Find me the grooms Ronin Petite, Sareyya Manin, and Canticle du Freysne. Bring them down to the Guardhall for questioning. Adrian says he was out walking the grounds all night – find me evidence. Go."

"On it." The man moved away fast, whistling sharply for the remaining Guard in the room. They tore away, leaving Rikyava, Dusk, Layla, and Adrian behind. Silence devoured the apartment as everyone stared at the dead body. At last, Dusk pulled a sheet from Adrian's bed, draping it gently over the luminous corpse, hiding it in draping folds. They continued to stare at the sheet, until Adrian raised his eyes back to Rikyava.

"I didn't do this, Rikyava."

"I believe you." She drew a deep breath, but her gaze was awful as it met his, then swept to Layla.

"I know who it was." Layla breathed, horror curling through her veins like liquid darkness. A memory of hunter-green eyes surfaced in her mind, and she shuddered.

"I know." Rikyava murmured back, something awful in her blood-red eyes. "I wondered when something like this was going to happen. Ever since he infiltrated the Hotel the first time, I was wondering when we'd finally have to clean up a mess of Hunter's. How long it would be before he decided to make a move and show us all how easily he could become any one of us – and take down someone we loved. I thought it was going to be Layla he made a move to harm… I never expected this."

Gazing back to the covered body, Layla felt something cold slither through her gut, swallowing her into a black despair. This was her fault. Sylvania's death was her fault. If she hadn't resisted Hunter at Samhain, if she had gone with him, the Head Courtesan's death would never have happened. And to make it worse, Hunter had framed Adrian. The one person Layla couldn't do without, the one person she died to be close to. Hunter had deliberately killed using Adrian's face, even the imprint of Adrian's magic.

Something that was supposed to be impossible.

Just then, the Madame and Head Courtier swept into the room. Etienne Voulouer's hands clapped to her cheeks, her feline eyes brimming with tears as she rushed forward in a purple and gold dressing-gown, stopping at the rim of the blood pool and covering her mouth with her hand.

But it was Reginald who rushed all the way in, kneeling without a care to his quilted blue silk robe in the blood beside the dead woman. Eyebrows knit and eyes wide in horror, he cast back the sheet quickly, baring Sylvania's haunting corpse. A tortuous sound came from his throat as he seized the dead woman's shoulders, hauling her up – clutching her to his breast. A terrible keening came from him as he cradled the Head Courtesan to his chest, rocking her.

And in that moment, Layla suddenly recalled that the Head Courtier and the Head Courtesan had been lovers. More than lovers. Primary mates – something that seldom happened between two people of different Lineages.

"*How could you have let this happen?!*" Reginald roared over his shoulder at Dusk, rage and pain in his pale blue eyes. "Sylvania!"

Dusk hunkered upon the other side of the dead woman, a matching pain in his bright sapphire gaze. "I didn't feel it, Aldo. I'm so sorry! Please – it all happened so fast."

"We *trusted* you with the Orb of Cephalus!" Reginald snarled, still cradling the dead woman. "You have *one job* here, Dusk! And you have failed, *utterly!*"

"Reginald—" Dusk's voice was a hard rasp now; tears stood out in his lovely sapphire eyes, though they didn't fall.

"Get out of my sight! Get out… all of you just get out!" The Head Courtier roared, a long, furious wail ripping from him again as he clutched the body to his breast. Keening now with hard, roaring sobs, he cradled Sylvania's lovely head to his face – kissing her pale lips over and over.

Dusk's dark eyebrows knit, pain suffusing his features as he closed his eyes, iridescence flashing hard through his hair and Dragon-scales. Layla watched Dusk's tears fall, awful. With steady stoicism, he rose, taking a deep inhalation. And then turned, striding out from Adrian's apartment into the hall.

Rikyava went after Dusk, her eyes returned to lavender and her blonde brows lifted as she stepped quickly to the hall. Moving to Layla, Adrian's eyes were bleak. Twining his fingers through hers, he nodded his chin at the hall also. Glancing back, Layla saw Reginald fall forward over the corpse, his entire body wracked with sobs. Waves of water manifested in the air around him, washing around the corpse as he screamed, as if his magic could cry for his dead lover.

Watching Reginald, the Madame sighed with pain in her eyes. Her demeanor was tired as she motioned Adrian and Layla out, stepping out behind them and closing the doors to Adrian's apartment. Everyone lingered in the hall, stunned, Dusk heaving hard breaths and wiping his eyes with the heels of his hands. Squaring her shoulders, the Madame beckoned, and everyone followed her to her apartment. Opening the doors, she ushered them in, then spoke low to a Guardsman, who gave her a crisp nod and rushed off.

Fires roared in four fireplaces around the Madame's apartment, outlining patterns of tiger-stripe and leopard everything. As if Layla had stepped into a cat sanctuary, the Madame's rooms had a wilderness to them, drowning in pots of vines with trees twisting their way through the vaulted space. Even the tiger-print bed reflected a feline aura, situated on a high platform one had to climb stairs to access. There were even decorations around the room that reminded Layla of tinsel-balls that house cats played with.

Though no one was playing now.

A midnight spread from Catering arrived quickly, though they had shocked faces as they set up an urn of coffee and plates of small bites. After they departed, the Madame sipped coffee from a china cup, though no one ate much, silence devouring the room. Just when Layla thought it couldn't get any worse, Reginald pushed in through the doors, his golden hair bedraggled, his dressing-robe stained with silver blood.

"Madame." He rasped, his gaze bleak and red-rimmed. "The Intercessoria Judiciary are here. They would like to speak with you and establish the crime scene."

The Madame blinked rapidly as she set her coffee down, smoothing her hands down her robe. "Of course. Of course…"

Tension spiked through the room as the Madame exited. Adrian sank into a seat by the fireplace, his hands laced hard as he set his thumbs to his lips, his face ashen. Dusk sat beside him but said nothing, though they both looked up as the Madame returned and summoned Rikyava and Dusk out to speak with the Intercessoria Judiciary investigators – to tell them what they'd discovered when they evaluated the body.

Nervousness clenched Layla as minutes stretched to an hour. The glow of dawn began to brighten the sky through the Madame's vaulted windows as Adrian sat silent, his hands still gripped tight as he stared at the fireplace. Layla could practically see his mind churning as he frowned at the curling flames. She watched him consider this event from all angles as he sat, pensive and waiting.

He'd not been called to speak with the Juds yet, and Layla knew he was keenly aware that he was their primary suspect. Layla shifted in her seat, worrying if they took him away for questioning, that she might never see him again. Adrian must have felt something, for he looked over. Their gazes connected and he gave her a sad, reassuring smile. Reaching out, he clasped her hand. But his hand was cold to the touch and Layla felt his energy swirling just like hers, dark and deep inside his body.

Reginald sat by one fireplace in a high-backed chair. He'd already been out to speak with the investigators, and now sat staring at the flames. Without any of his couture, he was truly striking, even in his grief. Reginald's aquiline features were stony, his gaze frigid as he stared at the fire, his full lips set in a hard line. Bright golden hair escaped around his face from his tight club, the glow of the flames making his pale blue eyes a haunting color. The high collar of his blue silk robe was open, his strong collarbones standing out in his artfully-muscled chest.

As Layla watched, he balled a fist in the silk of his robe and clenched it, then released it as if with a will. Moving over to him, the Madame sank gracefully down before his chair. His gaze flickered to her, and reaching out, she gripped his hand. But though he glanced at their fingers, something in his manner was still shellshocked.

"Aldo," Etienne Voulouer murmured softly. "We will figure out why this happened, and who did it. I promise. And we will have retribution."

Closing his eyes, Reginald sat still a long moment, beautiful and terrible like a marble statue. Flames crackled in the fireplace, the only sound in the room. At last, he gave a weary nod. Rising and reaching out, Etienne gathered the Head Courtier's head in her hands. She stepped close, and Reginald's shoulders heaved in a sigh as he rested his face on Etienne's belly. Etienne ran her hands tenderly through his hair, removing the elastic that kept his club back and letting that wealth of burnished gold fall free. Layla saw Reginald's shoulders heave again; saw him shudder though his face was hidden by his hair now. The Madame met Layla's gaze, though she did not cease combing her long fingers through Reginald's flaxen glory.

At that moment, Dusk re-entered the room. Glancing at Layla and Adrian, his gaze was bleak, triply so as he saw the Madame and Reginald. Lurching from the door, he moved toward the fireplace. Stopping just short of the Madame, he gazed at Reginald.

"Aldo, I swear to you—" Dusk began.

"Leave it be, Dusk." The Head Courtier's voice came muffled through Etienne's robe. He said no more and Dusk closed his lips, a woebegone look taking his face. It was clear the Head Courtier wasn't going to forgive Dusk for the lapse in Hotel security that had happened while Dusk and Layla had been out-of-contact in the crystal bathhouse. It had already been agreed that neither Dusk nor Rikyava would be fired because of this event, though Layla could feel Dusk's terrible guilt – as if he'd failed in his responsibilities at the Hotel, utterly.

At last, Dusk moved back to where Layla and Adrian sat, collapsing into a chair. Reaching out, he took up Layla's hand, twining his fingers through hers as if for comfort. It was comforting, and Layla sighed, Dusk sighing at that same exact moment.

"What are the Judiciary saying out there, Dusk?" Adrian's voice was low, tense.

"They think this was a hit," Dusk spoke, taking up the conversation as he toyed with Layla's fingers. "A hit meant to destabilize the Paris Hotel. I told them all about our interactions with Hunter a month back; told them our theory. Rikyava backed me up. They berated us for withholding information about such a dangerous creature on our premises, but at least the two investigators the Juds sent are civil. They're listening, gathering clues, weighing all options. The lead investigator is a stickler for finding out the perfect truth in any case he works. Which may be to our advantage."

"Who's the lead on this case?" Adrian asked softly.

"Heathren Merkami. Second on the case is Insinio Brandfort." Dusk's words were like stones dropping from his lips as he watched Adrian.

With a slow out-breath, Adrian rubbed his hands over his face and down his stubble. Layla hadn't thought he could get any more ashen, but he did, like hearing those names had stolen his soul, or worse. He swallowed hard, his gaze dark, the gold in his eyes intense by the light of the flames. "I'm their primary suspect, aren't I?"

"Yes." Dusk didn't mince words. "Rikyava and I had to tell them the truth of what we found in Sylvania's blood and final memories, Adrian, and the Guard's initial investigation. But there is an anomaly that may work in your favor. Apparently, both the Sphinxes and your guardian Dragons held an imprint of you and Sylvania ascending the stairs and going into your apartment together an hour before we found the body. But neither set of guardians imprinted with you ever *leaving* your room. So unless you jumped out the window of your own apartment or off the fourth-floor balcony to meet up with Layla and I outside the crystal bath-house…"

"And the Guard already reported that my apartment was secure when they did their first sweep. No windows or balcony doors were unlocked." Adrian blinked; something hopeful moved over his features.

"It may be your saving grace, Adrian." Dusk held his gaze with a level intensity. "Heathren Merkami won't let a detail like that slide, you know he won't."

"God, I hope so." Adrian wiped his hands over his face again in a tired gesture. Reaching out, Layla took his fingers in hers also, so one hand was holding Dusk and the other Adrian. Adrian looked up; a small smile flitted over his lips before it was gone.

"I'm sorry the night turned out this way." Layla breathed.

"Me, too." Adrian's smile was sad.

But before he could say anything else, Rikyava came back into the room. Glancing at Layla, her gaze pierced like a spear. "Layla. The Intercessoria Judiciary are ready for you now."

"Sure." Layla took a deep breath and rose. It was almost physically painful to let go of Adrian and Dusk's hands, but she managed. Her gaze connected to Dusk and she felt him give a reassuring rumble through the air. She glanced at Adrian, and his eyes were tired.

"Tell them the truth, Layla. Don't hold anything back. We're too far past that, and it'll only end up causing trouble." Adrian spoke softly.

"What if my testimony incriminates you?"

"It will." His gaze was bleak. "But to not tell the Juds the full truth at this point would dig us even deeper into the pit than we already are. It was my mistake to have not have reported Hunter's infiltration of the Paris Hotel to them back in October. I wanted to solve the situation internally; I was wrong. I have to own that now. Don't dig yourself into a hole with the Juds. Just tell them the truth."

Gazing into Adrian's sober face, Layla nodded. He was right. It was going to be a mess for them to sort out, but the more she could be honest now, the better chance Adrian had of not getting chucked into a dark oubliette for the rest of his days – or worse.

Taking a deep breath, Layla stepped away from her bound men toward the doors. Putting a hand to one gilded door-handle, she pushed out, stepping into the hall.

CHAPTER 10 – JUDICIARY

Across the fourth floor hall, Adrian's apartment had been cordoned off with some kind of strange, shimmering gold boundary. People of numerous sorts came and went from his rooms between the massive Dragon guardian statues. Wearing sleek white silk Twilight Realm versions of hazmat suits and investigative gloves, they all carried golden tablets to record notes on or spoke into golden smartphones for dictation. As Layla stepped out of the Madame's apartment, she saw an immense, burly-shouldered man standing near the gold perimeter turn her way, then tap a lean man standing next to him.

The one who turned first was tall, broad like a shield through the shoulders, strongly built with brush-cut black hair. His square jaw could have cracked skulls, his irises a vivid, luminous silver. Wearing black-buckled leathers with an immense broadsword angled over his shoulder and a harness of assorted knives, his leather breastplate had an ornate silver star set into the leather above his heart. His waist was strong and his leather-clad thighs enormous – clearly he had never skipped leg day.

The other man who turned was as slender as the first man was burly. Though as tall as his partner, he was lean in a heroin-chic way, but his florid beauty didn't say *drug addict*. Piercing Layla with all-white irises and black pupils that could have been the beauty of an angel or the darkness of a demon, he wasn't a Siren; his beauty precise rather than alluring, sharp like a blazing sword. Wearing the same leather gear as the first, he had two slender swords crossed at his back rather than one large one. His cheekbones were high and his features perfectly sculpted; beautiful and dangerous. A thick cable of sleek white-silver hair was braided over one shoulder, all the way down to his waist.

Though his features were masculine, they were the sort of perfection that was so intense it was otherworldly, and his lips held no smile of any kind. Layla saw his eyes were also silver as he neared, though far more pale than the dark-haired man's stunning gaze. Both had skin that was almost luminous, giving each man a breathtaking appearance as they neared. The only description that came to Layla's stunned mind as she watched them approach, was *battle angel*.

"Layla Price?" The big man asked in a rumbling basso voice as they arrived before her.

She nodded, her mouth dry. Both men were insanely attractive, but their impressive armor and commanding presences weren't to be ogled. Their demeanors screamed *cops* – and more than that, *military cops*. As they stopped before her, their twin power made her skin crawl, her Dragon hissing inside her on high alert. A fierce citrus-bourbon scent boiled off Layla's skin, and the slender silver-haired man lifted a straight eyebrow.

"Control your Dragon, girl," he murmured, in a voice that was smooth as silk and cutting as blades. "Or we will control it for you."

"I can't," Layla swallowed, more intimidated by these two men than by any police she'd ever met. "It's not really under my control yet, and I don't have a talisman any longer."

The two investigators exchanged a look. Narrowing his eyes, the lean man stepped forward, gazing down from his exquisite height into her eyes, intently. Layla realized he was nearly seven feet tall as she felt something sweep though her, like silver wings of light; searching, evaluating. The sensation breathed through her with a haunting movement, as if reading every inch of Layla's soul.

At last, the man's pale lips quirked. He raised a straight eyebrow with a slightly amused look as his magics sighed away. "The Royal Dragon Bind. They weren't lying when they said you were on fire. So new to your magics that you have no concept of how they work yet." Lifting a long-fingered hand, he gave her a look that brokered no resistance. "This won't hurt. Hold still."

Layla held still as the man set his hand over her heart. Closing his eyes, he drew a deep breath, and Layla had the strangest sensation like he raised seven sets of enormous silver-white wings from his back, though she saw nothing disturb the air. Raising his chin, he siphoned all that power though his palm and into her chest, though it wasn't a terrible sensation. Like a flood of evening starlight, it flowed into her body, warming her and cooling her at the same time – and causing her Dragon to curl right up inside her and take a very good nap.

Layla's heat calmed instantly. She was left blinking at the man as he opened his pale silver eyes.

"Come." He spoke. "The effect on your Dragon will eventually wear off, but that gives us enough time to digest your situation. This way." With an effete gesture that was also somehow battle-hardened, the lean man with silver-white hair motioned for Layla to step to a cordoned-off area in one of the hall's alcoves. She did, stepping over the golden boundary on the floor.

And instantly felt herself whisked away – right out of the Hotel altogether.

Disorientation swept Layla, a moment of blinding white light. And then she was standing in a white room with the two men, in the middle of which was a silver table and three chairs. Motioning to the single chair on one side of the table, the lean man claimed one of the two chairs opposite. The burly fellow didn't sit, just stood behind the final chair, crossing his enormous arms over his chest and watching Layla

113

with his intense silver eyes.

Fidgeting, Layla took the indicated seat. Gazing around, she saw the all-white walls shimmered with a golden grid, sigils and strange script set inside every grid-box. The grid itself was made from a golden script that actually flowed as she watched, as if the incantations written there were somehow breathing, or alive. The roughly twenty-by-twenty space had no windows and no door, though everything was softly bright. Looking up and down, Layla saw the same sigils and script running through the ceiling and floor.

"Ms. Layla Price, Royal Dragon Bind of the Desert Dragons of Morocco and the Mediterranean." The slender silver-haired man spoke, leaning back in his chair and interlacing his long fingers in his lap. "My name is Heathren Merkami, and this is Insinio Brandfort. We are Intercessoria Judiciary investigators, and have come to settle the case of Sylvania Eroganis' death. Which we are finding more and more complex with every testimony, unfortunately. Let us start with your name, for the record. And tell us how you have come to know Adrian Rhakvir."

All around the room, Layla watched the script and sigils brighten in a cascading wave, as if they were ready to record her testimony. Swallowing hard, she firmed her courage, knowing that only the truth would free Adrian of accusation.

"My name is Layla Price," she spoke in a strong voice. "And I first met Adrian Rhakvir in Seattle, at an art gallery. At least, that's when I can first recall meeting him."

The silver-haired man Heathren Merkami nodded peaceably, gesturing for her to continue.

Layla did. Her story came pouring out, everything that had happened since she'd first met Adrian back in August. Bleary, exhausted, she felt like she'd been awake thirty-six hours as she talked on and on. Nothing changed inside the white room except the slow scrawl of sigils across the walls and floor, writing themselves over and over in slowly-flowing waves of gold. Listening intently and interrupting now and then to ask clarifying questions, Heathren Merkami held an attentive patience, staring at her with his silver-white eyes. Still standing though he shifted occasionally, Insinio Brandfort listened just as attentively, though his questions were less frequent.

Layla tried to start her description of her association with Adrian with the art gallery. But when she mentioned her strange desert-scape dreams of him, Heathren's straight dark brows narrowed, and he asked Layla to go into an account of her childhood. That conversation led to Mimi, to Layla having been born at Adrian's home in Morocco, and the Rhakvir family's earliest awareness of Hunter.

By the time Layla got back to present day, Heathren was scowling with a dark, pensive silence, the big burly Insinio doing no less behind him. Heathren let her complete her tale of how she'd come to the Hotel, how Adrian was trying to protect her from the void-shadow, and everything that had gone down when Adam had shown himself for who he truly was. Layla finished with a brief account of her current situation training her magics under Reginald, and her relationships with Dusk and Adrian.

As she spoke, Heathren sat back in his chair. Crossing his arms over his chest, he tipped his chair back on two legs, crossing one long leg at his knee. His black leather boots had knife sheaths on the sides, occupied by daggers with silver hilts, and Heathren adjusted so the knife handle didn't press into his kneecap. His brows still knit, he regarded Layla with a quiet intensity as she finished. She was so bleary, she had a feeling she'd left something important out – though for the life of her, she couldn't remember what. Still standing, Insinio was a burlier echo of Heathren's intensity, his bright silver eyes narrowed though his strong posture seemed relaxed.

There was no good cop bad cop here. Just quiet cop and quieter cop, which made Layla squirm with discomfort more than a bad cop could have.

At last, Heathren drew a deep breath. Settling his chair back to the floor, he regarded Layla with a fierce directness. "Your tale makes a number of strange cases over the years become plain, Layla Price. The odd disappearance of Mimi Zakir, famous Royal Dragon Bind chanteuse. The sudden death of Juliette Rhakvir at her family home, still an unsolved murder to this day, though some would call it closed. The problem of Adam Rhakvir's magical imprint on official records changing after his sixth birthday, ever-so-slightly, from his recorded magical birth print. It was officially written off as due to severe trauma from when his family were assassinated in Italy, though I've never believed it."

"So... what does that mean?" Layla breathed, curious and also wary.

"It means," Heathren exchanged a glance with Insinio, and some accord passed between the two investigators, "that I am very seriously weighing the testimonies I have heard about this *Hunter* character. No record exists of this man; no magical birth-documents. Only tales like the wind which I have compiled over millennia. Tales of fear and darkness, death and tragedy. But he is like a ghost in the dark. The entire Intercessoria have no concrete proof of him. We didn't even have a name for this creature until now. Until it broke its own code of shadow and stealth to make itself known to you. Which could prove useful."

Heathren and his partner exchanged another glance, before Heathren's gaze retuned to Layla. "In any case, Adrian Rhakvir is not off the hook. He remains our prime suspect in this murder investigation until evidence proves otherwise. While we've been speaking, he has been taken into custody. Where he will remain until any new evidence frees him. I'm sorry."

Layla's throat became tight, shock flooding her that they'd already arrested Adrian. Her eyes stung, thinking of her last touch with him – holding his hand in the Madame's apartment. "But he's not guilty. He didn't kill Sylvania!"

Heathren's gaze weighed Layla, his long fingers interlacing upon the tabletop. "Perhaps not. But Adrian Rhakvir has many business ventures that lean on the edge of the law, Ms. Price. And your other beau, Dusk Arlohaim, murdered three villages of humans when he was young. Don't even get me started on Reginald Durant, starting an entire war between the Blood Dragons of Sweden and Norway and the North Sea Sirens because he drowned a town of Blood Dragons in his wrath. Or Rake André, implicated in five years of creating hallucinations so vivid with his magics that he drove eighteen humans to suicide. But the Red Letter Hotel has long held a truce of sorts with the Intercessoria. The Hotel was founded prior to our lawmaking system, and so its original charter still stands as its own law – unless dire circumstance necessitates Intercessoria investigation, which it does in this case."

"What are you saying?" Layla breathed, astounded to hear such accusations levied against her friends. She couldn't believe that Reginald had drowned a village, nor that Rake had killed people, not intentionally. Layla recalled her conversation with Dusk, that the Hotel protected more people than she knew – people who had once wound up on the wrong side of the law but were making good at changing.

As if reading her thoughts, Heathren Merkami gave her a level look. "Recovered lawbreakers who work at the Hotel are given amnesty as long as they can prove they are no longer a threat to society. The Paris Hotel has many yet-dangerous creatures within its walls, Layla

117

Price, which we are not currently investigating or clapping in irons because of the amnesty. You are one of them."

Layla stiffened, feeling a not-so-veiled threat behind Heathren's words. "Are you saying I could be arrested if my magic goes haywire?"

"I'm saying it already has, from reports we're gathering from Hotel Owners who were at Adrian's little shindig yesterday."

"Adrian's invoked the Magna Dicta. I'm his protectee." Layla fought back.

"I know." Heathren lifted an eyebrow, his glance one of barely-veiled disdain. "A claim that should have been reported to the High Court, but was not. Like his *oversight* in reporting your abduction at Samhain and the entire issue of Hunter. Adrian has secrets within secrets. He believes he operates above the law. I don't agree. I have brought down men like Adrian Rhakvir time and time again over my two thousand years in the Intercessoria, and I don't have any qualms about doing it. But I feel no lie from his soul when he asserts that he did not kill the Head Courtesan. And if I can use a small fish to hook a bigger fish, one that has slipped through every Intercessoria net for *tens* of thousands of years..."

Heathren Merkami suddenly gave a small smile, just a quirk of lips. It was the first time he'd done so, and something about it was so vicious that Layla recalled her first impression of him. Like an angel of darkness, he had a bright fury about him, something fallen and wild. Something that lusted for the hunt and battle, for victory and bloodshed. That smile was so dark that Layla shivered, her skin raising in gooseflesh all along her arms and spine.

"You're using Adrian as a bargaining chip," Layla spoke, understanding. "To secure our Hotel's cooperation against Hunter. My cooperation. And Dusk's."

"Sometimes secrets are currency," Heathren spoke, "and

sometimes truth is currency. My currency is *prisoners*, Ms. Price. Adrian Rhakvir will rot away in the Intercessoria's dungeons unless I know that you and your friends are doing everything humanly possible to lure this Hunter from his hiding-grounds. I don't want Adrian Rhakvir. Eventually, maybe, when he overtly breaks a law big enough. But right now, I want the bigger fish. Do I make myself clear?"

"Crystal." Layla breathed, fear washing through her at what all of this would mean.

"Good." Rising from his chair with an uncompromising fluidity, Heathren stared her down. Layla saw fire in his pale silver eyes as he regarded her. Something about it made her think of blazing swords – and wrath. "I will be in touch, Ms. Price. And when I am, I suggest for all your bound lover's sakes, and for the friends you are making in this new life of yours, that you cooperate with everything the Intercessoria asks of you. You may go."

Before Layla could so much as open her mouth, she was suddenly flashing through that white-blind space again, disorientation sweeping her. And with a sensation like being vacuumed through a funnel, she was thrust back within the golden circle on the Hotel's fourth floor.

It was full afternoon outside the high banks of windows, a dark and stormy winter grey. No one was about. The doors to Adrian's apartment stood ajar, the golden crime-scene boundary still around them. Layla had thought the hall was empty when Dusk suddenly rose from a chair in the alcove. Still wearing his tux shirt and pants but no jacket or bow-tie, he looked ragged as he moved over swiftly, waiting at the edge of the golden boundary until Layla stepped across.

And then he swept her up in his arms.

"Thank god." He breathed at her ear, clasping her close. "I thought they might hold you longer. I'm glad they didn't."

Layla's Dragon was sluggish in her veins, barely awake after whatever Heathren had done to her magic, and only a small surge of heat passed between her and Dusk as they held each other.

"Where is Adrian?" Layla breathed anxiously, a dark pit swallowing her.

"They arrested him a few hours ago, just after you were taken into interrogation." Dusk leaned back, brushing a curl from Layla's face, his face bleak. "I'm so sorry, Layla…"

Layla's heart sank. Inside, her Dragon coiled up, digging into a hole so dark Layla could practically taste emptiness on her tongue. It was a terrible place, black and devouring, but she was too exhausted to cry. She should have been feeling more, but after such an awful thirty-six hours, all she could feel was numbness.

It must have showed, because Dusk held her face gently between his palms and kissed her. It was just a press of lips, but as he gave a low rumble, Layla felt something wake inside her at last. As if the veils of bad and worse information that Heathren Merkami had trapped her in finally released, Layla heaved a sigh.

Dusk kissed her again, pressing her sweetly with his lips. "I could use some sleep. You?"

Layla nodded. She didn't feel like speaking. Dusk's lips quirked in a terrible smile as he slung his arm around her, escorting her down the hall. They wound up at his rooms, and as they pushed inside the modern 1930's crystal-accented space, Layla felt ease breathe through her at last. It wasn't much, but somehow entering Dusk's serene apartment with its wealth of crystal pillars, geodes, and greenery-framed altars made Layla feel a small release.

The sound of water burbling in the Anubis fountain eased Layla as they stepped into the living area. Moving to his sleek modern breakfast table with its scroll-worked ebony wood, Dusk rummaged inside his tux jacket, slung over a chair. Retrieving the opal stone, he murmured something to it, then slid it away again. Turning to Layla, he nodded at the spread of eggs, bacon, and sautéed kale on the table. "It's cold, but would you like to eat? Or I could order something new from Catering."

"What time is it?" Layla moved to the table, but nothing looked appetizing, not even the French press coffee.

Glancing at his platinum and sapphire Rolex, Dusk heaved a sigh. "Two-sixteen p.m."

Rubbing both hands over her face, Layla sighed. "They held me all morning?"

"You're lucky. The Intercessoria are known for interrogating witness for days sometimes." Moving over, Dusk rubbed a hand over her back. Glancing down, Layla saw quicksilver blood staining her yoga clothes from when Adrian had thrown her down on the soaked bed.

"She's dead." Layla spoke, finally processing it.

Sylvania was dead. Her friend, the woman who had healed her from illness, the Head Courtesan of the entire Paris Hotel and probably the kindest person Layla had ever met. And though she and Layla hadn't been the closest friends, Layla felt an enormous hole in her heart, a black reaping not just from her but from the entire Hotel. Sylvania Eroganis had been a treasure, a sublime creature that had been taken from the world far too early. It suddenly made Layla furious – all her sorrow rushing into a blistering sensation that screamed from her veins even though they were still sluggish from Heathren's ministrations.

"When I see him… I'm going to kill him." Layla spoke softly, feeling something far more than wrath slide through her. The heat scorching off her body made a shimmer of golden fire break through the air – real fire this time just like she'd produced down in the fight-hall, not the scintillating ether of her passions. Lifting one dark

121

eyebrow, Dusk moved a hand through that simmering aura, but it didn't burn him. It writhed around Layla, singeing the nearby plants, but it didn't hurt either her or Dusk.

That fire wasn't meant for him.

"Who are you going to kill?" Dusk asked, his fingertips dancing through her curls of flame as he admired their vicious beauty.

"Hunter." Layla's gaze found Dusk's and she saw him take a long, slow breath. Reaching out, he cupped her face with one hand, brushing his thumb over her cheek.

"Your eyes look like his…" Dusk murmured sadly.

"Whose?"

"Hunter's. Adam's." Dusk gave a small, awful smile. "His eyes would go this same deep green color when he was angry. So dark they'd nearly become black; just like yours now. The look of a hunter in the darkness – the look of a killer."

Layla's breath caught. Something within her screamed, feeling a precarious balance tipping inside her. As if she might fall into a terrible pit, which would turn the Dragon inside her utterly black, Layla felt how far Hunter had pushed her. She felt how deeply he'd manipulated her with Sylvania's death and Adrian's framing.

And how dark the road of retribution could be.

"Don't let me go bad over this, Dusk." She breathed softly, fear racing through her veins and cooling the simmering fire around her, making it curl out to nothing.

"Never." He spoke, stepping in and catching her close. She could smell him, his calm river-water energy easing out around her. As his strong hands held her close, one hand stole up to rub the back of her neck. With a sigh, Layla abandoned herself to it; her head relaxing to his shoulder. Breathing at his collarbones, Layla moved her nose beneath the open collar of his tux shirt, smelling him. Smelling steadiness, calm depth, and support.

"There's still a ring of gold around your eyes, Layla." Dusk murmured softly as her arms came up around his waist. "We can fight this. Hunter fights alone but we fight together. You, me, Adrian – and everyone else we love."

"What if I can't fight going dark like the rest of my Lineage?" She breathed. "What if my talisman was the only thing keeping me safe from that? What if Hunter keeps pushing me… keeps killing people I love to make me fall over that dark edge…"

"That's why you have me," Dusk spoke in her ear, gentle. "To keep reminding you what love feels like no matter what. And Adrian."

"Adrian's in prison!" Layla's throat choked as her hands gripped Dusk's shirt.

"He won't stay there." Dusk murmured. "If I know one thing about Adrian Rhakvir, he's got more outs from sticky situations than a cat greased in butter. His business dealings are shady, Layla, but he makes sure to stay clean of anything the Intercessoria can actually pin him with. He's stayed out of their clutches for a hundred and fifty years, though he's been brought in for questioning numerous times. Even though the evidence against him looks bad right now, there are too many anomalies surrounding Sylvania's death that Heathren Merkami is going to chew on like a terrier. They questioned the grooms at the barn: Adrian has an alibi and it's solid. The only reason Heathren's holding Adrian right now is to put pressure on us to cooperate."

A beam of light poured through the darkness in Layla's heart, Dusk's problem-solving words giving her hope. Looking up, Layla met his gaze. "If that's the case, then what do we do?"

"I have an idea." Dusk's eyes held a glint of devious planning – of course he'd been thinking through the tangle while she'd been questioned by the Intercessoria. "But we need sleep first. Come on. Adrian's not going anywhere for now; we can use that time to rest and address this fresh in the morning."

Stepping back, Dusk gave Layla a gentle tug at the hand. She came, following him to the massive four-post ebony bed with the crushed amethyst pad beneath the sheets. But when he reached down to gather up her tank top, Layla stopped his hands.

"Just sleep." She murmured, exhausted.

"Just sleep." He echoed, pressing his lips to hers in a sweet kiss.

CHAPTER 11 – DAMAGE

Dusk and Layla slept through the night and long past their usual wake-up the next morning. A fancy alarm by Dusk's bed went off with copper chimes at five a.m., but he merely whacked it and rolled over, tucking Layla closer to his warm body. They drifted off again and when they finally woke, the winter morning was fully light and swaddled in snow. Overnight, the Red Letter Hotel Paris had transformed from a barren tableau of topiaries to a shrouded garden of benevolence in the high morning. Stretching as she sat up in Dusk's bed, Layla marveled at it through the vaulted windows. From the fourth floor, everything looked like a fairy dreamworld, soft and bright.

Layla didn't feel bright this morning, but it couldn't be helped. Sliding out from underneath the covers, she padded to Dusk's walk-in closet and found a spare silk robe in striped taupe and grey. Slinging it on to prevent a chill, the fire in the fireplace long gone out and the radiators not on, Layla moved to the dining table, pouring a fresh mug of hot coffee from the new French press that Catering had brought while they slept.

She slid back into bed with her coffee and blew on it, watching steam curl up into the chilly air. Beside her, Dusk stirred, rolling to his front and throwing an arm across her lap, snugging her hips close. He buried his face in her hip, breathing deep. Layla admired the midnight ridges outlining the musculature of his strong back as he breathed. Dusk was built like some ancient god, deliciously robust but lean. A small smile quirked his lips and Layla knew he was awake, but he just laid there, breathing her scent and smiling into her hip.

"I know you're awake." Layla spoke, blowing on her coffee and taking a sip.

"I know you know I'm awake." He growled, giving her a rumble of pleasure from his lower-than-sound vibrations. "But I like it when you watch me."

"What can I say? You're hot. You know it."

"Hottest man I know." He rumbled cheekily.

"And so modest." Layla closed her eyes, enjoying his vibrations as she remembered two nights ago when they had been together in the crystal bath-house. A smile blossomed in her as she opened her eyes, leaning back in the pillows as Dusk pushed up to sitting beside her, the muscles in his arms rippling in a powerful movement. As he sat up, a flash of midnight iridescence passed through his sleep-mussed yet still surprisingly stylish dark hair.

"Hey, let me in at that." Reaching out, he snagged Layla's coffee mug from her fingers and had a sip. She opened her mouth in mock protest and he only waggled his straight dark eyebrows, swigging off more. Half the mug was gone before he gave it back, with a roguish grin. "God! That was the best sleep I've had in decades, despite everything."

"So what are we doing today about our situation and Adrian's?" Layla asked, sipping more of her coffee as Dusk's fingers strayed, stroking her thigh where her silk robe gaped.

"Today," Dusk spoke decisively, though he was still playing his fingers over Layla's skin, "we are going to start by approaching the Madame. I trust Etienne to keep a secret, and this is one she'll have to – from the Intercessoria if they come calling. Which is no small task."

"What secret is she going to keep?" Layla asked, her eyebrows arching as she took another sip of coffee.

"That you won't be in the Hotel for a few days." Dusk eyeballed Layla with a sly smile.

"And where will I be?" Layla blinked, wondering what in blazes he was planning.

"In Manarola." Dusk's smile became a grin, purposeful and reckless.

"King Falliro Arini." Layla knew exactly what he was talking about the moment he said it. She set her coffee mug aside on the ebony table next to the bed as she watched him. "You're sending me to the Phoenix King. So he and I can have a little chat about Hunter and give the Intercessoria some intel they'd be willing to bargain for Adrian's release."

"Tit for tat," Dusk agreed. Pushing up from the bed, he moved to the dining table butt-ass nude and poured his own coffee, then returned. Layla couldn't help but ogle him. He was magnificent, with striking muscles and perfectly-proportioned shoulders and hips – not to mention a tantalizing groin even when it wasn't erect. Leaping back to the bed, he managed it with catlike grace, controlling his coffee mug so he didn't slosh a drop. Settling in against the pillows next to Layla, he drank with rogue abandon, setting his head back on the wood with a relieved expletive.

"Fuck, I love coffee! Anyhow, you've got that feather from King Arini, I figure we get you to Manarola discreetly, then gather as much information as we can on what Arini learned about Hunter while he was being stalked, then get you back to the Hotel and arrange a meeting with the Intercessoria. All done very discreetly of course, so we can get Adrian back before the Owner's Ball. Which is scheduled to happen the final day of their residence, in a week."

"What happens if we don't get Adrian back in time?" Layla asked, frowning.

"Bad things." Dusk scowled, taking a generous swig of his coffee. "I really don't want to think about what may happen to our Hotel if Adrian can't be present for the final night of the Board's visit. We're already in a precarious enough position with that fuckup of Bastien Durant's, plus *everyone's* heard about the murder of the Head Courtesan by now, and a number of the Owners have even been questioned by the Intercessoria. Sylvania was a treasure here, Layla – very few Hotels can say they have a Silver Passion on staff. And now we can't, either."

But Dusk's dark frown said far more. He and Sylvania had been close. Maybe not lovers exactly, but it was clear he'd had a tremendous respect for the late Head Courtesan, and Layla felt the same. It was a loss they were all going to have to process in the coming months. But now, there was too much at stake to take time to grieve. Dusk was in problem-solving mode, and Layla couldn't have agreed more.

"So we get me to Manarola via human routes where I'll be harder to track, before Heathren's calming of my Dragon wears off and anyone can feel me." Layla picked up the conversation.

"Planes, trains, and automobiles," Dusk agreed, a pensive look on his face now as he cradled his coffee mug in both hands. "Hunter has shown a weakness for tracking people in the human world. He didn't find you until Adrian and I did, and only then because Mimi Zakir's death was made public. Either he doesn't have access to human systems like scanning passports, credit cards, and such, or he doesn't give a shit. Some older Twilight Realm beings feel that such modern methods of keeping tabs on people are beneath them. Which is where we win."

"I take it you have methods of keeping tabs on me?" Layla lifted an eyebrow.

"You'll take your special smartphone with you; it's a magically-infused system that can track you as you travel, sending a vibrational signal back to the Orb of Cephalus, a security element here at the Hotel that I monitor." Dusk nodded, his gaze full of machinations. "And if you're ever in trouble, like you're being stalked, you just have to swipe the Hotel credit card I issued you at any location in debit mode and enter a special PIN, which will notify me at once of your situation."

Layla whistled, having had no idea that the security systems Dusk had access to were so extensive. "Holy shneikies, Batman."

"Batman ain't got nothing on us." Dusk's smile was pleased, though still intense. "Even if I'm not with you, I can track you every step of the journey, Layla. We can't get a new talisman to hide your magical imprint on such short notice, but the rest will do in a pinch."

"You're not coming with me?" She blinked, suddenly worried.

Reaching over Layla to set his coffee and hers on the bedside table, Dusk settled his body between her legs. Pulling her down by the hips so she was laying flat on the bed, he moved up in a lithe motion so he trapped her beneath him. Layla's Dragon roiled inside her veins to be so pleasurably corralled, though it was still much lazier than usual from the after-effects of Heathren's magic. Lowering down, Dusk kissed her deep, and Layla heated as they kissed, her hands stroking the serrated muscles of his sides. Pressing himself down upon her, he ground their bodies together until she squirmed with pleasure, lacing her arms around his neck and pulling him down to kiss her deeply.

By the time they finished, their scents were careening through the room, hot and wild. Pulling back, Dusk gave Layla a dark, amazing smile before his face got serious. Propped on his elbows with his hot body splayed out atop hers and only her silk robe between, he stroked back one of her sable curls.

"I can't come with you, even though I want to. We need you to keep a low profile as you travel, and I have to be here to prove to the Intercessoria and the Owners that we are operating on *business as usual.* No Hotel jets, no fancy cars, just you and a suitcase and your Hotel credit card and smartphone so I can track your whereabouts."

"What if Hunter or the Intercessoria can track my Hotel credit card or phone also?"

"It's a risk we'll have to take," Dusk breathed, kissing her lips again. "They're the only methods I have to track you on such short notice. If we had known this was coming, I could have gotten Rikyava to help me imbue a Blood Dragon-crafted item with my magical imprint, so I could follow you as you travel. But those things take weeks we don't have. I'll be with you every step of the way, though, I promise. Every time you make a purchase, be it a coffee at the airport or a room at a hotel, I'll know where you are. And if you use that unique PIN, I can focus a special transportation item we have here at the Hotel for emergency use, to get you out pronto."

"How pronto?" Layla lifted an eyebrow.

"Within seconds." Dusk's gaze held no lie. "Run to a gas station, a grocery store, an ATM, wherever. Swipe, enter that PIN, and I've got you. OK?"

Layla took a deep breath, then let it out. A deep worry moved through her at this plan, even though she'd never feared traveling alone before. She'd traveled alone dozens of times, in as many countries. Layla was a pro at navigating planes, taxis, trains, and hotels in the human world. So why was she feeling so squirrelly all of a sudden?

"I just hate to think that you and Adrian won't be with me." She spoke, knowing her words for truth. "I've become so used to you both being there for me, at different times these past months, that it feels strange taking a trip like this on my own during a time of crisis."

"I know." Dusk's words were gentle as he hovered over her, his face concerned. "But you're a pro, Layla Price – you've been training for this all your life. You speak Italian and French fluently, you've traveled on your own dozens of times, and through some pretty gnarly places. And you were raised human, so you navigate the human world with ease. Hunter has proven to us that he doesn't want you dead – only on his side. He's not going to harm you. And I have the feeling that even if the Intercessoria find out you've gone AWOL from the Hotel, they'll track you to understand what you're up to, but that's all. You'll be safe; I promise. If anything happens, anything at all, I swear I will move all of heaven and earth to get you back."

Drawing a deep breath, Layla knew her moment of judgement had come. Either she stood up for the people she loved, taking a risk in their high-stakes game and putting her own life on the line, or she played it safe and watched everything she loved get torn down around her. She was willing to risk her own life for something she believed in.

But she wasn't willing to risk the lives of people she loved.

"I'm in." Layla spoke, certainty in her voice as she stared up into Dusk's handsome face, her arms still clasped around his neck. "Where do we start?"

"We start by fucking you rotten while your Dragon is still lazy from the Ephilohim's charm," he breathed with a grin, though his sapphire eyes were serious. "And then we go to the Madame and tell her what we're up to, and make all the arrangements for you to leave this afternoon."

"Sounds like a plan." Layla agreed.

Staring up at Dusk, watching his beautiful face, Layla suddenly realized there wasn't anything she wouldn't risk for him, or for Adrian. They were a part of her now – a part of her she couldn't deny anymore. They had been woven into her spirit so fundamentally that there was no turning back. She would put her life on the line for both of them.

Anytime, anywhere.

Lowering down, Dusk kissed her, gently at first, then with heat.

There was time for passion and they took it, kissing hot but slow, embracing and caressing each other in the bright winter morning. Dusk slid Layla's silk robe open as they kissed, settling to his elbows atop her. Curling her into his arms as she slid her legs up around his hips, Layla stroked his sides with her fingertips as they sweetly devoured each other's lips. They both cried out together as he entered her, their foreheads resting together. Layla found herself breathing in rhythm with him as he tightened his core, pressing inside her deep. He didn't thrust or pull out, just stayed inside her, moving his body in fluid waves to gather her into him, deep and hard and slow.

They moved together, breathing together, making it last. Time stretched; the day seemed to expand around Layla in a halo of light as she watched Dusk while they made love for the second time in as many days. Because that's what it was – lovemaking. She'd not had this chance with Adrian yet, but with Dusk it was incredible; sweet and deep, solidifying something between them that had long been aching.

Layla felt her heart expand as he thrust deeper, slower, more firmly, watching her with amazement. Waves of light passed through his Dragon-scales, brightening him in blissful pleasure as he curled his strong arms around her and held her close to his warm, hard body. Layla felt that light passing through her also, even though Dusk wasn't plying her with his magics today – only the beautiful experience of making love to him, luminous in the winter day.

They rose to their climax at the same time; a deep, sudden quickening that took Layla's breath as she cried out in his arms. Dusk called out with a deep shudder, waves of light and vibration passing through him. Layla came again on that tremendous power, her hands gripping his back and her legs clenching him close as she cried out into his shoulder. Dusk made a purring sound like a cat as he cradled her, thrumming wave after wave of pleasure through her as she gasped, crying out against him and coming a third time. He stroked her nape, holding her tight, letting her crumble in his arms even as he gasped with glory. And with one last thrust and spasm, they collapsed to the bed like cut marionettes – Dusk propped on his elbows, kissing Layla gently, over and over.

Layla didn't ever want the moment to end. She held him close, still gripping him with her ankles around his butt and her hands on his sides in a way that was almost possessive, even though the rest of her had gone lax. Dusk tried to move, to slide out of her and Layla made a petulant mewl – straight from her Dragon.

He chuckled by her ear, kissing her neck. "I'm going to get a cramp if I stay locked inside you like this, Layla."

"Too bad." Layla spoke, her voice growly and breathy all at once. "You're not going anywhere, pal."

He chuckled again, brushing her curls back from her neck with his fingertips. "No, you're the one going somewhere today. We both should get dressed."

"Just a moment longer." Layla was enjoying the sensation of him still inside her. It was a moment she didn't often get to enjoy, and she was determined to make it last.

"Why, Layla Price." He chuckled by her cheek, lifting his head so he could see her. His entire being was smiling, cheeky and wonderful, and as Layla watched, a ripple of light passed through his eyes and sex-messed hair. "I do believe you're hot for me."

"Yup." Layla grinned, lifting up to kiss him again.

Dusk chuckled. But before Layla could lock him in more, he pushed up and off her with a bright laugh. With a cheeky glance back, he walked to the table nude, giving her a great view of his perfectly-sculpted back and ass, and the amazing lines of Dragon-scale and gold accenting that musculature. Dusk flaunted it for everything he was worth, taking up a piece of bacon and munching, turning half-back toward Layla so she could watch his lean, built muscles in the high winter light.

"You bastard." Layla pushed up from the bed as she grinned, cinching her silk robe closed.

"What?" He grinned back, lifting one dark eyebrow as he ate.

"You know what." Layla laughed, taking her coffee with her as she went to the table to get some breakfast at last. She couldn't resist stroking her hand over Dusk's perfect abdomen as she went, tracing the lines of serrated Dragon-scale that curled in over his hips. "We could be in the middle of armageddon and you'd still act like a cheeky dick, flaunting your sexiness."

"Hey, there's no better way to approach armageddon, really." Dusk finally fetched his midnight-blue silk sleep pants from a chair, pulling them on. Layla was sad to see his beautiful nakedness disappear, though there was still plenty left to admire. Pulling out a chair, he started filling a plate with his usual brusqueness. And just like that, he transitioned from languid lover to moving fifty miles a minute. Filling a plate for Layla with swift precision, he refilled her coffee and added a generous amount of cream, then refilled his own.

Clinking coffee mugs, he spoke, his gaze level as it had ever been in Concierge Services. "Here's to your first foray into the dangers of Dragon life, Layla Price. *May the odds be ever in your favor.*"

His reference to the Hunger Games made Layla laugh, even though it was serious. As she sipped her coffee and began to eat finally after forty-eight hours of hell and pleasure, she realized her life was going to be something like that from now on. The old her was gone, replaced by someone new. And though she was still technically the same person, she was now venturing into the unknown, even more than when she'd first arrived at the Red Letter Hotel Paris.

Yet something inside Layla smiled, vicious and ready. She would be known in this world; her Dragon would be known. And not for being a weakling, or an idiot, or arm candy that anyone could just throw around.

She wouldn't be a ceramic dinner plate.

She'd be a priceless Ming vase – one with bite.

CHAPTER 12 – PARTNERS

Layla returned to her room on the third floor to pack. Though her fancy clothes had been moved to Reginald's apartment when she'd moved in with him, most of her casual clothes were still back at her own place. It was strange returning to her rooms. Everything had a familiar yet stale feel as she moved through her space, gathering up jeans and sweaters and boots and stuffing them into a small black rolling bag that she could carry on a plane.

She and Dusk had met with the Madame and Rikyava, and though Etienne Voulouer had fretted immensely at Layla going off to Manarola alone, and Rikyava had hated the idea, all had finally agreed it was their best shot at getting Adrian returned without arousing suspicion. The plan was for Layla to go for five days, long enough to dig into conversation with the Phoenix King Falliro Arini, but not long enough that she would miss the Owner's Ball at the end of the week. Layla would travel by human means, starting with a taxi outside the Hotel's gates in the human world, then flying standby on a commercial jet to Rome from the Paris Charles de Gaulle Airport. Everything was to be scheduled on-the-go, to not give either the Intercessoria or Hunter any lead time as to where Layla was headed.

And hope that she'd make it there untraced.

Sliding her special smartphone from Dusk into her red leather purse, Layla was dressed in skinny jeans and tall fawn boots, plus a high-collared grey wrap sweater cinched at her waist. With a royal blue peacoat for nice winter days and a cream knit hat with matching gloves, she looked like any traveler going for a winter vacation through Europe. It felt strange to leave Mimi's jewelry behind, Layla wearing only a plain set of gold hoop earrings. Everything precious she kept on her, like her Hotel-issued black credit card, her US passport, and King Falliro Arini's cobalt feather – all tucked into a hidden silk pouch snapped to her bra beneath her shirt.

Closing her apartment doors, Layla walked down the hall, rolling her bag behind her. It was the first time she'd been dressed this casually in the Paris Hotel, and it felt strange as she passed other employees up on the third floor. But everyone just gave her knowing smiles – it was common for employees to take vacations in the human world. Layla looked like that was her intention now, like she was just using her vacation time to go off for a jaunt.

Rolling her bag to an ornate elevator used by Guard transporting luggage and by the Catering staff, Layla entered the crimson and gold décor of the lift and shut the ornate wrought-iron grate. Hitting the button for the fourth floor, she went up first to do one last errand. Stepping out, she had to pass Dusk and Adrian's doors to get to her destination, and noticed that Adrian's rooms were finally shut, no golden perimeter around the guardian Dragons anymore. It felt strange moving past, knowing Dusk was downstairs at the Concierge desk playing like everything was normal and Adrian was in prison somewhere. Stepping past, Layla moved to Reginald's doors at the far end of the hall and knocked.

"Enter."

A sensation of chill fog surrounded Layla as she pushed into Reginald's apartment. Stepping into his opulent living area of sky-blue drapes and nautical detail, a fire roared in a hearth of white stone. Done in 1700's Parisian style, every gilded table and niche was painted with ships; ships beneath storms, ships under blue skies, ships being devoured by leviathans. Coiling sea creatures rose from every baroque picture-frame; mermaids and giant octopi decorated the rugs – even a stunning rendition of H.P. Lovecraft's Cthulhu hung over the gargantuan fireplace.

Stepping in, Layla saw Reginald sat at his eight-seat formal dining table, staring out the windows even though it was late afternoon. Sitting before empty gilded china plates and untouched trays of lunch foods, he wore his quilted pearl-grey silk dressing robe and matching sleep trousers, his hair pulled half-back and showing his cutting jaw though a few golden strands escaped around his face.

He ate nothing; touched nothing on the table. As Layla entered, he looked around and pain flashed through his red-rimmed eyes, before he looked back out the windows. Layla hesitated at the door, her hand on the gilded door-handle. She almost backed out, but something about the stiff set of Reginald's shoulders drew her in, shutting the door quietly behind her. Something about the way he stared at the clouds moving over the darkening afternoon made Layla's heart hurt. Moving forward, a sense of rightness filled her that she had come. Leaving her bag by the door, mercy swept her forward until her hands slipped over Reginald's shoulders – smoothing down his soft silk lapels and slipping over his bare chest.

"You are a mess, Courtesan, and you smell like sex." He spoke coldly. A sensation of chill water sluiced around him, though Layla recognized it for what it was – pain.

"I've come to say goodbye. For now, at least." Layla spoke by his ear, her hands still touching his lean-muscled chest. He was warm beneath her hands; warm yet chill, as if he was drowning his body heat in icy water.

"I've heard the plan from the Madame." He grated in a voice that sounded like he'd been crying. "Just go. Go save your beloved."

"Reginald." Layla pressed her cheek against his, her nose brushing all that incredibly soft, silken hair. Something about his posture, his distant elegance drew her like a mariner to the sea today. They'd spent nearly a month together, sleeping in separate beds, separate rooms. Picking at each other and fighting as he'd sluiced her with never-ending disdain. But something about the past forty-eight hours had shown Layla Reginald's humanity. There was a person beneath all that arcane silk and cold distance.

A person who had been hurting – for centuries.

Emotions moved deep inside Layla, a feeling like her Dragon was twisting up inside her, keening. She didn't hate Reginald. He was awful but he was also beautiful, and his quick generosity had saved her in the past days. She found herself stroking her hands over his smooth chest, her energy flaring. As if her Dragon could feel his pain – and wanted to soothe it.

"You should go," he rasped again, his impeccable icebergs still not breaking to her touch. "There are direct flights from Paris to Genoa in the evenings. You don't want to miss them."

"I'll go when I'm good and ready." Layla spoke, still touching him.

Something about her defiance affected Reginald, and he stiffened beneath her touch. Turning towards her, the planes of his face were haughty; expressionless.

Only his blisteringly cold eyes told her his fury.

"Don't pretend to know me, Courtesan. Don't pretend to know what it is that can soothe me today." Chill rage spiked deep into Layla's fingertips as he spoke. Her compassion was wiped away as he turned, a cold-as-ice Royal Siren sitting in the chair now rather than a man in pain. With a slow, dominant rise, he pushed up, facing her. His body was full of grace and power, and just watching that dangerous movement made alarms ring inside Layla's mind. She shrunk back, her hands slipping from his skin. But Reginald's slow, elegant rise merely took him to standing before her, his ice-blue eyes narrowing, his lips twisting in a haughty sneer.

"Run to your bound men, Layla," he spoke, cold as midnight at the north pole. "Run to their arms, to their beds. Run to the ones who love you and hold them close, for you may never get another chance. And if you don't, you'll understand how I feel. You'll understand a Siren who gives you no quarter – because none was ever given to him. You'll finally understand the curse of magic, and how it destroys us; heart, soul, and humanity. Go. Try to save what you love. But if you can't, don't come begging back to me to help you pretend the world is still beautiful. Because it's not."

Layla's mouth opened, wanting to protest. But Reginald saw the defiance in her eyes and stalked closer, staring her down, fury pummeling from him in chill waves that surrounded Layla like Arctic currents – ready to rip her apart if she spoke even a single word.

She didn't. Layla shut her mouth as the furious Royal Siren advanced. She didn't know what Reginald would do right now in his grief, and it terrified her. Her heart was pounding, her lungs couldn't get a breath as she stared at him, her Dragon writhing deep within her with fangs bared now as if it agreed that he was dangerous.

"Go." He hissed, nodding at the door. "Now."

She did. Stepping back, Layla moved quickly to the door, her Dragon on high alert and hissing deep inside her veins, even though it was still mild compared to her usual. Reginald didn't follow, but Layla tightened her shoulders all the same, hating to turn her back on him. If he'd been surging with wrath, if he'd pummeled her with oceanic power, she could have understood. But he was out of control right now in a way Layla had never seen him. And this cold, hateful creature was something dangerous, something Layla instinctually knew she shouldn't provoke.

Quickly, she stepped to the doors, taking up the handle of her rolling bag. She was about to exit and leave the scathing Reginald Durant behind, when she paused. A chill fury sluiced through the room, as if it pushed her to go. Shivering, she felt Reginald's dark tides making her Dragon want to curl up and die from that terrible power. As if it swept through her with fear and darkness, she suddenly felt Reginald's influence upon her emotions. He was encouraging her to go; he was causing her to retreat from him.

He was creating a tide of fear so Layla would run – and leave him, drowning and alone.

But feeling his dark tides, Layla suddenly understood. He was forcing her out because having someone be kind to him right now was too much. It was too frightening to have someone stand here and accept his pain. And though everything inside Layla told her to leave Reginald alone with his woe and darkness, she knew she couldn't.

Removing her hand from the door, Layla turned. Reginald fixed his gaze upon her and she felt his wrath like a spear of ice in her heart, giving her a horrible shiver though she stood her ground. Layla remembered that Reginald had started a war between two powerful Dragon-clans because he'd drowned a city with his magics. And seeing him standing there so cold and austere, Layla had that vision flash through her mind again. The same vision of that beautiful raven-haired woman with lavender eyes standing on a far-north beach. Laughing, as a far younger and innocent version of Reginald swept her into his arms.

But he wasn't innocent anymore. Pain bled through Reginald's haughty gaze as he re-lived the vision while Layla saw it. His breath caught and the vision was sluiced away in a white wave. But not before Layla had seen, and understood. Maybe not the entire story, but the

141

thing he hid – the reason he'd killed an entire Blood Dragon village.

The pain of love lost that lurked beneath Reginald's chill, dark oceans.

"Those are not your memories, Layla Price." Reginald spoke coldly, though she could see he was shaken.

"No, but they're yours." Stepping away from the door, Layla approached him again like one approaches a wild animal – with caution but with uncompromising love. "They're the deepest part of what you hide every day, because it hurts too much to tell anyone where you've been. It hurts too much to tell anyone how much you've loved… and how much you lost."

"What do you know of love and loss?" He spoke with cold wrath, though Layla could see a tremor starting in his body, as if he couldn't contain all the emotions now pouring through him.

"I don't know about your love and loss." Layla stated, feeling his misery like a deep ocean around her now, crying with lonely gulls. "But I want to. I want to know who you are, Reginald. The real you, beneath the façade. We're Partners. Shouldn't your true Partner know your pain? Isn't that what made Sylvania different from the rest of your lovers? Because she knew what you hide – and loved you anyway? Isn't that why you loved her, too?"

Reginald went very still. Gazing at her, she saw him war deep inside; disdain slipping over his haughty face, then agony. As he took a deep breath, Layla felt his chill tides ease until she wasn't being pummeled anymore. And as that massive tide finally rolled back, she felt Reginald's true pain, deep beneath the rage.

Sadness drowned him to his core. Sadness filled him like a lonely ocean, an endless isolation like a man stranded on an iceberg in the frozen north. This was no pretty Gilligan's Isle. This was endless suffering, and as Layla felt it, her hand flashed to her heart, clutching her jacket as it choked her. Deep inside, her Dragon roiled, keening with a strangled sound as it thrashed through all that sadness; as it tried to heat it into anything but agony and failed.

Reginald watched her, his lips parted as he felt her Dragon react to his pain. For a long moment he did nothing, then at last stepped forward, moving to Layla and taking up her hand. They didn't speak as he gave a heavy sigh, then escorted her to the dining table, leaving her as he stepped to a copper side-bar near his towering apartment windows.

Layla watched him as his rage finally came unwound. He idled at the side-bar, letting her see him in all of his wretchedness as he turned and poured two crystal tumblers of brandy from a decanter. His face was clean of powder and rouge, and as Layla watched him pour, he reached up and picked the elastic band out of his golden hair, letting it tumble free.

And suddenly, his devouring sadness heightened all that amazing perfection – making Reginald Durant beautiful as a high-north dawn.

Silken strands of hair like sunlight dazzled Layla as Reginald poured the brandy with a deft elegance. She had seen him in his natural beauty before, but now with his true emotions bared, he was absolutely stunning. Barefoot in his pearl-grey silk trousers, his matching quilted dressing-robe hung open, his chest bare. His dancer's body was gloriously lean with sinewed muscle; his skin a creamy white with only a touch of golden hair at his chest, leading down to his navel between sculpted hips. His abdomen was a sleek, muscled dream, that perfect V-shape men would kill for, lower things hinting in his silk trousers. As Layla stared at his impossible beauty, Reginald gave her a deep look – making her blush.

"Sorry." She mumbled, feeling like she should face the door.

"I'm not." He held her gaze, something fierce and calm in it now.

"It's nice to show someone who I really am. Beneath the powder and rouge, and rage."

Layla swallowed. Heat stirred deep inside her, not her roar of fire around Adrian or Dusk, but a strange clear space where she could both feel her attraction to Reginald and also observe it. As if she had stepped outside her body but was inside it at the same time, she felt like she stood upon a sea-cliff observing the waves, yet also feeling herself moving within those waves. Picking up the tumblers of brandy, Reginald approached, stepping close to Layla and offering one.

"Thanks." She nodded, taking it. Their fingers connected on the glass and Layla paused, not because she was swamped by the vengeful sea or her own inner fire, but because she felt the simplicity of his touch. Their fingers hesitating, and Reginald watched her – his fingers slowly moving over hers; caressing hers. Layla swallowed, feeling her strange attraction rise. She pulled her glass away and he let her go, his gaze deep upon her now like the ocean.

Layla took a sip of brandy, feeling its sweet burn slide down her throat. She was grateful for it bolstering her shakiness, pushing back the events of the past days and Reginald's strange, intense mood. For a moment, she closed her eyes, reveling in the orange peel flavor of the alcohol.

It was a basic thing, a scent without magic – a taste without passion.

Opening her eyes, she found Reginald watching her. He was quiet now, and he didn't swirl or sip his brandy, just stood there watching her. Something about it reminded her of Luke in his calmer moments, and Layla realized Reginald was a lot like Luke. Clean, tidy, impeccable. Observant, determined, responsive. Dominant, and critical. But Reginald had had a few hundred years of life to influence his destructive side – a few hundred years more heartbreak. The image of a

Scandinavian harbor surfaced again in Layla's mind and a wash of white surf from Reginald rolled it away, the scent of sea-brine easing off his skin.

"You stay with me despite all my fury and punishment, Dragon Bind," he spoke softly, watching her. "Wanting to know the real me despite all the cruel ways I've demeaned you, harangued you, and tortured you these past weeks. You want to know me in a way no one but Sylvania ever asked to do, her Ephemeral nature unable to spurn a tortured heart. Why?"

Layla swallowed, but her answer was on her lips, warmth easing from her as she spoke. "Because I don't believe the costume you show the rest of the world, Reginald. The man I felt that first day you helped me control my magic during my entrance interview held me safe in the harbor of his hands. You did the same when your brother Bastien set my magic free the other night, holding me with a strength and tenderness I've felt from no one else in my life except maybe Dusk. The persona you show the world is cruel, but only because of heartbreak. But the real you, the man I see in your memories with that woman on the beach, and the one I feel when you hold me – he is something else. Someone amazing."

"And do you presume to know me, Layla Price?" He asked again, with his calm distance.

"If you'll let me." Layla spoke, feeling his misery.

"And do you want to know me?"

"Yes." Layla knew it was the truth as soon as she said it. "I want to know who the strongest Royal of the North Sea Sirens is. I want to know who the man is that I call Partner. I want to know *you*, Reginald, the real you. *Sivvir*."

That last word startled him. Layla didn't know where it had come from, it had just been there upon her lips. But as she spoke it, she knew

145

it was right. Somehow, that was Reginald's real name, the name he hid from the world and the persona he hid with it.

Layla saw him shudder. As if all the fight went out of him, as if the fury of the north suddenly died, Reginald's black tides washed away. Something vulnerable moved through his eyes, changing them from ice-blue to a stormy pearl-grey. But Layla felt sunlight upon those deep tides now. As if her words had thawed his heart, flecks of golden sunlight danced within his grey gaze. With the most broken smile Layla had ever seen, Reginald raised his brandy glass to her in a salute.

And then downed it entire, in the most uncouth motion she'd ever seen from him.

CHAPTER 13 – CONTROL

Reginald's gaze was faraway as he stared at Layla, something complex moving through his pearl-grey eyes. Reaching out, he stroked her curls, up in a twist at the side of her neck for traveling. Something beautiful blew through him like the first winds of spring as he played his fingertips gently down Layla's neck above the collar of her peacoat.

"*Sivvir.*" He sighed at last. "No one has called me by that name in a very long time."

"What does it mean?" Layla asked.

"It means *beloved*, in Brut Hathne."

"The language of the Blood Dragons." Layla blinked, understanding. "It's what she used to call you, isn't it? The woman in your memories."

"Yes." Taking a deep inhalation, Reginald set his brandy glass on the table. He paused, tapping his long fingers on a chair before turning and moving to his walk-in closet. Disappearing from view, he soon returned, holding a small box of sky-blue velvet like a jewelry case, tied with a cream silk bow.

Moving to Layla, he held it out. "This is for you."

"What? What is it?" Layla set her brandy aside on the table. Having no idea what was happening now, her brows furrowed as she took the velvet case. Undoing the bow, she opened the top to see a stunning choker of saltwater pearls and diamonds nestled on a pad of blue velvet with a matching bracelet, plus diamond and pearl earrings. A note on the Hotel's exquisite stationary was tucked in beside the jewelry and Layla lifted it out.

I'm sorry. Please forgive me. – R

"Reginald…"

Layla stared at the elegant angle of Reginald's calligraphy on his apology note. Lifting out the note, she ran her thumb over it, then reached into the case and lifted out the pearl choker. The saltwater pearls were dove-grey like a misty ocean, in six long strands that spanned an inch tall, studded at intervals with diamonds. It was set with platinum-filigree clasps, each clasp encrusted with diamonds also. Reginald's gift was tremendously elegant, beautiful like a bridal necklace; and something about it made Layla swallow hard. She glanced up but before she could say anything, Reginald lifted the choker from her fingers and stepped behind her, clasping it around her throat.

It was sensually tight upon her neck, and Layla felt herself flush with heat. It felt like Reginald's hand had clasped around her throat with the pearls – as if he was choking her lightly, deliciously. As he set it in place, Layla heard the call of gulls in her mind and felt a slow movement of ocean surf in her veins. Leaning down, Reginald placed a soft kiss upon the side of her neck just above the choker's band, then took out the earrings, affixing them in her ears as he slid out her gold hoops. Last was the bracelet, bound around her wrist.

"I've imbued these items with my magic," he breathed as he finished affixing the bracelet. "To keep your gifts from exploding at random moments while you're in public. It's not as effective as your talisman once was, but it should keep your powers from being felt in the human world once Heathren's charm wears off. The pearls and diamonds also carry a Siren-glamour. To humans, they will appear as inexpensive bangles. But Twilight folk will see them for what they are, and to them you will appear to have accepted the *Louenou Virdii.*"

"The *Louenou Virdii?*" Layla breathed, touching the choker as she glanced up at him.

"It is an ancient tradition among my people," Reginald smiled sadly as his fingers lifted to the choker also, touching the pearls as his fingertips caressed softly over Layla's. "It is the gift of a Royal Siren to his First Concubine – to his chosen mate. The implication of the gift will keep most Twilight Lineages from bothering you, and the color signifies the North Sea Sirens, my clan. A powerful clan not to be crossed. I do not imply that you must be my mate, Layla. But this farce will keep you safe in the Twilight Realm, as far as anything can. The pearls also carry my signature, and I can trace their energy from afar and feel your whereabouts. Please wear them while you travel – for me."

"Of course," Layla breathed, the choker deliciously tight at her throat; the thoughtfulness of Reginald's gift tightening her throat more. "But what is the note for? The apology?"

"Because I was wrong." Reginald's sea-grey eyes pierced hers, deep and honest. "I was wrong to take you immediately into my care to train as a Courtesan at Samhain. I was wrong to deny you access to your bound lovers this past month. I thought it would build your magic and make you stronger. And while it has done that, I now realize my overzealousness was cruel. You need your bound lovers; you need their love. To be with them as a trio brings you steadiness. I can help control your magic with an iron fist… but I can never give you what they provide. And it is wrong of me to deny you the love that I lack, in my deep and bitter jealousy. Forgive me."

Layla's heart clenched. Her eyes stung, feeling his honesty. Feeling his apology. And that he'd gotten this gift for her sometime prior to their conversation today proved that he was the person she felt beneath all his severity and disdain. "Reginald, I—"

Lifting his fingers to her lips, he stopped her words. And then leaned down, placing a kiss upon Layla's lips.

It was the most sensual kiss she'd ever felt. As if his lips held the full softness of an oceanic breeze and the cry of seagulls, Reginald's kiss was the smooth allure of the oyster and the rocking of deep tidal waves. It held oceans of pain and pleasure, and depth, and Layla found herself kissing him back, tasting what sunlight felt like in the blue deeps. Opening his mouth, his tongue found hers, and its smoothness made Layla catch her breath. Or perhaps Reginald stole her breath as he pulled gently away, gazing down at her with a deep passion in his eyes – and pain.

"I don't believe in gods or monsters, paradise or hell," he murmured softly. "I believe life is what we make of it; that all we can do is become better – more impeccable – day by day. I had forgotten that, until you called me *Sivvir* just now. I had forgotten that I made a choice to become who I am, to develop the control over my magics that I have now. I am not the strongest Royal of my clan, but it is a truth I must someday face that I am not far from it. Like you, this Hotel is my sanctuary. But here you are, brave enough to risk disaster by venturing forth from these halls for the ones you love… while I rot here, too afraid to even show people who I really am underneath the wig and powder and rouge."

Gazing up at Reginald, Layla was taken by his honesty and his passion. Reaching out, she stroked back his golden hair, feeling it soft as the finest silk beneath her fingers. "I believe you'll find that courage. When the time is right. Maybe sooner than you know."

"Maybe." Reaching up, he clasped her hand, moving it to his lips. Kissing her knuckles, he gave a sad smile, all his storms spent now. Stepping to her side, he wound Layla's hand around his quilted sleeve to escort her. "We should hurry. I believe a taxi is already waiting for you."

"Are you escorting me downstairs?" She blinked at him. "In your dressing-gown?"

"Why not?" Reginald spoke with a glint in his pearl-grey gaze. "If the Hotel Owners don't like it, they can fire me. Are you ready, Layla Price?"

"Ready, steady, go." Layla spoke, wondering if he was really going to go down into the Hotel dressed in just his bedroom attire.

But Reginald only gave a slight smile, leading her out of his rooms and taking up the handle of Layla's bag in his free hand as he passed. They stepped into the hall and he shut his doors, then led Layla to the stairs. Rather than take the elevator, he hefted her suitcase to his shoulder like it weighed nothing, then continued escorting Layla down.

As they arrived at the main level, people stared with incredulity at the Head Courtier's attire, guests and employees alike gaping, astounded. Reginald breezed through it all like he was the best-dressed royalty among plebes with Layla on his arm. As they arrived at the main Concierge desk, Layla saw Dusk's gaze fix on them, his eyes going two degrees wide and wider when he realized it was Reginald standing before him without wig and powder and dressed in silken sleepwear. Expertly dismissing a group he was talking to into the hands of Jenna and Lars, Dusk rounded the Concierge desk, stepping quickly to Reginald's side.

"Aldo!" He spoke low, his sapphire eyes enormous as he took in Reginald's sexy barely-dressed attire. "Have you gone mad?! What if the Madame sees you? Or the Owners?"

"Let them see." Reginald spoke regally, turning and escorting Layla toward the place one could catch a taxi at the south side of the palace quadrangle, Layla's bag still hefted effortlessly at his shoulder. "I am Head Courtier here. It's time I began dressing as I please, rather than pleasing Hotel tradition. Most of the Hotels ceased dressing their Head Courtesans and Courtiers in Imperial garb a hundred years ago. With Sylvania gone now, it's time we began doing the same."

Layla blinked, realizing for the first time that Sylvania's sheer outfits had been a kind of standard costume as much as Reginald's 1700's couture. In his grief, Reginald was no longer standing on any ceremony he didn't care for, and Layla suddenly wondered how he might dress if allowed to do as he pleased.

But walking down the hall with Dusk beside them now, Reginald was imperious in his silk sleepwear, and somehow more comfortable than Layla had ever seen him. Whispers abounded; stares followed the Head Courtier. As Layla watched guests and employees all stop and gape, she realized the Siren held an overwhelming power over those around him. Even without using his magics, even with Layla's luggage on his shoulder, there was something magnetic about Reginald. And now, moving down the hall with a bearing more regal than any king, his golden hair swept over one shoulder, his incredible dancer's body bared by the quilted robe and his arrogantly beautiful features shining through, Layla saw the truth.

Reginald Durant was quite possibly the most royal person in their entire Hotel.

Walking through it all, Reginald exited a side door, then moved to the wrought-iron gates where one could pass to the human world. Before they went through, he halted, setting down Layla's bag on the snowy walkway and gazing down at her. Reaching up, he stroked her cheek, then leaned down and gave her a gentle kiss, right in front of Dusk.

Layla heated, but it was chaste and Reginald soon pulled away.

"Be careful." Stroking the pearl choker at her neck, his eyes met hers, sea-grey and stern. "Don't take these items off, even to sleep.

Make sure that they, and you, return home safely."

With that he turned, nodding regally at Dusk and moving off, back toward the Hotel. Dusk watched him go, then turned to Layla with a wry grimace. "Well, I'm afraid Reginald's little show ruined any chance we had of getting you off clandestinely. It's probably for the best. He's demonstrated fair and square that you're under his protection, if Hunter has any spies in the Hotel."

"You mean the pearls?" Layla asked, touching the choker.

Dusk's dark brows knit in an intense look. Reaching out, he stroked the choker with his fingertips. "Do you know what gems you're wearing, Layla?"

"Reginald said they signify the concubine of a North Sea Siren."

"These pearls are more than that." Dusk's gaze was complex, deep with emotion. "These are Avri's pearls. The set Reginald had made for the Blood Dragon woman he chose to be his wife when he was young. He hunted these pearls himself, for over a year to find the most perfect ones in all the ocean. He sold himself into slavery for another year to a horrible Crystal Dragon, to obtain the diamonds and platinum. It's Siren tradition to toil for your first beloved's bridal set. Avri wouldn't take them off when she was around her clan. It's part of what got her killed, her devotion to him; to wearing his token in public. It's what started his clan's war."

Layla's eyes went wide. She reached up, touching the choker again. "Why does he want me to have them?"

"Because you mean that much to him." Dusk's gaze was sad now, wry. "I'm afraid you've imprinted upon yet another Royal Dragon, Layla. He's not bound to you... but he cares for you. I suspected before that he was fond of you. This gift proves it, beyond all doubt."

Layla's throat suddenly felt tight. She could feel Reginald's magic in the pearls, sighing through her body like sad northern winds. She could feel *him* suddenly, walking back up the stairs inside the Hotel to the fourth floor. She felt him pause on the stairs; felt him give a soft smile. And then the sensation was sluiced away with a slow wash of tides and she felt nothing more.

"Keep these on at all times, Layla," Dusk spoke, and Layla glanced up as he took her hands, pulling her close so he could wrap his arms around her. "Reginald's gift is precious not just because they're an additional measure to keep you safe, but because they're precious to him. It would be devastating for him to lose them, even though he's technically gifted them to you."

"I'll never take them off." Layla murmured. "I swear it."

"Good." Lifting his lips, Dusk kissed her forehead, then set their foreheads together. They shared a moment, breathing in the darkening winter day. Long shadows fell across the snow now, painting the world in cool blues and stark whites at the curb.

Dusk drew a deep breath, letting it out in a puff of steam. "This is so hard."

"That's what she said." Layla grinned, and Dusk laughed in his lovely rolling baritone. Giving a rumble that thrilled Layla from head to heels, he reached up, caressing a stray curl back from her face.

"You've got King Arini's feather?"

"Yes."

"And your passport?"

"Check."

"And your Hotel credit card?"

"Yup."

"And you remember the emergency PIN?"

"I've got it." Reaching up to cradle his face in her hands, Layla smiled. "I've got this, Dusk. Everyone's been trying to protect me ever since I opened to my magics. Well, now it's time for me to protect them. The Hotel needs me to do this. For you, for Reginald, for Rake and all the others who depend on this place for safety. I'm doing this to free Adrian, but really, I'm doing this for all of us. Trust that I can. Trust me to be strong."

"I do." Dusk breathed, generous and heartfelt. "I know you're strong, Layla. I just don't want to let you go into potential danger alone. It goes against every instinct I have. Even though we're doing it to keep your journey as quiet as possible without alerting anyone of importance, I keep doubting the decision. I want to be there, protecting you in Manarola, even though Arini's Aviary is an impenetrable fortress. Adrian would tell you the same, if he were here."

"I know." Lifting up, Layla pressed a kiss to his lips, letting it linger. "But I have to go. I'm the red-shirt here, I'm the crew member of the Starship Enterprise that no one's going to notice is gone. Not until I'm already back."

"You are *so* not a red-shirt." Dusk laughed softly.

"No." Layla breathed, smiling slightly. "But I still need to go."

"I know." Dusk smiled, then sighed. Kissing her forehead, he inhaled her scent before he finally drew back. "Ready to get this show on the road?"

"Absolutely." Layla smiled back.

"I can't go through to the taxi stand at the Palace of Versailles in the human world with you. I don't look even remotely human without a glamour, and I didn't have time to get one today. So you'll have to go through alone." Though he spoke briskly now with his Head Concierge attitude, Dusk's smile was wry. And for the first time, Layla saw him regret what he was. He'd come to Seattle as himself back in August, but that had been on a residential street at night. Though it was nearly evening in Versailles, there was still light in the winter sky, and tourists would be lingering around the Palace for photographs.

He couldn't come with her, not even to escort her into the taxi.

Lifting to her toes, Layla set her lips to Dusk's one last time – pressing him with the deepest kiss she could give. She felt him startle; and then he wrapped her in his arms, crushing her close. Her arms wound around his neck as they kissed, incredible currents flowing between them. By the time they broke apart, both were breathless.

Dusk chuckled, then pushed Layla gently away. Gripping the handle of her rolling bag, Layla took him in one last time. Fit and delicious in one of his impeccable dove-grey suits, he wore a canary silk tie with midnight polka dots, reversed for his silk pocket square. Layla laughed, shaking her head with a smile.

"What?" He grinned back.

"You." She spoke, her smile softening. "I love everything you are, Dusk Arlohaim. Everything."

"You better make it back to get some more of this." He lifted an eyebrow, a ripple of light passing through his artfully-sculpted hair. "As I recall, we still have an unsettled breakfast date together. And more sex to indulge in."

"You better believe I'm making it back for that." Layla blew him a kiss, and he caught it theatrically with a wink.

And then she turned, stepping through the gates of the Red Letter Hotel – and back into the human world at last.

CHAPTER 14 – NORMAL

Traveling in the human world was a known thing for Layla. Riding in taxis was familiar, being deposited on the curb of the Paris Airport, navigating her way to the Air France counter to secure a standby ticket to Genoa or Pisa or even Rome if she had to. She was in luck. A first-class ticket on the next flight to Genoa was available and she purchased it with her black Hotel credit card, then navigated through security with her baggage.

The routine of being gazed at like a potential terrorist by security was familiar as they checked her ticket and passport. No one noted her expensive pearl and diamond jewelry, though Layla fretted as she removed her boots, sweater, and coat to pass through security, wondering if she should take Reginald's gifts off. But Dusk had said to never remove them, so Layla sweated as she passed through the body scanner. But neither the jewelry nor King Arini's feather in its silk pouch snapped to her bra were picked up by the human security systems, and with a bored glance by a security agent, she was waved through.

Relief washed through Layla as she claimed her carry-on, moving to a bench to zip her boots back on and don her sweater. Her hand stole up, touching the pearl choker as she moved away from the security area, rolling her bag behind her with her coat on top of it. Gazing around at other travelers, she wondered suddenly how many of them were aware of the Twilight Realm – and how many might be Twilight folk traveling in disguise.

Layla couldn't imagine she was the only person to ever have done so, and even as she had that thought, a short, dowdy older woman passed by – whose eyes suddenly sharpened on Layla's choker. The woman glanced at Layla's wrist, and her eyes became enormous as they tracked to Layla's face. Giving a deep nod, the woman hurried past – also giving Layla a wide berth. A scent like honeycomb hit Layla's nostrils and she saw the woman shiver in a way that almost buzzed. Layla smiled, realizing the short older woman was of Head Clothier Amalia DuFane's bee-type Lineage, traveling as human.

So Twilight people traveling incognito is a thing after all.

As she walked briskly to her gate, stopping to pick up a bottle of water at a newsstand, Layla kept her senses alert. Most travelers only gave her cursory glances as they hurried to their gates, but now and again she passed someone whose nostrils flared when she was near, or whose eyes fixed on Reginald's gift. Most only gave Layla vague traveler's smiles, but a few really looked at her as if trying to remember her face or discern if she had any glamour.

Layla had seen applications of glamour done at the Hotel on Twilight folk who looked distinctly non-human, so they could go sightseeing in the human world and blend in. She found she could pick these people out as she stepped to her gate, noting that it was still seven minutes until boarding. A tall Scandinavian-blonde woman to her left had a waver in the air around her face as Layla glanced over. They shared a look and Layla thought she saw curling red tattoos at the woman's temples and down her neck – badges of a Furie's battle-prowess. A hippie guy with enormous brown dreadlocks and a nose piercing glanced up from his seat, giving her a big smile. Layla saw a waver around him too, and suddenly saw the velveteen features, corkscrewing horns, and short brown billy-goat beard of a Satyr.

But glancing around the crowded pre-flight area again, Layla realized that the two Twilight Lineage people she'd noted were the only ones waiting for her plane. She went over to take a seat next to billy-goat boy, one of the few seats still available at the crowded gate, but soon learned it was vacant because he smelled intensely of patchouli and a goaty B.O. It was overwhelming, and swallowing back a cough, Layla opted to stand near a column with a panel of cell-phone chargers instead.

Just then, the call for initial boarding of first class passengers came, and Layla turned toward the gate. Only a few people were boarding first-class or with infants, and Layla queued up, getting her boarding pass scanned and moving down the jetway. Stepping into the plane, she found her grey leather seat in first class and hucked her rolling bag into the overhead bin, then settled in.

Layla had the window seat, and as she watched other passengers file by for coach, a well-dressed businessman with a black briefcase nodded at her and settled into the seat beside her. Dressed in a grey pinstriped three-piece suit and russet wingtip shoes, he was lean and tall; silvering with age though quite handsome. With exquisitely cut features, high cheekbones, and a masculine yet elegant jaw, he had an enviable, mature sexiness like some kind of high-powered lawyer or CEO, with a sharp intensity about his person. Glancing over with ice-blue eyes, he flashed a quick smile, though his gaze lingered upon Layla's choker.

"North Sea Sirens?" He spoke with a cultured British accent, keeping his voice low as the flight attendant moved past assisting people with luggage.

"You know it?" Layla blinked as she reached up on instinct to touch Reginald's gift, shock flooding her that she hadn't noticed the man at the gate.

"I am one. And you clearly are not." One corner of his haughty

159

lips curled into a smile, something deeply patronizing in it. Flaring his nostrils, he inhaled. "Desert Dragon. Moroccan and Mediterranean clan. Heading to Italy for business or pleasure?"

"Business. And none of yours, pal." Layla's scales felt instantly scratched. Whoever this asshole was, he was going to get some lip from her if he kept pushing.

"It is my business, actually." His gaze got frosty as he stared her down, something furious but composed in his ice-pale eyes. "If I'm going to help my brother Reginald protect someone from Paris all the way to King Falliro Arini in Manarola, I'd like to know just exactly why."

Layla blinked hard. Her gut dropped through her boots as she stared at him. "You're one of Reginald's brothers?"

"The eldest of ten. By a few hundred years." The older gentleman lifted a straight eyebrow. And suddenly, Layla saw the family resemblance. Though going sexily silver, he had once been golden-haired, and traces of it still showed. His angular jaw was the same as Reginald's, his lean, mean physique not showing even a trace of paunch. His blue eyes were the same icy color as the Head Courtier's when he was irritated or angry. As he stared her down, Layla had the distinct impression of power, though she heard no oceans in her ears.

"Why don't I feel any Siren-magic coming from you?" She frowned at him.

He lifted his wrist, showing an ornate wrist cuff of silver inset with pearls. "My talisman. Like you, I wear something in the human world to control my energy. Chafes like a manacle."

"So why are you wearing it?" Layla sassed, still shocked and uncertain about him.

"Because I'm a *Royal* Siren, darling." His gaze was impeccably withering as he stared her down. "Do you want an orgy to happen on this plane? No? Well then, I suppose I have to leave it on. Tempeste Durant, of the North Sea Sirens. And you must be the infamous Layla Price."

"How do you know me?" Layla crossed her arms, raising an eyebrow and trying to still the roil of furiously alarmed energy that roared through her Dragon.

"Intercessoria files, my dear." He gave a cold smile, his husky-blue eyes penetrating. "Plus, you were raised human, so your image is all over the human internet and social media."

"You're Intercessoria?" Layla's heart gripped with severe alarm now, knowing her and Dusk's plan had somehow been found out by Heathren and Insinio.

"Yes." Tempeste Durant's gaze went two shades of cold and colder. "And you are lucky I am. I'm here for two reasons. One, because my youngest brother asked for my help, and I have a soft spot for my headstrong little Siro. And two, because Heathren Merkami and Insinio Brandfort couldn't be here at the moment. Rather than clap you in irons for this stunt when he specifically told you to stay put, Heathren would like a man protecting you as you travel to King Falliro Arini. You neglected to tell Heathren about your connection to the Phoenix King during your interrogation, by the way."

Layla rubbed her arms, feeling a cold breeze move through her area. She looked up, seeing if the plane's air blowers were active, but it was just a chill wind easing off the pissed Siren next to her. "I didn't *neglect* anything. I'd been up for over thirty-six hours and was out of my mind from exhaustion when they interrogated me. I tried to tell Heathren Merkami everything I knew about Hunter, I really did. I want Adrian released. And I will do *anything* to make that happen."

Tempeste's gaze softened on her. At last he drew a deep breath and something seemed to smooth in his prickly energy. "Forgive me.

I've been callous. This missive interrupted my vacation with my husband and children in Paris. It's made me irate. Intercessoria don't get much time away, and when I do, I like to spend it with my family. May we start our acquaintance again?"

"You're... a gay Siren?" Layla blinked.

"That's very rude." He gave a rueful smile. "Not all Sirenni are heterosexual."

"Sorry..." Layla found herself flushing three shades of red as a whiff of orange-bourbon scent rose up around her.

But the tall silver-haired Siren just smiled, reaching to the inner pocket of his elegant suit jacket and pulling out an alligator-skin wallet. Opening it, he took out a photograph of quite possibly the sexiest Greek man Layla had ever seen, plus two gorgeous young women in their mid-twenties; one with golden hair, one with sleek black ringlets. They were at Disneyland in California, dressed in American clothes, each with a silver and pearl bracelet at their wrist. Taking a group photo with Mickey, the silver-haired Tempeste laughed in the photo with them.

"This is Giro, my husband from the Mediterranean Sirens. And our two girls, Julia and Salina."

"Your daughters are beautiful. Are they adopted?" Layla glanced up at him.

Tempeste chuckled with a kinder nature now, putting the photo back in his wallet and tucking it away inside his jacket. "No, my daughters are not adopted. All Sirens have both sets of anatomy in their Dragon form. Giro and I wanted children, so I spent three years in Dragon form during an estrus cycle, mating with him and waiting to see if I became pregnant. I did, twice. Which is very lucky for a male Siren. Though spending three years as my Dragon, and pregnant, was a special kind of hell."

"Wow." Layla blinked, realizing that she still knew so little about different Dragon Lineages, especially the offshoots like Sirens and Phoenix. "So you really are Reginald's eldest brother?"

"Fortunately or unfortunately." Tempeste's face softened, his gaze straying to the pearls around Layla's neck. "I helped him hunt those pearls, you know. He was so very determined to wed Avri. Our father was against it, but he eventually came around. He'd given them his blessing at last, but then Avri became pregnant. Her clan found out. The rest was tragic."

"Reginald hasn't told me the story," Layla reached up, touching the pearl choker. "I've only seen visions of Avri, briefly."

"Ah, yes, the Royal Dragon Bind." A deep wisdom came into Tempeste's eyes. "You would be able to read Reginald's thoughts. He's a powerful Royal; even a rival to our father. Though Reginald would refute that. He has a very negative opinion of his power, drowning an entire Blood Dragon village as he did when he was young."

"What happened with that whole situation?" Layla asked, intrigued. "Reginald hasn't told me hardly anything about it, only that he remains at the Hotel partly because of amnesty from the Intercessoria."

"Do you recall the tale of the Little Mermaid?" Tempeste asked, as he signaled the flight attendant and ordered a martini. The attendant raised her eyebrows at Layla also, and she ordered a Jack and Coke, the fixings for an Old Fashioned not available on flights.

"Of course." Layla spoke as the flight attendant moved away. "I think every girl knows that story since Disney made a mockery out of the Hans Christian Andersen original tale."

Tempeste's smile was amused but there was something deeper beneath it; a tired kind of sadness. "Imagine the Little Mermaid, except set it off the southern coast of Norway and change the handsome human prince to a beautiful Blood Dragon peasant girl, and the role of

163

the mermaid is now the youngest of ten Siren brothers, the son of a powerful King. Now imagine that their romance happened without any sea-witch taking the young Siren's voice – the only instrument he had to woo his beloved. And now imagine that she came to him, and they were forbidden to be together when her clan found out. And because she was found pregnant by him, her clan deemed it better to put her to death with the child still in her womb rather than create an impure cross-bred Lineage of Blood and Sea."

"Oh my god," Layla breathed, horrified as the memory of the beautiful raven-haired woman with lavender eyes surfaced again in her mind.

"And now imagine that when the young Siren prince found out his beloved had been put to death, drowned in the very ocean in which he lived while he was away, that his voice became the wrath of the sea-witch and King Titan both," Tempeste spoke darkly, "and pummeled the headland of that Blood Dragon clan until they were all drowned to every last man, woman, and child."

"Reginald." Layla breathed. "His actions started an all-out war between the Blood Dragons of Norway and Sweden and your North Sea Sirens."

"It did." Tempeste nodded sadly. "As Clan First and King of the Sirens, my father Léviathan Durant has been waging that war ever since, along with my brothers. Reginald went into voluntary exile, coming to the Hotel to train with someone who could help him contain his terrible gift – and eventually rising to the position of Head Courtier because of the control it gained him."

His story finished, Tempeste drew in a deep sigh and let it out like a rip-tide. The flight attendant returned with their drinks and Tempeste thanked her. The attendant bustled away as the doors were closed and the safety demonstration began. Layla sipped her drink as the

164

instruction finished, and then the plane began to rev its engines and taxi.

"So what's your story?" She glanced over at Tempeste.

"What do you mean?" He eyeballed her, taking a sip of his beverage, then cradling it as he crossed his long legs at the knee.

"Why are you Intercessoria, rather than heading up your clan?"

"Because my magic isn't strong enough to lead my clan, or even be Clan Second." Tempeste's smile was rueful. "Though I was firstborn, my magic is only fifth of my ten brothers. Besides, I enjoy the rigors of Intercessoria work, and I am a monogamous homosexual. Life in a Sirennic Court is not to my taste. It's rather... *incestuous*... to put it mildly."

"What about Reginald?" Layla pushed, curious.

"He could be our First, and leave father to only worry about the demands of being King." Tempeste spoke with a dark kind of wistfulness. "Reginald's magic is strong enough. But he's never shifted into his Dragon, and there are those who are worried about that point. Plus, he would be hunted by the Intercessoria if he ever left the Hotel, which would put me in a very awkward position. Reginald is an anomaly among Sirens, you must understand. Most Sirens glorify in their power and use it to their advantage. We're a very cutthroat Lineage. Like the Little Mermaid, Reginald has power he can't even comprehend in the songs he weaves. But like her fable also, he has tremendous flaws that prevent him from pursuing the fullness of his gift."

"He's afraid of it." Layla understood suddenly.

"Ever since Avri's death, yes. Reginald drowned an entire coastline with tsunamis for three days, and still didn't shift into his Dragon. Most Sirens can't create a single tsunami with their songs, let alone do it in human form."

Tempeste's gaze was pointed, and Layla got the point. Reginald was a force of the ocean, but like his natural beauty, he hid it away, fearful of the power it held. Thinking about that, she settled in as the plane turned onto the runway, revving its engines into takeoff. She gripped the arm of her seat, hating the sudden weightless sensation as the jet lifted off.

But then it was over and she was in the air – heading to Manarola with the Intercessoria at her side.

CHAPTER 15 – ITALY

Though he'd been prickly at first, Layla found Reginald's eldest brother Tempeste Durant to be a wonderful conversation partner during the flight to Genoa, and she found herself surprisingly grateful for his company. She'd assumed all Intercessoria were as cold and calculating as Heathren Merkami, but she soon found that Tempeste was a family man – he was only prickly because he missed being with his loved ones. They were soon laughing together, enjoying more drinks as the plane leveled out into cruising altitude.

"So are you going to accompany me all the way to the Aviary?" Layla asked as they began sipping their third in-flight drink.

"No, unfortunately." Tempeste set his dry martini with three olives down on his tray table with a precise gesture. "The Intercessoria still do not know the precise location of King Arini's stronghold. You'd think we would by now, but that place is protected by incomprehensible magics, ancient as time itself. As the story goes, Arini himself discovered it by pure luck, scented it out upon the sea-winds while composing poetry off the cliffs of Manarola. It remains a secret to this day, a place no one knows of except by invitation with one of Arini's feathers."

"Can't you just hold him down and pluck a feather to get invitation?" Layla snorted into her third Jack and Coke.

"No." Tempeste's amused grin matched hers. "Though that would make it tremendously easier to contact the Phoenix King. The feather has to contain the resonant energy of a personal *invitation*. Your feather, for instance, would not invite me to the King's stronghold. Only you."

"So I go in and you stay out?" Layla mulled that over, that even the Intercessoria had limits.

"Yes." Tempeste's gaze was frank and a sudden seriousness settled around him. "I cannot protect you inside Arini's fortress, Layla. I can get you safely to Manarola, but there I must take a B&B until your time with Arini is finished. You won't have any friends inside the Aviary, though the Phoenix tend to be peaceful unless their feathers get ruffled. And I know about Dusk Arlohaim's tracking systems. There are no credit card readers inside the Aviary, so his plan fails there, and advanced technology tends to go kaput inside the Aviary because of warding-magics. The only one who will be able to track your whereabouts within the Aviary is Reginald. He'll be able to feel if you're in trouble, and he has my Intercessoria number to alert me if he feels distress from you. But I'll not be able to get to you. If anything happens in there… you'll have to get yourself out for the Intercessoria to help. Am I clear?"

"Crystal." Layla thought that over as she sipped her drink. "Do you think I'll be in danger inside the Aviary?"

"It depends." Tempeste's gaze was thoughtful, and Layla saw his eyes subtly change from ice-blue to a light blue-grey. "Does Hunter know about the Aviary? Can he get inside? Does he have someone among Arini's Phoenix who does his dirty-work? The Intercessoria estimate that about a hundred individuals in the Twilight Realm have Aviary access. Not all of them are Phoenix, but most are, and you are now one of them. That feather Arini gave you is not a one-time pass. It is forever, unless Arini decides to revoke your access. He is placing a deep trust in you, Layla. Deeper than perhaps you know."

"I'm starting to get the idea." Layla sat back, frowning. "Why would Arini trust me this way?"

"Who knows?" Tempeste's smile was kind. "Perhaps he wishes to know you better, and this is his way of showing it. Arini is an enigma; he rarely shows his cards to anyone. He knows how to play the game of ruthlessness better than any King or Queen I've ever met. And yet, he is tremendously kind. Just not a fool."

"So what's our play?"

"There isn't one." Tempeste sipped his martini. "Once you're inside, there is no play. Speak with Arini, try to stay as close to him as possible once you're in. Trust no-one else. Get out as soon as you feel you have enough information to help us locate Hunter, or at least learn something about him that we can use. And then, Adrian is yours."

Layla nodded, feeling a sudden weight in her chest. This journey was so far outside her comfort zone. She'd never been in a situation of political intrigue or danger before. Sure, she'd traveled through areas where her safety had not been guaranteed, and she'd had to bribe her way out of a few tight spots over the years, especially traveling alone as a woman. Crossing her arms, she heaved a sigh. Glancing over, Tempeste reached out, settling a hand to her thigh. Layla felt a gentle ocean wave pour through her, not strong but calming.

"You'll do fine." Tempeste held her gaze with his grey-blue eyes. "You have more spark and quick thinking than many Judiciary the Intercessoria has sent in to do undercover work. And power; don't forget your power. I've seen the cracked sapphire door on the Paris Hotel's Vault, Layla. Your energy is wild, but it's there. If there's any emergency…" His gaze shifted to Reginald's choker, "cast away my brother's gifts. Rip them from your skin if you have to, tear them to pieces if you must, to unleash your magic. Better to have you alive. I'm sure my youngest Siro would agree."

Drawing a deep breath, Layla nodded. She knew what rip-roaring magic she carried in her veins. Even though it would be awful to ruin

Reginald's gifts, she knew Tempeste's words were sage. If it came down to it, she would rather have her power unleashed to be able to fight with it, not have it be hampered by magical restriction.

Just then, an announcement of descent came over the PA system, and she felt the jet begin to angle down. Their empty drinks were picked up and Layla and Tempeste Durant settled in as the jet descended steeply into Genoa, then landed with a smooth touchdown. They taxied to the gate and before long were stopped, the seatbelt sign dinging off and everyone rising to claim luggage.

Tempeste was gentlemanly, helping Layla get her bag down, though all he had was his briefcase. He motioned her in front of him, then trailed her like a bodyguard as they exited the plane and walked up the jetway. Once they were out into the Genoa airport, he walked at her side – though his gaze swept the airport, piercing, a cold wind easing off his skin like icebergs.

Walking through the airport, they made their way to the train system. Purchasing tickets from an automated kiosk, they waited for the next train to La Spezia, settling in at a well-used plastic bench and avoiding stepping in old gum on the concrete platform. Though it was nighttime now, it was warmer in Italy than it had been in Paris, and Layla left her jacket tucked over her rolling bag, massaging a cramp from her neck as she opened the collar of her sweater.

"So, we've got an hour-and-a-half train ride ahead," Tempeste spoke casually as he glanced over. "Is there anything else you'd like to ask, Layla? I've been cleared to give you any information you need about the Intercessoria, within reason. And as far as family matters, if you wish to learn more about Reginald, I'm sure he wouldn't mind me blabbing."

Crossing her legs and bouncing one boot as they waited, Layla considered it. "Actually, I do have a few questions, about both."

"Shoot." Tempeste spoke pleasantly. Reaching into his inner jacket pocket, he produced a roll of mint Mentos and popped one, then offered them to Layla. She took one with a smile and a nod of thanks.

"Well," she spoke, chewing the Mentos. "What is Heathren Merkami? I get the sense of wings around him and Insinio Brandfort, but not like a Phoenix or any other kind of bird-shifter."

"That's because Heathren and Insinio are not bird-shifters," Tempeste spoke pleasantly, even as his gaze continued scanning the gradually-thickening crowd on the platform. "They're Ephilohim. What you would call angels. Archangels actually, the both of them, though they are first-generation Fallen Ephilohim, both born on earth in the Twilight Realm. Though neither is originally celestial, they are extremely powerful and not to be crossed."

"Archangels?" Layla blinked, realizing how much that fit with her first impression of the intensely beautiful Heathren Merkami and Insinio Brandfort. As if they had something otherworldly about them, in a way that not even Dusk, Adrian, or Reginald could match. They were more on the level of Sylvania's beauty – as if they were something that didn't quite come from earth. "So do they come from the Ascended Realms? Like Sylvania Eroganis did?"

"Originally, yes." Tempeste nodded, glancing at her. "Ephilohim are an ancient race, and not limited to the earthly realms. But there have been Fallen Ephilohim in the Twilight Realm for quite some time – Ephilohim that decided to reject their ephemeral nature to have a more worldly experience. Heathren and Insinio both come from clans that Fell many thousands of years ago, in the area of the Caucasus Mountains and all around the Black Sea. Their Lineages are ancient and have engaged in terrifying purges over the years. Do you know the legend of Dracula?"

"I thought Dracula was a vampire?" Layla frowned.

171

"No." Tempeste shook his head, something dark in his eyes. "Vampires can get powerful, but their power is in manipulation and coercion. They don't have an Archangel's raw brutality. Vlad the Impaler was a Fallen Ephilohim – his true name in the Twilight Realm was Vladimir Merkami. Heathren Merkami is his first son. It was Insinio Brandfort that convinced Heathren to turn against his father and bring him down, before all of Eastern Europe in both the Twilight and Human Realms fell to Vlad's madness. The wars that happened both before Heathren turned against his father and after were mind-boggling. It's a terrible thing when a Fallen Archangel goes mad and has to be put down."

"I can only imagine." Layla tried to wrap her mind around it, that a legend she had known all her life was actually the terrible story of a Fallen Archangel. "So that explains the seven layers of wings I felt from Heathren and Insinio."

"You felt their wings?" Tempeste's gaze sharpened on her. "That's rare. Most Twilight species only get a feeling of tremendous power from Ephilohim."

Layla shrugged. But before she could say more, the train's arrival was announced in Italian, English, and a few more languages. They rose from the bench, though Tempeste held a hand out to forestall Layla from pushing through the crowd. Waiting in the back of the throng as the train arrived, they moved far down the line to a car that was mostly unoccupied.

Finding seats, Layla put her bag up on the luggage rack as they settled in, an old Italian couple taking the seats opposite. The old man stared out the window and the old lady yelled something at him in heavily-accented Italian that Layla couldn't quite track despite her fluency. The old man didn't respond and the woman whacked him with her cane, then shouted louder as he glanced at her, about *dinner* and *fish*. They shouted at each other for a moment, apparently discussing what they were going to eat when they got home to La Spezia. Their argument was so vocal with so many agitated hand gestures that Layla thought they might come to blows. But suddenly, they were kissing – cute little pecks of long-term love before he stared out the window again and she took up a magazine.

"God, I love Italy." Tempeste chuckled.

Layla grinned and they shared a smile as the train pulled away from the platform. Moving out of the Genoa station, they were soon rolling past a dark evening cityscape dotted with lights. Old Roman ruins were lit with modern yellow streetlights, combined with classical Italian architecture as they rolled through the city. They soon gained the countryside, moving through a wide landscape that would have been beautiful by day, but by night was simply dark.

After twenty minutes of silence, Tempeste glanced over. "You can sleep if you'd like. I'll keep watch."

"No, I'm not tired." Layla shook her head. "Hungry, actually. I could use a meal when we get to Manarola."

"I know the perfect place." Tempeste smiled kindly, like a father. "It's a five-minute walk from the apartment I've booked for us tonight, just down the main street towards the wharf."

"You booked us a place to stay?" Layla blinked, suddenly grateful that they had a place to rest tonight, in a small town where nearly everything probably shut down at 9 p.m.

"It's mostly for me to wait at while you're at the Aviary," Tempeste chuckled. "But you'll have your own bed tonight, and any other night if for whatever reason you decide to not sleep inside the fortress."

"Do you know where to access the fortress?" Layla asked him.

"It's off the cliff-walk." Tempeste shrugged elegantly. "That's all

173

we really know. The feather will guide you there once you get close enough."

"Tempeste?" Layla sat back in her seat, a few more questions on her mind. "Do you know Adrian?"

"Not well." He glanced over at her, alert to her sudden line of questioning. "Adrian Rhakvir and I have met on a few occasions. I had the distinct displeasure of interrogating him once on Intercessoria business. Adrian is close-lipped about his dealings, and quite resistant to magical coercion. We had to bring in six Vampires and still he wouldn't break to our questioning. Ultimately, we couldn't get a confession out of him, or any physical evidence on the case, so Heathren had to let him go."

"You interrogated Adrian?" Layla blinked, feeling fury suddenly rise in her as she looked over at Tempeste.

"It's my job." Tempeste held her gaze, his blue eyes frank. "Not a part I revel in, but a part of being Intercessoria Judiciary. In any case, there wasn't any overt physical torture involved. The Intercessoria do have scruples, unless extreme methods are warranted. You'd be well-informed to know that Adrian lasted ten days under our duress, including the elimination of food and water. He's stronger than he looks, that Royal Desert Dragon of yours. He breaks Heathren's immense patience, which is something to note. Few people can top the patience of a Fallen Ephilohim."

Layla digested that, both hating that she'd learned this tidbit about Tempeste, but somehow strangely comforted by the information on Adrian. It made her worry less about him being incarcerated, though she still wanted him free as soon as possible. "What was the case?"

"I'm not at liberty to share the specifics." Tempeste held her gaze. "Just know that it involved crimes against Twilight folk and Humans alike – a vast ring of people-trafficking that Adrian had been implicated in. He wouldn't defend himself during the interrogation. We don't know if that was because he was involved or because he was trying to infiltrate the traffickers to shut them down, and didn't want his cover blown. Knowing Adrian, it could have been either way. He's a renegade, and doesn't play by Twilight laws."

"So it seems." Layla's mood darkened, wondering if she would ever not be surprised by the things she heard about Adrian. She added this to her list of things to ask him when she saw him again. "Sometimes I feel like I barely know him at all."

Tempeste's gaze was deep as he contemplated her. "Adrian Rhakvir is a mysterious creature. But Heathren has confessed to me that he can't sense evil intent in Adrian. Clandestine activity, surely, omissions and even outright lies, but never malice. Heathren is an Archangel – it's his magic to know if a soul is tarnished or clean. And for whatever else he's involved in… Adrian's soul is still somehow clean of tarnish."

Taking that in, Layla crossed her arms. Thinking about Adrian, she suddenly realized she could feel him. Distant, a vision came to her as if she was looking out of his eyes, seeing a silver table in a white room that scrolled with gold sigils and script. Adrian's wrists were manacled to the table, the silver cuffs writhing with gold script like the room. She could see his crimson Dragon tattoo on his left forearm, beneath his rolled-up shirtsleeve. As she felt him, roiling with defiance despite an immense fatigue, she felt him startle. Adrian inhaled, and Layla felt him breathe in her scent across the distance.

She got a whisper of cinnamon-jasmine back, and a breath through her mind – *Layla*…

The vision fell apart and Layla saw no more. Settling back in her seat, Layla looked out the window at the dark countryside, dotted with lights as they passed northern Italian fields and farmhouses. Gazing out

175

at the darkness, she digested Tempeste's words; that Adrian had a soul clean of tarnish. And she realized that's what she felt from Adrian also, despite all his secrets. That he somehow remained morally clean despite his temper and ruthless decisiveness and clandestine activities. She had a million more questions about him, but didn't feel like asking at the moment, so she settled into silence.

Beside her, Tempeste Durant settled into silence also, though he kept alert on the train, watching everyone who walked by with his piercing, Siren-blue gaze.

CHAPTER 16 – AVIARY

The town of Manarola in Cinque Terre was glorious in the nighttime. As Layla and Tempeste walked down the cobbled main street away from the local train station and into town, the storied cliffside city was as beautiful as its photographs. Picturesque, the town perched on the hillside in steep tiers, winding down a rocky headland straight into the Mediterranean Sea. Nearing eleven p.m., the city was mostly quiet, every red, blue, and canary-painted abode glowing from city lights not only illuminating the night but also highlighting the town's beauty.

Tourists lingered at an open-air bar, drinking local wine and eating antipasti, and Layla's stomach turned over, ravenous. She'd not eaten anything since the afternoon, but Tempeste had promised dinner after they found their B&B. Down the winding main thoroughfare, dotted with wrought-iron porches, potted greenery, and winter dry-land mooring for covered fishing boats, they arrived at a four-story guesthouse.

Ringing the bell, a dowdy older lady in a floral print cotton dress answered the door and Tempeste announced his reservation in fluent Italian. The woman beamed, motioning them in through the wrought-iron gate and blue timber doorway. Entering a tiled hall with doors to either side, the woman fetched some papers and a key from her apartment to the left, a TV blaring Italian dramas inside, then ushered them up a corkscrewing wrought-iron stairwell.

They ascended to the fourth floor and the woman opened an ornately-carved door, leading to a modest apartment. It was homey, decorated in sea-themed bric-a-brac like any coastal retreat, but with a stately Italianate flare and bright colors. The apartment's best feature was a private rooftop patio through a set of French doors, crowded by potted plants and patio furniture overlooking the sea.

With a few words to Tempeste about house rules and quiet hours, the homeowner gave Layla a pat to the cheek and handed over the keys, departing with a kind smile. At last they were alone, and Layla heard Tempeste heave a deep sigh. She turned, watching him sling his black suitcase to the linen couch, then scrub a hand through his brush-cut silver hair.

"Want to settle in?" He glanced at her. "Or get food?"

"Food would be stellar," Layla spoke, already browsing through the apartment's kitchenette. It was moderately stocked for cooking and had a welcome basket on the table of local Cinque Terre products. Layla was already twisting open a jar of cured green olives and dipping her fingers in, then cranking open another jar of sardines in olive oil and eating them with a slice of pecorino cheese. With a chuckle, Tempeste moved over, taking up a fork from the table and having a few bites with a bit more style than Layla.

"You'll spoil your dinner," he joked in a fatherly way.

"I could eat six dinners right now." Layla spoke back, dipping her fingers in for more sardines. They were delightful, the olive oil flavored with garlic and dill, lemon and black peppercorns.

"Let's head down to Giuseppe's then," Tempeste spoke around a bite of olive. Screwing the lids back on both jars, he liberated them from Layla in a decisive maneuver just like Reginald, and stuck them in the mini-fridge. "Stow your things in whichever room you choose and we'll leave."

Layla nodded, then rolled her bag to the room on the left, decorated with a seashell theme and featuring a pretty lace bedspread.

Tempeste took his briefcase to the other bedroom. As Layla exited to the living space, she saw him liberate four silver knives with pearl-encrusted handles from the case, sliding them into a shoulder-rig beneath his jacket that she'd not noticed until just now. Also set with silver and pearls, the shoulder-rig was military-issue kevlar, though decorated with sigils Layla could only suppose were of Siren origin. Her eyebrows rose as Tempeste turned, the knives disappearing on his person with a watery mirage and the rig no longer visible even as she peered directly at it.

"You wear magically-disguised weapons?"

"Not through a human airport." Tempeste's glance was meaningful. "The case disguises them better and hides them from scanners, though my shoulder-rig and knives have a Siren-glamour on them. It's extremely rare, but there are humans who can see through a glamour. Usually, they have a bit of crossbreeding with a Twilight Lineage back down the line somewhere. Most of those wind up in asylums if they're not in the know. But you'd be surprised how many of them keep what they see a secret – and how many of those work in police or security, precisely because they know there's a world out there they can't explain, and aren't safe from."

"I never thought about that." Layla blinked, feeling glad she had a human visage as a Desert Dragon.

"Let's get some food." Tempeste moved toward the door, unlocking it and ushering Layla out. She wore her wrap sweater, the winter evening warm on the coast but with a slight wind. As they moved down the stairwell and out the guesthouse to the cobbled street, Layla breathed deep of the fresh seaside air. The nighttime breeze carried all the good smells she had once associated with her life in Seattle; ocean detritus and salt, brine musk and seaweed.

Moving down the thoroughfare in the late night, there were few

179

tourists about, most simply wandering, gazing up at the lights of the city upon the colorful buildings. Tempeste and Layla walked all the way down to the wharf, the crashing of the surf audible now as the thoroughfare opened up to a broad palazzo overlooking the ocean, boats bobbing in the harbor behind the cove's jetty. Turning left, Tempeste avoided the tourist bars and restaurants, issuing Layla up a nondescript flight of outdoor stairs with a wrought-iron trellis covered in winter-dormant grape vines and featuring a candle flickering in a blue votive dangling from an iron chain. Ascending the white-washed steps, they arrived at a bare outdoor patio with rusting furniture.

But as they arrived, Tempeste brushed his fingertips over a wrought-iron mermaid post to their left, and Layla experienced the disorientation that signified passing through from the human world into the Twilight Realm. Suddenly, the sprawling patio before them was adorned with party-lights, lively music playing inside a building to their left. An assortment of Twilight Realm people laughed on the patio, dining and drinking at garishly-painted wrought-iron tables. The entire patio had an arbor of fully-leafed and fruiting grape vines, twinkling with colorful strings of lights and creating a whimsical fairy-like bar.

Not only was the bar new, but Layla gazed from their high vantage with a surprised smile, seeing a whole new Manarola as she overlooked the thoroughfare and the harbor. As they stepped to a hostess podium carven with frolicking mermaids, she noted the city was taller as it perched on the cliff; more precarious with bridges of old Roman stone arching far out over the water to sea-stacks piled with more abodes – all of which didn't exist in the human world. The color and gaiety reminded Layla of a cleaner Venice and she laughed, feeling a thriving, vibrant city all around her rather than a sleepy tourist town.

"Welcome to Manadora, Manarola's sister-city in the Twilight Realm." Tempeste gave her a sly sidelong smile. "I imagine you've never seen it?"

"Wow! I mean… wow!" Layla was breathless, admiring the sea-stack city all around her, something she might have seen only in dreams. She was still gaping stupidly as a pretty flaxen-haired waitress with silver scales at her temples greeted them, then showed them to a wrought-iron table near the stone wall overlooking the harbor.

They settled in and Tempeste thanked the hostess, then handed a menu to Layla. Scorched into some kind of thick fish-skin, the menu was written in a script so archaic it looked like pirate handwriting, though it was thankfully modern Italian with an English translation just below each item. Perusing the menu, Layla saw all the regular Italian coastal antipasti and delicacies, plus a few things like *Perpetuate Tentacle on Garlic-Misssendra Crostini with Pecorino*, which made her eyebrows rise.

"What do you recommend?" She asked, glad that Tempeste was here to show her this place. The Siren Jud was proving far more of an asset than a hindrance, and Layla was starting to appreciate his company. The waitress moved by, filling their water glasses, and Tempeste ordered two cappuccinos and a carafe of local pinot grigio. The waitress whisked off with a smile, and they went back to the menus.

"Some of the items will taste strange to you here," Tempeste spoke as he perused the menu with a brisk efficiency. "I wouldn't recommend the *Royal Crab*, unless you enjoy excessively bitter food. It's not like crab in the human world."

"Noted." Layla looked the selection over. "What about the *Sea Slug Wine with Cuttle Shark Scale and Innocent Brine*?" It was quite possibly the weirdest-sounding thing on the menu.

Tempeste grinned at her slyly. "Not unless you want to have an orgasm in your seat. *Innocent Brine* is far from innocent."

"Ok… no-go on the Innocent Brine." She blinked, blushing. "What about the *Shipwright's Classic with Olives, Raccini, and Liquid Shrimp?*"

"Mmm… I might have that one myself." Tempeste smiled in a bright way that made him stunningly handsome, making Layla rather sad he was gay. "You'd probably like it. It's a tomato-based seafood soup, like a *cioppino*. Raccini are like chanterelles and Liquid Shrimp are like a scallop, except softer. They soak up all the flavors of the stew and burst in your mouth when chewed; delightful. Looks like it comes with a fairly normal olive tapenade on crostini. Should we order a pot of stew to share? They generally serve family-style here."

"Sounds perfect." Layla set her menu aside and took up her wine as it arrived. It was delightful, crisp and sour like all good pinot grigios. Taking a sip of her cappuccino next, served with a sugar cube, Layla smiled, delighted. It was the best coffee she'd had outside of Seattle.

The server came around again and Tempeste ordered in fluent Italian with an odd guttural twist to it. Not writing anything down, the server nodded as her lovely gossamer ear-fins fluttered. Layla saw opalescent fins at her collarbones flutter also, and pegged her for a Saltwater Mermaid; a Lineage that frequently lived in coastal towns, whereas only Freshwater Mermaids were seen at the Paris Hotel. The pretty Mermaid server smiled as Tempeste finished his order, then hustled off.   As their server moved away, Layla dug into her crostini, finding it perfectly toasted with a generous soaking of extra-virgin olive oil beneath the delicious olive tapenade. Ravenous, she had three pieces before she spoke again around a bite. "So. How do we find the Aviary?"

"Shush." Tempeste glanced around, though the other tables near them weren't occupied. "Let's refer to it as… the Hope Diamond."

"Isn't that a bit obvious?" Layla frowned.

"People here don't know or care about the Hope Diamond," Tempeste snorted. "You were raised in the human world, remember?"

"Oh." Layla chewed her crostini, then swallowed. "So how do we find the Hope Diamond?"

"We can go looking for it tonight, if you like." Tempeste looked like he was about to say more when their seafood stew suddenly arrived, in a big ceramic crock. Bowls and deep spoons were set down and Layla salivated, smelling the most delicious *cioppino* she'd ever encountered. They nodded their thanks to the waitress and ladling generous amounts of stew into Layla's bowl with a delighted smile, Tempeste continued as they dug in.

"Once we get close enough on the cliffs, you'll feel a call from the feather, in the direction of the Hope Diamond. It'll get stronger the closer you get. We have to be in the human world to feel it – the Hope Diamond is hidden in that realm rather than this one, another reason it's so hard to find."

"Yeah, why is that?" Layla asked around a bite of tomato-rich broth. A scallop-like object in her mouth popped as she chewed and she sighed in bliss, reveling in the exquisite texture and flavor. "Why are things harder to track magically if you're in the human world?"

"Because the human world vibration is inherently without magic." Tempeste chewed, wiping his lips with his white napkin in an effete gesture that reminded Layla of Reginald. "Magic is a finer vibration than the resonance of the human world, closer to the vibrations of an etheric realm. The human world is coarser, and finer resonances are generally lost there. Thus, they're harder to track. It's why your mother Mimi Zakir was able to hide herself, and you, in the human world. She had a talisman to aid her, but when someone of the Twilight Realm lives in the human world, their finer magical vibration essentially disappears into a coarse sea. Imagine slapping your hand into a bowl of water, and vibrating that water with a tiny diode at the same time. The fine vibrations from the diode will essentially become lost in the coarser vibrations of your slapping."

"So how can glamours be applied in the human realm?" Layla took another bite of stew, enjoying a chewy nugget of mussel or oyster in the broth.

"They can't." Tempeste gave her a look. "Glamours have to be applied in the Twilight Realm, then you go into the human world and the glamour remains. They have to be re-charged, unless stabilized by a talisman, which holds the magic inside gems and rune work. It's one of the many mysteries of the Hope Diamond, that it exists in the human world yet remains under a glamour so strong it's practically un-locatable. And from the stories, magic is able to be worked there in full strength – don't ask me how."

"So how come I felt Adrian's power when he and I touched in the art gallery back in Seattle?" Layla countered, digging into anything Tempeste would answer.

"Did you feel Adrian's full strength that day?" Tempeste gave her a knowing look over his next bite of stew. "I'd wager not. And though your own power can rage in the human world, it will never be at full strength there. Why are there only ancient stories of Dragons among the human world? Because no Dragon has been able to shift in that magically-dead world for ages."

"Could I have controlled myself from shifting if I'd remained in Seattle?" Layla asked, curious as she sipped her wine.

"Perhaps; perhaps not. Just because a Dragon hasn't shifted in front of humans for centuries doesn't mean other havoc can't be wreaked."

Finishing her wine, Layla conceded that was true. Reaching the end of her formidable bowl of stew, she sat back, breathing the fresh sea-scents and reveling in being full. As she and Tempeste sipped their cappuccinos, Layla gazed out to the twinkling lights of the sea-stacks with their precarious towers of houses perched on sheer cliffs. It all looked so impossible, the way those abodes were piled on top of each other, and yet she knew they had been secured by magic – probably stronger than any cement or steel available in the human world. Magic was confounding sometimes, and sometimes dangerous, but as she stared out over all the winsome glory, Layla realized it was also beautiful. Tempeste re-filled her wine from the carafe and they sipped, enjoying the deepness of the night.

At last, their meal was finished. Layla didn't have room for dessert so they skipped it, paying with her Hotel credit card and sauntering from the cliff-bar with a hail of thanks to the waitress. As they moved back to the steps, Tempeste touched the mermaid post again. In a wave of light and disorientation, the cliff-bar disappeared, replaced by an empty swath of patio. With it went the colorful nighttime sea-stacks – the bustling city dying to a sleepy port-town once more.

It filled Layla with an indescribable sadness to watch it all disappear. As if the human world were darker with less color and gaiety, she felt the transition back to the place she'd once called home like a mist had rolled in through the harbor. It was as if everything had been swaddled in shades of grey, and moving down the whitewashed stairs, they meandered to the quay in silence.

Lights of boats twinkled in a placid sea beneath a sprawling dome of stars. Moving northwest along the old stone cliff-walk, they circumnavigated the headland, most of Manarola's light soon disappearing from view. But as they lost sight of the city, Layla suddenly heard a call of birdsong in her ears. Halting, she blinked, realizing that they sounded like a tropical forest rather than anything active on the coast at night.

"I can hear them... Arini's birds." She spoke, reaching up to touch the silk pouch under her shirt. As she pressed the pouch to her chest, she suddenly felt a thrilling tremolo from Arini's downy feather vibrating within.

"We're close, then." Glancing around, Tempeste motioned her on before him. "Move slowly along the cliff-walk. Find where it gets strongest."

With a nod, Layla moved forward. As she stepped further along the stone walkway, high cliffs on one side and a sheer drop-off to the ocean on the other, she heard the birdsong in her ears crescendo, then fade. Retracing her steps, she found where the musical cacophony became strongest, at a piece of grassy cliff that jutted out past the stone walkway. Sitting on the retaining wall and sliding over to the unprotected side, Layla stood, listening to birds riot in her mind. She thought she felt a tug from the feather at her chest, as if it had connected to her heart and pulled her forward.

"Here." She nodded at the short spar of grass, to where it dropped off to ocean nearly a hundred feet below. "This is the spot."

"Walk forward, slowly, carefully." Tempeste nodded at the place where the cliff dropped away in the midnight darkness. "If the bridge into Arini's stronghold is active right now, you'll step into his realm as you reach the end of the promontory. If not, I'm here to catch you."

"What do you mean, active right now?" Layla glanced back with one eyebrow lifted, to glimpse Tempeste haloed by the stark glow of a porch-light far above the stone walk.

"Rumor has it there are certain times of day and night when the Aviary can't be accessed." Tempeste's smile was wry by the light of the dwelling above. "Another precaution of the ancient magics that guard it. If the Aviary-access is active, you simply step onto the fortress bridge from the end of the promontory."

"And if not?"

"You plummet to your death in the ocean." Tempeste's direct gaze was meaningful.

"Awesome. Fucking awesome." Layla breathed, her heart hammering suddenly as her Dragon roiled in her veins, wide awake beneath Reginald's gifts now that Heathren's charm had finally worn off. But though she was terrified of simply stepping off into thin air and falling to her death in the crashing ocean below, her Dragon was strangely thrilled by the prospect of the test – like it was all some big, fun game.

"You said you could catch me if I fall? If the bridge isn't active?" Layla eyed Tempeste, setting her hands to her hips and taking a long, deep breath.

"You won't like it, but yes." Something glittered in Tempeste's eyes, some dark humor that Layla couldn't quite read. "You won't die. I promise. By my dear departed mother's scales."

"Great…" Moving forward with another deep breath to steady her terror, along with her Dragon's thrill-seeking eagerness, Layla stepped out onto the slim promontory. A sheer drop-off cascaded down to the right, another just as sheer to her left. Moving forward carefully in the wan light of the stars and that single porch-light high above, Layla put her concentration in her feet, glad she'd worn boots with low heels tonight but wishing for sneakers.

As she stepped to the edge, trying not to gaze down at the water crashing on rocks a hundred feet below, she felt a scorching rise in birdsong, like they screamed in her mind. The feather at her breast pulled again, and Layla took a breath, knowing this was the spot.

"What now?" She called back over her shoulder.

"Take a leap of faith, Layla Price!" Tempeste called out to her, still waiting by the stone wall. "And see what is revealed!"

"A leap of faith. Awesome." Layla closed her eyes. Setting a hand between her breasts and clutching the silk pouch with Arini's feather through her shirt and sweater, she said a little prayer.

And then walked straight forward – off the cliff.

CHAPTER 17 – DROWNING

Layla didn't get far in her leap of faith. One moment she was on land, the next she was plummeting toward the dark rocks and crashing surf. Panic slit her veins in a roar of fire – but then in a vast surge, the midnight ocean suddenly rushed up. Thrust into a hard wall of water with a violent slap like a belly-flop, Layla was inundated by the ocean and heaved back up – over the promontory and straight into Tempeste Durant's arms. He seized her in an iron grip as the ocean rushed away, leaving Layla spluttering and gasping, clutched close to his warm body as the strangely singular tsunami washed back out.

"What the fuck?!" She coughed, wiping brine and seaweed from her eyes, soaked.

Tempeste laughed, roaring with humor, holding her close as the last of the water flooded off the promontory in a white rush beneath the stars. "I told you that you wouldn't like it!"

"I didn't know you were going to *wash me back out of the fucking sea!*" Layla spat, rounding on him. He released her just enough that she could turn, but didn't let her go completely, the promontory soaked and slippery. Reaching a hand up, he brushed her wet curls from her face with a beaming grin that was less like Reginald and far more like Dusk.

"Well, I guess we know King Arini's bridge isn't active right now."

"Fuck you." Struggling out of his arms, Layla sat on the low stone wall and slung her legs over, back to the path. With a chuckle, even though he was just as soaked as she was, Tempeste sat and slung his legs over also, currying water out of his short silver hair with both hands. But rather than look pissed at being sodden, he looked exhilarated, a pearl-grey color flecked with gold shining from his eyes now by the light of the far above porch-light.

"There's a reason my mother named me Tempeste, Layla," he chuckled as she began marching back toward the harbor and their abode. "I have a fairly wicked sense of humor. Something all my younger brothers learned early in life."

"Haha, very funny." She grumped, hating that she was sodden. Even coming from Dusk, a joke like that wouldn't have been very amusing. She was learning that Sirens had a cruel sense of humor – Reginald and his eldest brother had that in common. An orange-bourbon scent lifted around her and Layla was suddenly aware that it was stronger than in the past hour. With a pang of alarm, she checked the pearl bracelet at her wrist, then the choker and earrings – and found one missing. "Reginald's earring!"

"Don't fret, I have it." Moving forward, he placed the earring in Layla's palm. "From the sea, to the sea. Such items can never be lost around a Siren, especially not in the ocean."

"Fine." Layla was terse as she looped the earring back into her lobe.

"I can see why Reginald loves you," Tempeste spoke as he watched her with a very frank look now, intense. "You have a temper to match his own. My brother has only given those pearls to two other women in his life. And the second one, Sylvania Eroganis, returned them as kindly as everything else she did while alive. She taught Reginald everything he knew about control, pleasure, and healing, when he arrived at the Paris Hotel a broken man. Avri was his youngling love, but Sylvania was his maturation. You, I don't know what you are, but you mean enough to Reginald to receive his most precious gift for the third time in as many centuries."

"The pearls?" Layla frowned, reaching up to touch them. It was news to her that Reginald had learned his control from Sylvania, and that he'd once tried to gift these pearls to her but been kindly denied. The deep and tender relationship between the Head Courtier and Head Courtesan was something Layla would have to ask Reginald about eventually.

"Not the pearls, those are inconsequential." Tempeste shook his head. "It's his *abandon* Reginald's beginning to gift you with."

"His abandon, what do you mean?" Layla retorted, wiping water from her cheeks.

"Reginald was once as headstrong and tempestuous a creature as you'd ever meet." Tempeste eyeballed her frankly in the midnight darkness, sounds of the sea crashing far below. "He learned fear of his power, and thence became severely inhibited until Sylvania taught him how to control it. Now after her death, he begins to show his power once more – don't think I didn't hear of him striding through the Hotel barely dressed with you on his arm. And not just because of Sylvania."

"Is that meant to worry me?" Layla cocked her head, crossing her arms over her chest as a cold wind blew off the ocean. She shivered as it chilled her, her inner Dragon languishing deep beneath the waves of Reginald's magic now that she was soaked.

"No, only to open your eyes." Tempeste's gaze was less austere by the high light of the stars. "Come on. Let's get you back. We'll return in the morning and see if we can get you into the Aviary."

"Awesome." Layla grumped as she moved forward, rubbing her shoulders with her hands now. It had been a long while since she'd last felt chilly with her Desert Dragon-magic. But the combination of sea water and Reginald's pearls seemed to accentuate each other, and as Layla stepped up beside Tempeste, it was as if she could hear the

191

crashing of the waves echoed through her bones. She began to shiver hard, and he slung an arm around her casually as they walked, and Layla didn't shrug him off. The Siren was impossibly warm, as if the touch of cold ocean had made his temperature rise like a fever. As they gained the cobblestone thoroughfare back up the hill, Layla had ceased shivering, snuggled close under Tempeste's arm like huddling by a radiator.

They moved back up the hill in silence. Unlocking the guesthouse door, they were soon inside and moving up the corkscrewing stairs. Once they were back inside the apartment with the door locked, Tempeste turned and gestured to the shared bathroom. "You should have a hot shower. Reginald's magic in his pearls is synergizing with the ocean water. The sooner you can get the salt off your body, the better. Freshwater won't have the same effect. I'll make us some hot tea."

"Could have told me you were going to wash me back up out of the ocean like a dead fish." Layla grumped, though she was less sour now, a smile creeping in at the edges of her lips.

"You have to admit that was humorous." Tempeste grinned at her as he moved to the kitchen, shucking his sodden suit jacket to a chair. "Besides, if I hadn't controlled your fall, you'd be dead by now. You're welcome."

Layla smiled a little more, knowing it was true. Tempeste's fast action had saved her life. And his control of the ocean, to make it wash her directly back up into his arms, was impressive. "You're right – I'm alive because of you, and I know it. You'd think Arini might have warned me there'd be such a dire trick to finding his Aviary."

"He's a mysterious creature, Layla." Tempeste eyed her as he took down a teakettle from the shelf. "Few people know the whys of King Arini's movements."

"Do you think he meant to kill me?" The thought suddenly struck Layla, that if the Phoenix King had wanted her dead, what better way than to act like her friend and give her his feather, then leave her to plummet to her death trying to find his Aviary. Tempeste frowned, blinking a few times as he turned and leaned back against the kitchenette counter, crossing his arms. Layla could nearly see his knife-rig now that his jacket was gone, like a watery mirage against the lean cut of his shirt and vest, and his thoughtful poise plus the weapons suddenly reminded her that he was Intercessoria Judiciary.

"I honestly don't know." He spoke at last. "Finding the Aviary has always required a leap of faith, that is something about it that is infamous. Those without invitation can sometimes feel its presence, but they are the ones who find the site and then walk off into the ocean and die. Do any with an invitation ever fall to their deaths? Would magic of Arini's have interfered if I hadn't been there to catch you from hitting the rocks? I don't suppose we'll ever know. You might ask King Arini when you speak with him. Though that man has even more secrets than Adrian Rhakvir."

Thinking about Adrian made Layla sigh, a dark hole opening in her heart. She suddenly remembered her mission and all the reasons she was here, and they swamped her. Tempeste Durant saw it and his face softened. With a wry smile, he gestured to the bathroom. "You should get cleaned up. I'll have tea ready soon."

"Thanks."

Moving to her room, she began to strip off her sodden garb, not bothering to close the door. Tempeste was gay; she figured he wouldn't care if she got naked. He didn't, bustling about the kitchen and starting the kettle boiling. Moving to the shared bathroom with only a white towel wrapped around her, Layla showered with the door open like she'd once done when Arron had been the only one home in the Seattle house, then bustled back to her room with a towel wrapped around her body and one twisting up her hair. By the time she was dressed in the yoga pants she'd brought and her old comfortable grey v-neck shirt, Tempeste was pouring two steaming mugs of chamomile and having a seat at the small dining table.

Tempeste slid her mug over as she sat. Though he'd taken off his jacket and knife-rig now, which Layla saw laying upon his bed, he'd left on the rest of his sodden outfit as if he didn't terribly mind being wet, though the shirt was half-unbuttoned with the sleeves rolled up now. Layla saw how beautifully sculpted the Siren's chest was, lean and graceful just like Reginald's, though Tempeste was taller and more slender through the shoulders like Adrian. She tried to stop staring at his nearly opalescent white skin as she sipped her tea, but it was hard.

Sirens were just so fetching, gay or not.

"Damn. Why are your kind so attractive?" Layla blurted out suddenly, curious.

Tempeste chuckled as he blew on his tea, pleasure flashing through his grey-gold eyes. "It's our way. Sirens are the most attractive Lineage in the Twilight Realm, besides Ephilohim and Ephemerals like Sylvania."

"Is it wiles? Or just natural beauty?" Layla mused, her gaze drifting to Tempeste's sculpted chest.

"A bit of both." He smiled, letting her ogle him but not responding to her gaze. "We have a natural allure. Sirens are mesmeric, it's why you hear stories of mariners wooed to their death upon the rocks not just by Siren-song, but also by a Siren's beauty beneath the moonlight. Male or female, it doesn't matter. We're all this way."

"I've not met any female Sirens yet."

"Prepare to be astounded." Tempeste gave a secretive smile, blowing on his tea. "If I wasn't entirely gay, I'd have mounted dozens of them by now. They're incredible creatures. Though the birth-rate for female Sirens is about one-in-twenty. There's a reason Siren males are able to breed in Dragon form. Because the females are very hard to come by."

"Huh." Layla pondered that, seeing the crazy hand of evolution at work. "I would have thought from human stories that Sirens were all women."

"No, but female Sirens are the most powerful." Tempeste blew on his tea and sipped. "Nearly each one that gets born has Royal abilities. And they can be very cruel, reveling in causing mayhem over their beauty. Hence, enjoying luring human mariners to their deaths, before such things were banned by the High Court and enforced by the Intercessoria."

"Interesting." Layla sipped her tea. "So is the Intercessoria the High Court's right hand?"

"Yes." Tempeste set his tea down, regarding her with a level directness. "Just like your human judicial system, we have ours. The Intercessoria are called on to investigate many different issues, from immigration concerns between Realms to missing persons reports, to stolen items, to dealing with clan wars."

"Do clans have their own internal policing systems?" Layla wondered, thinking back to Rachida Rhakvir and her frightening position in Adrian's clan.

"They do." Tempeste nodded. "Though if a clan can't solve a particular issue according to their own internal laws with minimal disruption to the outside world, the Intercessoria get involved. We were originally created to be a policing system between clans, to aid the High Court in solving disputes and putting out fires that might lead to inter-clan wars. That is still largely what we do, though we address many other issues as well."

"What about the war between the North Sea Sirens and the Blood Dragons of Norway and Sweden?" Layla asked pointedly. "Isn't that currently ongoing?"

Tempeste heaved a sigh, his long fingers tapping his mug. "If a clan war threatens the general populace, or humans, the Intercessoria get heavily involved. But if it occurs in a fairly remote region in the Twilight Realm…it's generally allowed to run its course. Our clan's war is being let burn because it's raging up in the North Sea and in less populated areas of Norway. Clan wars can be brutal, and ours has been, but not as brutal as some. Crystal Dragons are famous for clan wars so terrible, they kill nearly everyone on both sides within a day of non-stop battle."

"Like Dusk's Egyptian Crystal clan. Was their war with the Tunisians allowed to rage because they had their battle out in the desert?"

"Partly." Tempeste's gaze became thoughtful with sadness. "But also partly because the Intercessoria heard about that battle too late to stop it. Crystal Dragons have long-simmering tempers, and they take deep offense at slights. Clan feuds can simmer beneath the surface for centuries. And then – pop – an affront happens, and suddenly everyone in a clan is rushing to battle within minutes. That's what happened with the Egyptian and Tunisian Crystal Dragons. Crystal Dragon battles are hard to predict and even harder to control, as they often happen deep underground. They frequently spill over into the human realm, as earthquakes, tsunamis, and volcanic eruptions."

Layla wanted to ask Tempeste more, when she suddenly yawned from the long day and the chamomile tea. Even though she hid it with her hand, Tempeste smiled, then pushed up from the table. "You're tired. It's been a long day for both of us. Go get some sleep, and we'll return to the cliffs in the morning."

"Sounds like a plan."

Rising, Layla moved to her room. For some reason, she felt safer leaving the door open a touch with the Jud nearby rather than closing it. Sliding into bed, she turned out the shell-encrusted bedside light. She could still see light from the kitchen and hear Tempeste puttering around, washing their mugs and straightening chairs. She heard him check the front door, then saw him check the French doors to the rooftop patio with the impeccability of a bodyguard. Closing her eyes, Layla heard him at last retire to bed with a creaking of mattress springs.

Like her, he left his door open, and she found it comforting.

Snuggling into the crisp sheets, Layla found herself lulled by the sound of the ocean outside. Soon it was inside her mind, and for the first time in ages, she did not dream of the desert. Instead, she stood upon a rocky headland high above the ocean, watching seagulls wheel and cry in the fresh salt spray. A luminous dawn surrounded her, glinting golden off the waves. As she stood, feeling her heart lift in the new day, she saw a man step out of the sea. Far down upon the beach, he emerged from the water naked, draped in strings of pearls and seaweed. His only true ornament was a pearl and gold belt woven around his sculpted hips. As he walked out from the surf with a dancer's grace, his long golden hair flowing down over one shoulder like a river of sunlight, Layla felt her heart catch in her chest.

His eyes found hers, up where she stood upon the promontory. Grey light with flecks of gold smote Layla upon her high perch, shining out from his achingly handsome face. Far below, he smiled softly to see her – a winsome smile full of bold pleasure and oceanic desire.

And then he opened his lips. A song emerged from his throat, colored by all the orchestrations of the sea. Impossible harmonies flooded Layla; beautiful melodies as ephemeral as the crashing waves far below. As she listened, her body began to melt into that sound, becoming spray and salt, sand and pearl.

And as he wooed her, she fell forward off her rocky promontory – down into the crashing surf below.

Layla woke with a start, the taste of brine and the smooth flesh of the oyster in her mouth. Reginald's oceanic scent from her dream drowned her and she gasped, her eyelids fluttering as she tried to struggle beneath that towering wave and lost. Gasping for air, she felt him rush in – kissing her like the entirety of the ocean rushing into her body, dark and darker. Layla struggled for breath; she struggled for consciousness.

Falling beneath the enormous weight of Reginald's passion.

She gasped, clutching her throat as Reginald's kiss and his magic drowned her from afar. There was motion in the hall – Tempeste suddenly rushed in, throwing himself to the bed and ripping Reginald's choker from her neck. The clasp broke; pearls scattered through the room with a terrible rattle as Layla finally gasped a clear breath. Cradling her close, Tempeste poured a freshening breath in through her lips in a similar way to Adrian, until she could breathe again.

Layla's heart hammered in her chest. Fear burned through her as she gasped in Tempeste's arms, as he flicked on the bedside light and cradled her face in his hands, gazing from one eye to the other. With a growl, he slipped both earrings from her ears, and Layla's breath came easier. He set them aside on the bedside table, and though he inspected her eyes again, he didn't reach for the bracelet.

"Are you all right?" He spoke softly, intent.

"I don't know." Layla gasped, rubbing her neck where the choker had been – so tight and pleasurable in her dream of Reginald that she'd wanted it to take her down. "What happened?"

"You were resonating with my brother, strongly, through the pearls." Tempeste's pale gaze was intense as he scanned her eyes again.

198

"He was dreaming and so were you. You connected, through the jewelry. Reginald has always had terrible control in his dreams. He nearly drowned you with his unrestrained power."

"The choker...?" Layla glanced around. Seeing the choker laying upon the coverlet, she picked it up. Five of the six strands of pearls were intact; only one had broken. But the clasps were ruined; there was no way it was going back around her neck without a jeweler to fix it.

"I'm sorry. I didn't have time to take it off properly." Tempeste's gaze was sad as he looked down at the choker also. "I'll find the pearls and store them safely. They call to me; even if they rolled far, it won't be any trouble to collect them."

"Is it safe to fall asleep again with these things on?" Layla glanced at the bracelet doubtfully.

"Your irises are back to their normal color." Tempeste smiled. "They went ice-blue for a moment there, full of my brother's power. If your power is once again dominant, it should be safe to sleep with just the bracelet. I'll store the earrings and the choker in my briefcase until tomorrow."

"Good plan."

But though Layla was relieved, something inside her also felt bereft. The sensation of Reginald kissing her in her dream had been so profound, so hot with passion and deep with his oceanic pull that she found herself slipping back into the sensation after Tempeste gathered up all the scattered pearls from the coverlet and the floor. Saying his goodnights, he turned off the light, stepping back to his own room with the broken choker and earrings in his palm.

But like a command had been left inside her with the fury of the sea behind it, Layla found herself drifting back into dreams of the ocean after Tempeste left. Though they were still vivid, they were also calmer – intimately pleasant as Reginald's soft lips found hers again on the edge of sleep. Falling hard into his power though she didn't choke on it now, Layla surrendered to his kiss – tasting oysters and ocean water and sunlight with every breath.

Feeling the surge of his body all around her in the night.

CHAPTER 18 – PHOENIX

Layla woke early; too early. The sun was barely up over the mountains, lighting a screen of mist that coated the morning ocean. As waves crashed outside in the harbor, Layla could still feel the crashing of her dreams. She lingered in bed, staring out the misty window; feeling Reginald's passion surging around her still. She didn't think she'd dreamt of anything else, all night. Being in his arms, moving with him, kissing him – a thousand pleasures still washed through her, making her heat and shiver.

It was confusing, and as Layla pushed up from bed, she could feel her vast unrest. As if Reginald had somehow gotten under her skin, he lingered all around her with the fresh scent of the morning ocean. Going to her purse, left the night before in her room when they'd gone out for dinner, Layla found the phone Dusk had given her, magically encrypted to connect her to the Hotel. Pulling on her now-dry sweater from the back of a chair, she dialed Dusk's direct line, then padded out to the main room.

Glancing into Tempeste's room, she saw he was still asleep. Sleeping naked, he'd cast the covers off his upper body, and Layla couldn't help but stare. He was chiseled perfection just like Reginald, though Layla could see how his skin was slightly thinner; more mature. He stirred as if he felt her watching, and as the phone continued to ring, Layla stepped quickly to the patio doors, unlocking them and stepping outside.

As she did, the phone was answered. "Layla? Are you all right?"

"Hi Dusk." A relieved smile blossomed over Layla's face to hear him. Everything suddenly seemed alright with Dusk on the line. Her twisting, heated dreams of Reginald were banished as Layla inhaled the fresh salt air, feeling her connection to Dusk strengthen now that his voice was on the other line. "I'm ok. Just checking in. I forgot to do it last night."

"Understandable." He murmured gently. "You had a long day of travel. Thanks for calling me now, though."

"Sure." So many unsaid emotions breathed between them in that moment of silence, until Layla spoke again. "How are things at the Hotel?"

"As well as can be managed." Dusk's voice was low, and Layla got the feeling he wasn't alone. She heard him move as if going to a quieter location, before he spoke again. "In all honesty, it's a shit-show. The Owners are demanding to see Adrian, and we can't produce him. Thankfully, the Intercessoria haven't told any Owners that they have Adrian in custody, but they're still pouring all over this place looking for clues about Hunter, and there's not much we can do. Reginald's brother Bastien is causing trouble, and meanwhile, Reginald's conveniently begun to explore his independence as Head Courtier."

"Independence?" Layla thought again of Reginald's kiss, and his exquisite nakedness in her dreams. "What do you mean?"

"I mean, he's just doing as he fucking pleases in the last twenty-four hours." Dusk sounded peeved, but also impressed. "He's wandering around like Hugh Hefner at the Playboy mansion, and no amount of cajoling is changing his mind to act just exactly how he wants to right now. The Madame is fretting. She believes it's a power play against his brother Bastien, but I disagree – I think Aldo's facing some intense identity crisis. And to make it all worse, we still don't have Sylvania's body back to do a memorial as the Intercessoria are holding it for investigation. I wish you were here, Layla. Things are just so convoluted right now."

This last was said with such a sigh that Layla's heart went out to Dusk. She rarely heard him so stressed. Dusk was the consummate problem-solver, yet it seemed that he'd finally met his match – too many problems of too great a magnitude that couldn't be solved.

"Easy, breathe." She spoke gently into the phone. The morning wind whipped and Layla tucked her curls behind her ear. "You can keep it all together, Dusk. I know you can."

"Isn't that usually my line?" She heard him smile through the phone.

"Well, now it's mine." Layla smiled back, walking to the edge of the patio and looking far out over the morning ocean, watching the mist begin to lift. "We're all facing new territory. I can't say what the Paris Hotel is going to look like from here on out… but I'm going to do my damnedest to make sure we're all safe."

"You sound like the problem-solver now," Dusk smiled again. "How is the search for the Aviary going?"

"Pretty good." Layla scanned the cliffs below, spying the grassy promontory where she'd walked off into the water the night before. "I found the cliff-access last night, but no bridge materialized. I'm going to try again this morning."

"Be careful." Dusk's tone held warning. "Even Reginald's pearls can't keep you from falling off a cliff and drowning."

"Well thankfully, Tempeste has been a big help in that area." Layla smiled, enjoying how protective Dusk was of her. Just then, their connection began to fray, cutting out with static. She heard Dusk's voice come tinny and fractured as he spoke again.

"Come again, Layla? Who did you say was helping you?"

"Tempeste!" She spoke into the phone, louder now. "Tempeste

Durant! Dusk? Are you there?"

The line was fraying dramatically now, with electric whines and pops. Glancing around, Layla looked for the closest cell phone tower, but didn't see one on the cliffs. Moving to a different spot, she kept speaking Dusk's name and heard her name come back from him, but the line was truly fucked now. Turning, she glanced at the balcony doors to see Tempeste was awake now, watching her out on the patio with a concerned frown. She waved and he waved back, then set a hand to the doorknob and came out, dressed in just his slacks from the day before.

"Layla? Who are you talking to?"

"Dusk." She growled. At last, the phone line finally cut out, replaced by a busy tone. With a harsh sigh, Layla touched the screen to hang up. "Or at least I was. Fucking cell phones."

"I don't think there's a cell tower nearby. Reception's probably spotty all through this area." Like her, Tempeste glanced around, scanning the adjacent hills as the early morning sun began to flood down the crevasses. Golden-rose rays lit hilltop vineyards as far as the eye could see along the coastline, showing the grand beauty of Cinque Terre. Though the morning was glorious, Layla felt darkened. She tried dialing Dusk's line four more times but got a busy signal each time, and the same for the Hotel's front desk. Her belly rumbled, and with a growl Layla finally gave up, resolving to call Dusk back later.

"I need something to eat. How about you?" Layla spoke as she turned to go back inside.

"I could eat. So how are things at the Hotel?" Tempeste asked casually as he followed her, moving to the kitchenette and starting some espresso, though his husky-blue gaze was wary.

"Shitty, apparently." Layla sighed, flopping to a seat at the formica breakfast table and setting down her phone.

"And Heathren? Does he have any leads on Hunter?"

"Not that Dusk said." Layla watched Tempeste's lean, elegant hands move through pulling espresso and steaming milk at the fancy little espresso machine on the counter. "Your people are still crawling all over the Hotel, looking for clues."

"I'd expect no less." Tempeste finished their espressos, then brought them to the table. Going to the fridge, he pulled out the local delicacies they'd snacked on the day before, opening them for a casual breakfast. Layla began to eat, finding that sardines and olives made a surprisingly good breakfast. Moving to the small stove-top, Tempeste sliced a crusty loaf of bread and toasted them in a pan with olive oil and herbs, making crostini. He brought them to the table and Layla dug in with the olive tapenade from the welcome basket, creating a repeat of their appetizer the night before.

"So, down to the cliffs again this morning?" Layla spoke around a bite, determined to find the Aviary.

"Indeed. Intercessoria reports suggest that Arini's fortress is most approachable after dawn."

"Seriously? Why didn't you tell me that last night?" Layla set her crostini down with an incredulous look.

"It was theory I had yet to test." Barely suppressed laughter curled Tempeste's lips. "Now we know."

"You're very cavalier for Intercessoria, you know." Layla shot back with irritation.

"I enjoy Disneyland and Six Flags, Layla." Tempeste grinned around his tasso of espresso. "I like a thrill. It's one of the reasons I joined the Intercessoria, to do field work. I love being with my family, but I also love having a thrill ride. On this job… it's always something different. Different places to go; different issues to solve. Different dangers."

Layla could see it. She was learning that Sirens had a push-pull between control and recklessness, almost moreso than any other type of Dragon. Shaking her head, Layla rose from the table. "I'm going to get dressed."

"Meet you out here in ten, and then we'll go down to the wharf."

Layla turned away without comment, truly irritated now that she knew Tempeste had used her as a test last night. It pissed her off, but didn't seem to bother him in the slightest. As Layla dressed in a plum wrap sweater and skinny jeans that hadn't seen any seawater, Tempeste went to dress also. Re-packing her rolling bag, she glanced at her possessions. Taking up her passport, her Hotel credit card, and Arini's blue feather in its silken pouch, Layla snapped it back inside her shirt on her bra, then slid her phone and the rest into a zipper-pocket of her jeans. She'd leave everything else behind with Tempeste, just in case things got hairy at the Aviary. Moving back to the living area, she saw he was fully dressed now, but in a clean navy pinstriped suit, different from before.

"How... did you pack a second suit in your briefcase?" Layla blinked.

"Magic." He smiled, his blue eyes amused. "Intercessoria Judiciary always pack light, but our briefcases can hold a surprising amount of belongings and weapons. I always bring at least one change of clothing on assignment. Come on, let's get down to the cliffs."

"Wait." Layla did an internal inventory. "Reginald's earrings?"

"Ah." Tempeste gave a rueful smile, then went to his briefcase. Opening it, he fetched out the earrings and handed them to Layla. "Here. I'll keep the choker safe while you're inside the Aviary."

"Fair enough." Fixing the pearl and diamond earrings in her lobes, Layla heard a vague surge of ocean sound in her ears before it died away. The earrings felt heavier today, as if something about her intimacy with Reginald last night had changed the weight of them against her skin. Layla frowned, touching one, then adjusting the bracelet at her wrist – wondering if everything just felt odd today because she was missing the choker to complete the set.

"Something wrong?" Tempeste frowned, watching her fidget.

"It's nothing," Layla dismissed, straightening. "Let's go."

"Certainly."

Moving to the door, Tempeste unlocked it and they retraced their steps of the night before. Except today, the cliffside town of Manarola was glorious with morning's first rays beginning to ease over the eastern hills, painting the colorful buildings in a golden glory. Tourists in hats with cameras were already up and about as Tempeste hurried Layla down to the quay, citing that he wanted to get to the cliff-walk before anyone interrupted them.

Soon, Layla was back on the grassy promontory, facing the ocean. White cruise ships passed far out in the aqua seas, colorful fishing boats trawling the near shore for a morning catch. As Layla stepped to the rocky edge and a brisk morning wind stirred her hair, she felt a sudden panic. The last thing she wanted to do was step off this damn cliff again, but she knew Tempeste had her back now, even if it was a fairly uncomfortable salvation.

Taking a deep breath, Layla set her hand to King Arini's feather in its silken pouch between her breasts.

And then stepped off the cliff, into the abyss.

She stumbled. Where there had been nothing before, there was now an arching stone bridge leading from her promontory three hundred feet over the water and ending at a tremendous sea-stack out in the swirling tides. It hadn't been there before, and as Layla gaped at it, she saw there was not one but five sea-stacks in tight formation at the end of the stone causeway, all connected by high stone bridges. An enormous fortress spanned all five sea-stacks, gulls wheeling around its towers in the golden morning sunlight.

Glancing behind, Layla saw the stone bridge ended in a grey mist behind her. Tempeste was gone; so was the headland and the town of Manarola. As if this place existed in a bubble, the same grey fog surrounded it about a mile in circumference, though the sky was blue above and morning sun smote the towers. As if the fortress was part of the human world but heavily hidden in a glamour by the mist, Layla began to walk forward on the stone bridge, marveling at the Aviary.

Because it was an Aviary. At once the solid stone of an old Roman fort but also supported by the whimsical magics of the Twilight Realm, towers soared up at impossible, broken angles, dangling in midair. Rope bridges connected these to the main halls, even higher stones floating in midair as if suspended in the sky. Enormous cocoons of what looked like nests dangled from these floating stones, swaying in the morning breeze.

As Layla watched, a magnificent bird with gold and crimson plumage launched from one egg-shaped nest, taking wing on the sea-air. Enormous as a lion but sleek and graceful, curling feathers streamed from its wings and tail and from its long crest-plumage – a Phoenix, in its Dragon-form. And then a second Phoenix followed from the same nest, launching into the breeze, this one a luminous silver-grey that flashed like a fish as it flew through the sky.

As Layla watched, they careened on the air, rolling and diving in movements that were at once serpentine and also eagle-like. A raptor's screech split the morning air, with the deeper roar of a Dragon beneath it. As Layla watched, she saw a flash of sleek scales through the cascading plumage – the diving beasts like a primordial combination of Dragon and bird. They were the closest thing Layla had seen to depictions of bird-dinosaurs like the archaeopteryx, and as she stood on the bridge in stunned silence she realized they had plumage that brought to life Mesoamerican stories of Quetzalcoatl.

Layla blinked, wondering if those stories of the feathered serpent god had been Phoenix.

Moving forward, she found herself entranced by the beautiful creatures as more joined them in the dawn sky. Colored in incredible jewel tones, they soared through the blue, playing in the golden mists. Layla saw them dive beneath the sea, coming up with fish in their talons and curved raptor beaks; sometimes even small sharks seized in their cruel grips. As Layla neared the vaulted doors of the fortress, bound with gold that shone in the morning sun, she saw them crank open.

A sluice of birdsong flowed through Layla's mind as the Phoenix King Falliro Arini himself moved out from the fortress. Stepping down the stone stairs, he took up Layla's hands, kissing them in a wave of grace. "Layla Price. I felt you coming. Be welcome in my Aviary."

"King Falliro Arini. Thank you so much for inviting me." She responded.

"It is my pleasure."

The Phoenix King's golden eyes glowed in the morning sunlight as he regarded her, and Layla found herself soothed by his presence. Naked but wearing a cascading robe of midnight-blue feathers with a high collar that was open at the front, King Falliro Arini's sleek cobalt plumage shone with a rich array of colors in the high morning. In his human form, he towered over Layla, nearly eight feet in height. His lean body was covered in a silky blue down, a crest of long cobalt feathers like hair fluttering in the sea-winds. His smile was bright, his chiseled features outlined by dark lines of feather at his cheekbones and temples, like Dusk's Dragon-scales. Cruel black talons tickled her hand from his fingertips, the same jutting from his bare feet with their high arches and birdlike structure.

Listening to King Arini's lovely birdsong in her mind, seeing him beaming at her with his perfectly radiant smile lightened Layla's heart. For the first time in days, she felt safe and calm, and all at once it seemed impossible that he would have invited her here just to send her to her death in the ocean. As he smiled, clasping her hands warmly, Layla's heart suddenly expanded. King Arini was a good man. She could feel he was an ally, and Adrian was right to trust him.

"I need to talk to you." She spoke suddenly. "About Hunter."

"The void-shadow." King Arini's golden gaze was deep with knowing. "I can feel questions moving all through you, Dragon Bind. I will answer as many as I may, though I sense your time here is short. Your friends are in danger, aren't they?"

"Adrian's been captured by the Intercessoria," she breathed, her heart twisting. "They'll release him if we give them everything we know about Hunter."

"Then we will give them everything we know." King Arini's eyes glittered, wry but calm. "Come. Your body has not had a proper breakfast. Walk with me and see our fortress. And we shall speak of details to free your mate. This way, honored guest."

Tucking her arm into his, King Falliro Arini escorted Layla toward the fortress. Walking on the balls of his feet like a bird, he moved up the stone steps, guiding Layla into an enormous vaulted receiving-hall. Though the old Roman fortress was half-tumbled, it had been repaired with magic, shimmering mirages of light and air shoring up every broken arch and tumbled wall. Set with banners upon all sides woven from colorful feathers, there were dream-catchers of feather and sea-bones dangling from every arch.

The effect was of a broken, abandoned palace that yet breathed with airy life. Gazing around the gargantuan hall, Layla saw more birds than she'd ever seen anywhere. As she watched, a pair of cliff-swallows zoomed in through one of the open-air walls, chirruping up to a high nook and feeding a clutch of viciously peeping chicks. Birds of paradise rested upon high ledges; peacocks strolled around the Greco-Roman tiled floors. A wall of vines held hundreds of parrots in blue-canary colors, making a ruckus in the bright morning.

Layla saw every kind of bird, seed-eating or fruit-eating or carnivorous, even a pair of golden eagles perching out on a dead tree branch over the sea, scanning the water below for breakfast. The Aviary had every kind of plant to support its teeming, beautiful life; fruit trees growing up through the cracks in the floor and vines winding through the broken walls. The vegetation shored the Aviary up as much as Phoenix-magic did, and the overall impression was of a ruined cathedral – sacked long ago and returned to life in the most beautiful way.

As Layla had that thought, the sun caught upon a high round window at the far end of the hall. The emblem of a screeching Phoenix with dark violet plumage was illuminated, made of stained glass as large as the famous rose windows of Notre Dame. Layla stood, overpowered by its glory, as King Falliro Arini paused by her side.

"This was a stronghold of my people in olden days," he murmured. "And to the Phoenix it has been returned in my time. But come, that is a story to tell over breakfast. This way."

Still unable to speak from the glory all around her, Layla nodded. King Falliro Arini smiled his beaming smile, then led them through an arch to the left, the doors to the fortress closing with a boom behind them.

CHAPTER 19 – NEST

Layla and the Phoenix King moved into a vaulted dining-hall nearly as enormous as the receiving-hall. Inside, Phoenix moved about in their human forms, taking bounty from a massive trestle-table piled with dishes of every sort – pomegranates and persimmons, swordfish and mussels, roast boar and fresh nuts, seeds, and chutneys. In all the ostentatious opulence of the breakfast spread, however, Layla noted an absence of eggs or bird-meat. All around, Phoenix nodded to their King, dipping their heads gracefully as he escorted Layla. He nodded back, moving Layla to the giant table and taking up a gilded plate for her.

Handing it to her with a smile, he nodded at the spread. "Take what you like. It is magically-preserved, do not worry about anything going to waste. This mound will feast the entire Aviary for a month, and when it wanes, we shall hunt and forage to replace it."

"Thanks." Layla didn't quite know what to say. As she rounded the table, boggled by the excess of gilded platters piled with delicacies, she felt almost shy. She'd been in the presence of opulence at the Red Letter Hotel Paris, but this was the dining hall of a King, and a powerful one. But as Layla selected a spread of Italian meats and cheeses, plus mango and sliced persimmon, she realized that this hall was informal. Phoenix mingled, taking what they wanted, then sitting at smaller social tables to chit chat or suddenly manifesting enormous wings in a half-shift and launching into flight, taking their breakfast up to the vaulted arches to sit and watch the morning.

As she glanced around, Layla realized each Phoenix was as different as the birds they mimicked. Some had ostentatious feathers like peacocks grown into long fanciful gowns around their downy nakedness, some were a sleek pearl-grey like mourning doves, while others were entirely black with an iridescent sheen like crow feathers. Birdsong chirruped through the hall as Layla took her plate to a long table with a gilded wooden throne at the end. It was Arini's high seat, though it was modest, and as he claimed it, he beckoned for Layla to take the chair at his right. She did, listening to the lovely trilling speech of the Phoenix mingling through the hall with the calls of real birds. Though as Layla settled in and King Arini poured a chalice of water for her from a copper ewer, he continued to speak in heavily-accented English.

"I am pleased you came to us, Layla." He eyed her with the full wisdom of his stunning gold irises and black pupils. "I have wanted to speak with you again. Tell me, what is the situation at the Paris Hotel?"

"Not good, I'm afraid." Layla sighed.

King Arini gestured for her to continue and Layla launched into the full tale as she ate, conscious of keeping her voice low in the echoing hall. Through it all, King Arini nodded sagely. When she had finally finished her tale of Hunter and the mayhem he had caused by killing Sylvania as Adrian, the Phoenix King heaved a sigh.

"I wondered when something like this would happen." He spoke softly, his golden gaze penetrating. "For that was how it was long ago, when the Hunter stalked me. Over and over, he would take the faces of those I held dear, slaughtering others who were close to me. Leaving me terrible gifts of the dead, trying to befriend me with false visages to get me to join his cause as a Royal Dragon Bind. He does not seem to understand the concepts of trust or friendship, and thus has no sanctity for life. I perceive, as I did of old, that Hunter is a solitary creature,

213

lonely and dark in his heart. As dark as his eyes when he is angry."

Carefully filing all this information away to tell the Intercessoria later, not to mention Adrian and Dusk, Layla nodded. "I've seen his eyes when he's crossed. They're terrible."

"And yet, he has an agenda I cannot fathom." King Arini sat back in his wood and gilt throne. "He seems to wish to unite the Dragon Binds under his banner, yet… he has no banner. He is a more clandestine creature even than I, and that is saying much. If he never steps out of the shadows to show his true face… which of the remaining Dragon Binds will come to him?"

"Remaining Dragon Binds?" Layla's brows rose. "Only Hunter has ever said anything to me of other Dragon Binds still living. I thought he was lying."

"Oh no," King Arini's gaze grew piercing and sly. "He was not lying. They are out there. Do not think your Lineage is entirely extinct, though they may seem so. They have gone into hiding so deep over the years that even the blackest arts of the Intercessoria cannot find them. But I can."

"You can?" Layla sat forward.

"I can smell them on the winds." Arini smiled slyly now. "Do you think it was mere coincidence that I was there at the Hotel the day you arrived? I had scented you out in the human world many years before, just as I have scented out a number of other Binds. But waiting to see you casually at the Hotel to satisfy my curiosity about you was the right move. As a Phoenix, I need an intense amount of glamour to travel the human world. And those with Twilight blood can often see through it."

"Where are the rest of the Binds?" Layla spoke breathlessly. "How many of them are out there?"

"Perhaps a dozen, hidden in both the human and Twilight Realms." King Arini spoke softly. Reaching out, he stroked a black talon over Layla's cheek. "You are the youngest, but not the weakest. Not by far."

"How do I contact them?"

"Patience." King Arini smiled gently. "There will be time for that. In the meantime, I must relate to you everything I know about Hunter, and everything I have presumed over the years. Come, walk with me. Let us explore my Aviary and enjoy its many heights, and I will tell you the deepest part of what I know about our mutual nemesis."

Rising from the table, Arini extended his hand. Layla took it, finding the touch of his black talons somehow thrilling upon her skin. Wrapping her hand around his lean arm, he led them out of the hall and up a stone staircase with no railing that curved around the side of a massive turret. Heading to the top, they came out upon the roof of the world. It was actually only a few hundred feet above the sea, but it seemed like a mountaintop as Layla took in the wide vantage of sun and glimmering water. From here, she could see the mainland, though the near shore was still obscured by rolling grey fog. Far above, other turrets towered, but as Layla shaded her eyes and glanced above, she could discern no way of getting up to them.

"How does one get all the way up there?" She asked.

With a sly smile, Arini glanced down at her. "Do you trust me, Layla Price?"

"I'm here alone with you, aren't I?" She spoke, wondering where this was going.

With a delighted laugh that trilled like thousands of birds, King Falliro Arini suddenly scooped Layla off her feet into his arms. With a startled *eep*, she clung to him around the neck as enormous cobalt wings suddenly flared from his back through slits in his robe, moving the air in a gale wind. With a powerful launch from his strong, lean thighs, he catapulted them up into the morning sky – a screech of

215

delight issuing from his throat with the roar of a Dragon.

Layla clung to him, terrified of flying so exposed and so far above the ocean as they wheeled upwards with powerful beats of Arini's wings. He moved them fast through the morning air as if Layla weighed nothing, holding her firmly against his chest so she wouldn't fall. As her heart hammered from fear and exhilaration, and her Dragon roared to feel so weightless and free, King Arini flew them up to the topmost turret of the five islands – a floating turret not reached by any bridge. As they flew up to a wide patio of flagstone, Layla saw there were no egg-shaped nests dangling from this turret, but that the entire rear of the tower had fallen away and been replaced by a woven bower of feathers and sticks, grasses, shells, and sundry.

As King Arini touched down on the wide balcony, a lush Persian garden of fruit trees and vines sprawling through the broken stone all around, he gave a laugh of delight. His eyes sparkled with gold as he made a flexing motion and those enormous cobalt wings whisked back inside his shoulders, leaving him in man-form once more. But his gaze was pleased as Layla gaped at his shift – amazed that he could accomplish it so easily.

"How do you do that?" She spoke, as a morning breeze whipped the height of the broken tower. "Transform so easily?"

"Phoenix are one of the few shifting Lineages that need no down time." He chuckled, birdsong rolling through his laugh. "We can also partially-shift with ease, experiencing no discomfort. As the smallest of the Dragons, it gives us an evolutionary advantage to be able to change into our beast on the fly, so to speak, or partially change as I did just now."

"Where are we?" Layla glanced around the wide balcony and garden, seeing three vaulted entrances of stone enmeshed with the enormous bird-basket on the side of the tower. Over each arch, a thick screen of cobalt and gold silk fluttered in the wind.

"This is my private bower." Arini smiled. "Here we can speak of your troubles, and not even the winds will hear us. Come."

Leading her by the hand, King Arini escorted Layla to the centermost arch and pulled the silk aside; admitting them to a space that was both whimsical and homey – and not at all what Layla would have expected. She laughed as she entered; she couldn't help it. About fifty feet in diameter, King Falliro Arini's bower consumed the end of the turret, though the vaulted windows overlooking the sea were open to the air, rippling with the same barely-visible barrier keeping the fortress together in the lower levels. It permitted a gentle breeze, though the space wasn't chilly. Between the archways, up into a pinnacle far above like a Russian onion dome, the bower had been woven full of branches and grass, feathers and shells, bleached bones and even long strips of colorful fabric.

But it was the décor that amused Layla most. Cascading from the ceiling on long threads of silk were the most garish and lovely decorations. Collections of shiny beach-glass shimmered in nets of fine silk. CD's had been strung up in the thousands, creating a rainbow-shimmer everywhere Layla looked as they spun in the sea breeze. Strings of Swarovski crystals hung next to Mardi-Gras plastic beads in every color. Enormous fetishes of feathers had been strung up, spinning and fluttering in the wind.

The overall effect was intoxicating, and it was a moment before Layla realized King Arini was gesturing her over to an enormous sleeping-area overflowing with colorful silk, giant pillows, and soft down. The huge nest was corralled by woven pinion-feathers, and Layla grinned as she stepped over the retaining barrier and into all that softness and fluff. She sighed in delight as she sank to her hands and knees in it, feeling that perfect, springy nest swallow her. King Arini had splayed out on his side in his nest, at ease. He didn't make a move to touch Layla as she slid down to her belly, reveling in all that softness – only smiled at her enjoyment, beaming at her with his very gold eyes.

"I like your style." Layla grinned, still running her hands over everything. "But my visit here is platonic, right? No ulterior motives?"

"I would be lying if I said I do not find you attractive," the King spoke pointedly, "but yes, this is all quite platonic. I brought you here because we can speak freely inside my bower. It is fortified with magics even more intense than the rest of the fortress, against prying ears and eyes. Even if you looked out the windows and yelled to the winds, no one would see or hear you."

"Good to know." Even though his words satisfied Layla, that he wasn't going to try and put the moves on her, some part of her was disappointed. She could imagine herself splaying out in all this softness naked with King Arini's tall, strong body laying out atop her, rubbing her skin against all that luscious cobalt down. Just the idea of it made her Dragon stir eagerly inside her, and with only Reginald's bracelet and earrings to contain it, a generous wash of bourbon-orange scent simmered up around her.

King Arini chuckled. His lips parting, he inhaled the air with a very masculine look. "I can smell your attraction to me. No need to be shy about it. Phoenix are similar to Sirens in our attractiveness, though where theirs is mesmeric to the mind, ours is the allure of touch and texture. Rather like petting a cat – how it calls to the hands."

"I'm not embarrassed about being attracted to you," Layla spoke, "it's just new for me to feel this much heat around so many men. Especially so many powerful ones."

"Being a Royal Dragon Bind is a strange thing," Falliro's gaze softened. "I remember it well, the sensations of uncontrollable attraction to powerful people. It is not a thing to be ashamed of, Layla, only to be aware of. Your magic will crave all men, and even women, with power. Though it is your deeper choice of partners that will shape your destiny."

"I don't know if any of it has been my choice, exactly." Layla sighed, stretching out on her side and pulling a pillow up beneath her so she could prop her head on her hand. "Adrian, Dusk... they both seemed like accidents with my power."

"And yet, would you say that having them both in your life is a bad thing?" King Falliro eyed her knowingly.

Layla was silent a moment, pondering that. "Having Dusk in my life is definitely a good thing. I never would have thought when we first met that he'd be almost the perfect partner for me, but it's true. Adrian... I love Adrian with all my heart, but he's challenging. I can't get enough of him, yet he infuriates me."

"Safety and challenge," Arini spoke with a knowing glitter in his eyes, "they seem like the perfect balance of opposites. For we must have both a safe haven in our lives and a driving rod that challenges us to grow, if we are ever to become who we are truly meant to be."

Layla had never thought about it that way before, and suddenly having both Dusk and Adrian bound to her made the most sense it had ever made. "That's a good point. When I think back to other lovers I've had in my life, they were never balanced. They were always too extreme, in one way or another. Being with Dusk and Adrian together... well, we've not quite managed it, but the beginning of it was the most amazing, most balanced heat I've ever felt."

"Then keep your bound men close," King Arini spoke levelly, "for they will be a boon to you in hard times. If you can manage their tempers, and manage to Bind them together with you into one inseparable unit, your power will go far."

"It's not my job to manage their tempers." Layla frowned, not liking the sound of those words. "They're grown-ass men, they should be able to manage their own tempers."

King Arini chuckled, petting one taloned hand through the cobalt down of the nest. "Truer words were never spoken. I did not mean to offend. It is not a woman's job to smooth the tempers of irate men; too many women have endured terribly abusive situations trying to do so. What I meant was that as a Bind, you have the ability to overcome differences in your men's ideals, their jealousies, and the worries that trigger them to become bullish. You have magic that is specifically intended to overcome all obstacles, and all fears. Many Binds have used this power over the millennia to engage in acts of domination, Binding and then subduing those with power to their will. But there is a better way, one I would have explored more thoroughly had I not been stalked by Hunter."

"What better way?" Layla asked, curious.

"A Bind of equality and mutual respect that addresses the fears and needs of those bound to you," King Arini spoke knowingly. "It creates a compassionate kind of love. That is the strongest Bind. And one I have learned from, though I do not possess your magic anymore. Understand this, Layla Price: the ability to Bind another exists in all of us, and there are many types of Binds. Fear, need, grief. Honor, respect, duty. But the strongest of all of those is honest love; compassion. Find *that* aspect in your power… and you will have more strength in this world than any other Bind has ever achieved."

"Is that what Hunter wants?" Layla asked, mulling Arini's words over. "Does he want to Bind everything that lives with that kind of power?"

"Hunter." King Arini sighed, petting his hands over the soft down of the nest again. "We must speak of Hunter. For I know many things that may be useful to you. And to the Intercessoria, that I have long withheld from them. Though I despise their organization, it is time for me to admit their usefulness in this matter. Perhaps if I had enlisted them long ago, I could have stopped Hunter while his powers were still immature. But I fear his powers have grown terribly since he and I last met... and the task of finding him has become immeasurably difficult now because of it. Come, listen to my tale. And then we may decide how we can move forward against our mutual enemy – together."

CHAPTER 20 – MIMIC

King Falliro Arini's golden gaze went dark as he spoke of Hunter, all birdsong from him dying abruptly as he adjusted his reclining posture on the sprawling nest of feathers and silk. Something dangerous slid through his eyes, and suddenly his slender height seemed menacing, even lounging in his feathered robe as he was. But it wasn't menace toward Layla he displayed, only toward their mutual enemy. Like most Phoenix, Falliro Arini had a reputation for being peaceable, but Layla saw in that sudden change of intensity his other reputation – that he was also a furious warrior with a long history of success in battle.

"You have heard how Hunter infiltrated my most trusted hundreds of years ago," King Falliro Arini spoke quietly as he began his story, "but you have not heard specifically how he managed to gain access to my Aviary. And that is the tale I must tell you now, so you may understand his power."

"I thought your Aviary was impenetrable, except to those who have a personal invitation from you." Layla frowned.

"That is so," King Arini's gaze was acute as he smoothed one black-taloned hand over the downy nest. "And it still is the case. All except for Hunter. Which, unfortunately, is an ongoing problem for my security team."

Layla blinked hard, her heart hammering as she realized what he was saying. "You mean Hunter can still get in here? He still has access to your fortress? He could be in here right now, masquerading as one of your Phoenix?"

"Why do you think I've fortified my bower with all the most catastrophic magical spells I could find over the years?" King Arini's golden gaze glittered with a terrible wrath as he gestured around the whimsical dome. "My Phoenix know to never come in here unless led in *by the hand*, by me. Had I not led you in just now, all that mess above," Arini nodded to the suspended mobiles and fetishes, "would have focused the light from the windows upon you, like putting an ant under a magnifying glass. It works even with starlight and moonlight. You would have charred to death, no matter the time of day you tried to enter without my permission. Even for a Phoenix, the death would have been permanent. We burn hot to regenerate in ash and flame, but this fire burns hotter; melting flesh and bone into glass."

"Holy shit," Layla spoke, glancing up at all that glittering opulence and feeling like the hand of death was suspended above her now.

"Nothing I do is whimsy," Arini spoke darkly, his gaze intent upon her. "Not on the battlefield, and not in my home. All those luminous barriers you see shoring up my fortress contain spells of destruction for anyone not invited. Every feather fetish and mobile contains blasting-power to char an enemy. Spells researched, practiced, and incanted by me over thousands of years. Phoenix are the most talented *drachans* spell-masters outside of Blood Dragons. And I use that talent, to its utmost degree."

"So how can Hunter get in your fortress?" Layla asked, curious as to where all this was going. "If it's so well fortified with magical spells, how does he dodge them?"

"Because he doesn't need to dodge them." Arini sighed sadly, smoothing his talons over the nest again. "Hunter is the ultimate mimic of faces, irises, even scents. And not only that. When he kills someone… he can mimic their magic."

"What?" Layla breathed. Inside, her Dragon roared up in anger, though it was still stifled by Reginald's pearls. And yet, though King Arini's revelation was shocking, it also made sense. Hunter had killed Adam Rhakvir as a child, and had been able to mimic Adam's magic to such a degree that not even his own clan had suspected the imposter.

Only Heathren Merkami had suspected, though he'd never been able to prove anything.

"I do not know how his magical mimicry is done, for such a thing is thought impossible." Arini spoke again, a hard set to his lean shoulders as he gripped one taloned hand into the feathered nest. "Whether Hunter is some anomaly of magic or simply a great study, he has found a way. When he kills someone, he learns the vibrational imprint of their magic to such a degree that he can mimic it with near-perfect precision. And he once used that mimicry to gain invitation to my fortress. From which we have subsequently never been able to block him."

"How?" Layla asked, breathless with interest, though a dark trepidation writhed in her. "If he killed one of your Phoenix and mimicked them, wouldn't you have been able to find a body and figure it out eventually? Or discover Hunter through questioning or something?"

"No. Because the person he killed – was me." Arini spoke softly.

Layla gave a slow out-breath, seeing the depth of the problem and how much it destabilized the Aviary. "He can mimic you. He can wear other faces but mimic your magic when he comes in here, or just simply *be you*… and the wards in the Aviary don't know the difference. No matter how much you change them, those wards are imprinted to you. To your magic."

"And to Hunter's magic, when he takes my imprint." Arini spoke darkly, his gaze digging into Layla. "Though my wards keep the rest of my enemies out and keep the fortress hidden, my efforts are useless against Hunter."

"But how did he kill you?" Layla asked. "And how are you not actually dead?"

"That is a long tale." King Arini gave a wry smile, adjusting his lounging posture in the nest. "It was on the battlefield during the War of Five Giants, over a thousand years ago. I was leading the Phoenix army with my most trusted against the Blue Giants of inner Mesopotamia. We were in the middle of a vicious battle, when one of my generals turned on me. He tore into me with beak and talons, his eyes bled to a dark hunter-green from their usual gold. I didn't understand the change at the time, though I do now. We plummeted to the earth out of the sky as we fought, and at the last moment, Hunter released me to crash upon the serrated rocks below."

"He broke you, but it wasn't enough to kill you," Layla breathed.

"Oh, but it was." Arini eyed her darkly. "I was crushed, my insides pulped and my flesh rent from Hunter's talons. He flew down to my side as I died, placing his beak over mine and inhaling. I felt like my very essence was being ripped away. All the deepest parts of myself twisted, screaming in a way I'd never felt before. I'd died over the years, but this was something else – a dark magic I had never faced. As he ripped my Phoenix-essence away, devouring it, the last spark of my magic resisted. I burst into flame, charring into ash. He couldn't inhale me any longer, but the damage was done."

"He had mimicked your magic."

"Yes." Arini nodded. "By devouring and digesting it, I believe."

"But why did he want your magic? Was this when you were a Bind?" Layla asked.

"No. This was before I ever became a Bind. I don't know why Hunter wanted my magic; he did not act upon his new abilities right away. Centuries later, when I did resurrect with Bind powers, he finally used my resonance. He was able to get inside my fortress, simply by becoming me and walking right in. Every feather on his body pointed the way; every resonance inside him allowed him to cross my barriers. And then he killed, and hid the bodies, and took their faces. And so it went – a madhouse of mimicry that decimated all those closest to me at that time, as he tried to convince me to partner with him in his aims."

"But…" Layla's mind spun, trying to process all this information and store it to tell the Intercessoria later. She pushed up from the nest, sitting cross-legged as she chewed her lower lip, thinking. "How could Hunter imitate Adrian's magic to kill Sylvania? Adrian's not dead. Hunter never killed him."

"Adrian believes it was Hunter who killed his mother." Arini's glance was pointed as he replied. "Adrian and Juliette had very similar powers. Hunter was powerful when I knew him centuries ago, to be able to imitate the magic of someone he'd murdered. But now… I believe his power has matured, to be able to imitate the magic of the *family* of those he kills. Killing Juliette would have given him Royal Desert Dragon magic very similar to Adrian's, and an ability to make a deeply educated guess at the imprint of Adrian's magic – if he'd been allowed access to Adrian for a long enough time."

"Hunter took the form of Adrian's cousin Adam since they were kids," Layla spoke quietly, horrified as a black pit of fear and rage opened up inside her. "We thought he'd taken a person close to the Rhakvir family just to learn Adrian's secrets and business dealings. But what if… what if he did it so he could stay close to Adrian, long enough to mimic Adrian's magic? And kill using Adrian's face? Or maybe even Dusk's?"

That last thought sent shivers through Layla, her whole world feeling like it had suddenly turned upside-down.

"It seems likely," Arini spoke darkly. "Hunter is a cunning creature, Layla. I would put nothing past him, not even such a long-con as growing up for one hundred and fifty years as a Desert Dragon in order to study Adrian and become able to kill like him. Or anyone else he had significant contact with during that time. Dusk Arlohaim lost his father during the Egyptian-Tunisian Crystal War. We have no proof that it was not Hunter who killed Dusk's father Omar Arlohaim during that conflict – perhaps learning Arlohaim family abilities also."

"My god." Layla breathed, glancing up at Arini. "When Dusk examined Sylvania's body, he said it had been *vibrated apart* from within. It held Adrian's magical imprint and scent, but Adrian professed up and down that his power couldn't do such a thing."

"But Dusk's power can." King Arini took a deep inhalation. "Dusk can vibrate someone apart from deep inside; I know, because he has confessed this to me. He is afraid of his Crystal King learning the extent of his abilities and coming after him. He wanted me as an ally, if that ever came to pass. And yet, we may be comforted that Hunter cannot be in two places at once. We know one of his most recent aliases as Adam Rhakvir. Anywhere that you or I have seen Adam around company, we can be reasonably certain that that company was not Hunter."

"But just because we saw someone in Adam's company once doesn't mean Hunter hasn't killed them and stolen their magic since." Layla countered. "Or killed one of their family and become able to imitate them."

"True." King Arini's words were soft, his gaze tired now as he pushed up from his lounging position into a cross-legged seat like Layla. "Why do you think I am so cagey, Layla Price? It's not because I fear the world. I don't. It's because I don't know whom I can trust, and I can only make guesses these days as to who really is whom they say

227

they are, and who is not."

"Can your scenting of the winds still pick out Hunter?"

"Yes." King Arini spoke, a fierce glitter in his gold eyes now. "I still smell the void-shadow when he changes faces. At least he has not been able to hide that, not completely."

"What about this chamber?" Layla asked, glancing around.

"Hunter cannot enter here." King Arini's smile was smug now. "It may be the only place he is truly not permitted. He imitated my magics hundreds of years ago, and since then, my imprint has changed with every new body. I cannot undo the spells laid upon the fortress that his imitation of my old magic can access, but I can create a new bower free of that imprint. This bower was begun only seventy years ago. The magics laid into it are only my most recent."

"That's a small comfort." Layla chuckled wryly, though she wasn't smiling.

"Indeed." Taking a deep breath, King Arini rose elegantly to standing, then held out a hand. Layla took it, rising also, and together they stepped from the nest's soft confines back to solid stone.

"I have more that I wish to relate about Hunter while you are here," Arini spoke, cradling her hand in his. "We could speak of him for days and still not tell everything, and perhaps we should. I know your time here is limited, but my time is precious also; I have a Lineage to rule and many issues must be attended today. Take your rest a while; I will have one of my most trusted bring up food and leave it just beyond the doors. I must have audience with my generals now. If you need anything, set your hand to that stone there," Arini nodded to a large ruby set into the wall of the bower, gleaming with sunlight, "and someone will arrive to attend you."

"Thank you." Layla spoke. "When will you return?"

"This evening, as the sun sets." Reaching out, the Phoenix King cradled Layla's face in his leathery palm, his black talons tickling her jaw as his gold eyes pierced her to the quick. A small smile lifted his lips, and Layla heard his beautiful birdsong wash through her mind once more as they gazed at each other. It made her heat, feeling a deep pull between them. She could feel her Bind-magic struggling beneath Reginald's gifts as it tried to reach out to Arini, wanting him for her own. He was a powerful man and a powerful Royal, and as Layla watched him in their quiet moment of mutual understanding, she also knew he was a powerful heart.

She saw him realize what was happening. A wry understanding filled his eyes as he stepped in close, taking both her hands in his. She thought he might kiss her, the pull between them strengthened so much, but then Layla felt King Arini ease back from that intense, carnal attraction with a soft chuckle. Lifting her hands to his lips, he gave them each a kiss, brushing the cobalt down of his cheeks across her hands and making her sigh with gentle pleasure instead of hot lust.

"You are an amazing woman, Layla Price." He spoke softly. "I have no doubt you will do tremendous things in your lifetime. Though I feel us pulling together by your magics, I wish to give you the power of choice in Binding me. I am content to wait, and not come to you until the time is right, if it is ever so. Until then, know that you have a friend in me, and Adrian Rhakvir and Dusk Arlohaim do also, this I swear until the end of my days."

"Thank you." Layla reached up, setting her hand to his cheek, feeling the beautiful softness of his cobalt down beneath her fingers.

"You are welcome."

With that, King Arini stroked her face gently with one taloned hand, then turned, walking gracefully out through the silk-hung doorway. Leaving Layla alone in the bower, with more questions than she had answers.

CHAPTER 21 – GOLDEN

Layla gazed around King Arini's bower after he left, restless. She hadn't counted on him having duties while she was visiting, but of course he did. Moving about the elegant space, Layla examined its details to pass the time. The nest took up the greater part of the bower, but along one wicker wall, a gilded Italianate armoire held long frock coats of cascading feathers and soft silk. An ancient writing desk from the 1700's held court by the vaulted windows, and behind a set of hand-painted Italian bathing screens decorated with birds, Layla found a bathing pool set into the stone floor, with crystal phials of oils lined up on a gilded stand. The water was cold, and though there was a gilded mirror, there was no toilet in the bathing area.

"Maybe he just perches his ass out the window?" Layla mused.

But just as she spied a clever hole in the floor covered by a round slab of stone with a foot-pedal next to it, she heard King Arini return in a wash of birdsong. Frowning, Layla wondered if he'd changed his mind about his duties or if they were already complete. Stepping back around the bathing-screen, she opened her mouth to speak – and stopped dead in her tracks. Tempeste Durant stood just inside the central silk-hung doorway, watching her. Or at first glance it seemed like Tempeste Durant.

Only the eyes were different – that terrible dark hunter-green color that seemed to devour all of time.

In an instant, Layla's magic seared up to roaring, her Dragon screeching with fury inside her veins. Layla burned like an inferno, everything inside her snarling to fight. A wind whipped deep inside her as her Dragon roiled, lashing its tail and baring fangs at her enemy. At the trickster; the impostor wearing the face and skin of Tempeste Durant – and the same navy suit Tempeste had been in when Layla had seen him just this morning.

But with Reginald's pearl bracelet and earrings on, all that happened was a blistering scent of burned orange peels that roared up around Layla. Her magic was still contained enough that if she wanted to fight Hunter, she'd have to shed Reginald's jewelry. She saw the impostor note it. She saw Hunter's black-green eyes flick to the pearl bracelet still at her wrist, before his gaze returned to hers.

"There's no need to scream." Hunter spoke quietly, calm. "Arini's magics have made this chamber soundproof."

"Did you kill him?!" Layla hissed, prickling with heat all through her body. "Did you kill Tempeste Durant, you bastard?!"

"I've been the one traveling with you these past days, Layla." Hunter held her gaze steadily from Tempeste Durant's haughty, beautiful face. "I found out about your plans and decided it was time to speak with you again. It's why I had to interrupt your phone call with Dusk on the apartment balcony. Because Reginald's eldest brother was killed on an Intercessoria job five years ago, and Dusk knows that."

"You killed Tempeste Durant, didn't you?!" Layla seethed, ferocious power ripping through her as her mind spiraled at how Hunter had tricked her – yet again. It made Layla feel sick inside, knowing this killer could so easily show her faces and personalities that made her feel compassion, just like he had done as Adam Rhakvir. As the extent of Hunter's deceptions staggered her, Layla felt her blistering red rage darken to something impossibly black. She felt her horror and fear and fury coalesce – into a pit so dark that demons and cold wrath roared in those depths like a nest of poisonous snakes.

A feeling unlike anything she'd ever had before.

"Yes, I killed Tempeste Durant five years ago." Hunter held her gaze, calm before her fury, his posture at ease inside Tempeste's tall, lean body. "He was getting too close to me with one of his investigations. I couldn't allow that; not with the Intercessoria. I assume Falliro Arini has told you something about me by now. I tried to get in sooner, but even I have to be cautious with the faces I take around Arini's security personnel."

"At least you have some limitations," Layla growled, feeling a biting wind stir around her, though it was still somewhat tamed with Reginald's jewelry still on.

Carefully, she slipped the earrings out of her ears, then unfastened the bracelet. Watching her, Hunter let her do it. Layla stuffed them into a zipper pocket of her jeans, keeping her eyes on him. Scorching power surged from her now, liberated by Reginald's gifts. A crimson and gold ring of fire burst into the air around her – her fighting fire. As she squared off with Hunter, humming with tension now, she felt her Dragon roar inside her veins. The fire around Layla brightened, singeing feathers of Arini's nest and fetishes dangling above. Hunter watched her, calmly. Just as before, her wrathful power didn't touch him – as if he had some invisible barrier all around him, or could simply negate Layla's power.

Layla balled a fist, sliding a foot back into a fighting-stance like Rikyava and Dusk had been teaching her. She had no idea if she could hit Hunter with her power, but damned if she wasn't about to try. But without Reginald's pearls on, she knew he couldn't feel what was happening with her right now, or pinpoint her.

Hopefully, her shock at Hunter's arrival had been enough to alert him that something was wrong.

Bad wrong.

"How are you not burning up right now from Arini's protection mechanisms?" Layla growled, aware that King Arini's wards were not functioning as intended.

"Because I can assume Falliro Arini's vibration completely." Hunter's words were said with a tone so dead that Layla wondered if he had any heart left at all. "Even the vibration of his most recent physical body is something I can approximate."

"So what do you want from me?" Layla snarled. "Why all this subterfuge – again?"

"Because I want you to see my side, Layla." He spoke quietly, still making no threatening moves towards her. "If I came to you as just me, would you ever hear me out? If I didn't trick you, make you feel close to me, would you ever give me a moment of your time? I just want to talk, Layla. No more games – just a conversation."

"Why did you even let me come to the Aviary, if all you wanted to do was talk? Why not just talk in Manarola or back in Paris?" Layla growled, furious.

"Because Arini's bower is the most magically-protected place I know from prying ears and prying minds." Hunter's gaze was still level with her.

"Whose?" Layla spat.

"You'll understand if you listen, if you hear me out."

"Fine. If you want to talk, talk now or talk never, bucko." Layla spoke, a furious nimbus of scalding air building around her now. Her lungs felt like they were on fire with her hatred of him; her veins burned with dark fury as her entire body trembled with a rigid tension. As she breathed, a hot mirage began to waver the air, as if it might create a wall of fire around her.

She saw Hunter note it, a smile touching his lips. "That mirage. You're channeling Adrian's ability to fire-breathe," he spoke softly.

233

"It's mine now." Layla growled back, her voice dropping an octave into a dark, nearly non-human register. It was a sound she'd never made before; a sound Adrian and Dusk made when they were channeling their Dragons, close to shifting for a fight.

"Not quite." Hunter corrected as he regarded her with Tempeste's face and his own hunter-green eyes. "But your power is growing if you're learning to adopt the abilities of your bound men. I wondered how you were able to crack the sapphire door in the Paris Hotel's Vault. Now I see you were channeling Dusk's formidable talent. But there are still countless mistakes you might make with your magic, Layla, and I wish to save you from that darkness. If I can."

"Don't act like you give two shits about me." Layla spat back, furious, balling both hands into fists now.

"But I do care about you." His green eyes deepened, so dark they were nearly black. "And I will do anything I can to make you see just how much you mean to me."

"Like killing my friends?"

"If I must." His eyes really were black now, only a trace of green still shining from them in the light reflected off the thousands of dangling baubles. "May I tell you my story?"

Layla paused. Hunter hadn't made a move to touch her yet, or lobbied any threats against her personally. It was clear he was here to talk, not to attack, perhaps unless he was provoked. Plus, the more Layla kept him talking, the more time there was for someone to discover what was happening in Arini's bower. With her mirage of power still seething around her, Layla glanced at the large ruby set into the outer wall of the bower, wondering if she could get close enough to touch it and raise an alert. "Ok. Talk."

"It would be easier... if I showed you."

"Showed, what do you mean?"

But before Layla could say anything else, Hunter lifted his hands, steepling his index fingers between his eyes. Drawing a deep breath, he closed his eyes. And on his exhalation, a wave of memory suddenly pummeled into Layla. One moment, she was standing in the bower with Hunter.

And the next, her mind was spinning; careening back through the ages.

Vast deserts rolled away from her. Vistas, arroyos, canyons; a land before time had ever been counted. And yet, the desert had beautiful oases – amazingly green and lush, Layla felt that they were her home. A Desert Dragon clan filled her mind; a tribe of caramel-skinned, dark-haired people dressed in luminous silks, living like Bedouins out in some nameless desert. Fighting in enormous temples of sandstone, practicing their powers, they laughed and danced out under the stars and the swaying palms; celebrating life around the fire at night.

She felt the ancientness of Hunter's memory – magic had been young when Hunter was born long ago. Powers had been volatile; Lineages had not been charted. There was no Intercessoria and no High Court, and she saw his clan traveling as nomads through the desert, fucking and fighting as they flew from oasis to oasis conquering rival clans.

She saw Hunter's parents, dark-eyed and caramel-skinned; beautiful. Tall and elegant, they wore cascades of red and turquoise beads and little else in their human forms, and she saw how they adored their only son. She felt how they knew he was different from the rest of their tribe; how they had tried to keep it a secret from their King and Queen. But young eighteen-year-old Hunter was magnetic and compelling. Fire burned in his green-black eyes and passion in his heart, the young Royal Desert Dragon possessing an ability to draw others to him with a power his parents didn't understand – a charisma that was unprecedented.

Layla saw them take him to the tribe's human shaman, to see if he could help the young man contain his magics. The shaman found out Hunter could imitate others; could change his face and body as he willed – and had heard of a Seer deep in the desert who had this strange ability also. Layla saw the young man taken from his parents, to find this Seer. She saw the caravan waylaid; two enormous black Dragons with red-gold stripes burning the shaman's belongings and camels. Layla felt terror consume her as those Dragons touched down to the desert sands, though it wasn't Hunter's terror. He ran to them, and Layla understood what they were. His Bound lovers, his two Bound mates, one female and one male – snarling as they faced off with the shaman to take Hunter back to the tribe.

The shaman resisted them, but he was a human, and they burned him to death. When they brought Hunter back and the tribe's King and Queen learned of their precious shaman's death, they feared Hunter's influence over his Bound lovers. Layla saw their stern faces; their rejecting gestures. She saw the clan vote – Hunter had to go train with the Seer or be banished for his unpredictable otherness.

With wrath in his heart, he went, roaring up into the skies as an enormous black Dragon with golden stripes – forsaking his beloveds to learn at the feet of the Seer. But what Layla saw next was pure torture. Hunter, chained in the bottom of a cistern, drowning as magical manacles prevented him from shifting into his Dragon and escaping. Hunter, starving out under the cruel desert sun in a deadly fatigue, two breaths from death and hallucinating. Hunter, buried up to his neck in a copper tub full of scorpions – stung over and over and screaming in pain.

Abuse, denigration, and misery had been inflicted by the tall desert Seer with the corkscrewing white dreadlocks and jagged teeth.

236

The tests had been meant to break Hunter, to make him rage and flare his powers as far as they would go. Layla felt fury build inside the young man. She felt his rage; black and horrible at the abuse he suffered. She saw the cruelty of the Seer – and how he was able to convince Hunter over and over with his terrible mind-magics to engage these tests.

She saw the final straw. She saw how the Seer took the face of Hunter's female Bound lover, how he came to Hunter in her body, making the sweetest love. And how he brought it all crashing down, exposing his true form in the middle of it.

Tricking Hunter; driving him mad.

That night, when one of Hunter's actual Bound lovers came in the dead of night and broke him free, flying him far out into the desert so Hunter was away from the Seer's mind-influences, Hunter did not know the man. Layla saw how Hunter thought it was yet another trick; how he argued with his male lover out beneath the midnight stars. She saw how Hunter had changed; the vicious, tortured creature he had become as he attacked his male Bound lover.

Fighting him in their Dragon-forms – killing him.

Only when Hunter felt the Bind with his lover break with a terrible howling in his soul, had he realized the man had not been his teacher in disguise. Layla's heart screamed, feeling it as Hunter had felt it, though she was watching the scene as if looking down from the midnight desert breezes. Something inside Hunter had still been beautiful until that moment. Insanity took him then, and Layla could barely hold her mind back from the same as she collapsed to her knees on the bower's stone floor, clutching her heart with both hands.

Hunter was screaming in the memory. Layla was screaming in King Arini's bower. Hunter was sobbing, fallen over the corpse of his beautiful dark-skinned beloved as the man somehow changed back into human form after death. Layla fell onto her hands and knees, dry-retching so hard she thought her insides were going to come out. She felt a hole of darkness open up inside Hunter – the void opening inside of him. She felt the hollowness in his soul, in his heart, in the very essence of his being.

And she felt it open wide inside herself also.

The rest of the memory was inconsequential. Layla came to a sudden stillness on her knees, staring with blind eyes as the rest of Hunter's vision careened in. His other lover, flying in and finding them. Her fury; she and the male lover had been a mated pair before Hunter had Bound them. Her and Hunter's Dragon-battle; terrible. But though Hunter was stronger, he was empty as he fought, and already wounded. Layla watched the battle come to a stalemate as dawn rose over the dunes. She saw them both limp away – but not until after the female lover had cursed Hunter, to wander the world alone forever for what he had done.

Layla felt those words smite Hunter's heart, what was left of it. Imprinting him with loneliness in addition to the emptiness.

It was then that he became the void-shadow. A void inside a shadow of his former charismatic self as the sun rose over the desert. Hunter had flown to an oasis to heal, but the dark emptiness inside him never would. Layla felt the rest of his memories as a blur; Hunter, returning to the Seer to kill him. Hunter, wandering for years learning mystical arts and how to change his resonance to mimic others. Learning that he could kill; inhaling and digesting other people's powers to imitate them.

The memories flickered out, leaving Layla gasping in the silence of King Arini's bower. All of her fire had died, her heat-mirage gone. The mobiles above fluttered in a sea-breeze and some part of her was astounded to realize it was still morning. She knelt on the stone floor, her mind still a thousand years away, her Dragon stunned and coiled up tight inside her from the inundation of awfulness that had been Hunter's memories.

From the awfulness of his madness.

"She was always out there, my Nadia, after that battle over the death of our Nimir." Hunter's voice was like a slap to the face as he broke the silence. "She spent thousands of years finding other Royal Dragon Binds as powerful as me – turning them against me to wreak her vengeance."

Layla glanced up at him, her eyes wide, still shocked.

She didn't speak, couldn't speak.

"In those days, I was the Hunted." Hunter continued with a sad gaze. "Nadia was not a Bind, but she was persuasive. She sought other Binds and twisted them with her words, making them believe I was evil – making me fight for my life when they came after me. I began to win some to my side, and then a great battle was waged among the Binds by Nadia, destroying many. In her wrath after losing that battle, she summoned a being from the Otherworld, the Realms that lie beyond even the Ascended and Demonic Realms. She made a deal with it – that if she gave it her body, they would make of her loins a child that could destroy me. They mated; that child was born. But the Otherworld Being gave that child a holy curse: it would either destroy me or it would be destroyed by me, and from its bloodline would someday be birthed a Golden Dragon Bind that could undo Nadia and I's ancient war. A magic that could restore what we had lost – our Nimir."

Layla's gaze had fallen to Hunter's knees as he orated the last act of his story, picturing it almost as if she was still inside Hunter's memories. As he spoke his final words, she looked up, seeing a flash of Hunter with his hand turned into cruel black talons, standing in the shadows of some ancient desert abode behind a slender young man. She saw those talons run red – as the young man collapsed to the adobe floor with his throat slit.

"You killed the child." Layla spoke softly, horrified.

"I did." Hunter nodded. With a sigh, he hunkered before Layla, gazing deep into her eyes. "I killed the godly child of my beloved enemy. But not before it reached maturity, mating with a female Crystal Dragon and passing on its bloodline. That bloodline became fractured amongst many different Dragon clans, and I have followed it through the years. For a long while, I thought Falliro Arini was the Golden Dragon Bind, as his mother held the bloodline. Then I watched Adrian and Dusk as children, though they managed to withstand my machinations to push them into their power. They all held the bloodline in generous amounts, but none were volatile enough to be the Golden Dragon Bind I sought."

"And now you believe it's me." Layla breathed, her heart dropping like a stone. "How are you so certain?"

"Because when you were born, I felt a golden fire consume my mind." Hunter spoke softly, his dark eyes penetrating as they bored into Layla. "I felt it flare like a beacon in my heart, Layla, inside my very soul. Inside the utter blackness of everything I am – leading me to Riad Rhakvir, to you. It was something I had never felt before with any of the others; a confirmation. Both your father and mother carried the bloodline of my ancient enemy and her godly consort. And now their holy curse has reached its pinnacle. You are the one who can restore my Nimir, Layla. You are the one who can help me unite the Binds and calm Nadia's wrath. You are the one… who can make us all whole once more."

CHAPTER 22 – RUIN

Layla stood staring at Hunter as a sea-wind blew through the bower. All she could hear in her ears was static. As if Hunter had just taken everything she knew about the world and turned it upside-down, Layla had that out-of-body experience again, like she was hovering at the upper reaches of the dome watching herself. A moment stretched between them, full of a strange tension. Before, she had wanted to kill Hunter for harming her friends. But to truly know the depth of his insanity, and how much ruin had come from so much love, made her cold inside with fear.

"That's impossible." Layla spoke, slowly rising to her feet like she would with a rabid animal, feeling something strange move between her and Hunter. "I can't be descended from some god-born Lineage. I don't believe in God, or gods."

"Don't you?" Hunter eased to standing also, his green-black eyes intense though his posture was still calm. "Is it so impossible to believe that your bloodline carries a godly anomaly? You've seen powers in the Twilight Realm that other humans could only describe in terms of gods and demigods. Why is it so impossible to imagine that your ancient ancestor once mated with a being so unique as to be considered a god by Twilight Realm standards?"

"I can't make your broken Binds whole again, Hunter." Layla breathed. "I can't resurrect the dead. Isn't there some Twilight Realm Lineage with that kind of power?"

"It is a godly ability," Hunter spoke, his gaze beseeching now.

"None have it but the truly blessed."

"So find one of them to do it."

"Don't you think I've tried? Don't you think I've hunted down every Ephemeral I could find to see if they could summon a god to hear my plight?" Hunter returned, moving a step closer. Layla startled at his sudden motion, taking a fast step back, her hands flashing up to a warding stance. He eyed her ruefully, and with a sad look on his face, suddenly morphed. One moment he was Tempeste Durant, and the next, his entire body wavered in a whirling mirage. For a moment, Layla saw a flash of light in his core, followed by a cavernous blackness. And then, standing in Tempeste's elegant three-piece suit was the tall, broad-shouldered Adam Rhakvir, running a hand through his thick golden mane and down his short beard.

"Are you less afraid of this visage?" Hunter asked softly.

"It's not your faces I'm afraid of, Hunter," Layla spoke, her hands still up and ready. "How about showing me your real self for a change?"

She saw a terrible woe seep into Hunter's eyes then, a look she had glimpsed twice before. In all his personalities, this one element had bled through each time; that terrible pain. Not a pain of the body or the heart, but a pain of the soul. As Hunter watched her with his pained eyes staring out of Adam Rhakvir's Roman-brigand handsomeness, Layla suddenly understood.

"You don't remember your own face." She breathed, shock flooding her.

"No." Hunter's response was soft, his gaze bereft. "I could try to blame Nadia's god for that curse, but the truth is that I cursed myself. I have been so many people over the millennia that at some point, I could not exactly recall my own face, or the details of my body. After a time, it became simply easier to be a persona, rather than trying to be myself and failing."

Layla couldn't imagine anything more horrible. To lose one's identity so completely; to never be able to come back from the masquerades. Something inside her screamed, feeling that pain. Feeling the madness and sorrow of losing oneself so utterly. "My god. Has no one ever been able to help you recall your own true image?"

"No." Hunter spoke softly, the saddest smile Layla had ever seen upon his lips.

"How will your lost lover know you, even if you're able to resurrect him?"

"I don't know." He breathed. "Perhaps my only hope is that my soul is not as far gone as my body or my heart, and that Nimir will still recognize the essence of me."

Layla's heart screamed. Deep within, her Dragon roiled with a tortured surge of coils. Not because she was furious now, but because she was feeling Hunter's pain. Adrian's face flashed in Layla's mind, then Dusk's. Layered upon them, she suddenly saw the caramel-tan faces of Hunter's beloveds, Nadia and Nimir. She heard how sexily Nimir chuckled just like Dusk, ribald with joy. She saw how Nadia's eyes flashed gold like Adrian's when pissed or impassioned. She felt Nimir's hard muscles beneath her hands, how cut they were like Dusk. She touched Nadia's body and it was like touching Adrian's honed musculature, fight-hardened and intense with energy.

They were hers in that moment, as she felt them, touched them. Layla felt them torn from her; she felt their Binds ripped apart by murder and heartbreak. Looking down, she saw blood on her hands – Nadia's blood, and Nimir's.

Adrian's blood, and Dusk's.

A black hole devoured her and Layla gasped, staggering backwards with a cry, one hand gripping her heart and the other covering that endless hole in her center. But it was as if her hands were still covered in blood, the center of her life torn out and replaced by darkness as she staggered to the bower's wall.

Through Layla's merged memories, she saw herself – tall and lean, caramel-skinned and incredible, honed from a life of fighting out in the desert. Masculine and beautiful, she was a god among lesser creatures, even though her body was rent and torn from fighting, her hands stained with blood. It was Hunter's body she was seeing; Hunter's original form as he gasped from his fight with Nadia, holding his bloody hands over his rent middle as he gave up. Layla's hand slapped to the massive ruby in the bower wall to steady herself, and she saw her caramel-skinned hand leave a smear of blood; blood that wasn't actually there but was.

Blood from Hunter, blood from Nadia – and blood from Nimir.

She heard Hunter cry out. Layla's head whipped up as she gasped, seeing him doubled over, gripping his chest and middle just like she was; staring at her with wide eyes. "What did you do?!" He rasped, gasping.

"I didn't do anything!" Layla coughed, feeling a terrible void eating out her middle; Hunter's cavernous darkness resonating from her sudden understanding of his pain.

"You showed me my body!" He rasped, staggering towards her as if everything inside him hurt. His eyes blazed a pure green now, and deep in their center Layla saw his irises suddenly swirl with gold. "*How did you show me my body?!*"

"I don't know!"

Shuddering with Hunter's pain, Layla staggered to a defensive posture in front of the ruby. Holding one shaking hand to its faceted surface, she raised the other up before her, tightening her fingers. But she couldn't make fire. A humming vibration passed through Layla as her Dragon roiled inside her, coiling in agony, distracted. Something was happening between her and Hunter, some kind of unstable resonance.

Something that made Layla's own fighting powers unavailable.

Still holding a hand to his abdomen as if she'd raked his guts out, Hunter began to vibrate hard like Layla. Like he had a palsy, he began to shake with it, his knees buckling as he crashed to the stone floor of the bower. All of a sudden, his body began to shift, furiously. A mirage roiled through him in disastrous surges of light and darkness, flooding him. Hunter screamed, gripping his fingers hard into his flesh, tearing Tempeste's navy suit, and Layla saw his face morph through ten, twenty, thirty different people as his body did also. He was screaming in waves now as he changed and changed again, still shuddering like the resonance between himself and Layla was going to rip him apart.

And though Layla shuddered with something close to a seizure now, she managed to keep a hand on the ruby as Hunter's voice began to roar. Resonating with impossible overtones and bass notes, she saw him coil in upon himself – and heave outwards into a massive body of black and gold scales.

Layla shrank back as much as her shuddering would allow, against the wall in a crouch. She gasped, wide-eyed with horror as Hunter became enormous inside his whirl of heat-mirage. Surging up on powerful forelimbs, he heaved into the heights of the dome with a thundering roar, smashing his enormous head of gold and black corkscrewing horns into the dome's wall. Black talons bigger than Layla's thigh punched into the floor, gouging up stone, flinging chips everywhere. Muscled coils as tall as Layla and forelegs like an armored tank heaved furniture aside as the enormous black Dragon slammed into the walls of the dome.

Slammed its head into the dome over and over – as if it had gone insane.

The bower's walls cracked with thunderous retorts. Sticks and silk, CD's and glass crashed down around Layla in a torrent. She cried out as a shark skeleton was liberated from the dome, careening down – and by a fast movement of her hands, Layla thrust a barrier of wind up, sending the bones careening through the shattering walls instead.

A hard churning of bird-wings came from outside as the enormous black Dragon heaved his blocky skull against the wall again, blasting one side of the dome out into the sea below. As the wall was blasted away, King Arini alighted through the gap with wings wide – his feathers ruffled up into a serrated prickle, his golden eyes blazing like a raptor of death as he drew himself up tall like a battle-commander.

"Hunter! Cease!" Arini roared, his voice half eagle-screech, half Dragon-thunder.

But the massive black Dragon still roiled like an injured snake inside the bower, a mad thing with no mind left. Layla saw Arini note it with wide eyes. One moment, King Arini stood in the blasted-out gap – and the next, he was launching at Hunter in full Phoenix-form.

Enormous and lithe, King Arini was a magnificent cobalt bird-Dragon. And though he was lean and fast, with sleek feathers that could maneuver like a falcon, Hunter was ten times larger. Magic cascaded in a furious whirlwind as they connected in a surge of coiled muscles, vicious barbs, and ripping fangs. As King Arini and Hunter hammered each other with powerful muscles, renting and biting, they slammed each other into the bower's dome. The walls shuddered, then shattered. One moment, the bower had a dome, and the next it was exploding from the Dragons battling inside it – everything cascading down from the tower's heights into the sea far below.

Hands above her head, holding her ward to protect from debris careening down, Layla ran toward the garden. As she rushed out, plants and fruit trees shuddered all around her from the blasts heaving the tower. Suddenly, the roaring Dragons careened through the tumbled dome – smashing pots and trellises as their battle spilled out onto the terrace.

King Arini shrieked like a raptor as his feathered tail was bitten by Hunter; Hunter roared with the sound of storms as his gold-streaked snout was raked by Arini's long, cruel talons. Over and over they tumbled, hammering each other into the broken bower and the tower's balustrades, cracking each other on the garden's flagstones. Blasts of magic careened everywhere; Layla hunkered in the middle of that fury, down on one knee and holding her hands spread at her sides in a maneuver Dusk had taught her, creating a personal dome of protection with her winds.

Lightning flashed around Hunter in a whirling funnel like a sandstorm as it swept up all the dirt from the garden into its spin. Flashes slit the falsely-darkened afternoon under Hunter's storm; thunder deafened Layla as lightning cracked all around the tower, stabbing at the Phoenix King. But King Arini was faster than lightning; faster than sandstorms. As their fight shuddered the foundations of the old tower, Arini darted in, locking himself around Hunter's neck. Hunter bit like a snake, King Arini's wing now savaged in Hunter's jaws – but Arini's talons and fangs were locked in Hunter's breast, digging for Hunter's heart and making blood fly.

Blood splattered everything now; crimson from Hunter and cobalt from Arini. Other Phoenix were hurtling in from every direction, shrieking like harpies as they dove to aid their King. Layla was bowled to her knees from the next impact of lightning as Hunter tried to lance Arini off of him and missed. She watched in panic as cracks spiderwebbed through the stone all around her. She heard stones beginning to crack free below as shrieks rent the air, other Phoenix diving in to harry Hunter and free their King. Hunter's storm sliced everything in a confusion of concussions like cannon fire as he struck at them with his magic, keeping the lesser Phoenix away.

Locked in battle, the Royal Dragons shredded each other in washes of crimson and cobalt blood now. And then Layla heard a crunch – King Arini's body going limp. His crested head hung from Hunter's enormous jaws, which had somehow gotten around his neck. And with a triumphant roar, Hunter ripped Arini's head free – decapitating the King of the Phoenix in a wash of cobalt blood.

Layla screamed. A surge of power roared from her, slamming into Hunter like an exploding volcano. She saw his green-black eyes widen; saw the shock in his Dragon's face as her surge blistered his scales, snapping the bones of one foreleg. But as that hard explosion knocked the enormous black Dragon backwards into the attacking Phoenix, shrieking for murder at the death of their King, the tower sundered with a last massive *crack*.

Stones fell – and Layla fell with them, plummeting to the sea.

A roar went through her as her Dragon tried desperately to shift as she plummeted. It roiled as she fell, making Layla scream from its powerful thrust of talons and barbs inside her body. But as the sea flashed near, she knew it was too late. In a fast reflex, her Dragon had only enough time to thrust blistering talons through the fingertips of Layla's left hand – shredding her jeans and closing her fist around Reginald's pearls in her pocket as she hit the water.

Layla felt every bone in her body break as she smashed into the sea from hundreds of feet up, Reginald's pearls flaying her skin as her hand clenched around them in shock. Her eyes were washed open beneath the water, peaceful blue sunlight glimmering through the ocean as her body was consumed by pain. Layla couldn't move, couldn't breathe as she slowly sank. Her lungs spasmed with pain, drawing seawater deep into her throat – choking.

Drowning.

Far away, something flashed through the deeps. As enormous blocks of stone crashed into the water all around from the crumbing tower, a massive creature of the ocean surged in. Darting through the deeps, it dwarfed Layla with its size, coiling around her in a sheen of luminous silver-white scales. Long filaments like ghostly seaweed surged around her, curling in. She felt her body enclosed in a massive fist of smooth scales and long white talons – an oh-so-careful grip. An enormous fanged snout flashed up beside her, an ice-blue eye flecked with gold boring into her. As she stared into that enormous eye, her consciousness fading, she felt the massive creature turn its head. Snuggling her face close to its neck just behind a mantle of streaming silver-white filaments, she felt fins brush her face. The creature pressed her close, forcing her lips and nose to those gossamer slits.

Breathe, Layla. Breathe, Courtesan.

Breathe.

She did. As a surge of energy shot through her ruined body from the creature's talons and filaments wrapped around her, Layla felt her heart re-start in a thundering heave. She coughed hard, and though her body was broken, water was ejected from her lungs. Her breath, pressed into the creature's flowing fins, was full of air upon her next inhalation.

Full of life.

Layla gasped as fresh air flooded her lungs from the creature's exhalation. Her vision cleared as enormous gill-slits fanned open, flooding air in through her lips and nose as it pushed away the water. Layla gasped its exhalations, each air bubble exhaled from the leviathan larger than her chest as its gossamer fins brushed her face, its talons and filaments cradling her. Only when she'd coughed out the majority of the seawater from her broken lungs, did it flash its thick neck away fast, curl her in its grip – and explode upward through the deeps.

Launched up through the water in its powerful talons, Layla gasped as she broke the surface, even though pain rioted through her broken body. But as if the creature's life-giving breath had given her opiates also, Layla felt her pain dampened. With an exhilarating rush, she was skimmed along the surface of the water, through a dark mist and back out into sunshine. Layla felt herself curled into the creature's massive, warm body as it coiled up from the water like a Dragon of the deeps. A speedboat roared nearby, and Layla was laid gently down upon the speedboat's rough deck by the creature's smooth coils.

Cries of dismay came; a rumbling voice she knew, along with terse curses from two others. Laying on her back, Layla opened her eyes just as two enormous sets of white-silver wings curled around her, enveloping her in a cocoon of shimmering layers. Kneeling inside that cocoon were the Intercessoria Judiciary Heathren Merkami and Insinio Brandfort. As Layla gasped true air, the two Ephilohim touched all their ephemeral wingtips to her, pouring a blissful light into her broken body.

And within their cocoon knelt Dusk, right beside Layla, setting his hands fast to Layla's broken form and pouring a healing resonance deep into her bones.

"Hold on, Layla," Dusk rumbled, holding her gaze with his diamond-light eyes as he held her life steady through their Bind. "I've got you…"

CHAPTER 23 – RELEASE

One moment, Layla was dying on the deck of a speedboat in Italian coastal waters, and the next, she was waking in her apartment back at the Red Letter Hotel Paris. Blinking her eyes open, she saw Dusk laying in bed beside her. He stirred as she woke, moving with a smile to cuddle her close under one muscled arm. She was naked and so was he, and though every bone in her body screamed, nothing seemed broken any longer. Layla curled in to Dusk, inhaling his fresh river-water scent as he thrummed a soothing resonance deep into her bones.

"There's my girl," he rumbled, giving her a gentle kiss on the lips. "Welcome back."

"How long have I been out?" Layla asked, enjoying Dusk's deep warmth like a soothing balm.

"Only twenty-four hours." He murmured, kissing her forehead. "You're healing fast. Getting the light of the universe poured into you by two Fallen Ephilohim helps."

"Heathren and Insinio." Layla blinked, recalling that the Juds had been there for her rescue. "But how did I get to the boat? What was that creature that brought me up from the ocean?"

"It was Reginald." Dusk spoke with a deep rumble, a strange look in his eyes. "When I told him Hunter was masquerading as his deceased eldest brother to trap you, he was furious; he insisted on coming with the Intercessoria and me to pull you out of the engagement. As King Arini died, Arini's boundaries around the Aviary failed. Reginald was on the cliffs of Manarola when he felt you hit the water with his pearls clenched in your fist. He dove in off the cliffs; got you out of the Aviary's waters."

"But, I thought it was some kind of leviathan that rescued me…" Layla spoke, astounded.

"That was a Siren, Layla, that's what they look like." Dusk's gaze was deep. "Reginald shifted for the first time when he hit the water – to save you. He's never done it before. It was instinctual; instantaneous. And thank god he did, because it was the only way for him to get to you fast enough before you drowned."

"He shifted for the first time to save me?" Layla spoke, amazed. "But… how were you there? And the Judiciary?"

"Remember the call you made to me?" Dusk brushed her curls back from her face. "The line was breaking up, but I heard you say *Tempeste Durant*. I knew there was no way you would have known Tempeste, and I notified the Intercessoria at once, knowing we had a problem. We got down to Cinque Terre through Intercessoria portals, fast; we had boats patrolling the Aviary's boundary and Juds in Manarola when the battle happened. But without Reginald's transformation…"

"I'd be dead. But instead of me, it's King Arini who's dead – isn't he?" Somewhere deep inside, Layla's Dragon screamed, knowing the Phoenix King was gone. Yet another casualty to Hunter's crimes, though Layla felt this one intensely, feeling like the possibility of something beautiful had been ripped from her – forever.

"He is." Dusk's words were awful, his sapphire eyes bleak. "Phoenix can't regenerate from decapitation. Hunter was severely attacked by Arini's people for it, but he managed to escape. The bastard has some kind of portal-making ability – yet another of his dark tricks. The Aviary is exposed now without Arini's blood to power the wards. Though fortunately, it's melded back into the Twilight Realm from which it was originally built, rather than the human realm."

"What will happen to the Phoenix?" Layla asked, feeling tired and sad.

"They're restructuring," Dusk spoke softly, petting her curls back again. "There will be a lot of dominance-battles in the near future, to decide who will be the next King or Queen. Arini was their lead for over two thousand years. He was a force of nature, and rarely challenged."

"Except Hunter was stronger than Arini."

"He was." Dusk lapsed into silence as he held Layla, the both of them breathing quietly in the mid-afternoon. Beyond the vaulted windows, snow swirled down in lazy drifts, brightening the world to soft hues. But all Layla could think about were Hunter's enormous fangs crunching down on Arini's neck.

"He's a Desert Dragon."

"What?" Dusk glanced down at her.

"Hunter. He fought King Arini as a black Desert Dragon, his own ancient Lineage." Layla looked up at Dusk. "Something happened between us, Dusk, some kind of resonance. Hunter showed me his memories, and I tapped into them so deeply that it rebounded on him, I think. He told me he didn't recall his human form. But he saw it when our magics interacted. And it triggered his shift. I don't think he meant to shift, he just wanted to talk with me. But it seemed like he went mad... smashing his head against the walls of the tower as if regaining the memory of himself was too painful to bear."

"Maybe it was." Dusk spoke softly. Layla could practically hear the wheels churning in his mind. "Maybe being so many people over the years was easier than recalling his own visage; facing himself. Facing what he'd done. Did he tell you why he's been hunting you Layla, and Adrian and I?"

"He thinks my magic comes from some god," Layla spoke softly. "He thinks I'm the culmination of a bloodline descended from his ancient enemy, a woman named Nadia and an Otherworld Being she mated with to screw him. Hunter was stalking you and Arini and Adrian, messing with you all because you three have traces of that bloodline, same as me, and he was trying to trigger that magic in you. But when I was born, Hunter felt me in a different way than the rest of you. He thinks I have some foretold ability to restore the one thing most precious to him that he's lost."

"His sanity?" Dusk snarked softly, though he was listening.

"His beloved, a man named Nimir." Layla continued. "A Desert Dragon from his tribe that he Bound in his youth but then killed in a case of mistaken identity. Hunter's been at war with Nadia, the third of their Bound triumvirate, ever since. I think he believes that if their lost lover is resurrected... that he'll get the love back that he lost. All three of them – together again."

Dusk whistled low. He snugged Layla closer, sliding a hand over her hip beneath the covers. "Hunter went insane when his Bound trio was fractured? And he really believes you can what, bring his lover back from the dead?"

"I think he and Nadia both went insane when their third died." Layla breathed. "Maybe they never came back from it. In any case, Hunter truly believes I can perform some Jesus-like maneuver, Dusk. You should have seen the belief in his eyes. It was scary. Like, Waco Texas scary."

"Well if losing one third of his Bound triumvirate drove him insane... let's try to keep you and Adrian and I alive then, shall we?" But though his comment was glib, Layla heard the truth in it. She felt Dusk's deep fear – that if their trio of power was ever fractured, it would drive the surviving two mad.

"Let's." Layla murmured as she recalled her vivid image of their blood on her hands – the entire concept too horrible to even think about.

Just then, her apartment doors opened. In strode the two people Layla least wanted to see, but who had saved her life – the Ephilohim Judiciaries. Moving to the bed with his lithe, smooth walk, Heathren Merkami reached out, touching his knuckles to Layla's cheek. He was warm and Layla felt the sensation of seven-layered wings rise up in his aura as he closed his pale silver eyes, inhaling deep. When he opened them, a smile crossed his lips.

"You're healing well. Another few days of soreness, but it will pass. We'd like to interview you now about the things you saw and heard during your travels, before anything fades. Starting from the moment you met *Tempeste Durant*. Do you feel well enough? We can remain here in your chambers and the Head Concierge may stay present to bolster you – this briefing concerns him and the Hotel's welfare also."

Though it was the last thing Layla wanted to do, recounting all the horrors that had happened from Hunter's scheming, the sooner she told the Intercessoria, the sooner they could get Adrian back. Pushing up against the pillows with Dusk's support and tucking the duvet around her nakedness so nothing showed, Layla eyeballed Heathren. "And I have your word that if I give this testimony, you'll release Adrian? No tricks?"

"I give you my word." Heathren Merkami spoke quietly, his pale silver gaze piercing. "Adrian Rhakvir shall be returned to you immediately upon completion of your testimony. If you learn anything about me from our dealings together, Ms. Price, learn this: the word of Heathren Merkami is feared in the Twilight Realm, because I *always* keep it."

Layla watched him, thinking back on the story Hunter had told her about Heathren's origins. Seeing the Fallen Ephilohim now, so regal and deadly before her, Layla suddenly wondered if Hunter's tales had been true. "Just tell me one thing. Are you the firstborn son of Vladimir Merkami, who was called Dracula? Is it true Dracula was actually a Fallen Ephilohim?"

"I was Vladimir Merkami's *only* son, and my father is dead by my hand." Heathren's pale eyes sank into her soul, a sensation of righteous viciousness seething off him as his eyes glittered, dangerous. "I promised him I would bring him down, and so I did. No Vampire was ever as ruthless as my Fallen Ephilohim father the Impaler. And no Ephilohim will ever be allowed to go mad like that ever again – not while I am watching. Now. May we begin?"

Layla nodded, satisfied that Hunter had at least told her some truths in his tales. The proof was standing before her, austere in his black Judiciary leathers and silver weapons. But how far Hunter's truths went was still a question. Taking up a glass of water from her bedside table, Layla drank as Heathren Merkami liberated a small white cube from an inner pocket of his leathers. Gold script scrolled across it as he set it on the bedside table, pulling up a chair with Insinio Brandfort taking up a standing posture behind him. Dusk had risen from the bed naked as a jaybird, moving to Layla's closet to fetch her cobalt silk robe and get himself some sleep-pants. Returning to the bed, he helped her into the robe as the Juds turned away briefly, and once Layla was settled and clothed, she began.

Layla briefed the Juds on everything she had experienced during her trip to Manarola. Over the next hours, they asked questions, circling back often to note precise details of how Hunter had behaved as Tempeste Durant. Heathren Merkami wanted to know the things Hunter had told her, the evidence he'd used to confirm his identity as Tempeste and also his history as Hunter. Insinio spoke up in his big, booming voice, asking numerous times about how it felt when Layla's magic had resonated with Hunter's memories, what Hunter had looked like in Dragon-form, and any special powers she may have noticed.

Through it all, Dusk sat with her, bringing her food and water and coffee, stroking her back and pouring his bolstering vibrations through her. Layla learned about the real Tempeste Durant, and that he'd been almost exactly as Hunter had impersonated him; an Intercessoria family man with a moderately cruel sense of humor, devoted to his loved ones and doting on his youngest brother Reginald. When Tempeste had been killed on duty five years ago, his knife-rig, wallet, and Intercessoria briefcase had all disappeared. Those items had actually been Tempeste's and Hunter had stolen them, using them to further his impersonation to a frighteningly accurate degree.

As the conversation turned to Hunter's memories, Dusk asked clarifying questions about the god-infused Dragon Lineage Hunter was tracking and his belief that Layla was the person who could re-unite him with the dead third of his broken Bind. Heathren and Insinio had frowned at that, sharing a glance Layla didn't understand and was too tired to ask about. Layla had also recounted her vision of blood on her hands after Hunter's battle with Nadia, and how it had layered Hunter's lovers with Dusk and Adrian.

Dusk had scowled deeply at that, a hard wash of refraction flashing through his hair.

But at the end of it, Heathren Merkami was as good as his word. The moment they wrapped up conversation after nearly six hours, he put the white-gold cube away in his leathers. Taking out a vial of golden dust, he stuck one of his silver boot-knives in the vial, then stepped from the bed to trace a circle on the floor. Layla watched him, seeing the dust solidify into the same golden perimeter she had traveled through during the murder investigation. Heathren stood inside it and spread his seven-layered aura, though Layla saw no actual wings sprout from his back like she'd seen on the boat. Murmuring something, he stepped out, then snapped his fingers – and Adrian was suddenly shunted through in a pop and whirl of magic.

Adrian stumbled to his knees as he arrived. Disheveled and weak, he was still wearing his shirt, vest, and pants from the Owner's party, though the shirt was deeply stained with sweat, the collar stained with dried blood. Barefoot with a five-day stubble, Adrian's breath heaved as if he'd just been released from some sort of magical or physical trial. His entire body trembled, his face drawn and his lips parched as if he'd had no food or water for days.

As he came through, he shuddered and began to fall down to his face. Dusk rushed to him and hauled him up under one arm before he could collapse to the floor, and Layla saw numerous bite-marks like fangs over both sides of Adrian's neck, the origin of the blood on his collar. Red blisters and raw, chafed areas ringed his wrists – manacle marks, with more deeply-bruised bites on his inner wrists, even through the coiling red dragon-tattoo on his left forearm.

With a cry of indignation, Layla struggled up from the bed. Though every bone in her body screamed, she rushed to Adrian. Supported by Dusk and still on his knees, Adrian could barely keep his eyes open. But his gaze went a beautiful Mediterranean-gold when he saw Layla, and as she fell to her knees before him, they embraced – kissing tenderly right in front of everyone.

But though his lips were so sweet beneath hers, and kissing him such a divine relief that he was alive, Adrian's body and magic were so exhausted from whatever he'd endured that his Dragon barely stirred in his veins. He smiled as their lips parted, resting his forehead against Layla's with a sigh. "Thank god you're safe! I love you so much,

Layla…"

"I love you too, Adrian…" she breathed, seizing his haggard face in her hands and kissing him again, tasting her own tears as they rolled down her face. She wore Reginald's bracelet and earrings, and though her Dragon stirred with rage at Adrian's condition, only a wash of bourbon-heat lifted up around her. But Adrian inhaled her scent, opening his lips and flaring his nostrils to capture it. Layla saw his eyes brighten; with a slow roar, she finally felt the muscled coils of his magic surround her – as if her scent had fed him strength.

"Thank you," Adrian breathed at her lips.

But Adrian slumped against her, exhausted, and Dusk began pulling him up with generous support. Layla rose also, though she had to clutch one post of the bed to not fall over from her own exhaustion. As Adrian came to standing, Layla watched his gaze lock on Heathren Merkami. The depth of mutual hatred that simmered there took Layla's breath away as she watched the two men face off, Adrian inhaling Layla's scent again. She felt it surge through him, spreading his coils in a writhing, furious wave. And though he was still exhausted and keeping Dusk close for support, Adrian rose to his full height, staring Heathren down with fire in his Mediterranean-gold eyes.

"Using thirteen Vampires to break me was too few, Heathren." Adrian spoke coldly.

"I'll get more approved for next time." Heathren's voice was just as cold, a dark sensation of nightmares easing off him. In her mind's eye, Layla thought she saw the Ephilohim's seven-layer wings again. Except this time they weren't white or silver, they were black – dark as death.

"Do that." With a regal nod to the Intercessoria, Adrian stepped past, though he still had to lean heavily on Dusk. He held his hand out to Layla and she abandoned her bedpost. As he gathered her in his arms, he kissed her deep and she kissed him back, tasting desert spices upon his lips. Adrian inhaled her scent again, his coils and barbs of Dragon-energy strengthening more. At last, he set his forehead to hers, then reached up to stroke her face.

"I'll be back soon," he spoke softly, a wry twist upon his lips. "I promise."

"You'd better be." Layla smiled sadly, knowing he needed to rest from whatever he'd gone through, but hating that he had to leave.

"I'll take him up to my apartment," Dusk spoke, making eye contact with Layla. "I can resonate the crystals there to heal him faster. Rikyava's just outside the door, Layla. If the Intercessoria—"

"We're finished here." Heathren and Insinio moved to the doors, opening the second door to give Adrian a wide berth. Making stern eye contact with Layla, Heathren continued. "If you recall anything else, Ms. Price, Dusk knows how to contact me. In the meantime, we will continue to maintain a presence at the Paris Hotel in case Hunter shows up again. With the Hotel Head's permission, we would like to make modifications to your security systems, in order to potentially track the energy fluctuations around Hunter that King Arini discovered."

Heathren watched Adrian, waiting for an answer.

Adrian's gaze went icy as it dug into the Ephilohim. "I'll think about it."

"Don't think too long," Heathren's gaze was a dark match to Adrian's intensity. "Every hour of delay is another hour for Hunter to kill again."

With that, Heathren turned, flicking his fingers for Insinio. The two Judiciaries departed in a flow of deadly elegance, and Adrian watched them go with cold hatred in his eyes. Outside Layla's rooms, eight Hotel Guardsmen in crimson watched them leave also, the tall blonde Rikyava giving a growl as the Ephilohim finally turned a corner, lost to sight.

"I fucking hate angels." She snarled, her violet eyes flashing a bloody crimson. Glancing at Dusk and Adrian, she said, "Adrian! Jesus, you look like shit! You guys need some help?"

"I've got this." Dusk spoke, as Adrian shook his head.

"Stay with Layla, Rikyava," Adrian murmured. "Please."

"Of course." Rikyava's gaze became sweetly all-violet again as she smiled at Layla, then flicked her fingers at two of her Guardsmen. "Bruno, Lars. Help Dusk get Adrian up to the fourth floor."

They moved off, Adrian giving Layla a tired, though reassuring smile as they went. Rikyava bustled Layla back to her room, shutting the doors and hustling Layla back to bed. Still weak with her own exhaustion, Layla crawled in as Rikyava went to the table, fetching a spread of food and coffee on a tray. Moving back, the Head Guardswoman climbed up beside Layla, plunking the tray down and giving Layla a sad smile.

"Girl's night tonight, chica. Hope that's ok."

"Just what the doctor ordered." Layla smiled, meaning it.

CHAPTER 24 – AFFECTION

The next morning Layla still felt pain, though it was rapidly improving. Rikyava had departed and Layla sat in her cobalt robe at her breakfast table, eating bacon and eggs Benedict, when a brisk knock came at the door. With a large bite of Benedict in her mouth, Layla startled, coughing as she tried to speak but inhaled instead. But before she could say anything, swallowing her bite, someone bustled in. Layla smiled as she smelled Dusk's crystalline river-water scent, glancing over as he entered.

"Good morning." Moving to the table and stepping behind her chair, Dusk kissed her on the neck, lingering and smelling her scent with a smile of his soft lips against her skin.

"Hi." Layla smiled also, reaching up and winding her hands behind his neck. As she turned into him, their lips met, and they kissed a long moment. Dusk was grinning as he pulled away, a sexy diamond-sapphire fire in his eyes. Even with Reginald's pearls still on her wrist and in her ears, Layla's magic gave a delightful simmer of orange-bourbon scent as her Dragon rippled eagerly inside her, delighted to be home in Dusk's arms.

"Someone's feeling recovered today." He grinned, nuzzling her nose. "I can smell your Dragon partying like your breakfast's an open bar at a wedding."

"It's not breakfast she's celebrating." Layla smiled as Dusk stepped to her side, hauling out a seat at the gilded French Baroque table and settling into it. "My bones still hurt like I got run over by a

Mac truck, but seeing you makes my day brighter."

"Lucky me. And you practically did get run over by a Mac truck." Dusk smiled roguishly, teasing and bright. Dressed in one of his impeccable dove-grey Italian suits, he was resplendent as always, rakish and sexy as hell. "High-diving into the ocean from three hundred feet up doesn't tend to be healthy. I'm glad you're improving."

"How's Adrian?" Layla asked, taking a bite of bacon with a worried frown.

"Better." Dusk nodded more soberly, sitting back in his tall dining chair. Crossing one ankle over his knee, he showed tasteful grey and maroon argyle socks beneath his suit, matched by a maroon tie and pocket square today. "He'll be in bed today, but I imagine he'll be well enough to deal with the Owners by tomorrow. Rake and I are giving him healing treatments in shifts. I can't stay long right now, but I thought I'd just pop in and see how you were."

"I appreciate it." Layla smiled, taking up her coffee. "Adrian looked like hell when he came through. Were those Vampire-bites on his arms and neck?"

"Yes." Dusk's energy spiked, churning restlessly as Layla saw a flash of fury in his eyes, though she could tell he was trying to control it. "Heathren likes to play a little game of *how many Vampires can I sic on Adrian before he breaks* when he has Adrian in custody. You'd think he'd learn by now that Adrian's remarkably resistant to them. Heathren could torture Adrian himself, using his own magic, but so far he's not gone there. He may, though, next time. Being drained physically and mentally by thirteen Intercessoria Vampire Interrogators is a lot. I'm actually surprised Adrian wasn't in a coma when he came back through."

"Heathren does what he has to, to achieve his aims, doesn't he?" Layla spoke, feeling a seething bitterness rise inside her at the way

263

Adrian had been treated.

"You have no idea." Dusk's dark glance held it all. "He operates within the letter of the law, technically, but the law is very broad when it comes to how much force Juds are able to use when investigating a case. It's a good thing you cooperated with him, Layla. I think we all got off far more easily because you were forthright and honest with them, and willing to help the investigation into Hunter."

"I couldn't have been much help if they treated Adrian that badly." Layla growled, sipping her coffee.

"Adrian and Heathren have history, Layla." Dusk lifted a straight dark eyebrow at her. "Heathren was going to lay into Adrian no matter what you did. But because of your help, we got Adrian back in a week rather than a month or three. How much worse do you think he'd be after a whole season in Intercessoria care?"

"Not good." Layla hated to even think about it. Dusk gave a sober nod, an understanding passing between them. Even though Adrian was powerful, he wasn't immortal. He had weaknesses, and in that moment, Layla knew that part of how Dusk looked out for his adopted brother was by keeping Adrian safe. Layla felt grateful for it suddenly, and reached out, taking Dusk's hand on the table top. He smiled, a beautiful smile that lit his eyes as he set down his coffee and curled his strong, warm hand around hers.

They shared a moment, feeling each other's closeness as Dusk's thumb brushed over her fingers. But then with his usual restlessness, Dusk glanced around the room to Layla's walk-in closet. Rising, he stepped over, throwing the doors wide. Moving in, he rifled through her dresses. Picking out a sexy royal purple cocktail dress with an Audrey Hepburn boat-neck, he hung it on the door. It was stretchy with a subtle shine, attaching across the shoulders and leaving the back bare. Picking out a royal purple silk thong and a matching strapless bra from her underwear drawer, then a pair of creme silk heels from her shoe-rack, he hung those from the door also.

"There." Dusk's critical gaze glanced over the outfit, before he nodded.

"Why are you prepping my wardrobe? Am I going somewhere?" Layla spoke, still sipping her coffee at the table.

"I thought you might want to visit Reginald."

"What?" Layla blinked, setting down her coffee cup.

Dusk turned, watching her with his crystal-blue eyes. "He did save your life, Layla. You might want to say thank you."

Complicated emotions sluiced through Layla. Suddenly, she recalled her night of sex dreams with Reginald, where they had rolled in deep waters with each other all night long. She could still feel that delicious abandon rushing through her, and not just because she still wore his pearl bracelet and earrings to control her Dragon's urges. A wave of heated bourbon scent washed up around Layla and she blushed, fidgeting with the bracelet.

"What if that's not a good idea?"

Frowning, Dusk stepped back over to her. "You don't have to go see him if you don't want to. I just thought it might be a nice gesture. He's been recovering these past days as much as you and Adrian – from changing into his Siren to save you."

Layla fidgeted again, her fingertips feeling the silken texture of Reginald's pearls. Part of her wanted to go see him, but part of her was afraid. She hadn't told Dusk and the Intercessoria about her sex dreams with the Head Courtier. She had only mentioned that she'd woken dreaming of a drowning wave and choking on it, when Hunter had rushed in as Tempeste and snapped the pearl choker from her neck. Now that omission seemed enormous, as if that wave of passion and darkness had returned for her and she couldn't escape it. Layla heard the sea rushing in her ears with a call of gulls. But she'd not dreamt of Reginald since that night and rubbing his bracelet again, Layla debated what it meant.

"No... you're right. I should go see him."

"As long as you feel well enough." Dusk had picked up that there was something strange going on. As she looked up, he lifted his dark eyebrows at her. "Layla? Are you ok?"

"Yeah. Just... give me a moment."

Though he frowned, Dusk stepped back with a nod. Moving to the closet, Layla closed the doors so she could get dressed. The stretchy satin dress Dusk had picked out was cozy enough for winter and fit her curves well. The undies and heels were comfortable, and Layla felt herself re-adjust to Hotel life as she did a tad of makeup from her makeup kit in the wardrobe, then combed out her curls and spritzed them with shiner, twisting them up with Mimi's diamond hair-pins.

Stepping out of the closet and approaching the table, she adjusted Reginald's pearl and diamond bracelet at her wrist. The pearls were snug, the feel around her wrist deliciously restricting. But the choker, the best part of the set, was still missing – maybe never to be recovered. Although the Intercessoria had searched the apartment in Manarola, they'd not found Tempeste's effects, nor Reginald's pearl choker. Layla's bag had been there, but that was all, plus a fridge full of half-eaten food.

"Layla?" Dusk furrowed his brows, watching her.

"Hmm?" She blinked, glancing over, her strange reverie interrupted.

"Are you sure you're alright?"

"I... still feel odd. Probably just recovery." Shaking her head to dispel the fog in her mind, Layla moved to the table. Her royal blue peacoat was there, and Dusk held it out for her.

"You'll need this. Reginald is staying in the Crystal Cathedral out in the gardens right now, rather than his apartment."

"Why?" Layla frowned as she donned her coat, buttoning it.

"He had his first shift," Dusk's face was grave as he adjusted her coat like a butler, pulling her hair out from the collar. "When a first shift happens, the likelihood of a second one increases exponentially. The Madame's moved Reginald to the Crystal Cathedral, because with the Vault out of order, it's the one place with enough concentrated energy to contain a Siren-shift. You and I were lucky that time you tried to shift at the Dragon party, that you were standing in that hall. It helped me stabilize you and stop the shift. Plus, you're a Desert Dragon – a lot smaller if you shift than a Siren."

"Do you think I'm in danger around Reginald right now?" Layla looked up at Dusk.

"Not at the moment." Dusk shook his head, though his brows were furrowed. "He's got his emotions on lockdown, and the Cathedral is helping. Plus, Rikyava's stationed a cadre of Guards outside with shift-stalling abilities and Dragon-stopping weapons. If anything gets out of hand, all you need to do is shout."

"Where will you be?"

"Adrian needs me. In between healing sessions, we're strategizing about how to deal with the Owners Board." Dusk smiled softly. Reaching out, he stroked one of Layla curls back from her neck. "So many problems... so few of us to solve them."

"Us? Am I on your problem-solving roster now?" Layla lifted a cheeky eyebrow at him.

"You took a big risk to get Adrian back for us. Not just for you and me, but for our entire Hotel." Dusk's gaze was grave. "If what you did wasn't the epitome of problem-solving... then I don't know what is."

Smiling, Layla stepped forward. Dusk's arms wrapped around her as they kissed, long and delicious. When he pulled away, his eyes were shining, and Layla could feel his lovely diamond light shimmer through her bones as the same refracted through his artful dark hair.

"I'll come find you up in your rooms when I'm done." She murmured.

"I'll be waiting. But Adrian's in my bed, so no hanky-panky." Dusk grinned.

"Unless he wants to join in. As I recall, we're still missing out on the little three-way we started before everything went to shit…"

"Everything's still shit," Dusk brushed his lips over hers with a chuckle and a sexy smile. "But I'll never turn down a three-way. Not if you're at the center of it. I'll talk to Adrian today. You never know…"

"I want to know."

"I'm sure you do."

But something complex moved through Dusk's eyes then, as his fingers stroked her curls. A wave of refraction passed through his scales as he watched her, his lips turning up in a sad, wry smile. "I do hate it that you have so many men competing for your attention, you know." He spoke softly. "But to restrain a Royal Dragon Bind from having powerful men is like cutting a Crystal Dragon off from the earth. If there's one thing I've learned from Hunter's story, it's that denying those Binds is almost a fate worse than death for you. I don't want you to become like Hunter, Layla. Even if it means sharing you, I will do whatever it takes to make sure you stay as bright and beautiful as you are right now. And never become dark, like him."

"Thank you." Layla's smile was a match for his, sweet and sad. An echo of what she'd experienced with Hunter's memories hit her, a dark sensation like a pit opening up inside her. But that was a place of deadliness and cold rage, not a place of love. Held in Dusk's strong arms, Layla was able to banish it, lifting up to kiss his soft lips.

"It won't be this way forever." She spoke quietly. "I'll get control of my magic, and then Binding lovers will be my choice, not the magic's. When I do… you're the first person I'm going to come find. And we're going to have some *serious* alone time together. I promise."

His smile twisted, though that sadness still lingered in his bright blue eyes. "Don't make promises your ass can't cash, Layla Price."

"I'm not. I mean it."

He sobered, watching her. And then smiled more naturally, cheekiness returning to his eyes. "Off you go – to the Siren's cave. But when you're done training with him and your magics are under control, Layla, you're mine. I'm going to haul you off to Barbados and we're going to fuck on the beach and drink rum right out of the bottle for a month straight. We clear?"

"Crystal."

Layla grinned at him and Dusk grinned back. Setting her palm to his cheek, she lifted up and kissed him once more, then turned and headed for the door. Taking a deep breath, she stepped out into the hall and shut the door firmly behind her. Hotel Guards posted on her door came to attention, stepping forward as if to follow her, but Layla waved them off. They glanced at each other but hung back, and Layla set out.

The Hotel was bright in wintertime. As she headed down the opulent French Baroque hall with its writhing porticos of Dragons, Satyrs, and sundry, Layla glanced out the vaulted windows. Everything was bright, fresh snow reflecting the light until the entire Hotel glowed from every gilded rail and silvered mirror. Heading down a grand crimson-carpeted stairway to the first floor, she pushed out through an ornate double-door into the gardens.

Snow created fanciful shapes of the winter-dormant topiaries. The walkways had been swept clean and salted, and Layla took a flagstone path in her high heels with confidence. Walking past ponds and fountains, Layla circumnavigated beds of dormant roses and barren lilac trees. Though the vegetation was now dead, fairy-lights twinkled everywhere, lighting the paths and the snow and the bare trees. It made the gardens luminous in the grey day, and Layla knew it would be even more spectacular at night.

Rounding a row of hedges, she came to the Crystal Cathedral where she had once nearly shifted into her Dragon at Samhain. Fourteen Guards in uniform with a full regalia of weapons were posted on the door, each holding a long black spear made of ebony wood and tipped with an obsidian blade. They were the same spears Layla had seen in Rikyava's office, the ones that could stop a Dragon. Golden sigils ran through them, and something about those sigils reminded Layla now of the script she'd seen moving through the walls of the Intercessoria interrogation room.

Stepping to the doors, enormous and fashioned of rose quartz, citrine, and aventurine, Layla nodded to the Guard. They must have been expecting her, because they nodded back, then stepped forward to open the doors. Layla entered and the doors were shut behind her. The vast space of the Cathedral was open, all the ballroom furniture moved to one side and stacked behind a series of silk dividers. In the center of the hall, ringed by the crystal columns that supported the vaulted roof, sat a four-post mahogany bed, an armoire, two bedside tables, and a breakfasting table.

The only person in all of that enormous space was Reginald. The Head Courtier sat at the table eating and reading a newspaper, dressed in a highly elegant ensemble. Cobalt rather than sky-blue, his sleek outfit was a mixture of Victorian and modern attire. A cravat of white silk was set with a diamond and pearl pin at the open collar of his shirt.

Slender black riding-breeches were tucked into tall black boots shined to perfection, a cobalt riding-jacket gracing his lean frame. His waistcoat was quilted cobalt silk set with pearls, a gold pocket watch flashing on a chain. Bound half-back, his golden hair shone in the morning light that flooded through the high crystal vaults, his chiseled face exquisite.

Hearing the doors, he lifted his gaze from the newspaper, piercing her. As Layla stared at him, undone by his incredible beauty, he gave her a subtle smile, his pale blue eyes flashing with golden sunlight and grey mist. Layla shut her mouth, heat flooding her as her Dragon gave an eager roil through her veins. Her dreams came roaring back, smashing into her like a tidal wave.

Frozen to the spot, she couldn't move, couldn't even breathe.

With a wry smile, Reginald lowered his newspaper and rose, moving towards her with his dancer's grace. Sidling close, he didn't reach out to kiss her hand, but instead slid his long fingers around her waist – gathering her in. Flooded with desire and roaring with bourbon-orange scent, Layla could only stare up at him stupidly as he held her close. Gazing down into her eyes, Reginald gave a soft laugh, a look of pure pleasure lifting his handsome face.

"If you looked at me like that everyday, I would die a happy man." He spoke quietly.

"I... um..." Layla's mind still wasn't working right. She didn't know if it was Siren's powers or just the severe hotness of the Head Courtier, but it had blindsided her. "Thanks for saving me at the Aviary."

Reginald stepped in, his hands around her waist, pressing her close to his sleek clothes and the hard, exquisite body underneath. His eyes were luminous as he gazed down, a small smile lighting his perfectly sculpted lips. "Thank you for wearing my gifts so I could find you in your time of need."

"Sure." Layla still felt stupid to his beauty. She blinked hard, but her Dragon roared inside her, as if ceasing looking at Reginald was not what it wanted. Her beast slid through her veins with a restless heat, coiling in a slow, sinuous motion. She felt it surge up, eager to try its heat against the Siren's – and felt it sluiced back by a wave of Reginald's cool power.

"Sorry." Layla breathed. "My Dragon's restless."

"Magic does as it will." Reaching up, Reginald brushed his knuckles across Layla's cheek. Their gazes locked and with their bodies pressed close, his grey-gold eyes pierced her to the quick. "We learn to control it, but sometimes it controls us."

"Is your magic controlling this, our attraction?" Layla breathed. "Those dreams we had when I was in Manarola?"

"No." Stroking her cheek, Reginald gazed deep into her eyes. "I felt those dreams just as much as you did. And our resonance is not happening just because of your magic or mine, but because of a connection between us."

"I feel it," Layla breathed, feeling him so near. "It's been like this for weeks, hasn't it?"

"Months." He spoke quietly, his gaze wistful. "I felt it the first day you arrived at the Hotel. When I stepped out onto the promenade to greet you with the Madame, I felt this attraction hit me like a forge-fire, making my seas boil. I *wanted* you, unlike I had wanted anyone in so very long. It made me fear you – and made me doubly cold in our subsequent interactions. Forgive me."

"You were trying to deny it." Layla swallowed, knowing she'd been trying to do the same for a while now.

"I was trying to deny what was happening, yes." He nodded. "I was trying to avoid what I felt, just like I've been trying to avoid facing

272

my true power for centuries. But you felt me, the real me, the first time we danced. I didn't mean for you to, but you fell into my eyes and my body – and I saw you recognize the man beneath the mask. I spoke long hours with Sylvania about it. She urged me to embrace it, but still I resisted. But now, because of my Dragon's response when your life was in danger, I know how I feel about you. And I will never deny it again."

"You give me strength." Layla spoke before she knew what she was saying. But as her words tumbled out, she knew the answer to the riddle between them, and why they were calling each other – why her Bind magic was calling him.

"I give you strength?" Reginald spoke quietly. Reaching up, he smoothed his knuckles over her cheek, his sea-grey eyes deep. "Whatever do you mean?"

"When I met with King Arini, he helped me realize that each Royal my Bind-magic calls gives me something." Layla spoke, knowing she had to face it at last, this formidable attraction between them. Taking a breath, she firmed her courage and continued. "Your control, your austere impeccability – it gives me strength, Reginald. Adrian gives me challenge and passion. Dusk gives me safety and clear problem-solving. But you give me cold, raw power. You have the ability to control my raging magic. The way it wants to wreak ruin and Bind every Royal in sight – whether I want it to or not. And I value that, Reginald. I value you. I think that's why my magic has been seeking you out. Because without you… I'm less than I could be. And without me… you're less than you might be, also."

"Less than I might be…" Reginald Durant breathed, his sea-grey eyes infinite.

And then he cupped Layla's face in his palm, lifting his lips and kissing her, deep and strong.

CHAPTER 25 – POWER

At last, Reginald released their kiss. Gazing down, his look was so breathtaking, so fiercely tender, that Layla's chest caught as he slid his hand back to cradle her neck. Silence breathed around them in the vaulted hall of the Crystal Cathedral, and as they watched each other, Layla saw that memory again in her mind, of Reginald's Blood Dragon lover.

Before he washed it away in a wave of white sea-foam.

"Why do you hide that memory from me?" She asked, knowing now that when she saw someone else's memories through her magic, that they experienced them also.

"Because it was my power that ruined everything, back then." Pain lay in Reginald's eyes as he gazed down, still stroking her neck. "A power I couldn't control at the time – my rage. Even though you've heard about my past, Layla, it is not something I wish you to see. I lost control back then. I did not have the strength you feel in me now, not like I have learned over the years. And the result of my lack of control – was terrible."

"That's why you insisted I become your Partner, isn't it?" Layla searched his eyes. "Because you knew that only you had the control I needed, over catastrophic, unpredictable magic like mine."

"Like ours." Reginald's smile was wry as he gazed down, his body quiet with intensity as his fingers continued stroking her. "I became what I am because of that terrible day. Just as you will come into your power more fully because of what happened at the Aviary, disastrous though it was. I thank Ummo and all the gods that your lesson did not come with such a high death toll as mine. Not all Twilight Lineages have the power you and I possess, Layla. When I lose control, my passion goes cold. And then it does not just kill, it wreaks ruin. I ruined that day – hundreds of people who did not deserve it. I have had to live with my terrible deed ever since."

Layla saw it then, her magic viewing the memory as Reginald finally released it. A young Reginald, furious with grief and rage, standing on a haystack rock in the harbor with his eyes red-rimmed, his hair whipping long and glorious in the brisk sea-wind. A sound flooding the harbor, like a cacophony of reed flutes being smashed in a storm as Reginald screamed. And then a true storm whipping the cove; swamping boats, driving people inland – called by Reginald's power and the dark fury of his voice.

Layla thought she might see a tidal wave then, but what she actually saw was far worse. An image of the Blood Dragons in the village came, clutching at their throats. All throughout the cove, they fell to their knees with eyes bulging as seawater rushed up from inside them; flooding them. They twitched like fish out of water in the stony fields, in farm-houses of wood beam and thatch, in their lodge-houses of worship and gathering.

Drowning – dying.

It was only then that Reginald had pummeled the cove with tidal wave after tidal wave in his horror, washing their corpses out to sea to hide what he had done. But Layla had seen the truth. Everyone thought he'd killed the village with his tidal waves, but the terrible truth was that he had caused seawater to bubble up inside those Blood Dragons – killing them where they stood long before he'd summoned any ocean waves at all.

Tears stood out bright in Layla's eyes. Staring down at her as she watched the memory, Reginald's eyes tightened though he shed no tears. Reaching up, Layla cupped his face in her hands, even as she gasped with agony from the vision. She could feel Reginald's woe; so impossibly deep. He'd not meant to kill them, only to destroy their ships and pummel their harbor. But he'd been furious with grief and his magic had raged, doing for him what he could not – taking retribution.

Drowning them from the inside out by the sheer power of his wrath.

"It wasn't your fault!" Layla gasped as she cradled his face. "Gods! It wasn't your fault, *Sivvir!*"

A bourbon-orange scent careened through Layla as her Dragon rose in a wash of deep mercy, keening for him. Reginald's eyelashes fluttered at hearing that name from her lips. His breath caught hard in his throat as his eyes sparked with a glorious grey-gold light. And then he seized her behind the neck hard; kissing her again.

Drowning her in his oceans.

Lust broke between them like a dam flooding open under heavy spring snowmelt. Layla felt them both give in to it for the first time – truly give in, neither of them holding back now. As if the fury and passion of centuries drowned them, all the tension that had been building between them these past months suddenly exploded.

Layla's Dragon scalded through her veins with a devastating heat as Reginald devoured her, and Layla devoured him back in a heady wash of passion. Picking her up under her thighs as they kissed, his oceans roared around her as he held her effortlessly aloft, hauling her short skirt up so she could lock her legs around him. This was no effete, clever courtship. This was no demure touch of passions restrained. This was wild, raging heat, and as Reginald tore away Layla's dress, breaking her bra in his roaring passion, he took her breast into his mouth, hard and deep.

Layla cried out, arching in his arms as he held her aloft while he sucked her breasts. Her passions and his were a tidal wave now; obliterating all restraint and logic as fire met water. Slamming Layla up against a rose quartz column, Reginald's hands ripped her underwear as he sucked her, making Layla gasp with abandon as he tore his breeches open also. Arching for him, her energies howled like a desert funnel in the tides. Tearing his pearls from her wrist and slipping her earrings out fast, Reginald set her free.

And then he thrust inside her, strong and deep, and Layla screamed out his true name – *Sivvir*.

The sea roared around Layla, devouring her with every thrust. Gripping her by the throat, Reginald fucked her as power screamed out around them in a furious golden flame rushing through a hurricane of water, his gaze rabid and his energy roaring just like hers. Layla felt their magics twist together; she saw it happen in the air as an enormous white-silver Dragon coiled through her red-gold one. With powerful muscles and fangs, Reginald's Siren wrestled her Dragon in its coils. She saw the dominance in Reginald's eyes as he fucked her; saw the way they sparkled like an ocean of light to master her as he threw her magic over on its back. And made her surrender to his power even as she slid her talons deep into him.

Twining them both together.

Reginald roared as he felt it; how their Dragons twisted into an inseparable coil, mastering each other and being mastered. With a growl unlike anything Layla had ever heard, he heaved her higher as he tore away his shirt and waistcoat – fucking her in only his breeches and riding-boots. An ocean of death and light streamed through Layla as he cored her harder; deeper. Her lips were in his hair as they fucked; she couldn't stop breathing him. His lips were at her neck, mad with abandon as he kissed her, bit her. He was a roar of passion and power as he bound her with his ferocity and she bound him back with her unrestrained magic. Layla felt her power twine into him as he thrust as deep as he could get, pinning her wrists up on the column as he kissed her and she gasped for heaven and high water.

But then – he stopped.

Breathing hard, Layla felt Reginald master himself with impeccable control. In a wave of glory, he mastered her also, sluicing her almost-Bind in his vast oceanic power. Arresting her body, mind, and magic, he pinned her with his gaze, his hips, and with his hands. His eyes burned grey-gold as he heaved for breath – as he gave her a glorious, dominant smile.

"Not yet!" He gasped. "Not yet!"

Breathing just as hard as he, Layla couldn't say anything, only nodded. She was sea-foam in his arms as he gathered her up off the column, cradling her naked body close as he walked them to the bed. Laying her down, he pinned her to the coverlet with one hand upon her chest, making her feel his tremendous power as he settled his weight upon her. Sliding his hand up to grip her throat, he mimicked what his pearls had once done – controlling her, making her writhe and gasp beneath him. Bracing one hand upon the bed as he kept her secure, he watched her eyes, making her wait for him.

And wait for him.

And wait for him.

Layla gasped, writhing with need, delirious with it. Keeping her pinned by the throat, Reginald somehow shucked his boots and breeches, then moved over her again, his glorious body entirely naked now. Layla could feel him, so hot and hard, resting against her – sliding against her royally slow. Making her feel him as he devoured her with his eyes; as he kept her waiting upon his dire tides like a becalmed fishing boat at sea.

With his free hand, he lifted her leg, sliding her ankle up to his shoulder. Layla's breath caught as he positioned himself at her opening; watching her, holding her in a tightly bound position with his hand around her throat and his lean, hard body bearing down on her thigh. Layla squirmed beneath him, whimpering softly, desperate for release.

But this game was a pleasure for both of them, and she saw Reginald's lips curl up as he held her, as he made her taste him but need so much more. Teasing her, he pressed the last bit of himself into her, then pulled away, making her gasp. Watching her as he turned his head to kiss her inner ankle, he teased her again and Layla writhed on the bed, trying to push her hips up onto him only to be denied. Tears beaded in her eyes now, tears of need as she mewled, gripping her hands like talons into the bed and giving a short scream of frustration.

Massaging her neck, Reginald soothed her with his magics, flooding a calming sensation through her raging lust. Pressing down hard on her thigh and spreading her wide for his pleasure, he slid his power in through her lips with his eyes as he choked her gently, licking his pleasure into her mouth with his oyster-smooth magic and making her devour him. And when he finally thrust inside her, it was with the sweet, slow slide of the ocean, thick and firm. Fucking her royally slow, impeccably slow as he kissed her with his magics, hard and aching and deep.

Pinned by his hips and body, by his eyes, his hand, and his phallus sliding deep inside her, Layla gasped in bliss as he sheathed himself to the hilt. And although she was the one tamed beneath him, her pleasure flooding out in ripples of golden fire that danced through the room on tides of seawater manifested by Reginald's power, he was tamed by her in return. His eyes shone as he pressed blissfully deep inside her, kissing her with his power. As he thrust again, Layla arched and he let her, his hand more gentle at her throat now. Massaging her firm and slow, he built his oceanic energy inside her, undulating with deep thrusts until she could barely take it anymore, crying out with the need to release.

And then he began to sing.

Soft and low, an impossible sound issued from Reginald's beautiful lips as he fucked her, as he took her. Like waves flowing in sunlight, it was the same sound she'd heard in her dreams the night he'd nearly drowned her with his passion. As Layla arched beneath him, feeling his grip on her throat, his body sheathed within her, his song so sweet inside her, something within her finally released. One moment, she was writhing with pleasure.

And the next she was screaming with it.

Surging in a bright wave as Reginald's Siren-song set her passions free, Layla spilled over into climax. With one last, sundering thrust, Reginald spilled himself deep inside her with a matching cry. Layla's Bind-power rushed out in a torrent; Reginald's power swirled out like a typhoon. Twining into each other, they cascaded into a blissful coil – shooting high into the sky like a geyser and flooding the morning with bliss.

Layla cried out again and Reginald's hand spasmed from her throat so she could sing free. As he came breathlessly down, he rolled her atop himself, still sheathed inside her. Layla heaved with sweet sobs as he cradled her close, singing his tender song in her ear. Gradually, the power of their Bind sighed away – though it was not gone, and never would be now.

Reginald's song faded out as he set a kiss to Layla's temple. Cradled close to his warm body, Layla felt him slip out with a delicious sensation, and she gave a small shudder as Reginald gave his own.

"My god!" Layla gasped, her lips at his neck.

"My goddess…" Reginald spoke softly, low and spent.

Combing her curls, Reginald's fingers touched Layla gently; reverently. Brushing across her back, he explored every curve with his touch until she was utterly serene where she lay on his warm chest. An image of sea-caves came to her; a Dragon of red-gold fire inside them, curled up in the sand with its nose beneath its tail. Peaceful, the beast winked at Layla with one lazy golden eye before it snuggled deeper into its cavern of sand and saltwater and soothing ocean sounds.

"Me, too…" she murmured with a smile.

"Hmm?" Reginald opened his eyes. With one lazy hand, he stroked her sable curls, a bemused expression on his face.

"I bound you." Layla breathed.

"I know." He spoke with a secretive, pleased curl of his lips. "I wanted you to."

But before Layla could ask questions, he shifted gently, rolling her down to the coverlet. Coming atop her again, Reginald eased his body against hers once more. The sensation of his pearl-smooth skin sliding over hers made Layla arch. Everything felt heightened in her post-Bind ecstasy. Skin had never felt so good as he moved her, sculpting her to his slow, regal waves and making her writhe against him. It was cool and clean and erotic, and Layla's breath caught as he slipped his hand over her hips; pulling her close so she could feel the press of him growing hard once more.

She squirmed against it and he smiled; *that* smile. Dominant pleasure shone from his eyes as he slid his phallus between her thighs but not inside her; rubbing her gently between the legs as she shuddered with pleasure. His lips came to her neck, kissing her softly beneath her curls, and Layla spasmed against him – her body too pleasured to resist his power.

"Please," she breathed as he continued to kiss her, sliding himself against her, a slick sweetness between her thighs. "Please, *Sivvir*…"

"Please what?" He whispered at her neck with a cruel little smile. "Please stop… or please continue?"

A small sound left Layla's mouth, as she found herself unable to decide which was worse and which was better. But Reginald enjoyed her heady torment, chuckling by her ear as he pinned her by her hips, still sliding himself against her gently. Layla's whole body surged, her breath fast once more. Curls of etheric golden fire manifested around the bed, and Layla knew the Dragon inside her was far from finished. Stirring, it opened its big golden eyes. Its coils writhed inside her with a sinuousness that made Layla's body move with a serpentine undulation on the bed, needful.

Through her heightening arousal, Reginald held himself contained, still sliding against her slow and sweet. With the skills of a man who had controlled his passions so thoroughly over the centuries that he could do anything with his body now, he controlled their dance, even though Layla controlled their Bind. As she surged beneath him with all the need of the darkest ocean, he watched her, holding her back from cresting – to his utterly dominant delight.

"What is your truth, Layla Price?" Reginald murmured as he moved her. "Do we continue our pleasure this morning… long into the night perhaps?"

"Yes!" Layla whispered, trembling hard with need. "Please, Reginald! Please, *Sivvir*. My Partner…"

"My Bind."

Sliding his arms around her, Reginald brought her up, kissing her as he sat her in his lap facing him. Layla was weightless in his arms as he settled her legs around his hips. Pulling her back gently by wrapping one fist in her hair, he lifted her up with his other arm tight around her waist.

And then he slid her down – deep upon himself.

Commanding their lovemaking with his hand wound up into her curls, fucking her sweet and slow, Reginald controlled Layla's passion like the deepest currents of the ocean. And when she crested into orgasm again in a wave of glory, he crushed her to his chest and to his lips with strong arms.

Devouring her screams with his Siren's kiss as he devoured her power through their Bind.

CHAPTER 26 – GAME

Layla was affixing Reginald's pearl and diamond earrings in place at her bathroom mirror, when she heard a knock on her apartment door. Dressed in an expensive stretchy silk royal blue cocktail dress tonight, Layla moved out of the bathroom. Lifting a hand to the diamond and pearl-encrusted sweetheart bodice of the sexy, short gown with its long close-fitted sleeves, she adjusted the bodice, then slid her hand down to straighten the hem at her mid-thigh. Checking Reginald's pearl bracelet at her wrist, she set a hand to the door to admit Dusk, here to escort her to the Owner's Ball tonight.

But instead, it was Adrian standing there when she opened the door – tall and perfect as he gazed down at her.

"Hi, sexy." Adrian breathed, a pleased smile curling his beautiful lips. He was stunning tonight in a white tux with royal blue satin lapels, wearing the collar open as was his way. Rakish and elegant, Adrian's thick hair was sexily styled, no stubble on his angular jaw tonight as he stood before her with graceful nonchalance, his hands shoved casually in his pants pockets. Diamond and pearl cufflinks flashed at his French cuffs, his Mediterranean eyes a vivid blue-green as he smiled down at her, arresting with his high cheekbones and straight dark brows.

"Adrian!" Layla didn't even know she'd moved until she was in his arms, kissing him. Holding her close, he kissed her back, passionate and reckless. Everything fell away as they reveled in each other; as their Dragons coiled together in a fire-bright dance. Layla's hand was behind Adrian's neck, pulling him into her as etheric golden flames burst through the air around them. When Adrian at last pulled away, it was with a breathless laugh, his Mediterranean-blue eyes on fire with gold.

"Someone's glad to see me!"

"You have no idea." Layla curled into his arms, holding him tight. Inhaling his cinnamon-jasmine musk, she let his desert heat surround her. Being with Dusk was a deep pleasure, being with Reginald had been a dark joy, but being with Adrian was like coming home. He had her scent, he had her fire – in so many ways, they were the same. Breathing him in, Layla gripped him tight and he chuckled, kissing her temple as he ran his hands deliciously over her bare spine.

"May I come in?" He chuckled. "Or are we just going to stand in your doorway making out all night?"

"Tempting," Layla grinned up at him, "but come on in."

Layla stepped back with a smile, admitting Adrian to her apartment. Her Dragon still roiled with pleasure, curls of golden fire moving through the air as he shut the door behind them. Lifting a straight dark eyebrow, Adrian ran one hand through that golden flame.

"You've gotten better control of your magic since you bound Reginald two days ago."

A sharp spike of fear made the curls of flame around Layla snuff out. She'd not had a chance to speak with Adrian about that yet, though she and Dusk had discussed it. Although not surprised it had happened, Dusk had been wary of her Bind to Reginald. But Adrian seemed surprisingly calm facing the truth tonight, and Layla blinked, having expected him to be unhinged.

But as she watched him, a wry smile lifted his lips. "You thought I would be mad."

"Aren't you?" Layla blinked, still surprised. "I mean... you were furious when I bound Dusk back in October."

285

"I admit, I am jealous that you bound Reginald. Intensely." Heat moved through Adrian's eyes though it was subtle, as he tucked his hands back in his trouser-pockets. "But it's really not like I didn't see it coming, Layla. Since August, actually, if I'm being truly honest with myself. I felt how much heat there was between the two of you at your entrance interview. And it was pretty hard to miss how Reginald's watched you ever since then. And how you've watched him back." As he spoke, Layla saw Adrian master his passion with a deep breath, the beast inside him settling.

"So why aren't you pissed at me right now, if you noticed all that since August?" Layla lifted an eyebrow at him, feeling her Dragon coil up inside her, eyeing him warily like perhaps this was some sort of trick.

"Maybe I should be," Adrian chuckled darkly, though his eyes were still clear of anger. "Maybe in another lifetime, if everything that's happened recently hadn't happened, I would be. But I realized something when I was being tortured by the Intercessoria last week, Layla. Something that's… made me think a little harder about what your Binds mean, for all of us. Including me."

"What do you mean?" Layla asked, crossing her arms. Though Adrian was being intensely reasonable tonight, she just didn't trust it. He'd erupted on her too many times with his passionate jealousy, and too recently, for her to simply take a change like this at face value.

But as she stared him down, Adrian gave a rueful smile, something sad in his eyes now. "I've trained you to not trust me, haven't I?"

"I admit, it's hard to take what you say at face value sometimes, Adrian." Layla breathed, though she kept her words gentle, not wanting to provoke a fight with him tonight. Her Dragon stirred in her veins with a far more peaceable attitude this evening, as if it agreed, simply watching the conversation but not heating to it. "You've fed me so many lies and half-truths these past months that I've had to wade through to figure out, and often from other people. And your emotions have been so catastrophic around me – and I admit, mine have been that way around you, too. Dusk was right when he said you and I spin each other's magics up through our Bind, even though Dusk's presence as part of it now has tempered our reaction somewhat."

"Which is where Reginald comes in." Adrian spoke softly, watching her.

"What?" Layla blinked, her arms coming unwound from their defensive posture, easing down to her sides as her brows knit.

Moving forward, Adrian slid his hands out of his pockets and corralled Layla around the waist. It was gentle rather than possessive, and Layla felt herself give in to him, stepping close to his body. Adrian didn't move to kiss her, just reached up, caressing back one of her loose curls as his smile went slightly sad. "Did you know that the last time Heathren Merkami set Vampires on me during an Intercessoria interrogation, I nearly broke?"

"No. How so?" Layla lifted an eyebrow at him, though she was enjoying being cradled close to his warm body and didn't pull away.

"Heathren brought six Vamps last time, when I was interrogated a few years ago, and I struggled hard against them." Adrian continued, watching her with his steady gaze as he clasped his hands around her low back. "I was like a drowning man beneath their powers, and they would have broken me, except Heathren got pressure to release me at the eleventh hour. But this time—"

"This time, you could withstand more." Layla blinked, understanding what he was telling her. "Because of our Bind... you were able to take far more of Heathren's torture last week."

"That bastard kept adding Vamps to drain me, but I just kept riding those waves, Layla." Adrian nodded, his gaze intense on her though calm, the highly-aware version of Adrian that Layla saw leading Hotel Departmental meetings. "They sapped my energy, but not my will. I felt your rage, flowing through me and keeping me strong. I felt your defiance along with Dusk's crystalline strength holding me grounded, letting me take my willpower straight from the earth itself. And all of a sudden, even delirious as I was, I realized we're stronger together – able to borrow each other's power through our Bind. And when you bound Reginald…"

"You felt it, didn't you?" Layla breathed, wondering at this deep change in Adrian, impressed by it.

"It *filled* me with energy while I was healing." Adrian spoke softly, shaking his head with a look of amazement on his face. "Deep power and control the likes of which I've never had before. I was entirely well within an hour, Layla. Reginald's power made me well. Your… sex with him… healed me. And somewhere during that time, as I felt the two of you together, I realized that your gain is our gain. All of us."

"So you're really not mad?" Layla held her breath, wondering at this intensely reasonable Adrian standing before her. She could still feel desert passion in him, she could still feel his raging jealousy deep down, but she realized she could also feel the ocean flowing through him now – stabilizing his emotions just as it stabilized her power since Reginald's Bind.

"I can't say I'm not going to punch Reginald in his haughty face once we're alone together sometime." Adrian chuckled, his eyes flashing with dark humor and a hint of rage now. "The bastard deserves it for the way he's manipulated all of us this past month. But even I can see it was done for a reason – to push your power, to make it grow quickly. Dusk and I have talked about it, and I know this is the right course for me to try and support you, even though Reginald and I have a very tense history. So I'm willing to give this a shot, for all our sakes."

"Are you sure?" Layla lifted an eyebrow at him, realizing that Adrian was now speaking words to her almost exactly like she had spoken with Dusk in the crystal bath-house. "Because this intensely calculating Adrian sounds a lot more like Dusk than your usual."

"At the moment." He chuckled, something dark moving through his eyes as he cradled her closer in his arms. "I can't promise I won't flip my shit about it sometime when I'm feeling less magnanimous. I can't say I'll help you find time alone with the Siren, Layla. But I want you in my arms; in my life. Spending so much time away from you, interrogated by the Intercessoria and not knowing if I was going to come out of it alive this time… it made my priorities clear. You. You are my priority. And I don't want you to be afraid of me, Layla. I want you to be able to trust me, to talk to me about what's going on with you. To trust me to give you straight answers and keep my shit together when we talk. I want to try. I really do."

"So this is what Adrian Rhakvir's like when he's calm." Layla spoke with a soft smile, gripping him closer at his waist.

"I don't want to be a bastard with you, Layla," he spoke with a wry but gentle smile, nuzzling her nose. "I want to be a good partner. I want to be *your* partner… not someone estranged from your life because he's just a jealous fireball all the time."

"I want to trust what you're saying," Layla breathed, pulling back slightly so she could see Adrian's eyes. "I want to trust this change I'm starting to feel in you. And I saw how reasonable you can be after you and Dusk saved my life back in October."

"Dusk is my brother," Adrian spoke with a wry smile. "And though he and I have been contentious for years, we also trust each other deeply, Layla. There's no one I trust more in this world. And even though that Bind stung, it was easier for me to accept. But Reginald... Reginald is my enemy, Layla. And though that one is far harder to accept, I'm willing to try, for all our sakes."

"Is Reginald your enemy because of him, or because of you?" Layla asked, wondering if this was the reason Dusk had been cagey about her new Bind to the Royal Siren. Because Adrian had a past with Reginald that neither man had told her about yet.

"Because of him." Adrian spoke, winding Layla closer in his arms. "Reginald hates my guts. I don't have any reason to hate him, except he's always been a dick to me, trying to undermine me as Hotel Head every time I turn around. Like he did when he pulled that fast one on us at Samhain, moving you into the Assignations department. But while I understand his anger towards me, I don't think he'll ever understand my position, Layla. His Bind to you gives us power, but..."

"You worry that he's going to try and steal me away from you," Layla breathed, understanding at last. "In a way Dusk never would."

"Yes." Adrian's gaze was so vulnerable that Layla reached up, cradling his face in her hands.

"That's never going to happen, Adrian." She spoke firmly, her Dragon rising in her veins with a roar of heat, making him understand. "You are my mate. You. Dusk and Reginald are bound to me also, and I love Dusk deeply, and Reginald... well, he's Reginald... but you are the Drake of my heart. I see you and everything inside me smiles, Adrian. Everything. You stir my passions in a way I can't describe – and I love it. I love *you*. The Binds make it complicated, but... I want you in my life. And I'm not going to take no for an answer."

"I would never say no to this, Layla," Adrian murmured, his lips curling up in a soft smile as joy beamed from every part of him. "Never."

And then he was kissing her, slow and deep as their energies whirled, bursting with golden flame. Adrian's aqua and crimson coils surrounded Layla's, playing with her power as they kissed. Tightening around her, Layla was trapped inside Adrian's coils, feeling them slide in a muscled play of sensuality all around her. A large, thick coil slid between her legs as if she rode a massive serpent – smooth spines brushing up between her thighs, slipping over her most delicate places. Layla arched in Adrian's arms, shuddering with heat, and Adrian broke their kiss, chuckling at her ear, low and devious.

"I felt how much you liked power-play with Reginald the other day. You should try it with me sometime."

"Ok." It was stupid, but it was the only thing Layla could say right now, deliciously obliterated. She was entirely wet as the last of Adrian's etheric barbs brushed her then slid away, giving her one more delicious shudder.

"Are you angry that I've been with both of them before you?" Layla breathed hard, clutched close to Adrian's chest and loving the way he held her.

"I am." He murmured at her temple, his strong fingers stroking her back. "I was a roaring flame of jealousy when you had sex with Dusk before me. But when you fucked Reginald in that sudden heat of passion, I finally knew."

"Knew what?" Layla asked breathlessly, feeling smaller versions of Adrian's barbs sliding over the bare skin of her back with his deft touch.

"That tormenting you is far more fun." He spoke by her ear, low and sexy. "That making you want me with a roaring inferno from my every glance, my every glide of fingertips across your skin is more satisfying than a furious, sudden copulation. That making you wait for me, not knowing when I'll come to you, waiting with bated breath for my touch, is the darkest bliss. And when we are together at last… it will be you who is bound, desperate for my pleasure as you scream my name to the high desert winds. *When the world pushes you to your knees, you're in the perfect position to pray.*"

Adrian's sexy, intense words and final Rumi quote shattered Layla to her core, making her shudder deeply in his arms. Reginald was a seducer, but he was also broken in ways that needed mending. Adrian wasn't broken. Adrian had been through hell numerous times but had come out stronger for it each time, not shying away from everything that he was. He was still taking the world by storm each and every day, adjusting to the shifts and slides and dangers in the monumental game of power they all played.

Adrian knew he was still learning the full force of his magics, and he embraced it. Sifting through his powers like cards in the world's highest-stakes poker match, he was still finding the ones that would smite his enemies and bind his friends closer, everyday.

And make his mate want him – deeper.

As she pulled back, Layla saw that immense game shining in Adrian's golden-aqua eyes. She saw his vast pleasure in playing it, in making her ache for him, pine for him – lust for him. She saw how much he loved the game of power and seduction, of pent-up frustration and release.

And she also saw, that no one had the ability to play like he did.

"Are you ready to go down to the Owner's Ball, Ms. Layla Price, Royal Dragon Bind and Drakaina of my heart?" Adrian growled seductively, his piercing aqua eyes flashing sexy murder.

"Absolutely." Layla breathed, a deep passion shaking her to her core as she took his arm.

"Then let's do it." He growled again with a devious chuckle, turning them towards her apartment doors.

And feeling Adrian's hand as it slid hot over hers, trapping her to his arm, Layla suddenly knew that like her frustration with being celibate this past month, her withheld release with Adrian only strengthened their Bind. Like Reginald had been doing with Layla, making her need consummation desperately yet denying it, Adrian and Layla had been unconsciously doing to each other this entire time – raising the power of their unconsummated Bind to the screaming point. As she and Adrian stepped from her apartment, Layla felt an enormous aura spread from the both of them like muscled coils, as if they fed each other's energy like a wheel of fire, devouring their enemies as they came forth to battle.

And as they entered the Grand Ballroom on the first floor of the Hotel in a sweep of elegance, Layla knew they came with power – together at last.

CHAPTER 27 – BIND

Heads turned as the Royal Dragon and his Bind entered the game. The chamber orchestra in the Grand Ballroom faltered, and Layla saw from the corner of her eyes the coils of gold, aqua, and crimson flame writhing out from her and Adrian as they faced the long mirrored hall. Owners stared, forgetting their conversations and their drinks as they watched the power couple take center stage, moving gracefully forward over the parquet floor of the ballroom. Gold and aqua flames were reflected in every French Baroque mirror along every wall, simmering crimson as they licked up the marble columns.

It was already impressive, but suddenly, Dusk stepped to Adrian's side, formidable in a midnight blue tux with pearl-white silk lapels, and Layla felt their trio's combined power explode like an inferno. Like someone had taken Layla and Adrian's muscled heat and thrust all the power of the earth behind it, it made their combined magics surge up the columns to the vaulted crystal roof far above, spiked now with deadly crystal shards glittering in the air.

And then, from the other side, Reginald stepped up to Layla. Dressed in a modern royal blue tux with black silk lapels, he gave a haughty glower to the room and a lift of one golden eyebrow, dressed as a part of their Bind by the clever Head Clothier. As he took up a position at Layla's side like the world's sexiest, darkest warrior, she felt their quadrupled magics roar. A giant beast surged out from them, screaming a vicious note; and Layla felt that creature of fire, wind, earth, and sea flare wings wide through the ballroom. Silvered mirrors shuddered. Champagne flutes shattered from the stress. High above, every chandelier in the hall rattled and Layla inhaled, hoping none of them would come crashing down.

None did.

But the illusion of their smallness shattered in that moment. Once, Layla had not been able to manage the roaring intensity of the Red Letter Hotel Owners and their vicious magic, but now it felt like nothing as the Owners stared at the foursome, astonishment and dark hatred seething in their eyes as magic heaved out all around them. As Layla's group stepped forward to mingle through the party, she remained on Adrian's arm, no longer needing Reginald's touch to prevent her Dragon from flaring – and no longer troubled by the vicious sensations she felt stabbing at them from all around.

They were inconsequential now.

Because now, Layla had control over her Dragon – at last.

Conversation began again as Adrian took them into the crowd, nodding politely and playing a game of dangerous small-talk with Owners who were friendly and others who were downright hostile at this new level of magic. Drinking in his scent, Layla soaked up the heat of Adrian's hand on hers, feeling magic breathe between them like a roaring bonfire of muscles and fangs and talons. It was incredible. Never in her life had she felt such enormous, grounded power, and she felt herself drinking it in like the finest wine upon her tongue, reveling in it.

All around, Owners reacted to Layla and her Bound Royal Dragons, many throwing up shields against their magic, slamming them up as if they were afraid of that combined Dragon-power. A Satyr with corkscrewing ram's-horns did this, throwing up an ephemeral screen around himself like vines. A Lamia snake-woman with scales at her temples did also, throwing up a shield of venomous fangs bared in warning. While some Owners came from old-money families, others had clearly fought their way into Hotel Ownership with magic, enormous signatures of power cascading out from them. Layla became aware that both kinds of Owners hated Adrian with a passion as they bristled at him and his Bound group.

But no one hated the young renegade with new money and newer power as much as the person related by blood to their Bind. Regal in a white tux jacket and bowtie, Bastien Durant's pale eyes with their ring of blue were vicious upon the foursome as he stepped in, sipping a dry martini. "A pretty display. Was it supposed to be intimidating?"

"No." Layla spoke coldly before Adrian or Reginald could say anything. "It was meant to make you shit your pants, Bastien Durant. No more games this time, asshole. Try to roll me with your tides again and see how fast you sink, dick."

"And do you think you're more powerful than me, Dragon Bind?" Bastien Durant chuckled, though fury flashed through his pale gaze as it pinned Layla. "You and your bound toys?"

"Just try playing with us." Layla snarled, heat rising in a simmering mirage around her now. "And watch how far we ram our magic right up your ass."

"Layla." Adrian's voice was low with warning, though Layla could see him trying not to smile as his hand tightened upon hers at his sleeve.

"Control your *pet*, Adrian Rhakvir." Bastien was not smiling, power rising up around the Royal Siren now like a roaring tide. "Or I will control her for you."

"She's not my pet." Adrian spoke, a warning growl in his own voice as his piercing eyes flashed gold now. "And your disrespect at this establishment will not be tolerated, Bastien Durant. You are banned from this Hotel. Collect your things and leave, immediately. I'll not have your vicious hatred disturbing my guests, my employees, or my friends. And if you ever try to return, just watch how fast I have you skewered, by my own talons if need be. Or by Layla's magic, ramming right up your ass."

Bastien Durant trembled with fury. Setting his drink aside on a table in a precisely elegant gesture, he squared off with Adrian. Contempt filled his icy white gaze as an enormous grey-white energy surged up around him in a watery nimbus – full of barbs and strangling tentacles. "Have a care whom you threaten, *cur*. Or do you wish the full fury of the Crimson Circle to come raging down upon you? And upon those you love?"

Bastien Durant's white gaze flicked from Adrian to Layla. In that instant, his hand whipped out, seizing her wrist, and suddenly Bastien's mesmeric Siren-power was pummeling through Layla's mind. His ocean roared like a supersonic boom through her head and she screamed, doubling over with both hands at her ears. It was louder than a bomb; louder than sanity. But the sound was inside her, and as Layla screamed again beneath the roar of an ocean gone mad, Adrian and Dusk shuddering as they felt the power also, she felt someone step in front of them.

Seizing Bastien's hand and wrenching it from Layla's wrist.

"*Enough!*" Reginald Durant's voice was an icy roar as he stood before the trio protectively, murder flashing through his husky-blue eyes. A light seethed from Reginald like a watery white-gold forcefield, spreading out to protect Adrian, Layla, and Dusk from his brother's power.

"Or you'll what, little Siro?" Bastien snarled coldly, yanking his arm from Reginald's grip. "Run away, like you have all these years? Where were you when Alexandre was torn apart by Blood Dragons *brother*? Or when Orlando was burned in battle? Or when Tempeste was killed on assignment with the Intercessoria? Oh yes, you were right here *fucking for cash*. You are a whore, Reginald Durant. Just like your Blood Dragon was, and just like this little piece of ass is here. If I pay enough, I can touch those whores, Reginald. I can fuck them for a fee – and I will, the moment I am head of this establishment and this young whelp you call your Hotel Head is properly disposed of. Permanently."

Bastien's hateful white gaze was fixed upon Reginald, and Layla saw all the worst things roil through his blistering eyes – of inflicting rape and torture and cruelty upon the people Reginald cared for. Of wreaking his revenge on his headstrong youngest brother until he was utterly cowed and penitent, submissive to their father's cruel iron will. She saw that the elder Siren would never stop until everything Reginald cared for was utterly destroyed, and everything Adrian protected ripped apart to satisfy Bastien's terrible wrath. She saw that Bastien would have no mercy, if he ever took over the Paris Hotel.

And he would do anything he had to, to break the dominance of Reginald Durant.

Reginald saw it also. And in that instant he reacted, the Head Courtier's oceanic power suddenly expanding a hundredfold, screaming through the ballroom like a hurricane. As a roaring, furious power surged through the hall and a rush of seawater went crashing across the ballroom floor, Reginald's Siren rose. A Dragon of the deep, Layla saw it emerge in her mind like a shimmering creature, flashing with gold scales and white filaments through the blackest ocean currents. As Reginald roared with rage, she saw the leviathan of his true self blossom up; the apex predator of the oceans, the beast that killed in the depths of the Marianas Trench.

And then she saw it take him.

A tremendous shudder wracked Reginald, every muscle in rigors as if his body was trying to tear itself apart. Standing tall, he tore open his tux jacket and shirt as his body began to ripple with light. Surging over his flesh, white and gold scales devoured Reginald's torso, huge white filaments ripping up out of his spine in a wave and shredding his clothing. As Layla watched, Reginald transformed fast, his chest spreading, massive, his arms becoming tall as tree trunks, fantastic gold-white talons punching from his fingers and gouging deep into the parquet floor. Above her, his long neck was graceful as it arched, huge white spines lifting up to the ballroom's vaults and shattering chandeliers as he roared, a long white and gold tail of spines and flowing fins coiling out behind him where legs had been.

"Layla! Get back!" Dusk roared nearby.

But all around Layla, Reginald's muscles bunched and lengthened into enormous coils as bones snapped and grew. His body surrounded her, serpentine like an enormous boa constrictor, trapping her. White fangs as long as Layla's forearm showed in his enormous maw. White scales streaked his muzzle with ribbons of gold since their Bind, flowing into long whiskers and corkscrewing horns like a Japanese sea-dragon. His enormous head was long with angled grace, cunning eyes of gold-white fire roiling with grey storms and sunlight. Trapped with him, Layla saw his transformation become complete. As he breathed above her, his enormous chest heaving like a bellows, the talons of his forelegs punctured into the floor on either side of her and his coils wrapped around her body, his eyes suddenly focused.

Piercing her to the quick.

Layla gasped, terrified, exhilarated; standing very still with the beast. Guards with black spears ringed them in the flowing seawater, surrounding Reginald; Rikyava with blood-red eyes, her body set in a rigid tension as she held her own spear steady. Reginald's sinuous form looped around Layla as if in protection, and as he lowered his massive muzzle, he watched her with cunning mist-gold eyes. Sliding his snout over her chest, he inhaled her scent. Layla shivered at the touch of those impossibly smooth scales as coils bunched around her; securing her. His body was massive, his tail coiling around the room, barbed white filaments and gossamer fins breathing in a wave-like motion from his spine.

Those scaled lips eased over Layla's collarbones and neck, smelling her. Long white and gold slits in his neck rippled with gossamer fins; the gills that had saved Layla's life in Italy, though thin nostrils in his snout allowed an icy-warm breath to pass over her. A fang brushed her and she shivered. Her breath came fast from fear and delight – one part terrified he was going to eat her, the other part knowing he was merely making the acquaintance of his Bound mate.

She made a move to raise her arms. The creature above her snorted with a hard ripple of his body and flash of his eyes – as if it wasn't entirely a man anymore.

"Layla…" Adrian's voice came very soft through the shocked hall, Owners being quickly hustled out by Guards as silently as could be managed, though Dusk, Rikyava, Adrian, and all the Guards with black spears remained. "Don't move. Sirens aren't known for having much human memory during their first few changes. He feels you're his partner; he smells what you are, but he doesn't remember. Go slow."

Layla kept still, watching the enormous thing above her coil and contract, seeing its intelligent eyes. The Siren's head descended again, his lips and elegant jaw brushing her skin once more. Turning his head, Layla saw the side-view of his face, just like she'd seen it in the water before. Though he had changed utterly, certain features of Reginald's were the same. Golden ridges created straight brows over his cunning eyes. That angle where his jaw met his neck, so stern and striking, was entirely his. High cheekbones, cuttingly fierce and angular, held Reginald's moody yet arresting attitude. The appearance of smooth lips

300

covered in white-gold scales were utterly his.

As he smelled her, he shifted, the muscled swath of his body pressing Layla's legs apart. She couldn't fight it as an enormous coil settled between her thighs; sliding up against her groin and parting her legs. She shuddered, unable to stop it. A pleasured gasp came from her and the Siren's head rose to her face – snuffling her with those massive fangs at her mouth.

It slid its muscled coil up against her again and Layla cried out, her eyelashes fluttering as pleasure shuddered through her. As if it knew how Adrian had teased her already tonight with his magics, the Siren did him one better now, sliding that thick, tremendous coil slowly between her legs. Layla's skin heated with a flavor of orange peels and bourbon and the Siren inhaled, taking her scent deep into its muscled lungs like a forge-bellows. It breathed out over her face and Layla inhaled the sea; sweet and fresh.

Raising her arms slowly, Layla settled one hand to the beast's ridged cheek and the other to its long, muscled neck. It gave a snort as she touched it, white spines rippling all along its back and coiling tail. Undulations moved its body as it breathed, washes of ocean sunlight refracting through its scales. Stroking that impossibly smooth skin, Layla shivered as it adjusted its muscled drape, laying down along her belly and hips. She felt swallowed by the creature as it settled around her, yet cradled by it also. That coil pressed up against her groin again, slipping along her and Layla shuddered, breathing hard.

The Siren's lips turned up at the corners of its long, blocky snout. It was such a cruel, calculating smile that Layla laughed suddenly. Reginald was still in there somewhere, teasing her with his powerful new body.

But even as she had that thought, a harsh voice cut through her reverie. "Disgusting. She would fuck it as a human, even though his power would rip her apart."

The massive creature that was Reginald's Siren gave a furious snort. As if remembering why it had shifted in the first place, that enormous head lifted, swinging around to face Bastien. Safe and dry behind a barrier of his own power, Bastien stood his ground in human form, staring Reginald down with contempt upon his austere face.

As if recalling that it had an enemy to murder, Layla saw no mercy in Reginald's Siren-blue eyes as he swung around to face his brother, bristling like a viper.

And there was no mercy in Bastien's gaze as he bristled back – powering up into his own shift with a furious roar.

CHAPTER 28 – BEAST

There was no love lost between the two Siren brothers. If Reginald and Bastien had once been close, it was not the case now. Layla felt magic roar up into the air with death in it, from both Reginald and Bastien. Reginald's magic was powerful in his Siren-form, but Bastien's was horrifying, even as a man. The air was suddenly so thick with ice and vapor as Bastien powered up that Layla couldn't breathe. Dusk gave a shout, and as Reginald coiled like a serpent to attack, Layla rolled out from beneath his tremendous weight.

In that instant, Bastien changed. This wasn't some gradual process like Reginald. Bastien's body knew how to shift; had known how to do it for centuries. Like Layla had seen with the Phoenix King and Hunter, Bastien was one moment man and the next moment roaring fast up into his Siren in a mirage of watery light. He towered over Reginald, an enormous serpent of grey and silver scales with long, flowing tendrils cascading off him like a leviathan. Bastien had gossamer fins all along the length of his back, and a massive mantle of fins spread from his skull like a frilled newt as he roared, cascading spray through the ballroom as he reared back to strike with fangs bared.

As Layla kicked off her heels, dashing across the wet floor towards Dusk and Adrian and Rikyava, the battle began. One moment, the floor was slick with flooding seawater, the next it was shuddering into whitecaps as the enormous Sirens slammed into each other. The room concussed with power; chandeliers crashed down. Dusk and Layla raised their hands in the same moment, and above their heads crystal was suspended on a barrier of power and wind.

They shared a moment as their gazes connected – astounded at what they had wrought together on instinct through their Bind.

And then the fighting Sirens hit a marble pillar. Sections of the crystal roof were suddenly shattering down and Dusk rolled fast, seizing Layla in strong arms as Adrian and Rikyava launched out of the way the other direction. Roars shuddered the ballroom; silvered mirrors exploded as crystal, wrought-iron, and steel from the roof smashed down through the water, sending chunks of the wooden floor ricocheting through the hall.

It was a war-zone. Sheltered by a pillar of marble and one of Dusk's barriers at the edge of the ballroom, Layla and Dusk breathed hard as the Sirens careened through the space. Silver-grey and white-gold blood flowed as tails whipped, talons raked, and fangs tore. Over and over they coiled, hammering each other, strangling, biting and gouging and flinging deadly spears of water-magic to try and smite one another.

Being in the middle of the Phoenix King's battle with Hunter had been frightening, but this was terrifying. Layla breathed hard, her heart hammering in fear as she watched the two behemoths battle, each of them three times the size Hunter had been in Dragon-form, and far more deadly. She had no question in her mind now that Sirens were the most powerful of the Dragons as she watched them slam into each other and explode the ballroom's confines like tissue paper to a car-bomb. It was how she imagined people felt as they saw a tsunami coming for them from the shore – that it was nothing they could possibly flee from in time, or fight in any way.

Raging funnels of water tore through the hall as Reginald got a good bite into his brother's shoulder, but then roared as he was whipped in the head by Bastien's long, barbed tail and a spike of ice that shattered upon his armored snout. Bastien launched in as Reginald fell away with a dazed snort, Bastien's talons raking Reginald's underbelly and thrusting rapid-fire ice-spears into Reginald's middle. But Reginald was swift, writhing over in an eel-like movement as he roared in pain, hammering his head into his brother's injury with an armored shield of ice protecting his blocky skull and pulping Bastien's already-damaged shoulder like a meat mallet.

Bastien roared; his magic shuddered the broken ceiling and another rain of crystal and steel came careening down. Layla saw Rikyava and Adrian peer around from the far columns; their gazes connected with hers. Guards with black spears held defensive positions behind the columns, heaving hard breaths. Fear was in their faces; Layla was certain that a Siren-battle inside the Hotel was so above their pay grade. At the ballroom doors, a few braver Owners gaped from a semi-safe distance. Hotel Guards held them back, though Layla was fairly certain Reginald and Bastien could have this whole ballroom falling down in minutes flat.

And start rampaging their fury through the entire Hotel.

"Layla." Dusk spoke as the Sirens crashed by to the far end of the ballroom, trying to hammer ice into each other's bellies. "What would you do to save Reginald?"

"What do you mean?" She gasped, her magic screaming through her body now as Reginald completely lost his own control. Their Bind was worthless at the moment, but perhaps that was for the best. She saw Dusk flare his nostrils, scenting her scorched bourbon fragrance blasting through the sea-scents around them, though still somewhat trapped by Reginald's pearls.

"I need to catch Reginald in a crystal cocoon," Dusk breathed hard, peering around the column. "You need to support Adrian and Rikyava in trapping him, long enough so I can weave my power."

305

"What happens if we can't trap him?" Layla gasped, watching the Sirens roil by again, trying to strangle each other with nooses of seawater now. Removing Reginald's pearl bracelet from her wrist fast, along with his earrings, she saw Reginald was retreating, coiling through himself again and again in pain. Layla saw why; Bastien had raked his talons deep into Reginald's face and gold-white blood surged down into Reginald's eyes. Layla saw Bastien side-wind in to bite Reginald's throat while he was blinded, but Reginald whipped his tail and his brother was hammered back against another column – causing the column to crack with a deafening retort.

"If we can't trap him, Reginald dies." Dusk glanced around the pillar again as his hand moved quickly, taking Reginald's pearls from Layla and stuffing them into his pants pocket. "The Forbidden Spears are almost ready. If Rikyava can get even three of them into Reginald, he's dead. We can't let that happen."

It was then that Layla saw something she'd missed in the melee. Behind the pillars at the edge of the hall, the Guard hadn't been idle. Each person, no matter their Lineage, was vibrating with a violet light pouring through their hands and wrists now, deep into the spears. The gold sigils on each ebony spear and their obsidian tips glowed a shade so deadly that Layla knew it was poison – last-ditch control for a rampaging Dragon. As Layla glanced around, fifty more Guards with black spears sprinted into the ballroom, taking up defensive positions at the columns. Beside Adrian, Rikyava held up a hand, watching the fight get critical but stalling her men.

They were hanging back on the Head Guardswoman's orders, powering up to max.

And once that max was reached, she would send them in to succeed or die.

Layla saw the determined set of Rikyava's shoulders; she felt the focused sensation of battlefield scorch all around her friend as Rikyava's gaze went a bloody crimson. A whirling vortex of blood flared up around the Blood Dragon, and as Layla watched, Rikyava's eyes began to bleed like she cried pure death. Somehow, Layla knew that the Head Guardswoman was only a moment from changing into her own Dragon to stop this fight.

And Layla knew that if she did, the death toll would be high.

"What do you need me to do?" Layla spoke to Dusk, as a storm of blistering bourbon scent roiled through her. Her Dragon rose inside her, rolling through her veins with an eager roar. Layla was shuddering from the force of her own power now; curls of blistering golden flame rushed off her in simmering waves. Clenching her fists, Layla felt that heat concentrate in her chest, rushing down into her hands and causing a hot mirage in the air.

Though it was wild, she felt the focus of Dusk's crystal energy at her side – and further away, Adrian's furious winds adding to her heat.

"Get to Adrian," Dusk breathed as the Sirens slammed into the stained-glass cupolas at the far end of the hall, blasting them out into the night like cannon-fire had hit them. "Join your power to his. You both resonate with the same magic. I can hold my own; you two need to get a noose of fire around Reginald. Hold him. I'll do the rest."

"What about Bastien?"

"Rikyava and the Guard can handle Bastien." Dusk glanced at Layla, something complicated in his eyes. They flared with a diamond-hot brilliance, and as Layla watched, Dusk began to thrum with the power of earthquakes. Reaching out, he seized her behind the neck and kissed her hard – then thrust her towards Adrian. "GO! NOW!"

She ran. Sending a ward of energy down to protect her bare feet from broken crystal and wrought-iron, Layla sprinted towards Adrian at his column, as hard and fast as she could. Their gazes connected;

Adrian saw her coming. She saw him recognize the plan as he shouted at Rikyava, making a motion for the Head Guardswoman to take a different position at a nearby column and get a better angle on Bastien.

But then everything went wrong.

As Layla ran, an enormous silver-grey tail snaked out, hammering her in the back. Layla flew; she hit Adrian's column with a solid crunch and a blast of pain. Falling to her back in the surf; Layla gasped. She'd had her forearms up; it was the only thing that had saved her. Her power had made a sudden shield of wind as she'd hit the column, but still, everything hurt like hell from Bastien's powerful strike. But Bastien's hit had thrown her to Adrian, and as she lay there gasping, he hauled her up, pulling her behind the column with him.

"Layla!" He scanned her eyes fast. "Are you alright?"

"Yeah," she gasped. "Yeah, I'm ok. I'm ok."

"Thank god." Adrian kissed her fast; then he was watching the battle. Across the hall, Dusk was vibrating with power; he'd stepped out from behind his column, white crystals spiking up through the seawater all around him. Layla saw him close his eyes; his lovely dark eyelashes fluttered as he gathered power. Spreading his hands, Dusk gripped them into talons, shuddering the crystals around him higher. As Layla watched, light began refracting through him, blistering along his serrated midnight scales and golden lines. Lengthening his fingers into cruel diamond talons, that light heaved an enormous double-set of corkscrewing horns from his temples as giant armored spikes sprouted from his shoulder-blades, ripping through his tux.

"Jesus," Adrian swore softly by her side. "I've never seen Dusk shift this much. We don't have any time, Layla. Feel my energy; follow my lead. Raise your power to scorching, and keep it as high as you can."

"I don't know how!" Layla panicked suddenly, fear driving

through her as she watched Dusk's power escalate. He had so much power, so much control, but Layla had never been a warrior like he was...

Hauling her close, Adrian kissed her, roughly. With a growl, he poured his energy down her throat, roaring at her inner Dragon in a challenge. She felt her Dragon roar back. Suddenly, her power was spiraling up through her throat, chasing Adrian's as he pulled away with aqua-gold fire in his eyes.

As he gave a hard smile, whirling and stepping out from behind the column, Layla felt her bones thunder with power; Adrian's power and hers, chasing each other in an enormous figure-eight of play and danger. Like Adrian had reached inside and bitten her, hauling the power out for her to use, Layla's body was suddenly on fire.

As she stepped to Adrian's side, she wasn't afraid anymore. Curls of real flame were in her hands now, swirling in a blistering wind. The same were in Adrian's hands, as their twinned magics created an enormous heat-mirage before them, ringing them in a wide arc. As Adrian moved forward, Layla moved with him in perfect synch. She knew what he was about to do; feeling everything he'd ever learned about fighting with magic. As Adrian breathed deep, she felt him haul all that tremendous blister of their Bound magics deep into his lungs. And as he roared it out in one long breath, that vicious mirage before them suddenly caught fire.

Igniting a gargantuan wall of flame all along its length.

Layla moved as Adrian did, the both of them gripping their hands like talons into that enormous wall of flame. They spun in synch, hurling that flame at Reginald, causing a barrier of fire to rise up between the Sirens. Roaring with affront, the fighting Sirens were forced back from each other. Writhing from countless injuries, Reginald heaved back from the fire.

And was trapped as Dusk shot his crystals at the Siren.

White crystals ripped across the wet floor, plowing a path through the water and surrounding Reginald. He screamed as they encased him; a roar of rage. Reginald thrashed and fought Dusk's containment as the crystals towered, building into a jagged ring up over Reginald's hulking shoulders. Reginald shrieked like the ocean heaving, and it was all Layla could do to not release her hands from her and Adrian's barrier to cover her ears.

But as they caught their friend, Bastien was suddenly loose. Though bleeding from countless punctures and a number of ripped fins, he'd taken less damage than Reginald. With a quick sidewinding movement like a cottonmouth through the water, he came for Adrian and Layla. But in that moment, Rikyava gave the signal for attack. As her Forbidden Spears rushed in, six Harpies and five Furies flying in while the rest rushed through the water, they surrounded Bastien nearly a hundred to one.

Rikyava held point, transformed now into a blood-red Dragon with black geodesic lines running through her scales. Though huge, Rikyava's Dragon looked positively tiny compared to Bastien, like a sparrow-hawk facing down a condor. Raising red and black-tattooed wings, Rikyava launched into the air like a falcon. Gripping a black spear in either taloned grip, she hounded Bastien's head, whirling and diving as rivulets of blood shed off her into the air; the power of her magic as she spun and dove, slashing for his eyes.

It was working. As Dusk shuddered the entire Hotel, stacking his crystal barrier up around the thrashing Reginald, Layla and Adrian changed their postures to sweep their barrier of fire around the snarling Bastien. The Guards rushed in. Though Bastien smacked them from the air and gouged them with massive talons, hammering others back with his tail, Layla saw one Werewolf Guardsman hurl a Forbidden Spear. It stuck between two of Bastien's glossy back-plates and he roared in pain. Poison-bright violet sigils careened out from the injury, devouring their way across Bastien's scales.

But there was a lot of Siren to devour. And plenty of Bastien was still furious, even as Layla saw that section of his back become paralyzed. Hammering Guards away, he whipped his body in a fast flail; sending those nearby scattering like bowling pins. Rikyava shrieked as more than half her Guards fell motionless in the water. She dove fast, anticipating where Bastien's head would be.

And thrust one of those cruel black spears right through his left eye.

Bastien roared. He surged forward, hammering Rikyava with his broad, viper-flat skull even as he rolled his snout around in a fast movement. In a one-two devastation, Rikyava was stunned, then seized in Bastien's jaws. Layla heard Adrian roar beside her. Their barrier of fire was suddenly whirling as Adrian shifted. Swept up in a massive funnel of wind and crimson-aqua fire, Adrian thrust Layla back as he careened out from that funnel.

A fully-formed Desert Dragon.

As serpentine as the Sirens, Adrian's crimson and aqua Dragon had no wings but flew through the air in a rippling of coils and barbs upon a wind of his own power. Stripes of gold and black cascaded down his back with rippling spines, a double-row of horns arching from his skull like Dusk's. Larger than Rikyava but still only a third as big as Bastien, Adrian shot like his own kind of spear through the air, coiling around Bastien's neck like a viper, strangling him. Savaging Bastien's throat with enormous fangs, Adrian whipped Bastien's underbelly with a powerful spiked tail – digging in with massive black talons at Bastien's heart.

As Adrian attacked, Layla felt his and her magic diverted. With

311

powerful mastery, Adrian took their barrier of flame – and poured it down Bastien's throat like molten lava as he savaged the enormous grey and white Siren. The Siren choked and roared in pain, dropping Rikyava from its jaws like sticking fingers down the throat of a mauling cat.

And though Adrian couldn't bite all the way through the Siren's scaled throat, he and Layla's fire could. Layla felt her and Adrian's combined power pour down the Siren's gullet, deep into its body. The Siren burned from the inside, screaming now – and as Adrian bit deep into its throat, silver blood gushed crimson-gold like the Siren's veins had caught fire.

It was the end. Five more Guards got in. Black spears were thrust. Violet death-sigils spiraled deep into the Siren's flesh.

And with a last shudder and howl, it went limp – dead.

An answering howl came from Reginald's crystal prison. But as Layla gasped on her hands and knees in the flooding seawater, she heard that howl drowned out as Dusk's dome finally encased Reginald. As Dusk slammed his hands together over his head in a thundering clap, a massive tone rang through the ballroom, knocking Reginald unconscious. But Dusk's blast exploded what was left of the ceiling and marble pillars, and Layla thrust her hands up, unfurling an enormous screen of wind with her last bit of power.

As the entirety of the ballroom came crashing down, Layla's barrier held – casting away falling crystal shards and marble and steel and keeping everyone below safe.

Layla heaved with shock as the dust settled and she finally released her barrier, only the night sky with stars above her now. By their light and the glancing glow still coming from the Hotel proper, she saw her hands had transformed; gold seethed through her veins from her chest into her fingertips, her fingers now cruel golden talons. Spines had thrust from her back; her head dragged from the weight of long corkscrewing horns. As Layla sobbed from pain, power still seething through her, she saw that Adrian had fallen away from the dead Bastien, gasping in the water butt-ass naked and back in human form. Crawling to the motionless Rikyava, also human again, he checked her pulse. Adrian heaved in relief as Guards stumbled up from the wreckage, blinking in astonishment at the wide sky above as they realized the battle was over.

But something was wrong inside Layla. The fight was finished, but she was still vibrating with power, and couldn't stop it. She could feel a thread of her Bind remaining to the unconscious Reginald, but it wasn't enough to control whatever was happening inside her. Her entire body was thrumming with power, surging with it. Gasping with pain, her panicked eyes found Dusk's as he stumbled to her side. She saw him understand what was wrong – in an instant, he knew her problem and how to solve it.

Hauling her into his arms, Dusk wrapped his naked body around her. Cradling her close in the seawater that still flooded the now-quiet ballroom, he cupped the back of her skull and the back of her heart with his hands. Though breathing hard from exhaustion, Layla felt his power thrum through her in the most soothing shower of sound she'd ever felt – to stop her beast from rising.

It did.

As her Dragon roared one last time and gave up, settling back down inside Layla's veins, she felt those enormous spines from her back resorb into her body. As the burning gold inside her veins retreated, Layla fell limp. And as Dusk used the last of his power to put hers away, he collapsed on top of her – passed out cold.

CHAPTER 29 – GONE

The Grand Ballroom at the Red Letter Hotel Paris was a demolition zone. Seawater rippled across the blasted-out floor as Adrian and Layla worked together, breathing energy back into Dusk to revive him. Hotel Owners gaped through the doors of the blasted-out ballroom, their eyes enormous upon the dead Siren in the middle of all the damage, not to mention a handful of deceased Guards. Layla was exhausted to her marrow from the battle, but Dusk was worse. Though he jerked up to sitting with a gasp, he immediately reeled, raising both hands to his head and wincing in pain.

Adrian gripped Dusk behind the neck, setting their foreheads together a moment. Adrian murmured something so soft that Layla couldn't hear it, and with a grimace, Dusk nodded as if the very act of nodding speared him with ground glass. Layla could feel an echo of it in her own body; the terrible pain of a partial Dragon-shift that hadn't been allowed to come to completion. But Adrian had shifted fully, and though he was just as exhausted as Layla and Dusk, he was in slightly better shape – his wounds from his battle with Bastien at least mostly healed by his change back to human form.

Setting his lips to Dusk's forehead, Adrian murmured, "save some for yourself next time, you bastard," before he rose, moving through the sodden debris back to Rikyava. Adrian repeated his breathing to get Rikyava conscious, then hauled her up into the hands of her Guards. Ordering her to her rooms on the fourth floor, Adrian instructed the Guards to find Rake André to heal her. Rikyava's entire middle was a morass of bruises and puncture-wounds from where Bastien had bitten her, but she was tough, giving Layla a weak smile as she was helped past.

Staggering up, Dusk shook his head to clear it and Layla swept in, getting up under his arm. Together, they walked to Reginald's massive crystal cocoon and Layla watched as Reginald's beast heaved a sigh in its unconsciousness. As if it was as exhausted as the rest of them, it suddenly settled all that enormous weight down – and with a shivering ripple, its bones began to crunch and re-mold, sinews collapsing and muscles shrinking. In half a minute, it was only a man laying within the crystal sphere, naked with scales rippling away from his haughty, beautiful features. Like a burnished pearl, Reginald Durant shone within the crystal – unconscious and still bleeding from a plethora of wounds, though they seeped red now rather than gold-white.

Alarm raced through Layla, but then she felt him heave a breath. His heart pounded and Layla could feel it beat against her chest, as if she was inside the cocoon with him. Going to her knees, she reached out, stroking the crystal near his face, but he was out cold.

"Is he going to be alright?" Layla asked Dusk.

Still naked as a jaybird, a dire glint took Dusk's summer-blue eyes as he set both hands to the enormous dome. "This is only the second time Reginald's fully shifted. He might be out a few days. Sirens fall hard the first few times they change. It's not like them to change back quickly."

Layla watched Dusk shudder, his dark brows knit with strain as he began pouring a sonic resonance through the cocoon. Layla stepped behind him, steadying him to make sure he didn't fall over, and he smiled back at her, though it was tired. With a deep breath, Dusk sent a series of pulses through the crystal, condensing the sphere down as it shed layers, until it was only six feet high and Reginald was curled into

315

a fetal position inside it. Patches of crystal had formed over Reginald's wounds – containing the bleeding.

"Will he heal?" Layla knelt by the cocoon, watching the man within breathe gently.

"Slowly. But yes. Changing back from his Dragon-form will heal him faster than a lot of other Lineages who take this much damage in a fight." Dusk smoothed a hand over the crystal sphere, though his entire body was shaking with exhaustion.

"Did he know me, when he was his Dragon?" Layla asked, stroking the crystal near Reginald's face again.

"It's your scent a beast knows during its first few changes." Dusk sighed, turning and leaning back against the cocoon and setting his head back upon it. "The Dragon doesn't think like a person, not for a while. All Reginald probably knew were basic things like *mate, danger, save*. Just like when he saved you at the Aviary."

"That's why you screamed for me to get back."

"He would have attacked had anyone threatened him." Dusk nodded. "Any sudden move around a newly-shifted Dragon is a dangerous thing. Especially Sirens."

Dusk's eyelashes fluttered then, and Layla stepped in quickly before he could faint again. Gripping him close, she set her lips to his. He startled with a quick inhalation, his eyes fluttering open – but soon closed. Layla kissed him gently, pouring her fire-warm breath down his throat. Moulding close to his nakedness, Layla poured life and heat into him through her lips, deep into his tired body. He shuddered; his arms came up around her, holding her close, pressing their bodies tighter. Like a drowning man Dusk clung to her, drinking her kiss. But by the time Layla pulled away, feeling lightheaded, he was finally breathing easy and no longer shaking.

"God, that's better than heroin," he sighed.

"You've tried heroin?" Layla smiled, pulling back.

"Victorian era. It was all the rage." Dusk heaved a hard breath, then pushed away from the crystal cocoon. His gaze fixed on something and Layla turned, seeing Adrian. Naked also and not seeming to care, Adrian sloshed through the ankle-deep water, stepping lithely around broken iron and piles of shimmering crystal, towards them.

"We need to get Reginald out of here." Adrian spoke softly as he arrived, his aquamarine gaze dark.

"And you." Dusk spoke back. They shared a knowing look, and Adrian set his jaw.

"Fuck." Running his hands through his short black hair, it was one of the only times Layla had seen Adrian fret. Intense worry was in his gaze as he glanced to Layla, then to the crowd seeping back into the ruined hall, despite the Guards trying to hold them off. But no Guard was going to forestall an Owner of the Hotel, and all eyes were fixed upon their trio as other Guardsmen and women moved through the room, checking the fallen and getting those still alive up on hovering stretchers to be taken to the Hotel infirmary.

Dusk flicked his fingers at two enormously tall Red Giant Guardsmen, their skin entirely red like a sunburn, though it wasn't. Both over eight feet in height and ridiculously muscle-bound like bouncers, they trundled over and Dusk spoke with them as he leaned heavily on Layla. "Jacques. Benny. Get the Head Courtier to his rooms. Stay on the door – I don't want anyone going in or out until I get there. Are we clear?"

Both Guardsmen nodded, their faces a mask of professionalism. Heaving Reginald's prison into their massive hands, they trundled their burden through the Owners, parting them. Dusk sagged between Adrian and Layla, still on the brink of fainting, and Layla called for help. Another Red Giant came over, seeing the problem and scooping Dusk up in his brawny arms.

Adrian took Layla's hand; his arm was shaking, and she couldn't imagine how much energy he'd expended bringing Rikyava and Dusk back to consciousness – not to mention the fight. Helping Adrian across the ruined floor, Layla subtly breathed her energy into him as they walked. Adrian went with his head high through the crowd of Owners, giving them his most severe glare. Some of them shrank back. Some held their ground. As they passed the Vampire Quindici DaPonti, he shook his head, giving Adrian a knowing glance. Adrian didn't spend any time acknowledging it, though he and Layla both knew what it meant.

Adrian was so shit-canned from his position as Head of the Paris Hotel.

Moving into the hall, Layla found everything wet with seawater. The marble floors were slippery and she had to grab the arm of the Giant Guardsman to stay upright. He was kind, waiting until they were around a corner before he scooped Layla up into his other arm and hefted Adrian onto his back with a small smile.

"Where to, Hotel Head?" The Giant murmured softly.

"Fourth floor, Reginald's rooms," Adrian spoke back. "And when you get us there, please find the Madame, Raffino."

"She's already in conference with some of the Owners," the Giant murmured back as he mounted the stairs, climbing as if his three burdens weighed nothing. "Some of the more powerful ones. I saw them go as soon as the fight ended."

"Dammit." Adrian cursed for the second time in nearly as many minutes, sounding tired. Layla glanced over the Giant's shoulder to see Adrian clinging to the Giant's back with his eyes closed. "She's already in conference with the Crimson Circle members that were here. Wait at her door, then. Get her as soon as you're able, bring her straight to us.

Quietly as you can."

"Yes, Hotel Head."

The man said nothing more as they climbed the final flight of stairs to the fourth floor, then made it to Reginald's rooms at the far end. The other two Giants were there and nodded to Adrian, hustling them all inside, then backing out with bows of fealty as Dusk was laid on a pearl-grey fainting couch in Reginald's apartments. Layla had a feeling who the Giants would go to bat for if it ever came to a conflict over Adrian leading this Hotel.

But she had no time to think about it as Dusk stirred. He didn't linger on the chaise but rose, going to the crystal sphere. Setting his hands to it, Dusk shivered all the crystal away except for the patches that kept the Head Courtier from bleeding out, and then Adrian moved over, helping lift Reginald to the bed. As they tucked Reginald in, Layla found silk sleep-pants in the closet for Adrian and Dusk. They received them with sightly bemused glances, as if their nakedness hadn't bothered them, but they donned them.

Leaning over the bed, Dusk pressed up Reginald's eyelids with his thumbs, inspecting the Siren's bloodshot eyes. Layla and Adrian hovered as Dusk pressed his fingers to Reginald's neck, timing the beats as he watched the maritime grandfather clock in the living area.

"Is he healing?" Layla asked.

"He's in bad condition, but yes, his wounds are already healing." Dusk glanced her way. "He doesn't need my help; it'll be nothing but scars in a day or so, and nothing at all after a week. Rikyava will be the same, fortunately, with a little help from Rake to control her pain and speed things up."

Dusk and Adrian shared a look and Layla understood it. That bite Bastien had given Rikyava had been bad. It hadn't been quite as accurate as Hunter's bite that killed King Arini, but it might have

319

severed her spine or worse had Adrian not gotten his fire down Bastien's throat and forced him to let Rikyava go.

Layla watched Dusk place a palm on Reginald's chest, closing his eyes and lifting his chin. She felt a low rumble pass through the room, the same kind Dusk used to heal, though this was more subtle. As Layla watched, a bold presence swaddled in tiger-striped taffeta suddenly whisked into the room. The Madame closed the door quickly behind her, and stepping up beside Layla, she watched Dusk with Reginald, worry in her golden tigress eyes.

"How is he?" The Madame arched her Elizabeth Taylor eyebrows at Dusk.

"He'll sleep a while," Dusk pronounced, rising from the Head Courtier's bedside. "I don't sense any significant danger. He's just exhausted."

"Small victories, I suppose." The Madame gave a flick of her fan as she stepped to the living area near the leviathan-carved fireplace. Her brows knit as she swept to a seat at a high-backed chair in the living area. Her golden eyes were grim as everyone took seats.

"Well. We have the worst kind of problem on our hands, my dears. The Board is calling for your head, Adrian." The Madame's gaze was level, giving it to him straight. "They don't just want your resignation as Hotel Head for the antics unleashed upon our fair establishment today. They've already ousted you from Ownership and they're calling for retribution under the Old Laws. They want a patsy for everything that's happened in the past months, Adrian, and you are the most convenient target, dear boy. I'm so sorry. They've invoked the *Risorgimento*, the reorganization of this Hotel branch. A vote is already in progress among the members of the Owner's inner circle… to see if the destruction here merits the *Punizione Completa*."

"The *complete punishment?*" Layla growled. "Why don't I like the sound of that?"

"Because it's a death penalty." Dusk spoke softly, sharing a look with Adrian. Adrian had gone ashen, his hand at his mouth, his fingers brushing his lips. "They're literally calling for Adrian's head, by the oldest Hotel laws."

"Well, they can't have it!" Layla growled, incensed as a weak flare of heat simmered up around her, though her Dragon was exhausted. "What about the Intercessoria?"

"They don't get involved when the oldest Hotel laws are enacted," the Madame fretted with her fan, watching Adrian. "The Hotel pre-dates the Intercessoria, my darling. Adrian must leave the Hotel at once, before the vote ends – go into hiding for the time being. Dusk, Rikyava, and I may be able to smooth out Reginald's attack with the Board, earn him only a suspension, but—"

"Someone has to take the fall." Adrian glanced up, a hard decision in his eyes.

"No." Layla breathed, her hand reaching out and touching Adrian's. He twined their fingers together, his gaze infinitely sad as he held Layla's hand.

"I have to go," he spoke softly. "Bastien had a number of allies on the Board, especially in the Crimson Circle, their innermost elite. I don't have any friends there, Layla. If the vote goes badly…"

"They'll hunt you." Dusk breathed. "No matter how far you run."

"The Intercessoria might protect me," Adrian shared a glance with Dusk. "I'm still one of the top witnesses in their investigation on Hunter."

"Small potatoes," Dusk breathed back, something scared in his gaze now, "when we're up against the entire Hotel Board, including the Crimson Circle."

"Not if I have anything to say about it." With a decisive glint in his eyes, Adrian rose. Command roared from him suddenly, even though Layla could still feel how tired he was. As if this was all part of the game Adrian played, he suddenly adjusted, approaching this new development against his life with cunning intensity and an utter lack of fear. Turning to Dusk, he set his jaw, a searing every-color light flashing through his eyes. "Dusk. Is your portal through the Thin Ways still active?"

"Yes. I never shut it down." Dusk's gaze was knowing as a secret passed between them, something Layla wasn't party to.

"Leave Layla here with Reginald, keep the Giants on the doors for a little while." Adrian spoke brusquely, though he raked a hand through his hair again, his gaze determined. "Until you're certain no one will be seeking retribution from Reginald's flesh, or Layla's. I'll rendezvous with you when I'm done running. Maybe a few weeks."

"Be careful, Adrian." Dusk spoke softly.

But Adrian was already sweeping forward, gathering Layla up and pulling her into a hard embrace. Tears shone in his bright aqua eyes as he wrapped her in his arms and in the exhausted magic of his coils. And she felt it in him then – how much he loved her. As they held each other, for what Layla knew could quite possibly be the last time if the Board got their way, Adrian pulled back from their embrace, cupping her face tenderly in his hands. As he smoothed his thumbs over her cheeks, Layla watched his tears fall – as her own tears slipped down her cheeks.

"Wait for me." He breathed. "I'll come for you soon... I swear it."

"I will." Layla hitched a breath, trying not to sob. "I will."

With that, Adrian Rhakvir kissed her; hard. Layla kissed him back, feeling their Dragons swirl together for one final embrace; coiling tight, never wanting to let the other go. She felt the cord of their Bind brighten between them, so impossibly bright, burning like the sun in the cosmos. And when he finally released her, it was with a will – hauling himself back from their Bind with a desolate look like it was ripping out his heart.

It ripped out Layla's also.

Stepping backward, Adrian made it to the doors, though his hand spasmed up to his heart as if it hurt, pain in his gold-aqua eyes. Reaching out, he ripped a midnight blue peacoat of Reginald's down from a coat-rack and slung it on. His body was already wavering with a tired mirage of light and wind, turning him into a hunch-backed old man with a balding head and doughy, deep-set grey eyes, a man Layla had never seen before.

And in a quick moment, he was out the door.

Gone.

CHAPTER 30 – UNLEASHED

The Hotel meeting at eight a.m. Monday morning was held in the Diamond Ballroom, the second-largest in the Paris Hotel now that the Grand Ballroom was being rebuilt. The meeting included all of Concierge Services, Catering, the Guard, and Assignations, currently being headed up on a temporary basis by Rake André now that Reginald was on suspension and Sylvania was deceased. Standing beside a recovered Dusk and a newly-healed Rikyava in the crowded hall, Layla watched the gilded platform that had been erected at the far end. Shifting warily in her burgundy cocktail dress with the beige lace shoulders, Layla observed the panel of twelve people sitting in crimson throne-like chairs up on the platform, all of them Owners. Memorizing everything about them, both the ones she'd met in the past week and the ones she hadn't, it wasn't lost upon Layla that Adrian wasn't among them.

But standing out like warriors in black leather among the glamour of the Owners were Heathren Merkami and Insinio Brandfort of the Intercessoria. Their steely gazes swept the hall as people began to quiet. Noting Layla and Dusk near the front, Heathren's piercing gaze lingered. But then the Madame was stepping up to an ornate podium emblazoned with the Hotel's crimson "R" and golden crown. Dressed in a cream and silver zebra-striped gown, she cleared her throat, speaking into a magically-amplified 1930's microphone.

"My dearest darlings," she began as her golden tigress-gaze swept the hall. "By now you have heard of the tragic events of the past week, involving our dear Head Courtesan and our beloved Head Courtier. Please know that our Head Courtier is recovering well, though his leadership has been graciously taken over by our sweet Rake André for the time being." The Madame made a kind gesture to Rake, standing tall in one of his bartending outfits a few people away. Making prayer hands at his brow, Rake bowed gently, acknowledging the Madame.

"Needless to say," the Madame continued soberly, "that upon the heels of such terrible catastrophe a change of leadership in our Hotel has ensued. While we shall have services for our dear Sylvania in a few days' time, our darling Adrian Rhakvir has been removed as Hotel Head, and will be replaced anon. In the meantime, I would like to introduce Ms. Lulu Duvall of the Hotel Mediation Committee to speak a few words this morning to you all. Lulu."

"Thank you, Etienne." A stately Faunus woman that Layla recognized from the past week rose from one chair, stepping to the podium and speaking English with a gentle French accent. She wore nothing to disguise her long gazelle-legs and the tawny fur that covered them, nor her bare breasts and sleek midriff. But elegant bangles of gold graced her slim wrists, the same bound around her neck in a fetching torque, while long spirals of gold curved up her corkscrewing horns.

"Greetings, cherished employees of the Red Letter Hotel Paris," she spoke with a smile. With large, dewey brown eyes and a pleasantly low voice, she was the perfect communicator for the Owner's will. Layla had a feeling this woman could deliver even the worst news with her slow, gracious smile, and be utterly forgiven. Even as she listened to the woman speak, Layla felt herself being drawn into a comforting magic, like being curled up in a cozy forest nest.

"I bear the tragic news that former Hotel Head Adrian Rhakvir has disappeared. The Hotel Board of Owners is concerned, and if anyone has information relating to his disappearance, we appeal you to please come forward. I will be staying here at the Hotel as we arrange new management in the coming weeks, and will hear any information with unbiased ears. In the meantime, the Hotel Board will be voting on new leadership for this branch. We would like for all operations to be business as usual during this time. Cleanup continues in the Grand Ballroom and it has been screened off for impending construction, which we hope will conclude swiftly. Please know that we expect the Yule Ball to proceed as planned for Winter Solstice."

"We further hope, that each and every one of you understand how valuable you are to this Hotel." Ms. Duvall's gaze swept the crowd, her smile still serene even though a slight change in her energy let Layla know the next bit was bad news. "Please know that any changes to the personnel rosters in the coming weeks are made with the utmost respect to all involved, and will be conducted with the proper severance packages."

"I.e. don't be surprised if you get shit-canned when new management rolls in," Rikyava snorted softly to Layla's left, crossing her arms irately. "Fucking typical."

"With that said," Ms. Lulu Duvall finished, "we have full belief that this Hotel branch will once again reach the height of its glory in the weeks to come. Thank you for your esteemed service; you are all a treasured part of the Red Letter Hotel family."

Stepping back with a demure nod, she returned to her seat. Beside Layla, Rikyava was scowling, her posture tight in her crimson uniform. On Layla's other side, dressed in one of his impeccable dove-grey suits, Dusk's eyes were narrowed, the look he got when the wheels in his mind were churning furiously.

Stepping forward, the Madame was about to dismiss the meeting, when Heathren Merkami and Insinio Brandfort suddenly rose from their chairs. Moving forward, the Ephilohim hijacked the podium as the Owners shifted in their seats. Clearly, the Intercessoria hadn't been expected to attend this meeting, and they *really* hadn't been expected to speak. But as Heathren took the podium, Insinio standing behind him with a scary glower and his burly arms crossed, the both of them positively bristling with silver weapons, Layla saw Dusk smirk.

"Your doing?" She whispered.

"Just watch." He murmured back, giving her a sidelong smile.

Heathren's searing white eyes scoured the room, a sensation of angelic wrath emanating from him as murmurs moved through the ballroom. Unleashing his magic like a nightmare, Layla felt it roll out in a terrifying spread of silver-black wings, seething over the platform and rolling down into the audience like a horror-mist. People cringed back, even Layla shivering deeply where she stood, feeling that terrifying energy coalesce around her. Beside her, Rikyava's hand flashed to the rapier at her hip with a growl, though she withheld herself from flicking her fingers at her Guards to rush in and take the Ephilohim down for the magical demonstration.

It was an intimidation tactic, and it worked, silence enveloping the hall. A number of faces behind the podium scowled fiercely and Heathren turned, pinning the Owners behind him with his formidable archangel glare.

His next words were spoken directly to them, and not to the hall.

"Clan First of the Desert Dragons of Morocco and the Mediterranean, Adrian Rhakvir, has been declared under Intercessoria witness protection in an ongoing investigation. Anyone who interferes with an Intercessoria investigation will face punishment under the full force of High Court law. The Intercessoria will be monitoring this Hotel. Any news of Adrian Rhakvir's whereabouts will be reported *directly to us*, rather than to any Hotel-related organization. On pain of severe reprimand."

Layla didn't need to know what *severe reprimand* was, but watching a number of faces around her go ashen was testament enough. The gazelle-woman was scowling now, making her pretty face intensely ugly, all her gracious coercion completely undone by Heathren's blunt evisceration of the Owner's agenda. Beside Layla, Rikyava gave a soft, incredulous laugh, relaxing her stance. On Layla's other side, Dusk was smiling a mean little smile – and Layla saw his and Heathren's gazes connect.

The Ephilohim lifted one pale eyebrow. "That is all."

Heathren left the podium as swiftly as he had come, him and Insinio returning to their seats. The two Intercessoria Judiciaries showed no emotion as Hotel Owners scowled at them, emanating a furious magical wrath, not the least of which came from Ms. Lulu Duvall. Layla had the feeling a severe feud had just been kindled between the two organizations, as the Madame fretted her way back to the podium.

"Well, that concludes this meeting, I suppose." She fidgeted with her zebra-striped fan. "Please return to your duties everyone, and keep in mind your Departmental meetings scheduled for this afternoon. Dismissed."

With that, the meeting concluded just as suddenly as it began. People didn't mill, most speaking a few low words with others in their departments, then moving off briskly for another day. Layla was surprised how quickly the ballroom cleared out; no one wanted to stay in an arena where two powerful organizations were facing each other down. Severe tension bristled between the Owners as they took refreshment off to one side of the platform – sending daggers from their eyes and magic toward the Intercessoria.

The Juds didn't give two shits. Rising from their chairs, all of that magical rage simply washed off them as they stepped down the stairs of the platform, approaching Dusk, Layla, and Rikyava. But as they neared, Heathren's gaze pinned them, then slid by. He and Insinio walked right past their group, to the doors of the ballroom.

Layla moved to follow, but Dusk gripped her arm. "Give them a moment."

Layla paused, and Rikyava glanced at Dusk with a sly chuckle, stepping close and speaking low so no one else nearby could hear. "I'm needed elsewhere right now, kiddos, Guard shit is tense with everything going on. So – you two ok meeting with those jerks alone?"

"Yeah." Dusk nodded at her, his sapphire eyes keen. "You know where we'll be."

"And you know I'll have a few Guards hidden right outside, just in case."

"Thanks." Dusk and Rikyava shared a smile. As if they understood each other's minds, Layla watched a deep, renegade gaze pass between them. And then Rikyava chuckled, shaking her head and turning for the doors of the ballroom, making her exit. As she left, Dusk lifted his chin, closing his eyes for a moment as if feeling vibrations through the entire Hotel. And then he glanced at Layla, nodding his chin at a side-door.

"Ok. This way."

Following Dusk's lead, Layla exited the ballroom at a set of doors that would take them back to the main Concierge desk. But at the last moment, Dusk whisked them around a stand of potted palms and through a gilded smoking-lounge, out of the Hotel to the winter-lit gardens.

The gardens were covered in snow, bright under the heavy grey sky. Dusk walked them quickly along salted flagstone paths where their footprints wouldn't track, through dormant topiaries glittering with fairy-lights in the morning. Moving into the manicured forest, they arrived at the crystal bath-house where Dusk and Layla had first made love and Dusk whisked the door open, ushering her inside.

But rather than having another getaway, they were confronted with business inside. The two Ephilohim Judiciaries were there; Layla could feel their etheric seven-layered wings breathing through the mist before they stepped forward, emerging like wraiths beneath the crystal vaults.

"Heathren." Dusk proffered a hand; Heathren Merkami grasped his wrist as their gazes connected. "It's good to have a friend in the Intercessoria."

"You owe me, Arlohaim. And so does Adrian." Strangely enough, Layla saw the intense Ephilohim crack a subtle smile. There was camaraderie in his gaze, though Heathren's aura was still piercing as mist swirled around him, stirred by his long etheric wings.

"Do you know where Adrian is?" Layla asked, wondering what this meeting was about.

"I wouldn't be the first person he would call while on the lam, now would I?" Heathren glanced at her with chastisement. "No. Adrian has enough mechanisms to avoid the Intercessoria's gaze, in addition to the Hotel Owners."

"Adrian's promised to let us know his whereabouts once he deems it safe enough to settle at one of his strongholds, Layla." Dusk answered as he shared a glance with Heathren.

"How many strongholds does he have?" Layla raised an eyebrow, crossing her arms.

"Enough to keep his enemies guessing." Dusk gave her a meaningful look, before turning back to Heathren. "So. What's the plan to keep Adrian's head out of the chopping-block?"

"The Crimson Circle are adamant, unfortunately." Heathren

spoke coldly to Dusk, his pale silver eyes glinting through the mist. "Our sources say they won't take no for an answer on this one. The Circle come from old Twilight families and believe this ridiculous tenant, this *Punizione Completa* of theirs is justified and not simply outright murder. Most of them are ancient, and have been committing crimes against Twilight folk and humans for millennia. They don't care if they take one more head – and they want Adrian's."

"Why are they so intent on Adrian?" Layla asked, frowning. "What did he ever do to them?"

"We believe Adrian has crossed someone at the very top, somehow." Heathren glanced at her. "Which is interesting, because until now we weren't entirely certain the Crimson Circle had a pinnacle. But from the way they've coordinated their efforts across the globe to find Adrian and dispose of him, he's deeply offended their most central member somehow with his recent antics. Which is useful. If we could secure Adrian's cooperation, use him to draw this person out…we could learn much about the Circle and how it operates. We know the Circle are behind some of the worst crimes our Realm has ever seen, many of them ongoing. But until now, we either can't get close enough to touch them, or all our informants wind up dead before we can get testimony. Adrian gives us an opportunity to amend that problem."

"Use a small fish to catch a bigger fish, just like with Hunter." Layla breathed, arching an eyebrow at Heathren. "But Adrian hates you. I kinda do too, from what you did to him while he was incarcerated."

"That is the least of my worries." Heathren spoke as he watched Layla, unapologetic. "Thousands of people hate me, Ms. Price, for very good reasons. But what I need to know right now, is if you think Adrian will play ball with us?"

Layla took a deep breath, considering it.

"I can get him to play ball." She spoke at last, meeting Heathren's gaze. "I think he'll want to now, actually. Adrian's time making decisions solo is at an end; he basically said as much to me the night of the Owner's Ball. He and I are connected now, deeper than even marriage can connect two people. And it's not just me. Dusk is involved; Reginald too. Adrian realizes he's not a candle in the darkness anymore: that he needs to come out into the light. Showing our Bind to the Owners was the first step. I think he would work with people who can keep him safe now – so we can magnify his fire a thousandfold to raze all our enemies. Both inside the Crimson Circle… and outside, striking back at Hunter for everything he's done."

"Bold words," Heathren Merkami eyed Layla with something like approval in his white eyes. "Not many would say they can tame a Royal Dragon."

"Except a Royal Dragon Bind," Dusk spoke, a hard love shining from his sapphire eyes as he gazed at Layla. Turning to Heathren, he said, "I believe Layla can do what she says. I'm connected to Adrian now also, in a way I can barely describe yet that I know will prove useful if we have time to explore it. Reginald has raw power and control, I have depth and planning. Adrian has renegade moves that no one can predict."

"And Layla?" Heathren's gaze was thoughtful upon her.

"Layla has battle in her veins, and passion, both." Dusk reached out, twining his fingers in hers, warm and supportive. "She's the lodestone to draw out our enemies. Rikyava and I can get her trained up in fighting. Reginald can train her in seduction. She'll work with the both of you in espionage. We'll pose her as a dual-position Concierge and Courtesan, then move her up the ranks to infiltrate the Crimson Circle and find out the people who want Adrian dead, or person. And maybe catch Hunter while we're at it."

"Great. I'm the bait." Layla joked wryly, though she felt a certain satisfaction at hearing Dusk's plan.

She wasn't afraid of being the bait. In a way it felt exhilarating, and deep inside, Layla felt her Dragon stir with a rush of heat through her veins. The human part of her hated the idea of becoming a Hotel Courtesan, but something about it made her Dragon roar with eagerness. A Courtesan could choose which Assignations they took. And the prospect of using her passions for something more than money or power gave Layla a sense of satisfaction. Hunter was out there, hurting people she loved. The Crimson Circle were out there, raging for Adrian's death and building their power at everyone else's expense.

Suddenly, Layla knew this was what she had trained for, all her life. This was what she'd wanted to do when she'd gone for her PhD in International Studies. She'd wanted to make a difference in the world.

And she'd do it – by bringing the elite down from the inside.

"How soon do we start?"

Dusk laughed. Sweeping in, he pressed Layla with a luscious kiss, his eyes shining with pleasure as he smoothed back one of her sable curls. "God, I love you, Layla Price. Are you sure you want to do this? Once we start… there's no going back."

"I'm sure." Layla lifted up, kissing his lips again. And then she turned to the Intercessoria. "So. What now?"

"Do as you have been doing." Heathren's gaze was pleased upon her, a small smile curling his perfect lips now that everything was agreed on. "Be a Concierge. Finish your training under Reginald Durant to become a Courtesan by Yuletide, then maintain a dual position at the Hotel as planned. Keep your ears and eyes open as the Paris Hotel transitions into new leadership, and we'll feel our way forward from there. Until then, try not to make too many waves. We'll be in touch."

With that, Heathren turned to go, but it was Insinio who lingered. The big burly Ephilohim grinned, a recklessness shining in his white eyes as he regarded Layla. Heathren turned, watching his partner. At last, Heathren returned to Insinio's side rather than his usual place out in front. And Layla realized that Insinio wasn't just the brawny backup to Heathren's scary intensity. As Heathren Merkami watched his partner with a bemused curiosity, Layla realized that Insinio was the quiet observer of their duo.

And he'd observed something about Layla that made her suddenly very uncomfortable, wondering what it was.

"Biggest balls I've ever seen on someone raised human." Insinio spoke at last, answering her thoughts while still grinning at Layla. "You sure you don't want a job in the Intercessoria?"

"Don't I sort of have one already?" Layla joked, lifting an eyebrow.

Insinio laughed. He threw his head back and laughed in that big, genial way that Adrian had once done masquerading as John LeVeque. Except Insinio Brandfort was the real deal, and Layla suddenly knew whom it was Adrian had based his impression on. Layla grinned at the big archangel; he grinned back. She suddenly had a feeling she and Insinio were going to get along famously.

"Touché, girly." Stepping forward, Insinio offered a fist and Layla bumped it – flowing into a series of complex handshakes that just suddenly came to her. Insinio grinned, something very aware in his bright silver eyes. "Kinda knew you'd intuit my secret handshake," he chuckled. "You pick up on resonance like a fuckin' live wire. Can't wait to see what you'll do with a little training. When you're ready, you'll train in magical battle with me. Get ready to rock 'n' roll with the big boys. Wear some tight leather pants."

Layla was grinning at Insinio's suddenly-revealed teasing and attitude, loving the big, badass archangel. "Why tight leather pants?"

"Because I want to see your butt in them when you fight!"

With a last grin and a booming laugh, Insinio was out the door. Heathren lifted an eyebrow at Layla and gave one last pointed glance to Dusk. "We'll be in touch." And then he was gone also, out the door of the crystal bath-house and into the cold winter morning.

Turning to Layla, Dusk was one big smile as he seized her around the waist.

"What are you smiling about?" Layla grinned up at him. "Aren't we so fucked right now with everything that's going on?"

"Yeah, we're so fucked." Still grinning to beat the band, a diamond-passion recklessness lit Dusk's sapphire eyes.

"Then why are you smiling?" Layla laughed.

"Because there's no one else I'd rather face this shit-storm with." He grinned back. "And however we *rock 'n' roll* this like Insinio said – we're gonna do it in style."

"I like your style, Dusk Arlohaim." Layla stepped close, smoothing her hands over Dusk's slim dove-grey Italian suit. She slid her hands up, stroking the sides of his neck, feeling the ridges of Dragon-scale there. A ripple of light passed through Dusk's hair as he gazed down, his eyes luminous.

"I like your style, too, Layla Price."

And then he was kissing her, deep and delicious.

As their scents mingled in the mist of the waterfall, Layla suddenly felt a resonance expand out from her and Dusk's kiss. As if Dusk's ability had taken Layla's Bind-magic and flared it wide like a fan, she felt it rush outward, seeking her other Bound mates.

All of a sudden, she felt a flow of ocean currents, and saw Reginald standing upon a far-north shore, deep in his recovery-dreams.

Decked in strings of pearls with his woven belt, his golden hair flowed in a surging wind off the sea. His eyes pierced her, grey and gold as if seeing her from his dreams. As Layla kissed Dusk, she suddenly tasted the ocean in their kiss – Reginald's tongue sliding across hers with an infinite softness.

And then she smelled Adrian, his cinnamon-spice fragrance whirling in a warm wind that stirred the mist. Like she was drowning in jasmine and midnight desert scents, Adrian was suddenly there also, holding her as Dusk held her, pouring his hot kiss down her throat. Layla gasped, drinking Adrian's fire and lust deep into her veins as his hands held her close, devouring him back.

And as they kissed, her three Royal Dragons all kissing her at the same time through their Bind, Layla drew their energies into herself, braiding them into a strong golden cord. Her Dragon rose, roaring with fire through her every sinew, bright and dark all at once. As it rose, Layla felt her body harness its power like she gripped it in an iron fist – taking its magic and thrusting the full force of their combined power back down that braid and deep into each of her Royal Dragons.

Reginald gasped, twisting in his recovery bed as he slept.

Dusk gasped in her arms, devouring her lips as she thrust power deep into his body.

And somewhere far away, she felt it stagger Adrian. She felt him on a narrow boat with a shitty diesel motor and a makeshift rudder; saw him shudder as he navigated the boat up a jungle waterway somewhere in Laos or Thailand. She saw his piercing aqua eyes swirl with fierce gold as he breathed her in, as he drew all that combined power deep inside himself – and roared. Like a leviathan of fire and wind had been unleashed upon the world, Adrian roared to the heat and the trees, shaking them so hard that birds exploded from hiding-places all around the jungle.

And then Adrian laughed – his sudden explosion of joy that Layla loved so much.

Layla broke from Dusk's kiss, breathless with love and light.

And then she was kissing him again, reveling in the feel of her three Bound Royal Dragons – knowing there was nothing they couldn't face together.

The story continues in *Blood Dragon's Heat: Royal Dragon Shifters of Morocco #4*
A Red Letter Hotel Paranormal Romance

Loving this series? Help Ava write more in the Royal Dragon Shifters of Morocco series by leaving a review at your favorite online retailer!

COMING SOON!

Blood Dragon's Heat: Royal Dragon Shifters of Morocco #4 the next book in the Red Letter Hotel Paranormal Romance series is coming soon.

Learn more and sign up for newsletter updates at AvaWardRomance.com

ABOUT AVA WARD

AVA WARD writes hot & sexy paranormal, fantasy, and sci-fi romance, and is the pen name for Amazon bestselling and award-winning fantasy author Jean Lowe Carlson. From dragon-shifters to otherworldly hotties, there's no limit to the heat! Discover the Red Letter Hotel romances, the decadent world of four bad-boy dragon shifter billionaires and the one woman who keeps them in line! **Discover more at AvaWardRomance.com**

Loving this series? Help Ava write more in the Royal Dragon Shifters of Morocco series by leaving a review at your favorite online retailer!

Made in the USA
Las Vegas, NV
23 March 2021

20048663R00187